THE 5 MOONS OF
TIIANA

The Chronicles of Rez Cantor

A swashbuckling, science fiction epic
filled with adventure, mystery,
romance, and fantasy.

PAUL T HARRY

Printing History
A Desert Portal Book
Sphere Publishing, LLC
Paperback edition/May 2012
ISBN -10: 0615528317
ISBN -13: 978-0615528311

LCCN: 2011914893
CreateSpace, North Charleston SC

Internal Photography by Victor J Palagano III / Eyeful Images Photographic Arts, LLC.

Map of Boutal - Concept / Layout: Paul T Harry
Map of Boutal - Graphic Design / Artwork: Michael Redhouse

Dedication

To my father,
Thanks for introducing me to John Carter of Mars,
and for making me learn to type.

And M.D. Rollins, the best friend and co-pilot one could have.

Other Works
by Paul Harry

Acknowledgments

I would like to express my sincerest appreciation to Dr. Jennifer Dare for her invaluable insight, and creative direction in helping this work come to fruition.

And for the rest—thanks for your input, help, and guidance. It was most appreciated.

Amber Harry
Dr. Hannah Tracy
David Alpert
Craig Christensen
Anthony Casares
Brenda Steelman
Thomas Barcia Jr.

Martin Kinnaman
Aaron Ezell
Anne Ezell
Richard Vogan
Joshua Harry
Gabriel Marquez
Ellen McCart

Terry Foster

The 5 Moons of Tiiana /
The Chronicles of Rez Cantor

*. . . [this] story totally works. Great beginning,
middle, revisit and rip-roaring climax . . .*

DR. J. DARE

. . . can you say Star Wars? ★★★★ *Four Stars*

B. CHERNY, LL BOOK REVIEW

*I really enjoyed this book, and agree, there
needs to be a sequel . . .*

M. KINNAMAN

an intelligent, thought provoking novel . . .

C. CHRISTENSEN

expansive, well developed characters . . . a wonderful read . . .

A. YEN

. . . a page turning read.

J. MALLAS

CHAPTER ONE

Meleta

t *was overcast, the sky* dark with a cold drizzle, melancholic clouds hanging low over the city. I stood, looking out the window of my flat, caught up in my thoughts as I rested from my fencing workout. The view was monochromatic and depressing for a number of reasons. First, it was sorely cold. The winter storm that had swept down from the north had brought an icy chill to Corin, peppering my window with a mixture of rain and slush. Its bleakness made me shiver and yearn for warmer days and the bright, gay lights that normally winked on at this hour. It was odd not seeing my home's usual collage of color—the rainbow hues that painted the evening skyline. The lack of their sight was disheartening, depressing me further, for I realized the lights were dim for good reason—that my home was withering under a cold, failed sun, and there was nothing I could do about it.

I edged closer to the glass, searching the streets below for a measure of normalcy. There was nothing, no movement from anything or anyone—no cabs, no PMs, no ATs hovering overhead. It was unusually still; it'd been like this for days. Most everyone was gone—Corin evacuated. Everyone had fled, taking their families and belongings to the forests and mountains, or off-world, if one could afford it. It was only soldiers like me who remained behind; we had our orders. We were the last bastions of order, the ones left to protect the Imperial core even though that was a joke in itself. What were we protecting? Thirty-two planets had already been crushed under the boot of this enemy-Melela was just the icing on the cake.

Angrily I whipped my sword blade, wishing I could somehow cut the head off the dragon that was coming to devour us all, but there was nothing I or anyone could do. That thought festered in me, souring my disposition like the bitter taste of rask. I rested my blade, resigned to the fact that all I had left was my duty; my orders to ensure the safety of the Relcor during the transition. Already the liaisons for the new leadership were here, and things were tense. By tomorrow, their full fleet would be here, filling our skies—giving formality to our surrender.

I moved to my bedroom and looked over my dress uniform. Everything was laid out across my bed, my dress boots on the floor polished to a high shine; the buckles and decorations on my uniform shining brightly under the room's austere lighting. Sadly, this was the sum of my life; twenty-three years of military service laid flat across a bed. That sudden realization gave me a pang of regret. I was barely thirty-six and my efforts now seemed shallow and pathetic. Where had the time gone? So much of it seemed wasted. Undoubtedly that's what my father would say. By my age he'd already risen through the ranks to become a Lieutenant Major. And yet, why did I care? It was hard to say.

Perhaps if I had pressed harder, pushed for an off-world commission, or been given the chance to fight the Relcor, then things might have been different. A battle commendation would have provided me the opportunity to make Major first class instead of Captain-as if it mattered at this point. The truth was, I was lucky to be alive, safe and sound on Melela. Too many had already died in our strange and bizarre war with the Relcor-nine hundred thousand in the Qui quadrant alone.

No, on Melela I was secure with my commission and rank; the royal family had been good to me. Because of them, my tenure had always been assured, my assignments fulfilling, and the reality was, before the war, I'd seen more than enough adventure and travel to keep me from being bored.

The question I faced now was what I was going to do after our surrender–for tomorrow was to be my last day in uniform. With the Emperor's final decree, all remaining remnants of the Imperial government were to be dismantled; our military put asunder, our weapons destroyed. This was the end of our Empire, the very heart of our sovereign civilization and culture put under the knife. Already, many of our sister planets were dark and desecrated, disemboweled by the Relcor's feudal dictatorship. Planets, which had once been free, were being laid to waste by an alien species of which we had little comprehension or understanding. The very nature of it was cruel.

I began to undress and prepare for my shower, first pouring myself a glass of toka. The amber colored liquid held a sweet, minty taste, and I knew it would help me get to sleep quickly. I needed to be up early to oversee the security details for the Princess. Her care would be my last official duty until the signing, after which, she and her parents were to be sent into exile. I took a sip, allowing the liqueur to roll across my tongue–its bite seemed tart, my taste soured by the realization that I was going to miss my young charge. After seeing to her safety for twelve years, the fledgling Queen had wormed her way into my heart, and the thoughts of her banishment only darkened my mood. I started to take another sip to deaden my discontent, but was cut off by a knock upon my door. I moved to the door and opened it, finding a junior cadet awaiting me. He carried a sealed note in his hand.

"Sir," he said, with a quick salute. "A message from General Spires."

He handed me the envelope, then crisply turned and left, barely giving me time to return formality. I closed the door and tore open the note. Inside were orders to meet the General in thirty minutes. I crumpled the paper and threw it into the trash in aggravation. Of all times to be called on the carpet; the security detail was set. Was the blustering old buffoon going to change everything now? Exasperated, I moved to my bedroom and grabbed a fresh shirt from the closet. I buttoned it and threw on a light jacket, along with my military saber, tucking my pants into my boots. If the old goat wanted me there in thirty minutes, he'd have to accept me as I was. I was not about to satisfy him by showering and appearing in full dress. Such short notice did not warrant full protocol, even if it was our last day of military service.

Leaving my resiplex, I walked toward the Palace, and the senior officer's complex, my hair soaking up the rain—my boots sloshing through the puddles. It was dark and damn cold. I was shivering by the time I reached the outer security perimeter where my face and hand were scanned before admittance. Inside the officer's atrium, I shook off the effects of the rain. Then, grabbing a lift, I headed to the third floor and General Spires' office. The ride up was short and when the lift doors opened I rushed out, only to be stopped by two hooded guards—Relcor.

Instinctively, I drew out my blade warding off any further move from the two. In quiet response they held up their hands showing me their empty silver-metallic palms.

"Brother," said one. "We stand in peace. You have no need for your weapon."

I stared at the two aliens, both dressed alike in their ornate, blood-red robes. They were Lodans, mid-level custodians of the Rodan order—foot soldiers. I wondered if they were armed. Unsure, I challenged their presence by keeping my saber high.

"My sword will always stand ready against you, Relcor. Now out of my way. I'm here at the request of General Spires."

The two said nothing. They simply followed my movement, staring at me with cold, cat-like eyes—dull, yellow oculars that sent shivers up my spine. Both reminded me of zombies, stinking corpses that were long dead. Finally, one responded, waving his hand in the direction of the General's office.

"Go," he said, "your superior is awaiting you."

Given a reprieve, I backed away from the two while keeping my eye on them. Fortunately, my steps were unimpeded. There was no move by them, and I made my way down the hall toward the General's office unmolested though I was angry with myself for not bringing a blaster. As good a weapon as my sword was, it was no match for an autolock.

I reached the General's door and knocked. There was movement inside, visible through the opaque window that separated the office from the hallway. I then heard a voice bellow.

"Enter!"

Opening the door, I found General Spires at his desk; he was not alone. Another robed sentinel stood to one side.

"I might have expected you'd be late," said Spires, looking up from his chair.

I bit my tongue, wanting to respond to his remark, but not with the Relcor creature looking on. Instead, I stood my ground and saluted.

"My apologies, Sir."

Spires rose from his desk and approached me.

"Look at you ..." he sneered in disdain, his face reddened from drink, "... out of uniform, body unwashed, hair unkempt. I can't for the life of me understand why the Emperor keeps you on staff."

He jabbed his finger into my chest for emphasis.

"Yes Sir," I answered. "Again, my apologies. I came immediately upon your request."

Spires turned from me and looked at the Relcor who was standing nearby watching.

"You see what you're going to have to put up with? A bunch of lazy ploths like this one."

The sentinel nodded as Spires backhanded my chest. The impact was sharp, and I felt my anger rise. He had no right to strike me, even if he was a General. I clenched my sword hilt fighting the desire to strike back. His actions were inexcusable. Suddenly, and without warning, Spires turned toward me, his look catching me by surprise. The gaze upon his face was forlorn, his eyes moist. Was this a look of despair? I was caught off guard. This was out of character and I was taken aback; Spires was a belligerent pricworm. What was going on? Before I could react, he turned and walked back to his desk while feeding me his instructions.

"I called you here, Captain, as there are details that require my attention before tomorrow's signing." He sighed heavily with resignation. "And our honored guest here wishes a tour of the Palace and the Senate hall where the signing will take place. In the interim, I need someone to hold the fort down, so to speak. Do you think you can handle this simple task?"

"Yes Sir," I answered, more than ever curious to his request.

Nothing more was said and I waited at attention while the General gathered his paperwork from atop the desk. He stuffed everything into a briefcase and left the room with the Relcor following. I watched as the door closed behind them.

Alone in the room, I pondered what was going on. Something was definitely amiss. Spires was not prone to intrigue, nor would he treat me like a junior cadet simply out of bad blood. No, there was more to this. I looked about the room and saw nothing that gave a hint. The desktop was barren, the room stark—three of the four walls covered by heavy curtains. This office was a reflection of Spires himself—stifling. I moved to the desk and pulled open a drawer. It held only office supplies. I went to the one below it. Unexpectedly there was a noise behind me; a muffled voice.

"Lock the door and draw the curtains," it whispered. I whirled around, looking to see who had spoken. "And dim the lights ..."

The voice was feminine—and familiar.

Without further thought, I moved to the office door, locking it. I pulled the drapes covering the large crystalline windows that faced the hallway and turned down the lights. It was then that I caught sight of movement from behind the curtains. A woman appeared, simply dressed in a night robe; her dark, yet graying hair pulled back. I recognized her instantly. It was Lady Tasha, the Empress of Melela; I immediately started to kneel. She waved at me emphatically.

"We have no time for that nonsense," she snapped in a hoarse whisper. "Come to my side—now!" I obeyed instantly, moving forward to face her.

"My Queen, what is it?"

I lowered my eyes in respect; her sudden appearance had me at a loss. To say the least, I had never seen her dressed so informally, with her face unpainted. She looked older this way, and though the light in the room was dim, I could tell she'd been crying. Her face was fraught with fear, and her eyes filled with emotion. I listened as she spoke in quick, hushed tones.

"The peace signing tomorrow is a ruse," she breathed, heavily. "The Relcor have no desire to leave any part of our monarchy alive. We are under a death sentence."

"You must flee then," I responded.

"No, we are trapped. There are spies everywhere, including the palace. They hold us prisoner, and the Emperor—he's been drugged."

"My lady, what can I do?

She grabbed my arm with a firm, hard grip. "I need you to get Leanna out of there."

Stunned by her request, I sputtered weakly. "B-b-but how? I'm Shadow Guard—I.M. would never allow me in—I don't have the clearance."

"That's precisely why I'm coming to you, Captain. I.M.'s been compromised, and I've nowhere else to turn. I need you— you're the adjunct officer in charge of her care. She knows you, and I need you to get her out of the palace and off Melela. You must—I want her to live! General Spires says if anyone can do it, it's you."

I was speechless. My Queen was speaking to me as a mother begging for her child's life, and I had no idea what was transpiring. I needed more information. I started to ask, but there was a rustling out in the hallway. One of the sentinels was at the door; he spoke through it.

"Brother, why have you locked the door and drawn the curtains?"

I felt the Empress' hand press against my chest—she pushed on me hard—near the place where Spires had struck me. It was then that I felt the micro pin stuck to my jacket, its point pricking my skin. The Empress moved back and away.

"I must go before they find me gone." She headed toward the curtains, but not without one final plea. "Save my daughter, Rez. Please!"

I watched her disappear, slipping into a hidden alcove behind the draperies. I was alone again, bewildered, and off-guard. The Relcor were rattling the door knob; I sprang into action.

"What!" I yelled angrily, rushing the door. I jerked it open and glared at the two sentinels. "Can't a man get a lick of sleep? Fucking pricworms!"

The two aliens looked at me blankly; I knew their human side understood my meaning, but the alien infecting them was confused. This was my opportunity. I brushed past the two, pushing them aside.

"I gotta get some sleep," I snapped. "Tell the General I couldn't wait."

I didn't look back. I didn't dare—not if my gamble was to succeed. I moved to the lift and hit the access button. By the hand of fate it was there, waiting. The doors opened and I entered.

Outside in the rain, on the safety of the streets, I mulled over what had just transpired. The Empress' words rang in my ear, *spies everywhere, watching—waiting.* The news of this was inconceivable—*the Interior Ministry had been compromised*—but how? Security for the palace was layered precisely for this reason, to prevent outside forces from penetrating the inner circle. And yet, if the Relcor were in control of I.M., then there was no one I could trust. What was I going to do?

Plagued with a myriad of questions, I looked down at the micro pin sticking though the fabric of my jacket. It was more like a small nail about three quarters of an inch in length with a barbed tip on one end and a small green data crystal on the other. I left it in place. Undoubtedly it held answers, but I needed to find a place where I could decode it—someplace out of the exchange loop. If there was information on how to save the Princess, I needed to keep it private. Unfortunately, I was ill prepared. I had no weapons or the means to stage a rescue and I lacked discretionary funds. I carried few mercs and little coin on me. Like most soldiers I used the Imperial credit system to pay for everything, but using that system now would be a mistake. If there were spies watching the Imperial elite, a credit track would follow my every footstep—and returning to my flat was out of the question. Still, I needed money. Rescuing the Princess wasn't going to be easy or cheap. There were bound to be bribes; just how much was the question. With few options available I made my way to a CTM where I withdrew an advance—enough to get me by for a few days. I left my card in the machine hoping someone would find it and use it. It wouldn't hurt to have a vag create a false trail, giving me time to disappear off the radar.

Credits in hand, I walked the dark streets of Corin looking for a place where I could ensconce myself away from prying eyes. I wasn't having much luck. Everything was closed; the shops, the taverns, even the street vendors were gone. Everyone was scared pithless—and who could blame them. No one knew exactly what to expect tomorrow. The stories regarding the Relcor were chilling at best. Some considered them alien zealots whose mere touch could usurp a man's soul. And then there were the accounts of brutal sex rites, torture, and pagan sacrifices. Dark rumors flew about thousands being slaughtered for the pure pleasure of Juc T'Krola, the heathen ruler of Relcor Prime. These black horrors included stories of those who had vanished forever, including my father.

Long before the war started he had been sent to negotiate with Juc T'Krola, but he was never heard from again. His disappearance had plagued my youth, and I often wondered if he had been killed or consumed by them. Was he now a Relcor hybrid—a concoction of human and alien genetics—a pagan religious cleric who lived and breathed the debauched, sadistic teachings of Rodan? I would probably never know, but I secretly questioned if he would be at the signing tomorrow. I also wondered how much of his knowledge had aided the downfall of the Empire; he had been privy to much. Perhaps he had been tortured or coerced, for it took only twelve short years for the Relcor to conquer everything—all thirty-three planets. To this day it was a mystery that yielded no answer. For me, it was simply a thorn in my heart, giving rise to the whispers behind my back. I kept walking—everyone had skeletons.

My journey soon took me toward the darker corners of Corin, where the seeds of corruption grew without help from the Relcor. It was the only place where the city still breathed, where the poor and the criminal merged, their faces lurking in the shadows, for they had nowhere to run. I looked up the street. I was in the brothel district. Things were slow, but the lights were still on. I moved along searching for a hostel with a measure of cleanliness. Finding one, I ducked in.

The lobby was small and dark, befitting a place where no one wanted to be seen. There was a Lacta sitting behind the front desk. He glanced up at me with disinterest, and then returned to his business. I approached him.

"Yesss," he said, not looking up from his work.

I looked at his bald, crusty head. He was an old snik, molting, his scales falling off.

"I need a room."

Yesss, twenty credits. You want someone, yesss?" His black tongue flickered through thin lips. "We still have a good ssselection—businessss is ssslow."

He waved a bony finger toward the wall behind him. On it were pictures of men and women of varying ages—a slide show of entertainers—some were Melelan, others were from the outer planets. For a price I could choose one or two or more.

"No," I responded. I just need a room, and also a comm—an older unit, with memory pin access and a privacy DAAT filter."

The Lacta looked up at me, curiously surprised by my request. "Those are illegal," he slavered, saliva seeping from the sides of his mouth.

I threw a hundred on the desktop. "Make it legal then."
I unsheathed my sword and set it alongside the note, adding
weight to my request.

"Yesss, I think ssssomething can be arranged." He handed
me a key. "Room twenty-four, upssstairs on the right. I will
have the comm delivered ssssoon."

I picked up my sword. "Don't disappoint me," I said, the
edge of my blade coming dangerously close to his saggy-skinned
throat. His tongue flickered and his black eyes widened.

"No, it will be there quite ssssoon."

I left the lobby and headed to the room. It was sparsely
furnished with a bed, a night stand, and a chest of drawers. On
the ceiling was a large mirror and there were tattered curtains
hanging across the window. The place stank of musty sweat
mixed with cheap perfume. At the far end, facing the bed was a
large view screen. It displayed the same show I had seen in the
lobby; a parade of men and women for rent, only these images
were more revealing. I passed the time looking at them as I
waited.

After a few minutes there was a knock at the door. I opened
it to find a young girl scantily dressed with long braids of yel-
low-straw hair. Heavy makeup covered her eyes and lips; definitely not my type. She handed me the comm and the DAAT
filter I'd requested.

"Do you need anything else?" she cooed, posing in the
doorway. "I'm available for a small fee."

"I'll let you know," I replied, shutting the door on her.

I returned to the bed and sat, unfolding the comm in my
hands. I pulled off the back and looked for the internal data
transfer chip. I pulled it out and replaced it with the DAAT filter. I then put the cover back on and tried to place a call; it
would not go through. I then tried to access Corin's M.A. network; it was dead as well. The filter worked. The comm could
not send or receive data. I could now access the micro pin without worry.

Pulling the pin from my jacket I pushed it into the
access port on the side of the comm. There was a low hum

as the internal circuits read the device. Suddenly the comm screen flashed to life, producing a message. I looked at the screen not comprehending the gibberish I was reading; it looked like an array of hieroglyphics. I realized then that the message wasn't in Melelan, but Barsin, an obscure dialect indigenous to my mother's home world. This caught me off guard.

I peered at the message, unable to decipher its meaning, my panic rising as I noted that the message was linked to a degradation timer. It had started at ninety seconds and was counting down from there. I forced myself to focus. I hadn't spoken or read Barsin since my youth, and it took a conscious effort as my thoughts were hampered by the memory of my dead mother.

Seventy seconds.

I began to sweat. Ten more seconds passed. There were eight symbols grouped into six phrases. What did it mean? I bit my lip, studying each image. The first was a crest—an emblem of some sort. Four triangles joined in a point with intersecting lines in between each. That looked familiar. The next symbol was a vector clip holding a phallic symbol. The vector was pointing to the next symbol, a wavy line, perhaps representing water or waves. The next image was a snake dripping venom into a bowl. This was followed by a "Y" and a heart. Lastly, there was a picture of what I could only call a helix bracelet, a chain symbolizing continuity.

I glanced at the timer. Another twelve seconds had past. I ran my eyes over the symbols searching for the key to unlock the message's meaning. It then hit me. The first image was a family crest—my mother's. I remembered seeing it as a small boy when we lived on Barsin. But what did it have to do with water? And what did the bowl and snake represent—and the "Y" and heart? I began filling the meaning of the symbols with synonyms—ten more seconds past.

Crest—family, heritage, coat of arms, house of names, bloodline.

Waves—water, sea, ocean, fluid, current, movement.

Vector clip—mathematic—an arrow indicating direction. In biology, a carrier, transport or transmitter.

Phallic symbol—man, male, person, human. Together they were pointing to the snake and bowl. And the snake was dripping venom. Was it a poison or medicine dripping into the bowl? Did it represent nature, patience, fertility, or rebirth?

The "Y" and heart really had me for a loss. Of course, the chain was never ending, looping in circles, binding—immortality.

Suddenly a thought popped into my head. The crest was my heritage, my bloodline. It was followed by a phallic—male— that was me. Then water or liquid—fluid. The snake was spitting a fluid into the bowl. I then realized it wasn't the letter "Y" I was seeing, but a stethoscope placed next to a heart—and a heart pumped BLOOD.

It was all there and I understood—D-N-A—of course. The message was coded to my DNA which meant it needed a blood sample from me. The micro pin was actually a hypoduct. Shit!

I glanced at the timer. There were thirteen seconds left. Twelve ...

My heart raced. Only seconds remained. If I didn't act, the pin would wipe itself clean. I ejected the device from the side of the comm and jabbed it savagely into the fleshy part of my arm. The nail bit hard as the miniature barbs on its end snapped open like a tiny fish hook. I yanked it out, leaving behind a bleeding hole with bits of flesh and blood clinging to the pin's tip. I quickly pushed the pin back into the access port then waited—the timer froze in response at four seconds. There was a low hum, something was happening, hopefully an analysis of my DNA.

As I waited, I put pressure on my wound, nursing the jagged hole left by the hypoduct. The experience reiterated why these archaic devices were illegal, not to mention unpopular. Aside from spreading infectious diseases, they hurt. Leave it to Spires to be a sadistic pricworm. I glanced again at the comm screen; the timer was still frozen. Finally, a few seconds later there was a tone and Spires' face appeared on the screen. He looked tired. He began to speak, but his voice was so low I had to bring the comm to my ear to understand him. His words were sobering.

"... situation is grave. As you have learned, the Emperor and his family have been slated for execution. Even as I speak the Relcor are consolidating power. I.M.'s been compromised and there are traitors everywhere, including some who stood with the Emperor himself. With the utmost of reservation I am turning to you as a last resort. I know you are only S.G., but it is my hope that you can work a miracle. Lady Tasha has expressed her confidence, and I have little recourse but to agree. You've always been a pain in the ass Cantor, but you are the most resourceful officer in my command. So, here is how things lay."

"Underneath the palace is a small labyrinth of tunnels; passages that lead in and out. They are known to only a few, including myself, and the Emperor's immediate family. One of the passages you have already seen, it runs from my office to the Emperor's personal quarters. The others run from the throne room to the Senate, while another exits into a tea warehouse in the Brookshire District. It's called The King's Tea Company and inside you'll find a map, some weapons and supplies, also a ship with inter-dimensional warp drive. If you can make it there with the Princess you might have a chance to escape off-world. That's all I have, Captain. Save the Emperor's daughter if you can. She's the only remaining hope for our people."

Without further warning the screen went dead, and I caught a whiff of acidic foam. The comm and micro pin were dead, everything inside melted. I tossed it on the bed. What was I going to do now? I sat there, my mind racing with Spires' words playing in my head. Even using the tunnels he mentioned, how was I going to maneuver inside the palace and kidnap the Princess with no one finding out? Security inside would be a nightmare, and I had only a rudimentary understanding of the layout and no authorization clearance to access more information. Still, I had to try.

As I pondered my options I took note of the slide show on the view screen—the men and women parading naked to my

14

view. Suddenly an idea struck. I looked over to the intercom that rested on the night table next to the bed. Crossing to it I pushed the button for the front desk.

"Yesss," answered a raspy voice. It was the snik from the front desk.

"The girl who brought the comm to room twenty-four," I said. "Send her to me."

"Yesss," he replied. "Immediately."

A minute later there was a knock on my door. I answered it finding the young girl I'd seen earlier. She was barefoot and wearing lingerie which revealed more than it covered. My eyes ran down her body, taking in her augmented breasts and her well trimmed pubic region.

"Hello," she cooed, a smile running across her lips. "I was told that you wanted to play."

"Yes," I answered, opening the door for her to enter.

As she walked passed me I looked her over. She was about the right height, thin, perhaps a little anorexic; it made her look quite young. That met my needs. Her makeup though—it was too heavy; it plainly showed she was a seductive. That wouldn't do. And her breasts—well, there was nothing I could do about that. I looked at her braided hair. It was almost the right color. She stopped and pivoted as if she were a model, winking at me coyly.

"I like blonds," I said. "Can you lose the braids? And take off the makeup?"

That caught her off guard. I don't think anyone had ever asked her to do that before. I pulled a wad of credit notes from my pocket and handed her a twenty. She grabbed the bill eagerly, stuffing it into a hidden pocket inside her negligee. She then proceeded to undo her hair.

"You want plain Jane—suits me. I've had stranger bids. I'll wash my face in the privy, if that's okay?"

I stepped aside letting her have access to the room's lav.

A couple minutes later the girl returned, her hair undone, her face nearly clean except for the eyebrows. It seemed they were light brown tattoos permanently inked upon her face.

Still, without the heavy makeup, she looked even younger; that was excellent.

"This better?" she asked. She shook her head allowing her hair to fall freely about her face and shoulders.

"Much." I replied.

"You like your sweets young, yes? But perhaps—a little dirty?"

I didn't answer. I just moved about her, sizing her up. She watched me from the corner of her eye, taking me in. Then without warning she moved toward me, snuggling her body up to mine. I caught the scent of her cheap perfume.

"I like tall, clean shaven men," she breathed, in a low, husky whisper. "And I can give you anything you want for a price. I'm very good at what I do."

She then giggled and I felt her hand slide down to my crotch. I grabbed her arm and pushed it away, noticing as I did, the partially hidden track marks on her forearm. She was a hazic user. She pulled back; I couldn't tell if she was embarrassed, hurt, or angry.

"I don't care about that," I said. "Look, I don't like this room. Can we use yours?"

"What's wrong with this one?"

"It stinks," I replied.

"Okay—whatever you want. It's all the same to me."

She walked to the door. I grabbed my sword and followed her out into the hall, relieved to be out of the room. I had reason to believe that the billet was probably bugged and I had already caused enough intrigue with my request for a pin comm and the DAAT filter. It didn't make sense to take any chances.

The girl moved up the hall with me following behind. I noted her gait, her small, firm buttocks moving up and down in a smooth rhythm. She was young enough and definitely the right size. As we walked she queried me.

"Are you an off-worlder? We don't get many good looking ones like you—especially now."

I didn't answer.

"You look like you take care of yourself. Workout a lot?" She then giggled. "This should be a lot of fun. I might have to throw in some freebies."

"How old are you?" I inquired.

"Twenty-three," she answered.

Close enough, I mused.

At the end of the hall there was a juncture. We turned the corner and entered another hallway at which point she offered me her hand and another look of invitation. I wasn't interested, and I motioned for her to keep moving.

"My room's down here at the end of this hall," she said softly, giving me a wink.

She moved forward again, but not without advertising her wares once again. It was then that I got a good look at her legs and feet. She wore ankle bracelets; one on each foot—thin silver chains interwoven with percussion nodules. Instantly I knew she was an indenture—her movement tracked by a GP tracer with a detonator. This complicated matters.

"How much longer do you have?" I inquired.

She glanced back at me. I pointed to her feet.

"Seven," she answered.

"Would you be interested in getting out?"

Suddenly, without warning, the girl turned on me. She slammed her fists into my chest and pushed me back against the wall. I could tell from the fire in her eyes she was livid with anger. She snapped at me harshly.

"Listen, you fucking pricworm. I'm stuck here in this filthy rat's nest workin' day and night, fucking sickos like you for chump credit. I don't care what you think of me, but I won't be played with. If you got religion, take it somewhere else; don't come trying to save me. And don't pretend that you want to buy out my contract like some free-wheeling high roller; no one gets out, not from the Lacta."

I sensed the bitter resolve of those final words, her voice weakening as tears of hopelessness welled in her eyes. I said no more, but simply pulled my jacket back, then my shirt revealing my upper torso and the Imperial crest that was seared onto my left pectoral muscle near my heart. My chest bore the cauterized brand of the Emperor. The girl's eyes widened.

"I can make it happen," I whispered. "But only if you're interested–and it won't be free or easy. Now do you wanna hear more? Cause I'm in a hurry."

Hesitantly the girl drew back, uncertainty and hope over-powering her ire. She glanced nervously up and down the hall making sure it was clear. She then motioned for me to follow, her pace quickening as we moved down the hall. We climbed out a window and sat on the escape stairs where we had privacy. It was damn cold, but we were free to talk and I told her what I needed.

✿　✿　✿

Fear is a powerful motivator and no one is immune, not even the Lacta, and they carried a reputation for being one of the tougher species in the Empire. The old snik manning the front desk was no different. He thought he was tough, but he quickly collapsed into submission once he realized I was serious about skinning him alive. I nicked him twice, once in the arm, the other to his thigh, drawing blood. I then pressed my blade hard to his neck. He was eager to give me the percussion release codes and the location of a laser cutter. I waited as the girl fetched it and soon she was free. Of course, this was only the beginning. I knew that buying this girl from the Lacta under duress was neither legal nor wise. The Lacta were a vengeful people, known for reneging on their deals, and I needed a guarantee of safety. In order to buy us time I shot him up with hazic, everything the girl had in her possession. The snik would be out for days, but just in case, I took his laser cutter with me; it made a good weapon.

Out on the street I walked with the girl. Her name was Penta, and she asked far too many questions. But with her slight physique, face clean of makeup, and long flowing hair, she could almost double as the Princess—at least under cursory scrutiny. My only problem now was figuring where to go from here, so I put up with her prattle, even though it was driving me nuts.

It was well after midnight by the time we found The King's Tea warehouse. It was a large place, an exporting facility, situated in a trade center along with other commercial endeavors. Not surprisingly, it was heavily guarded by electronic surveillance. There were cameras everywhere, infrared, night focus and motion seekers. It was obvious that we weren't going to get inside the warehouse without notice. The question was—who would be watching? I decided to opt for the simplest route; the front door. I had nothing to lose. At the entrance I paused before an opaque scanning screen that read my facial features. Fortuitously, it seemed that my approach had been anticipated, for a second later I heard a heavy metallic click and the door slowly opened. I knew I had Spires to thank for this.

Penta and I entered the building. It was a typical warehouse, large and open, though dimly lit. Solar fuses were the only light source, providing just enough illumination for us to make our way around. Together Penta and I meandered through rows of pallets stacked high with tea while searching for the supplies left by Spires. As I led the way, Penta followed, whining incessantly, her voice turning my head from her blathering chatter. Literally, she was giving me a headache and I had much to concentrate on. I was overly concerned with the plan I was trying to formulate and I feared my chances for success.

After searching for twenty minutes, I found the supplies Spires had left in a small office. Everything was there as he said, packed in a small knapsack—a battery powered porta-light, a knife, a small nitro-blaster, and a map showing where the tunnels lay. I was good to go. There was no mention of the spaceship, but I assumed it was here someplace. Looking over the map, I began to plan my next move when suddenly there was a loud thump. I looked up to see Penta lying on the floor. She lay there shivering, her breathing labored. I made my way to her side; she was sweating profusely, her eyes shut. I lifted her head.

"Are you okay? I asked, patting her on the cheek.

Her response was unintelligible. I lifted her eyelids to find her eyes rolled back into her head, her mouth dry, and her tongue swollen. I felt like an idiot, realizing now what the problem was—why she'd been blathering on earlier. It was the drugs; withdrawal from hazic was like that. Under its influence one's metabolism was slowed, even lethargic, the mind coasting along in a peaceful, euphoric bliss, until you crashed. It was understandable why a girl in her profession might want something like that—it made sense, but withdrawal was another matter. I swore. This couldn't have happened at a worse time. If she didn't get more hazic soon, she'd probably die, and I still had to get us into the palace. This placed me in a quandary. What was I going to do?

I mulled my options. I wanted to leave the girl, and find another way in alone, but without a decoy they'd know instantly that Leanna was missing. Fuck. I needed a double on the inside; it was the only way, but the little critch was passed out. Damn it. I needed her up and functioning. She was willing—a whore seeking a way out. Without her, my chances for getting away were nil. I knew then and there what needed to be done. If this little critch needed hazic, then I needed to get it and fast.

With that decision I tried to make Penta as comfortable as I could. I found some water and a pile of burlap tea sacks. I laid a few down for her to rest on and covered her with the rest. Penta didn't resist—she couldn't, her will to fight was fading fast. I then left the warehouse with the knife and nitro-blaster tucked into my belt. I needed to find a hazic dealer.

Retracing my steps, I soon found myself back in the seedier areas of Corin where I purchased hazic with little effort—though I did have to approach several dealers. It seemed the level of fear was running high in Corin, and the hazic business was booming. Needless to say, the price for the drug was high. Three small vials cost me well over two hundred credits. It might have cost more, but the nitro-blaster in my belt kept things within reason. I just hoped I'd bought enough.

Unfortunately, the purchase of hazic presented a new problem. The dealers had no syringes, they were out, and I needed one to inject Penta. I'd broken hers when I shot up the snik. I was gravely frustrated. It seemed I was running into one obstacle after another and the hour was getting late. I now had to find a pharmaca where I could get my hands on a syringe. In a heat, I headed back toward the center of the city, cursing the fact that there were no cabs or PMs to rent or steal; anything that would make my journey faster. Worse yet, it was raining again, and I was wet, cold, and miserable. Still, as I walked I came to see a plus side to my ordeal. The isolation gave me time to plan and mull my options. I gave analysis on what I might find on entering the palace. Who or what would I face there? Would there be Relcor? Or would I find Melelan traitors holding the Emperor and his family? It was hard to say. In either case, I had my sword, a knife, a laser cutter and a small nitro-blaster; it wasn't much, but it would have to do.

For a brief second I toyed with the idea of acquiring an autolock, or several percussion gannas, but it would take time to obtain them and they would be useless if I wanted to maintain stealth and secrecy. Besides, I wanted to save the Emperor and his family, not blow them up. There had to be a better way. Then it hit me. A decent pharmaca would be stocked with numerous drugs and chemicals. Surely I could find some combination that would aid my mission. Perhaps etheral, a soporific or two, or better yet, asper-vem extract. What else? How about triacene? When mixed with colaia and water the reaction created a smoke-like fog. I made a mental catalog of things I might use.

It took forty minutes, but eventually I reached a commercial district where I was able to access a street registry. I looked up the closest pharmaca, pleased to find that there was one two streets over. Auspiciously it was a small, obscure place, sitting on a side street. It was dark inside and padlocked, its windows sealed by heavy wire mesh. Making my way to the back, I found the rear entrance secured by a metal door. I pulled the laser cutter from my pocket and cut through it like butter. Within minutes I was stealing all the drugs and chemicals I needed, filling my pockets and several small bags. With my blood pumping I made my way back to the street. Everything was silent, there were no alarms or sirens and I was free to leave without hindrance. I laughed quietly noting the lack of a no civil response to my break in. Undoubtedly I had triggered an alarm, but who cared? With the Relcor taking over tomorrow nothing mattered. Besides, ninety percent of Corin's civil security had already fled, along with everyone else.

Armed with my supplies I made it back to the warehouse where I found Penta unconscious. She looked worse than ever, sweat dripping off her as she convulsed, her lips blue, her mouth foaming. I took off my jacket and laid it under her head. I then went through the supplies I'd stolen and pulled out a syringe. I filled half of it with hazic, the rest with water, sorely afraid of killing her by giving her too much. Incapacitated as she was, it was easy to inject her, and within fifteen minutes I began to see results. Her eyes fluttered open and the color returned to her face. I gave her a couple tabs of anasin with some water. She was soon sitting, and babbling away. Now came the serious part.

CHAPTER TWO

The Palace

The tunnels under the palace were pitch-black, but Spires had seen to my needs. On my back, I carried the knapsack packed full of the drugs and chemicals I'd stolen, and in my hands the map and porta-light. With Penta following behind we made our way through the subterranean labyrinth to the heart of the Emperor's residence. The walk was long, but at the end we reached a twisting path of stairs that led straight up to their personal quarters. I glanced at my timer. It was three seventeen, and we had twenty stories still to climb. To my displeasure, Penta started to whine again; her muscles ached from her withdrawal seizures. Her complaints brought my blood to a boil. I turned to her, angry as hell.

"Listen you little critch," I seethed in her face. "I've gone to incredible lengths to buy your lazy ass and keep you alive. Now if you want your freedom and the rest of the hazic I carry, you'll shut up. Or else I'll give you back to the snik and let him fuck you over for another seven years."

Penta said nothing; she got the message, and we began to ascend. Our progress was slow and measured, for I wasn't sure how soundproof the walls were and we could ill afford any mistakes. Finally, we reached the top arriving at a small alcove about five feet square.

I handed Penta the light and began running my hands over the walls. I had no idea what I was looking for, but I knew there had to be something, a lever or pressure plate, something that would let me in—to where, I had no idea. All I knew was that this was the access juncture that had allowed Lady Tasha to reach Spires' office undetected. For several minutes I stumbled around feeling the cold, hard wall. Finally, I hit something—a small indentation, a tiny imprint no larger than my finger. I pressed against it and heard a soft click; the wall gave. I pushed against it, and it pivoted, admitting light to the alcove room. I stopped and listened; there was nothing. Pushing harder, the wall opened, and I stuck my head out. I saw immediately where we were. We'd entered a bathing chamber; a huge rock and tile spa facility, complete with showers, sauna and hot and cold pools. I looked around; the place was empty. I stepped out, thinking it was no wonder no one knew of this access. It was well hidden by the rock facade. I was impressed with the ingenuity of it. Who would think of looking for a secret passage in the Emperor's bathroom?

Stealthily, I moved to the sauna, ducking down behind the raised rock pit, with Penta following me. To my dismay, our shoes made too much noise on the tile, the room echoing our movement. This would not do, so I sat on the floor and removed my boots, along with my sword and the knapsack. I motioned for Penta to do the same. The girl complied, sitting next to me. She removed her sandals while I secured my knife and the nitro blaster in my belt. The two of us then crossed barefoot to the large doors that gave entrance to the spa. There, I listened for any sounds, again nothing. I cracked the door, and saw that the coast was clear. We then entered the next room, finding it to be a huge powder room.

Unexpectedly, I heard Penta blurt out. "My God, can you believe this ..."

I whirled around and slapped my hand across her mouth, pulling her in tight next to me. The glare in my eye was filled with reproach. "Do you want to die?" I whispered angrily in her ear.

She shook her head no.

"Then shut up."

I released her, the two of us standing frozen, until I was sure that we hadn't been discovered. I then whispered, "Stay here. And say nothing. I need to see what lies beyond this room."

Penta nodded her head, and I moved to the next door, but not before stealing a glance back. The poor girl was mesmerized, literally overwhelmed by the opulence surrounding her. To someone of her meager status this place was beyond comprehension; unlike anything she'd seen, and it was beautiful. The walls and ceiling of the powder room were hand-painted art, portions offset by delicate cloth paper and small tiled patterns. The hot and cold tubs bubbled softly, and like the sinks, were cast from fine porcelain and decorated with ornate gold fixtures. The countertops were inlaid with marbled silver and set with plush towels and fine linens. On the shelves was a colorful array of perfumes, soaps, lotions and talcum—enough to fill a small store. There were also magnificent, full length oil paintings and ornate mirrors, everything coordinated under the light of three gold-encrusted chandeliers, each one dripping with gleaming white crystals. I could see how she'd be taken by it all.

With Penta thoroughly preoccupied I made my way to the door. It was time to locate the Emperor and his family. I hoped I would find them alone and in time, but I wasn't overly optimistic. This place was huge; as large a mansion as one could imagine. Rumor had it that each family member had their own floor with separate guest accommodations. This was in addition to the reading libraries, game rooms, kitchens, fitness rooms and servant quarters—five full floors dedicated to their personal needs. What I understood less was the personal security system. Was it on? And, if so, what were its capabilities? And lastly, would I find everyone together in one location, and guarded by whom? There were so many variables here and much rested on the Empress and how much she had been able to prepare. She knew I would come and she knew what needed to be done. I could only hope for the best.

Widening the door a hair, I looked out onto a dimly lit hall. Things were dead quiet. I slipped out, relieved to find thick carpet under my feet muffling my movement. With my back against the wall I edged my way down the hall, noting that my placement was near to a series of bedrooms. At each doorway, I stopped and listened for signs of life. I heard nothing and my feelings were this area was empty; the Emperor was probably being held elsewhere. I continued on my course heading toward the center of the residence. Along the way I spotted several cameras. They were stationary and seemingly without power; this was good.

A few minutes later I turned down a new hallway which opened up into a large living area filled with elegant hand-crafted furniture, chandeliers, paintings and tapestries—none of the lights were on, so seeing was difficult. The only illumination came from a series of large picture windows that lined the room's far side; they overlooked the city of Corin. I noted the dim skyline and the dissipating rain clouds. The storm had broken; moonlight was percolating through the clouds, its subdued radiance aided by the approaching dawn.

I quickened my pace, darting across the room. There were no alarms and no indication of my being spotted by the security system—still, it was imperative to stay out of sight. I could ill afford to get caught at this point. Dawn was approaching and I had to find the Emperor and his family immediately. Fortunately, I caught a break. At the far end of the living area was an archway leading to another room. It was covered by full length curtains, but there was light seeping through the folds.

I made my way toward the arch and as I approached I heard garbled voices coming from the other side. I held my breath; this was it—first contact. I pulled out my knife and held it tightly. Then, inching my way to the wall, I moved to where the curtains joined the entrance. It was here that I stood, my blood pumping, as I parted the drapes ever so slightly with the point of my blade. I studied what lay on the other side; it was a dining room. At its center was a long, ornate table about twelve feet long, constructed of dark maloskiny. It was surrounded by heavy looking chairs with tall backs. They hindered my view, and I was forced to widen the curtain a bit further to garner a better look. What greeted me was beyond belief. The room had been trashed and was complete mess.

Plates and dishes were strewn everywhere, some still piled high with half-eaten food and drink. Bottles of wine and liquor lay half empty or spilled with a number of goblets smashed on the floor. It seemed a drunken feast had taken place here; but where was everyone? I then heard voices. They were gruff and heavy, definitely masculine, with a thick accent—Gatlic. To my frustration I was unable to tell who was talking. They were out of my line of sight.

In an effort to find out, I pulled the curtain back a fraction more, widening my perspective. The move allowed me to catch sight of the royal family. They were in the far corner of the room and quite alive. My heart racing, I studied their position. The three were shackled to a chair. The Emperor seated in the middle with Lady Tasha and Leanna standing on either side. The Emperor appeared to be asleep, drugged I'm sure, his head resting on his chest. I looked again at Lady Tasha and Leanna. Both looked like stiff mannequins, dressed in ceremonial garb for the treaty signing. I was impressed at how dignified they appeared in the face of this scene. My heart went out to both of them.

I then heard a gruff voice speak from the other side of the room. *"Gimmie some wine. I need more."*

"No" said another, *"You've had enough."*

The speech was definitely Gatlic, though I had no clue if they were Relcor or just off-world mercenaries. And worse, I had no idea if there were more passed out somewhere on the floor. Judging from the mess and the number of plates and empty bottles, a dozen or more must be guarding the Emperor, but the table was empty. Where were the rest? I took a step back, and tiptoed to the other side of the archway. There, I peeked through the other side of the drapes, spotting two men sitting at the table. They were both dressed in red robes and attacking the bounty spread across the table like gluttonous pigs. The noises they made were disgusting.

I was in a quandary. Only two were guarding the royal family, but they were halfway across the room, partially hidden by the table and chairs—out of reach for an easy strike. Making things worse, the only real weapon I carried was the nitro blaster; a small gas pistol, woefully sloppy in a fire fight. Its discharge would undoubtedly bring others into the fray. I fingered my knife; it wasn't much better. It'd be good for a quick stab or slice to the neck, but not much more. I needed something else—right now I had no advantage.

Fortuitously, something gave. I heard the sweet, young voice of Leanna speak; I strained to hear her words. She sounded small and fragile, asking to use the privy closet. I then saw movement from one of the captors. He threw down the piece of meat he was eating, stood, and walked in her direction. I noted the silver sheen of his skin as he crossed in front of me. I withdrew to the other side of the archway so I could follow him. What I saw made me livid.

With his silver-tipped fingers dripping with fatty grease, he stroked Leanna's yellow blonde hair and face. He then began to paw at her breasts, laughing harshly as she winced and crouched in fear. The Queen's reaction was immediate; she did her best to defend her daughter's honor. She flailed at the Relcor with her one free hand, reaching over her drugged husband to strike the silver-skinned lout while yelling at him. It did little good. Her actions were brushed aside, until finally, the Relcor sitting at the table could take no more; he interceded.

"Hold!" he yelled, to the lout causing the trouble. *"The master will be displeased if the girl is harmed. Leave her—Now!"*

Though I couldn't see the Relcor as he spoke, I did see the results of his words. The drunken one snarled at the order, revealing his displeasure, but he stopped fondling Leanna.

I then heard Lady Tasha speak to the one in charge. "My daughter needs to use the privy. I suggest you let her go. I don't think your Juc T'Krola will be pleased if my daughter shows up at the signing with her clothes stained with urine."

To that request, the senior Relcor granted leave. He threw a set of keys to the other whereby Leanna was released. I then saw my young charge rub her wrists and begin to walk toward the curtains where I stood. This was the chance I'd been waiting for. With the haste of a madman I rushed back across the living area on my tiptoes, quickly diving behind one of the settees before I was spotted. It was from this locale that I watched the Princess enter the room, accompanied by her Relcor captor. He held her by the shoulder. As I watched their silhouettes pass through the archway I readied my knife. This would have to be a clean kill. The room fell dark again and I felt my body tense as they moved in my direction. Suddenly the room burst into a blaze of light. It was the other Relcor. He stood in the archway, calling to the first.

"Hold there, Rakka!" he spoke in command.

The one with Leanna stopped and turned. *"Whaaat?"* he spit out in a drunken slur.

"The girl needs no one to hold her hand," said the one in the archway.

"But she might try to e-e-escape," whined the drunk one.

I then heard the sound of an autolock hammer being cocked back followed by the words. *"I fear your actions more than her escaping, Rakka. And I fear Juc T'Krola even more. Now return to the table or I will kill you where you stand."*

A small smile lit my face. This one definitely did not trust the other. I waited as the drunk one swayed back and forth, mulling his options.

"Fine," he finally responded. He then turned to the Princess. *"You can go! Be back in five minutes!"*

He then swaggered back to the dining room, but not before stumbling into several pieces of furniture and cursing.

I gave a sigh of relief—that had been close.

The room fell dark again and Leanna continued on her way to the lav. From behind the settee I watched her moonlit form cross. There was hope now, but I made no immediate move as I needed to be sure I wouldn't be seen. Fortunately, that didn't appear to be a problem for I could hear the angry voices of the

Relcor in the dining room. They were snapping at one another, and neither was happy. They were busy telling each other to go 'fuck themselves'—of which I concurred wholeheartedly. My attention turned back to my young charge.

At sixteen, Leanna had the spirit of a child, elegantly developing into a woman. She was a pretty thing with eyes of turquoise blue, a smooth porcelain face holding small dimples in both cheeks. I had known her since birth, and over the years my responsibility toward her had developed from being a shadow guard to eventually orchestrating all her excursions outside the Palace. During those sixteen years, I had come to know her exceedingly well, her rare tantrums, her endearing quirks and even her dreams. She was very likable and one day would have become the Empress of Melela if things had gone differently with the war. Now, it was impossible to say, and I was further concerned with the words I'd heard. Who was this master the Relcor mentioned? Was it Juc T'Krola himself? And what did it have to do with Leanna? In reality I knew the answer. I knew what happened to young girls when a brutal regime took over, especially the daughter of the losing ruler. It was the ugliest of fates and I had to make sure it didn't happen.

I waited until Leanna reached the end of the room. She was walking slowly, praying and crying all at the same time; I would not have expected less, her being under such stress. Seeing her like this brought my heart to bear. I had been on auto-pilot, planning this mission to rescue her, but now it was grave—it was real. As she turned the corner and entered the hallway, I slid my knife into my back pocket and bolted forward, scurrying up from the floor in an effort to fall in behind her. I almost didn't make it. I think she sensed me coming; she started to turn. In fear of her screaming, I leapt upon her, grabbing her by the head and mouth. I was overly rough, clasping my hands to her lips and neck—we fell to the carpet where we struggled. Harshly, I muffled her voice.

"Leanna, it's me—Rez!" I shouted in a whisper as she tried to elbow my gut. "I'm here to rescue you!"

I felt her body relax. She shook her head, recognizing my voice. I released her. She then rolled into my arms and I felt her breakdown, small sobs wracking her body. We had no time for this. I broke from her arms, stood up, and jerked her to her feet. She gave me a look of surprise.

"We've no time!" I said sternly. "We only have a few minutes. Now tell me—how many Relcor are guarding you and your parents?"

"Nine," she responded.

"Where are the rest?"

"Our servants took them to where my mother's jewels are hidden."

"Damn traitorous vags," I swore under my breath.

Leanna put her hand on my arm. "No, you don't understand. Mother instructed them—to give you time."

I felt like a heel. It seemed, not everyone in the royal court was out to betray the Emperor.

"How long have they been gone?"

"A good while," answered Leanna. "Most of them were pretty drunk. I fear some of our maids will be raped. They told mother they would do whatever was necessary to keep the Relcor busy, but I think our time is running thin. The guards have been rotating every four hours and that time is approaching."

"We need to move then."

I reached into my pockets and fumbled about, pulling out a number of small vials. Two contained Penta's hazic, another, asper-vem, and a fourth, a cobalt blue liquid—a soporific. I handed it to Leanna. "Do you think you can get this into their drink without them seeing? Maybe the drunken one?"

Leanna nodded her head as she fingered the vial. "I think so. What is it?"

"A sleeping potion. Now go. There's no time to waste."

I watched as Leanna headed back toward the dining room, slipping into the darkness. In turn, I ran toward the spa, praying for a miracle along the way. It was up to the young Princess to create the diversion I needed.

Reaching the bath, I reentered the room, catching Penta by surprise. She was stealing perfumes and bath salts, and the look on her face was both priceless and pathetic. I told her to take whatever she wanted. Indulging the young prostitute was meaningless at this point, and it allowed me the freedom to work. I moved to the sauna room and grabbed the knapsack filled with all the stuff I'd stolen from the pharmaca. I emptied out all its contents and began cramming what I needed into my pants pockets, including cotton wads, a hypo-spray, two sheathed syringes, and a dark glass bottle filled with etheral.

I wasn't sure exactly what I was going to need, but the drugs I carried had the potential to incapacitate more than a dozen men. I shoved the etheral bottle into my front pants pocket. I then moved toward the marble sinks where a number of cloth towels were arranged symmetrically on the countertop. I picked up one of the smaller facial cloths and shoved it into my back pocket. I then headed for the door, but not without giving one last word to Penta.

"If I'm not back in a half hour, take whatever you want and get out of here."

The girl stopped and looked at me. "What about my freedom?" she asked. "You said you'd get me papers."

"Then you better hope I get back," I answered, sliding out the door.

Outside in the hall everything was still deathly quiet and I made it to the living area with relative ease. However, as I approached the dining room, I heard a loud voice; it was heated and hostile in tone. I then heard Leanna yell.

"No, no, I didn't do anything!"

Something seemed to be transpiring. I immediately pulled out my knife and moved toward the curtains. There, I parted the folds a fraction to see what was happening. What I saw was unexpected and ill timed. One of the Relcor had the Princess by the arm. His back was to me, and he was striking her while yelling in Gatlic.

What did you do?

She shook her head crying. "Nothing, I didn't do anything. He just drank too much."

I glanced at the table; the other Relcor was passed out cold, his face in the food. I was late. I looked at the Relcor and the

Princess. The Relcor's hand was raised, poised to strike—in haste I reacted. I flipped the knife in my hand, and holding it by the point, I drew back the curtain and threw it as hard as I could into the creature's back. It caught him square between the shoulder blades, but it bounced off like a piece of rubber. I was floored; he was completely unharmed.

Surprised by the blow to his back, the Relcor turned in my direction and upon spying me, a look of disbelief crossed his face. He released the Princess and reached for his autolock, a move Leanna blocked by grabbing his arm. As she struggled with him I pulled my nitro blaster, but I couldn't fire without hitting her, so I threw it aside and bolted for the Relcor. I leaped atop the chair closest to me and onto the table, where I threw myself full force into his body, driving him back into the wall. His head hit hard with a crack, and the autolock fell from his grasp, but he was far from out. He began striking me with incredible force and I felt one of my ribs crack. Desperate to gain advantage, I pushed my shoulder into his chest and rammed him into the wall, knocking the wind out of him. We fell to the floor wrapped in each other's arms where we rolled over and over in a heated fury. If only I'd realized that Leanna had grabbed the autolock, my problems would have been lessened greatly, but I was engrossed in the fight of my life.

Wrestling with the alien I learned firsthand why we had lost the war. As a hybrid he was incredibly strong. His skin was truly protected by a metal hide and my blows fell with little effect. Worse yet, I did not have the same defense as he, and he pummeled me like a whipped ploth; I was no match against his armor and I was losing. Fortunately, I had something else; a broken bottle of etheral in my front pocket. The noxious fumes were pouring forth, filling the air about us. It was my only hope. In a desperate gamble, I wrapped my legs around his chest, locking him in a vice-like grip. I then grabbed his head with my arms, and with all my strength I pulled his face toward my loins while I held my breath. There, I smothered him, taking the blows he dished out as he breathed in the etheral liquid that soaked my pants.

Finally, after what seemed an eternity, I felt his body relax; he was not immune as I'd hoped, and he passed out. I pushed him off and sat back, my head spinning madly. I then saw Leanna holding the autolock.

"Cover him!" I ordered.

With her hands shaking, Leanna nodded. She pointed the weapon at the unconscious Relcor as I scooted back. Hastily, I struggled to undo my belt and zipper. I needed to pull my pants off; the sickening sweet smell of the etheral was overcoming my senses. Stripped down to my briefs, I threw my trousers toward the Relcor. They landed atop his face.

Leanna moved to my side and helped me up. "Rez, are you all right?"

"Yes, yes," I answered, steadying myself against the table. "Your mother, we must set your mother free."

"I'm already free, Captain," said a voice. "Thank you. I knew you'd come."

I looked up with woozy eyes, and to my delight, saw the Queen standing next to Leanna. Tears were running down both their faces. I glanced to the Emperor. He seemed awake now, but warily distant.

"He's still heavily sedated." I heard Lady Tasha say. "Captain, I need to re-set the security presets. The others are bound to return soon. We haven't much time."

I nodded my head and sank into one of the chairs. My head was spinning like a top, and my chest ached with every breath I took. How long I sat there I am unsure. I may have even passed out. At some point the Queen returned. She brought a stimulant which she waved under my nose; it brought me around. A minute or two later I sat with her face to face. Her words were direct and to the point.

"Captain, I need to know. What is your plan? Have you a way to get my daughter off Melela?"

I nodded, but before I could give any detail I heard Leanna exclaim in protest.

"No, No! I will not leave. Not without you and Father. You must come—both of you! You must. We all must flee together.

She then grabbed onto her mother and began crying.

I felt sick. Something in my heart told me that this was not going to go well. This child was not going to yield to the logic of the situation, and as thick-headed as I felt, I realized something had to be done. My response was going to determine the success of this mission. I looked to the floor where the body of the unconscious Relcor lay in repose, my pants covering his face. I stood and walked toward him. The closer I got the more I could smell the sweet stench of the etheral. I held my breath and picked up my pants, giving one last glance at the Queen as she held her daughter. Without a word, I grabbed Leanna from behind, wrapping my pants around her face. The fumes quickly brought her into submission. She sank limply and her mother took her from me. I threw my pants back onto the floor.

The look on the Queen's face was the saddest I've ever seen on any woman. With her unconscious child lying in her arms she wept. Though her own fate was sealed, she knew that this rescue was her daughter's only hope–that through my efforts, her precious child might be given life. She smiled weakly at me.

"You remind me of your father, Rez."

I was stunned. "You ... you knew my father?" I managed to stutter.

She smiled and nodded. "He was a brave man, too."

I wanted to know more, but the Relcor on the floor began to stir. He moaned and I realized that as a hybrid, the effect of the etheral was more than likely limited. I needed something else to keep him under control and tying him up didn't seem like an option. I grabbed the autolock from the table and pointed it at his head. I was ready to execute him on the spot, but something stopped me. Perhaps it was the noise factor, or simply the fact that I couldn't brutally execute this creature in front of my Queen and her daughter; there had to be another way. Suddenly, an idea hit.

Taking a deep breath I grabbed my pants from the floor and emptied the front pockets, dumping everything onto the table. Amidst the cotton wads and broken shards of glass there was a vial of hazic still in one piece. By some miracle it made it through my fight with the Relcor; all I needed now was a needle. I turned my pants around. In the back pocket was the facial cloth I'd grabbed from the bathroom, and tucked safely under its folds was a syringe still encased in plastic. I removed the hypodermic from its casing and filled the syringe with hazic.

Kneeling down next to the Relcor, I exposed his arm, touching and prodding his skin, testing his silver metallic hue. I was more than impressed; I could find no soft spots. His skin actually had a hardened metal cast to it, an iron finish given by the joining. Did it cover his entire body? It seemed so. All the rumors were true and no small needle was going to penetrate this metallic hide. No wonder the Empire had fallen to the likes of them.

I was about to give up and use the autolock when suddenly the Relcor yawned. It was then that I saw an opportunity. It appeared that his tongue still held a human-like quality—a soft and pliable pinkish tinge. Forcing the pricworm's mouth open, I stuck the needle deep within the underside of his tongue, emptying the syringe fully. Within seconds his body began convulsing, bouncing hard against the floor until it lay still. In my heart I hoped his death was hard and painful.

With this one dead I moved to the other who lay face down on the table. I refilled the hypo with hazic. Yanking the creature's head back I forced his mouth open with a butter knife. I then used a meat bone from the table to prop it open while I shot him up. His response was the same, convulsions followed by death. Neither one of the filthy alien heathens would bother the royal family again. Hopefully now we had more time. I looked to the Empress.

"There's a young woman awaiting us in the bathing facilities; she bears a likeness to Leanna. I promised her freedom, if she would act as our decoy. It's the only way to get Leanna out of here without raising suspicions."

"But too many here know Leanna," the Queen responded. "I.M. will recognize a double."

I approached the Empress and took her by the shoulders. Face to face I explained.

"We must dress her to look like Leanna. I brought a drug; a derivative that causes paralysis. Everyone must think that Leanna is dead—that you took her life to protect her. It's the only way. You and the Emperor must convince them all with your tears and sobs that you couldn't bear to see your daughter subjected to Juc T'Krola's vicious rule."

I saw the Queen nod. She looked at her daughter lying unconscious on the floor, tears again trickling down her face. She then looked at me and nodded.

"I knew you were the man for her."

The next hour that passed was one of the most intense that I've ever been through. The sun was beginning to rise and soon more Relcor would be arriving to take the Emperor and Empress to the Senate hall for the signing. With the security protocols reset to a priority defensive mode we moved to the bedrooms where we laid Leanna on a bed. The Queen stripped the clothes from her body and redressed her in pants and shirt. I too, had to make ready. With Penta's help we taped my chest with a bandage, for it hurt like hell every time I breathed. The girl then rinsed out my pants to dilute the etheral so I could wear them again. I then introduced her to the Empress.

Penta was overwhelmed by the presence of Lady Tasha. She literally prostrated herself on the floor groveling, though her abasement was due, in part, to the fact that she needed another shot of hazic. Sadly, it was her need for the drug that made the whole process easier, and she willingly complied with my request to don the Princess' clothes and move to her bedroom. It was then that I gave her the last remaining bit of hazic, which she immediately shot into her arm. I watched from alongside the bed as she fell into unconsciousness, her face contorting in an ugly manner—a side effect of the asper-vem I had mixed with her drug. Within minutes the young prostitute appeared seemingly dead, her skin growing cold, her heart rate and breathing falling to nonexistent levels. It was in this pose that I arranged the young girl's body under the cover of the Princess' quilt. In this disguise no one would question her identity.

The Queen entered the room and looked at Penta. "Is she dead?"

I checked Penta again for a pulse. It was extremely weak. "No," I said, "she's alive. In low doses asper-vem affects only the voluntary muscular system. I took into account her body weight and the fact that she's a hazic user—she'll live."

Lady Tasha smiled weakly. "How do you know all this?"

"It's an old trick—used on the battlefield to stabilize the wounded if no medical facilities are near. It looks worse than it is."

"They will kill her, if they discover this ruse."

I nodded. "That is a possibility. But it was a risk she was willing to take. She wanted a chance to start over."

The Queen nodded her head. She then crossed to the bed where Penta lay and knelt down next to her—there was something in her hand. She pushed whatever it was under the quilt and into the girl's bosom; then whispered to her.

"Thank you, Penta, for everything."

Penta did not move. She remained cold and stone-like as the Queen kissed her on the brow.

"It's time," I noted, softly. "I need to take Leanna and go."

Lady Tasha stood. "I know," she replied, her tears flowing once more. "I've already said my goodbyes." She looked at me with red and swollen eyes. "Take care of her, Rez. Give my daughter a chance to become a woman."

Knowing there was no reply I could give that would convey any real meaning I crisply stood at attention and saluted the Queen. I then turned and walked away, returning to the bedroom where Leanna lay unconscious. It was there, as I observed the Princess atop the bed that I realized everything was changing—that our worlds would never be the same. My only hope was that I would be there to somehow make a difference. Gathering the Princess up in my arms I slung her over my shoulder, taking with me with the knapsack and the autolock I'd taken from the Relcor. I then headed for the bathing room, taking us both down to the tunnels that ran below the palace.

By the time we reached the warehouse, morning had fully arrived and I was exhausted. I had over exerted myself. My chest ached and my legs were cramped; the Princess was a heavy load to carry. I lay her down on the bedding of tea sacks where Penta had lain earlier that night, and I brushed the hair from her face. She was pale and groggy from the etheral, and she carried the smell of vomit on her breath. My young hostage was not a pretty sight, but there was little I could do about that—I still had to find the ship. We needed to make good our escape.

Outside in a large courtyard, I found the ship resting on a docking platform under a camouflaged canopy. From its appearance, it was an old, weathered freighter used for transporting commercial goods. I took it in. It had definitely seen better days. It was dented and blemished from years of use. I seriously wondered if it was capable of flight. Spires had said there was a ship here with inter-dimensional warp capabilities—not this bucket. I entered the ship and soon discovered the reality of the situation. The exterior was a ruse. This was not an ordinary freighter. The interior was the complete opposite of the exterior. Inside the ship shone of the finest construction, a small luxury liner built for the comfort of the Emperor and his entourage. As I made my way down its corridors I saw fine rooms set for dining and sleeping. The ship required nothing and could easily handle a complement of a hundred people or more.

It was not until I reached the control room, that I realized I faced a major hurdle. Before me lay a starship panel filled with the latest gadgetry and weapons—all the technology our society mastered. This was no simple carrier with rudimentary flight controls like the ones used on the battlefield. The controls here were well beyond my capabilities. This ship was built for multi-dimensional interstellar travel, and from what I saw it was going to take more than one person to fly it. Simply put, I lacked the training and the personnel to handle it. I wanted to smack myself. Now what was I going to do? This placed me in a serious quandary. I had successfully kidnapped the Princess, leaving behind a decoy to feign our escape and now I was stymied in getting off Melela by a spaceship I couldn't fly. Fuck.

I wracked my brain, soon realizing the answer was obvious. I needed a master pilot to make this bucket fly, and the only place to find someone at this late date was back inside the Senate dome where the signing was to take place. What was left of the Imperial army would be there—and that included pilots and flight personnel. I just had to go back into the lion's den to get one.

Returning to Leanna's side I found her still under the influence of the etheral, though it was wearing off. I found some rope and tied her up, feeling guilty leaving her bound like an animal and sequestered in the warehouse, but I saw no other choice. I could only hope that she'd be safe until I returned. I grabbed the knapsack with the weapons and journeyed back into the tunnels, running like a wounded gazill toward the Senate building where the signing was about to begin. Glancing at my timer I saw I had less than an hour, and I was sweating like a ploth by the time I reached the underground juncture. My heart pounding, I climbed the two flights of stairs to the access point in the lower floor of the Senate building—a janitorial closet.

I opened the door a fraction and peeked out onto a wide hallway; it was empty. With my knapsack in hand I entered the hall, leaving behind a tally of mops, pails and cleaners—there I rested for a second, breathing heavy, holding my chest. I needed a minute to think and plan. Where would I find a pilot? I knew, of course, everyone was upstairs. How was I going to approach this?

Looking myself over I knew I stood out like a sore thumb. I was out of uniform, dirty, soiled and sweating—a complete wreck. And I needed a way to arm myself, but without drawing unnecessary attention. I removed my sword and pulled my shirt from my belt, draping it over my hips. Underneath this covering I hid my knife and the nitro blaster; the autolock was too big. I put everything back into the closet for my return. I then headed upstairs and quickly found myself surrounded by Imperial uniforms. Everyone was filing into the main rotunda for the ceremony. In an effort to find help, I bucked the flow of bodies and pressed forward, searching for a face I recognized.

I wasn't having much luck. Even more unnerving were the Relcor—they seemed to be everywhere, lining the walls, guarding the stairs and exits. The sight of their red robes and silver metallic faces caused my stomach to turn, for I knew what was going to happen. It was the strangest of sensations. Here we were, unarmed and ignorant, surrounded by conquerors that held ready their autolocks and blasters; I knew in my heart things were not going to bode well today. It was then that Kensey, one of my men, spotted me.

"Captain!" he yelled, moving toward me, a look of disbelief on his face. "Captain, you're out of uniform." He then realized his lack of protocol and saluted me. "Sir, sorry Sir. We just heard about the Princess. I'm sorry."

I returned his salute; then pushed him back against the wall. I whispered to him. "Where are the men?"

"They're waiting for you back at the deck. You weren't there so they sent me to look for you. Captain ... What's going on?"

"Listen, Kensey. Get the section—bring everyone here. We need to find a pilot."

"A pilot? Why?"

"Go! Do it—that's an order!"

Kensey saluted. "Yes, Sir." He then disappeared into the crowd, leaving me alone.

I ran my fingers through my hair. It was dirty, greasy and matted to my face. God, I was exhausted—and stressed. This was not the place to be. Turning in every direction I looked for a face, anyone who might help—anyone. I moved down the hall, suddenly spying Philip Golan. I couldn't believe my eyes, of all the pricworms in Melela.

"Fuck." I cursed under my breath. Fate was really playing me like vag.

Lowering my face I edged forward, pulling my knife from my belt. I hid it against the inside of my arm, slipping unnoticed toward Philip, reaching his backside before he was aware.

"Philip," I whispered.

His head turned, his face registering immediate disdain at the sight of me. He turned away, but I grabbed his arm and pushed my knife into his side; it was dangerously close to his liver. The move garnered the attention of his men. I pulled him back to the wall where I could watch their movement.

"Tell them to back off," I warned. He made a motion, stopping them.

"Captain," he said. "What can I do for you?"

"There isn't much time," I replied. "In a half hour this place is going to be a bloodbath."

"Captain, Captain ..." he replied, patronizingly. "You've always been prone to dramatics. This is a peace signing."

"Listen, you idiot. Look around. Who's armed here? I tell you—the Relcor intend a massacre." I then took a gamble. As big a pricworm as Philip was I didn't think him a traitor; I whispered to him. "I have the Princess; she's not dead."

He looked at me, I had his full attention. I then pressed.

"I'm going to give you a choice. I have a ship. Fly us out of here or I will gut you like a ploth, leaving your entrails on the floor."

"Where?"

"Brookshire."

I could tell from the look on his face, he knew I was telling the truth. He had probably built the ship and put it there.

Suddenly something unexpected happened. Two Relcor approached us from the other side. One had seen the knife in my hand.

"Brother," he said. "I see you are carrying a weapon. This is against ..."

Before another word fell from his lips I reached under my shirt and with my free hand pulled the nitro-blaster from my waist. Without hesitation I shot both of the metallic bastards point blank. The nitro-blaster blew a hole a foot wide in the first one and the shoulder off the second, sending blood and guts halfway down the hall. Both Relcor collapsed in a heap. And with that, all hell broke loose sending everyone scurrying. Amid the confusion, I pulled Philip with me. We had to get to the access tunnel.

There was chaos everywhere. Relcor were moving in to see what had happened and Imperial soldiers, angry and frustrated at having to surrender were not in the mood for any shit. Fights broke out with weapons fire ensuing. The hallway began to seethe back and forth and we had to push our way through it. I shoved Philip ahead, his men following behind. They weren't sure what was happening, but Philip gave no orders to the contrary so we moved with deliberation toward the basement. At the stairs we met my section—another ten men. Together, our two squads headed down to the basement of the Senate building. There was little resistance at this level, but behind us it was another matter.

All in all we had about twenty men as we entered the tunnel, and none had any idea of what was going on. They were simply following their leaders to an unknown destiny. Thirty minutes later we were in the warehouse where I grabbed the Princess. At this turn of events the men were befuddled. The Princess was alive? What was going on? Was I a traitor kidnapping the Emperor's daughter? My orders were quick and direct. I told them I would explain everything once we were airborne. Philip supported my efforts, and we moved toward the shipping dock.

Outside in the courtyard it became apparent we were in serious trouble. The sky overhead was filled with Relcor ships— hundreds of them. They covered the entire city. Unsure of our chances, I wondered if we'd be able to penetrate their defenses, but that point quickly became moot, for unexpectedly the ships overhead began to bomb the city. It was genocide.

We ran for the ship, pouring ourselves inside; each man responding to his training. I ordered mine to take the weapons batteries, and Philip ordered his forward to the cockpit and the ship's flight controls. If nothing else, we'd give the Relcor the best fight possible. In seconds we were bringing the ship to life, armed and ready.

At the rear of the cockpit I stood back out of the way with the Princess resting in my arms. I watched as Philip wrapped his forehead with the zero-link band—a wafer thin belt that gave him direct access to the ship's computers. It was his design and creation, and it granted him total control of the ship and its warp drives using thought patterns alone. I envied his gifted intellect and scientific comprehension. It was his family's genius that had brought our Empire to unparalleled heights. If only he wasn't marred by arrogance and a sick desire for young, prepubescent girls. That was the thorn, the nemesis between us—for I had caught him trying to fondle the Princess when she was only eight years old. Anyone else would have been castrated and sent to Irone, the outland moons of deep space, but not Philip. He was the great-grandson of Demitri Golan, inventor of inter-dimensional space warp. That detail, along with the war, and the fact that he was a genius in his own right had kept him free and in the service of the Emperor. God, I hated politics.

A jolt in the ship's movement brought me back to reality; we were now airborne, and leaving the safety of the canopy—unfortunately we were also a target. The Relcor saw us and we began to take fire. We returned the favor by surging forward and blasting our way through their defenses. Incredibly, this ship was far superior to anything I'd ever flown and with Philip commanding the helm we were at the edge of space in seconds. The only problem was there were more Relcor awaiting us in space and the chase was on. Under a bombardment of percussion and vacuum bombs exploding all around, our ship bobbed and weaved out of control, leaving those of us inside to feel like pebbles in a tin can. Still, through it all Philip worked his magic. With every blast, he countered the Relcor taking us further into open space. It was there that he initiated the inter-dimensional drive. I held my breath.

With the sounds of battle all around, I felt the Princess stir. I held her close, whispering words of comfort in her ear.

"We'll be safe soon," I said.

Unfortunately, those words were a lie; for as soon as they rolled from my tongue, someone began yelling the words I dreaded the most.

"We've been targeted—three nukes! Impact in five seconds!"

It was now or never and Philip knew it; he took the ship into inter-dimensional drive just as the nukes exploded around us. Our ship was hit and we were careening out of control, falling though the very dimensions of space itself. There were explosions both inside and outside our vessel, with sparks and debris flying everywhere, including us—we were like rag dolls being tossed in every direction. Unable to control myself or the Princess, I felt her torn from my arms. Suddenly, there was another huge jolt and I flew backwards—my head hitting the wall. At that point everything went black, and I lost consciousness.

CHAPTER THREE

Urlena

was on a beach—*that much* I knew. The sand kissing my
face was abrasive. I could taste salt, and there was grit in my
mouth. Struggling with self awareness, I wondered: Where
am I? Things weren't making sense. I opened one eye and felt
a stabbing pain. My head spun. God, I felt like shit. I tried to
move, but had little will. It felt like I had been beaten within
an inch of my life, and I ached everywhere. Squinting through
half-opened eyes, I lifted my head to see where I was—yes, it
was definitely a beach. This has to be a hallucination I thought,
my face sinking back into the sand—or a nightmare. A wave
crashed behind me and water rolled up soaking my feet; my
pants were wet. This wasn't a dream.

I forced my muscles into action, even though it felt like
they'd been ripped apart. My head was pounding, my chest
ached, and my stomach was one large knot. I was nauseous
and I wanted to throw up. The ground underneath me was wet
and I clawed at it, grabbing fistfuls of sand, forcing myself up.
Move, I said. Again, I heard the dull roar of waves behind me,

cold surf rolling up as far as my crotch. I needed to get away from the water.

Inching upwards on my belly, I made it a few feet before collapsing, where I lay panting, and struggling for breath. I rolled onto my back to ease the pain in my torso, wondering what had happened. Why was I here? And where was our ship? I searched the sky, but to my dismay, it did not provide any answers; it instead presented me with a new and more serious problem. I didn't recognize anything.

The sky itself was unlike anything I had ever seen before. It was covered by a huge, purplish cloud that stretched as far as I could see. The thing was downright ugly. Aside from its dark purple hue, it was plastered with immense splotches of glow-ing pink light that pulsed and flashed in an odd kind of pattern over its surface—a lightning of sorts. I watched as the splotches bounced back and forth in a quirky rhythm, rippling here and there covering the entire horizon. The whole thing seemed like a strange dance and it somehow made me feel uncomfortable. I tried to sit up and garner a better view, but as I did, I noticed the cloud changing. The splotches began to move in my direc-tion, coalescing over me; the entire beach around me was now lit up and glowing. I then saw the lights shrink, narrowing into what I can only describe as two large eyes. They seemed to look down upon me, centering on my person, and I felt as if I were burning under a magnifying glass.

I knew now beyond any shadow of a doubt, that the blow I had taken to my head was causing me to lose my mind. I shut my eyes, hoping against hope that the hallucination would stop, and that things would return to normal. I was only half successful. When I opened my eyes, the apparition over me was gone, but the cloud was still there. It had receded somewhat and was rotating slowly, looking a little more sedate, but then it belched, rather loudly, sending out a shower of tiny, white sparks, followed by a puff of blackened smoke. I covered my nose and mouth to stave off the putrid odor that was assaulting my senses, but the stench made me cough.

The sound I made seemed to stimulate the cloud, for with-out warning it began to change again, morphing into a kind of giant hand with funnel-like fingers. I watched as the funnels grew long and thick, spinning and whirling chaotically, inching their way toward the ground. They appeared now as miniature tornadoes, dark and looming vortexes with hollow interiors illuminated by flashes of lightning. The heat emanating within each funnel was substantial and I scooted back in fear. As I did, I was hit by a cold wave of water; it swept over me, its force dragging me back into the ocean. Fighting for dear life, I mustered every ounce of my strength and clawed my way back onto the beach. I then got up and bolted for a grouping of trees I saw bordering the beach some fifty feet away. There, under the safety of the branches, I collapsed while thankfully noting that the giant hand had disappeared.

Under the cover of the trees I looked myself over; I was pretty banged up. My ribs were still bandaged, but my clothes were torn to pieces, shredded rags barely clinging to my body. And my arm—it was burned pretty badly; how it happened I wasn't sure, but it hurt like hell. To say the least, I was a mess. I then noticed my boots. They were still on my feet, but the metal buckles were missing as were the buttons on my shirt. I was also missing the nitro-blaster, my knife, the laser cutter, and my sword. My first impression was that I had been stripped of anything of value and dropped off here on this beach and left for dead. But who could have done such a thing? Philip? The Relcor? I hadn't a clue.

I looked out onto the water. The sea was a dark, dirty green and the beach was littered with seaweed and shells—a collage of ocean discards strewn across the sand. There was no sign of civilization or familiar landmarks, nothing to give me a hint as to where I was. Worse yet, the air carried a horrid stench. It smelled like burnt electrical wire, and my eyes and sinuses were dripping in reaction to the acidic odor. I wondered if it was due to some type of air pollution, a byproduct of some type of industrial manufacturing or waste. Were there ships or vessels out on the sea burning some type of caustic fuel? I scanned the ocean listening for anything unusual. I saw or heard nothing. The only sounds assaulting me were the ocean's roar and the rumblings of the cloud overhead. It seemed I was quite alone.

Under the protection of the trees I lay back catching my breath. I had to piece together what happened and what I should do. It was all crazy. Of all the notions and scenarios I had envisioned when fleeing Melela, this was not one of them. After resting for a while, I got up and ventured out onto the beach. That's when I noticed my ripped and torn pants; they fell down to my knees. I pulled them up and quickly found that my zipper was gone. I then noticed my belt buckle; it was also gone. I was floored. What kind of thief would take the zipper and buckle from a man's trousers? It was beyond reasonable logic, and I felt like a vag walking down the beach holding on to my trousers like a common derelict.

As I walked the shoreline next to the trees, I took in my surroundings, particularly noting the vegetation: the plants, trees, and grass. They were very dreary looking, sporting pale hues of color. Most of the trees had slender, gray trunks and small canopies of long, thin leaves, their color varying from gold to a pinkish brown. This was not the lush, green foliage of Melela I was used to. Even more bleak was the brush and grass that poked up meagerly through the coarse white sand at my feet. Most of it was yellow and brown, with speckles of gray; it looked dry, like it hadn't seen rain in months. I glanced up at the cloud, wondering if it was casting a pall over everything, perhaps with its heat or radiation. As it were, everything seemed depressed and subdued under its cover; I didn't like the way it lingered there. This place really needed some rain.

That thought made things worse. I realized I was thirsty; I needed water. My lips were burnt and dry, and my stomach was still churning, and my arm needed a cool compress. Warily I looked around. I had no idea which way to go, but then I thought: What did it matter? If I truly was on some alien world, completely unknown to me, then all the rules had been changed. There could be danger anywhere—insects, wild beasts—even the vegetation might be hostile.

I began to trudge along, heading down the beach, pants in hand, my boots sinking into the sand. At every step I felt uneasy, a sense of apprehension lingering over me—it felt like I wasn't alone. A shiver ran down my spine.

Suddenly a strange, faint voice echoed in my head—a high pitched childlike squeak ...

"Man ... alone ... hurt ..."

I quickly whirled around and looked up and down the beach—there was nothing. Spooked and unsure, I moved on convincing myself it was the lack of water that was causing me to hallucinate. After plodding along a short distance it came to me that I was looking in the wrong place for water. Inland was the obvious choice, so I turned and headed into the vegetation.

Under the safety of the trees and thicker foliage I felt better—safer from the cloud. It was very quiet here. There seemed to be no life—no birds, no insects, only a hint of a breeze. I forged on, searching for an indication of water, a stream, wet ground cover, mud—anything.

For the next hour I combed the land, my thirst becoming unbearable. Finally, I had a bit of luck; I stepped on some kind of moss. It squished softly under my boot. I knelt on the ground and scraped at the brownish matted turf with my fingers, finding it damp underneath. I looked up and saw that the carpeted mass grew thicker in one direction so I followed it. Eventually, near the base of some glazed, black rocks I found the source nourishing the moss—a small tiny pool of water no bigger than a small bowl. I fell to my hands and knees. The water was clear and I was overcome with delirium. I could only hope it was safe and wouldn't kill me. I buried my face in the shallow pool and lapped the water like a greedy animal, gulping it down in mouthfuls until the water turned muddy.

My thirst quenched, I rolled onto my back and looked around—this was indeed a strange place. Perplexed by my predicament my thoughts raced. Where was I? How long had I been here? It couldn't have been that long—my wounds were still fresh. Was there anyone else here or was I alone? It was then that I turned and noticed the moss bowl I'd been drinking from—it was refilling itself. Tiny beads of moisture were seeping out from under the black rocks and trickling down through the moss. I was pleased. It was at least gratifying to know I wouldn't die from a lack of water. I pulled off my boots, and using one, I scraped away the brown carpet of moss making a deep hole. I needed it big enough so I could fill my boot. When I finished digging I laid my boot on its side to capture the runoff. It was a slow process, but when it became half full I took it and poured the water over my head, washing the dirt, sweat, and dried blood from my face, chest, and arm.

Momentarily refreshed I pondered my next move, and my thoughts went to the Princess. What had happened to her? Was she alive? Was she injured? With all my heart I hoped she was safe, but I had to wonder: If she was here, where could she be? God forbid, not in such a desolate place as this. I remembered my promise to her mother, and I kicked myself for failing to keep the young girl safe.

Suddenly, my musings were interrupted. I heard the child-like squeak in my head again.

"Man ... hurt ... come ... so alone ..."

I got up and looked around. Where was that voice coming from?

I put my boots back on and headed through the brush not knowing where I was going, but something seemed to be guiding me. After several minutes of walking I stumbled out onto the beach again. I realized now that I was probably on an island or peninsula—how big it was I wasn't sure.

The voice entered my head again. *"Man ... hurt ... hurry ..."*

It was then that I caught sight of movement in the water. A large fish or something shot out of the waves then quickly splashed back down. I was overjoyed—there was life here. I ran to the ocean's edge and saw the fish jump again, but this time further down the beach. I moved after it, following its direction, but came to an abrupt halt when I saw movement in the clouds overhead. Just ahead, the dark pink cloud was shifting, forming another one of those giant hands. I watched as several funnel-like fingers emanated from it, each narrow twister snaking down from the sky, whirling and twisting back and forth in an odd sort of dance. The funnels touched the ground creating a whirlwind of dust that obscured my view. Lightning bolts followed, striking the ground with resounding explosions. I fell to the ground in fear, but the voice returned in my head, urging me on. It told me to hurry.

In haste, I jumped up and ran toward the whirlwinds. And to my surprise, as I got closer, they unexpectedly withdrew, disappearing completely. Almost immediately the entire beach was calm again and I could see now that there was a dark lump lying in the sand. I moved closer–it was a man. I ran to him and knelt down; recognizing him immediately–it was Kensey. I rolled him onto his back and checked for a heartbeat. He was barely breathing.

I looked madly about. I needed to get Kensey off the beach before the funnels returned. I locked my hands under his armpits and pulled him into the safety of the trees. I then tried to give him aid—what little I could. Like me, his uniform was in disarray, shredded and torn–his lips dry and cracked. He tried to talk, but a hoarse, raspy muttering was all I heard. I bent down and spoke to him.

"Kensey, its Rez. You're going to be all right. I'm going to get some water. I'll be right back."

With undue haste I flew back to the shallow pool of water I'd found earlier. There, I partially filled one of my boots, returning to Kensey as fast as I could, but it was too late. As I knelt down next to his body I could see from his glazed, lifeless eyes that he had passed. Angrily, I threw my boots aside, watching as the water spilled out and seeped into the dry sand.

Alone once again, I buried Kensey, digging out a grave with seashells I found on the beach. As I covered his body, I noted the similarities of his clothing to mine. He had been stripped of his medals, dress ornaments, belt buckle and even his buttons, before being dumped here like me. This was unacceptable and I was furious. I looked at the sky and swore aloud; somebody, whoever was responsible for this outrage was going to pay— and dearly.

Over the next three days I explored the island, though I found it hard to judge time. The sky above me never seemed to change. It was constantly overcast, and even during periods where the daylight seemed to dim somewhat, the cloud's luminescence would counteract it, confusing my senses entirely.

Still, it was those brief periods that made me wonder: Was there nightfall here? I couldn't be sure. All I knew was that I had rounded the island twice and there was no one else to be found. I did manage during my exploration, to find some bitter tasting berries and more water, but that was all. And with my hunger becoming paramount, it soon became clear; I needed to find a way off this island or I would die here.

I climbed a couple of trees and surveyed the ocean in several places, and I thought I spotted another island about two or three leagues away—it was hard to judge the distance. I didn't like the idea of swimming. The water was dirty looking, but swimming beat starving. I decided it would be best to try after resting first.

Later, when the light faded a little, I lay down on the moss bed I'd built near my watering hole and fell asleep. I'm not sure how long I was out, but when I awoke it was to a stunning find—I saw stars shining through the trees. The ghastly cloud that had muted my spirits for days on end was gone. The sky above was clear and dark—not as black as nights on Melela, but still, it was nighttime and the sky was filled with stars. I raced for the beach and looked up—again I was stunned. Not only were there stars, but there were moons—three of them. However, that is not what struck me most.

Out over the ocean, rising like a small sun, was a monolithic gas giant—a huge planet, blood-red in color. It was radiant in its beauty and its size quickly swallowed the entire horizon. Mesmerized, I watched in awe as its form took control of the night sky. The reflective light from its body turned the sand at my feet red, and the sea waters before me a deep violet. In addition to its breathtaking magnificence I took notice of three moons whirling in orbit about her. They appeared like jeweled orbs, red, white, and blue in color, each one shining brightly against the night sky. I knew now beyond any shadow of a doubt I was nowhere near Melela, for these celestial bodies were unlike anything I'd ever seen. It was then that my ruminations were cut short—a new sight beset me.

From up the beach, I saw two small lights wink into view. My first thoughts were that they were fireflies dancing along the water's edge, but they continued to grow in size as they approached, and I soon realized they were too big. Both were about the size of a plum and they were spherical in their shape. Taken by their appearance, I wondered what they were. Were they insects of some sort? Or perhaps, exotic aves—who could say? Whatever they were they reminded me of fairies from a children's book, weaving and bobbing as they did, like butterflies.

As they passed by me I tried to garner a closer look, but the glow of their bodies and their erratic flight made analysis difficult. It seemed that they were covered with a thin, translucent membrane similar to that of a jellyfish. And this observation made me wonder if they were aquatic in nature—a possible explanation for their sudden appearance, and the fact that they kept themselves quite close to the water.

With little else to do, I followed the creatures down the beach and to my surprise they didn't seem to mind my company. In fact, they seemed attracted to me. Perhaps it was my body heat or even my breath. Whatever the reason, they soon were floating around me—darting in and out, almost to my nose. To say the least, I was fascinated by the attention.

"Hello," I said, in wonder as the two floated about. "Are you the local greeters for this island? If so, I must confess, I am very lost. Is there a chance you could help me find my way back home?"

I got no response—which was no surprise, the little glowers were soundless to my query. It seemed their only concern was floating on the night's cool breeze, and following their carefree path. I had no idea where they were headed or what their purpose might be. Nor did I care. They were simply a beautiful mystery taking my mind off things.

Our walk along the beach continued for several minutes longer, with one of the glowers eventually alighting upon my fingertip. I was most taken by that gesture and I wondered if there was a measure of intelligence within the makings of the two. Who could say? Suddenly, however, I had the misfortune of sneezing, and that changed everything. The two glowers began to zip around me like a pair of angry mosquitoes emitting a sharp, whining sound. It was obvious that I had disrupted their harmony, and I stepped back to avoid being stung, but nothing happened. A moment later they settled back down, and once again, the two began to dance about me. This continued for a few minutes more, and then to my disappointment, they turned and headed out over the ocean's waters, disappearing without a trace. I was saddened by their leaving as now I had nothing but my loneliness to keep me company.

I had no further contact with the glowers or anything else that evening. The rest of the night I slept on the beach under the stars only to be awoken the following morning by the sun. It was a young, yellow-white star, illuminating the sky above with warmth and hope. I welcomed its brightness and the new day that greeted me.

✵ ✵ ✵

With the morning sun high and the red gas giant shining brightly over my head my spirits rose. This was as good a time as any to try and make it to the next island. I knew I couldn't swim the entire distance, so I needed to find something I could use to float across. Searching the brush, I found a fallen tree in the undergrowth. It was an old thing, part of it decaying. I pulled it from the brush and dragged it down to the water, where I broke off a bunch of its scraggy branches and limbs. I was surprised at how easily I was able to manage this. It seemed I had regained a measure of strength since leaving Melela. I pushed the log into the water, and to my good fortune, it floated. So, I took off my boots and tattered pants and waded in after it. The ocean was cool, but not unpleasant. I draped my tattered pants over the log to protect my skin from the bark and pushed the log out to sea. That proved to be difficult. I only had one free hand as the other was holding onto my boots. Finally, with the help of the out-going tide, I met with success.

The rest of my day was a tiresome blur of kicking and pushing against the log, trying to make my way through the water. In all honesty I had no idea whether or not I was getting anywhere. After hours of struggling I began to feel I'd made a mistake, though the reality was, I had nowhere else to go. Eventually evening fell, and the skies became dark as I floated helplessly in waters that were dark and mysterious. I was worried. Floating in the depths was quite unsettling, and my biggest fear was that I would be eaten. Who knew what lay in this ocean? For the remainder of the night I struggled to stay atop the log, but it kept turning, and all I could do was hold on for dear life. Hours passed—I tried to sleep, but that was next to impossible. I was near the point of giving up, resigned to the fact that I was going to drown, when I began to think of the Princess. I wondered what had happened to her and the others. Suddenly, to my amazement, a visitor appeared. It was one of the glowers from the night before. What in the world was it doing out here and in the middle of the ocean? I stared at it as it lit upon the end of the log, where it seemed to watch me.

"Hello," I said, my spirits buoyed by its appearance. "Are you lost? You're not following me are you?"

There was no response—the little thing just rested on the end of the log, the two of us bobbing along in the water. I didn't care. For me, it was a nice distraction and I passed the time introducing myself, telling it my name, where I had come from, and who I was. It was a great listener and soon, thanks to its being there, I saw light cresting on the horizon. I had made it through the night.

Utterly relieved, I couldn't believe that I had survived—that the end hadn't come. With light breaking I looked around to see if I could see anything. Was I headed in the right direction? I couldn't tell—it was still too dark. Exhausted, I shifted my position, my actions causing me to splash in the water. This disturbed my tiny companion. Sadly I watched as it floated up into the air. I was certain it was going to disappear. Clinging to the log, I thanked it through salt burned lips.

"Thank you for being here," I sighed. "You were a big help."

Unexpectedly, there came a reaction. The glower bobbled up and down as it headed toward me, where it hovered close to my face. Through wet, bleary eyes I watched as it twirled around and around, spinning its light—I hadn't noticed that the night before. The effect was very calming—almost hypnotic. Then, without any warning the glower pressed itself against my sweat soaked brow, forcing my eyes shut. I felt a tingle. When I opened my eyes the glower was gone and I was once again alone in the water. What had happened? I was totally bewildered by what had just occurred. Suddenly, there was a voice in my head.

"Man ... swim ... bad ..."

My head snapped up: What was that? I looked around and saw nothing. Was it fatigue? Was I now hearing things? I was so exhausted—my legs were ready to fall off. I stopped moving and tried to rest, holding on for dear life, when something hit the log, jarring it. It then brushed against me, grazing my leg. Fear set in. I was about to become someone's breakfast. I struggled to get on top of the log, but it rolled and my head went underwater. I panicked, grasping madly for anything.

Something hit me again—this time pushing me up. I grabbed the log and held on; looking to see what was after me. There was movement in the water next to me, and I watched as something broke the surface. It was a very large fish, with a long snout, and it peered at me in a most curious manner. It then spoke, chattering in my head.

"Man ... Swim ... Bad ..."

I was stunned. It was— It was—a talking fish!

"No ... fish ... Dolla ..."

I couldn't contain myself, and I spoke aloud. "My God, you're a talking fish!"

"No ... fish ... Dolla ... No ... fish ..."

I stared at the creature floating next to me. Its skin was gray, and it had blow spouts atop its head and two very large, intelligent looking eyes. It stared back. Suddenly there was motion on my other side and another one of these fish ...

"*Dolla!*" objected another voice, similar to the first.

I looked at the second creature. I understood now. They were called Dolla.

"Can you help me?" I asked. "I am trying to get to that island." I pointed in the direction I thought I was heading.

I'm not sure if the two aquatic creatures understood me or not, but with no further prodding, they both began to push on the log. Within minutes I was being propelled across the sea with no clue as to where I was going, but feeling reassured that there was a measure of intelligence on this world.

For the next half hour I clung precariously to the log, bobbing up and down as the two Dolla spirited me forward. The ride was rough and the experience unnerving, for the further out we got, the colder and darker the water became. I felt vulnerable and out of my element. I think the Dolla sensed my fear for our pace soon quickened and we cut through the water with added speed. I was most impressed with their strength and quite curious to where we were going. At times I tried to pull myself up over the log to garner a view, but all I saw were waves ebbing back and forth with dark green water everywhere.

Making the best of the situation, I questioned the Dolla, asking them where I was, or if they knew how I got here. I received no answer and I quickly realized I was talking to myself. My rescuers were preoccupied and not in the mood for conversation. They just kept pushing me further out to sea.

A short time later we struck something hard—perhaps a rock or a reef. Whatever it was, it jarred the log and I slipped off—my entire body sinking under water. While under, I was struck by one of the log's branches and knocked nearly unconscious. Dazed and disoriented, I floundered helplessly like a sick norka, only to be rescued again by one of the Dolla. The creature grabbed my arm with its mouth and dragged me upwards. I broke the surface coughing and spitting sea water as I made for the log. I grabbed it and pulled myself up, and as I did, I found that I was no longer alone. Surrounding me now were more Dolla, only they weren't alone. Sitting atop their backs were men—at least, I think they were men. They were bare-chested creatures, a blueish-green in color, each with two arms and two legs, but they resembled fish as well. Their faces were thin and narrow, their eyes small and dark, and their noses sharp and bony. Oddly enough, their hair was even stranger looking; a wiggling mass of tentacle-like strands.

At my appearance the new creatures began to point and jabber, vocally issuing a series of clicks and high-pitched whistle sounds. In their hands they carried weapons, which they immediately raised and pointed at me. I was unsure of what they wanted or what I should do, so I just looked at them, taking in their appearance. I immediately saw that they were adapted to life in the water for their fingers were connected by a thin membrane of webbing–I couldn't see their feet. I turned about, trying to take everything in–this was incredible. In all my travels I had never run into creatures like these. I noticed from their profiles that they also had fish-like gills, flaps behind their ears.

For the next few seconds we all stood transfixed, looking at one another. No one knew quite what to do–suddenly the situation got tense and the fish men became more animated and vocal. I got the feeling they were arguing.

I decided to say something. "Hello," I said.

Their voices fell silent.

"I come in friendship."

To me that sounded stupid, but I knew they wouldn't understand it anyway. Suddenly there was a flurry of movement and sound–they raised their weapons aggressively and pointed them at me. I raised my hands above the water to show that I was unarmed and my head went under. That's when several of them dove in—grabbing me.

CHAPTER FOUR

The Aquella

was bound and tied to the rear of one of the Dolla in a most undignified way. It was torture of the worst kind. I was dragged through the water like fish bait, gasping for air as I twisted and turned helplessly on a rope line. It was a hideous feeling–choking on salt water, my life flashing before me, and no one willing to help–well, except the Dolla. They seemed sympathetic to my plight. They understood my terror, and when the need arose, they pushed me to the surface so I could breathe. Their efforts saved my life. The fish-men or Aquella as I later came to know them, were not nearly so sympathetic. They were a nasty lot, and I quickly came to hate most of them.

How I survived the entire ordeal was beyond me, but I managed to live long enough for us to reach a rendezvous point of some sort. I was half drowned, barely conscious and not fully cognizant of what was going on, but due to the efforts of the Dolla, the Aquella finally realized I couldn't breathe underwater. They were perplexed by this, and as I was buoyed by the Dolla, the Aquella argued over what to do with me. It was finally decided that I should be taken to their city under the sea.

In order to survive the journey I was encased in a bubble of elastic skin or membrane—I wasn't really sure. There was much going on that I did not understand, and I had little will to fight or resist in my present condition. The material they wrapped around me was extremely strong and resilient, yet very pliable—and it held air. Oddly enough, I was sealed inside this bubble with a large pile of wet seaweed, a purple colored plant that stuck to my body and face like glue. It was not a pleasant experience; the leaves were slimy and they gave off a rancid odor.

After being secured inside my elastic prison, my hands still bound with rope, I was then pulled under the water. I immediately noticed the temperature dropping as we sank deeper, and it also got darker. I am not sure how long we traveled; time seemed suspended. Much to my frustration, my view was limited by the opaqueness of the material around me and I was disoriented. I was also perplexed by the fact that I could breathe with so little trouble in my small prison—I would learn later that the purple seaweed supplied oxygen.

The trip to the ocean bottom was serene—at least I wasn't drowning, and we traveled a good distance. Toward the end of our journey I got the sense that we'd entered a cave or dark cavern—I saw no light at all except for an occasional flash of luminescent color—perhaps fish or algae. Finally, we stopped—I wasn't sure why—I just lay in my prison in quiet solitude, buoyed by the membrane bubble around me. Suddenly, there was a rapid surge of movement and I felt myself shooting upward—the motion made me sick. Without warning, I broke the surface of the water, where I bounced several times, slapping the surface before coming to rest. It was disconcerting, and I lay there wondering what would happen next. I didn't wait long—a knife suddenly punctured the bubble, slicing it open. The air whooshed out and I sank into the water. Two fish-men grabbed me, and pushed me back to the surface.

When we broke the water I saw we were in a large cavern. The light overhead was subdued, but I could tell the place was big, in fact enormous. I was given little time to observe my surroundings, however, as I was abruptly shoved toward a rocky outcrop—a dock or landing of sorts. Standing there were more fish-men. They grabbed me and hoisted me onto the landing where they dropped me like the catch of the day. I was then kicked, jabbed, poked and rolled across the rocks as the men inspected me. I felt like a lab specimen and I glared at my gang of captors who prodded and jabbed me in ignorance. They were a band of hoodlums who spoke in harsh clicks and whiny pitches that left me angry and wishing for my sword. I wanted to fillet their slimy, blue-scaled skin and roast them over an open fire, but I was powerless. I was totally at the mercy of these creepy, sea swimming bultocks.

My abusive treatment went on for some time, and I was spitting blood from my internal wounds when someone finally came along and ordered the fish-men to move me. I was yanked up and shoved in the direction of some structures. It was the first time I got a look at where the Aquella lived. To my surprise, and in contrast to their harsh treatment, the city of the Aquella was beautiful. The homes, buildings or whatever they were, were gorgeous. The structures were built from the material you would find inside sea shells. They looked of porcelain or mother of pearl and reflected a rainbow of multi-colored hues from some light source I couldn't identify.

I was taken inside a building and forced to lie upon a table, where I was restrained and my tattered clothes ripped from my body. As I lay there naked more fish-like creatures began to arrive. I was an unexpected surprise which invited an ongoing parade of fish-men entering and leaving the room. Some would look me over, gesture and jabber wildly, leaving me to assume that they'd never seen someone like me before. Others were slightly more professional, and I pondered if they were doctors or scientists. They were dressed in long white tunics, and they held odd looking devices in their webbed hands. I was examined and prodded thoroughly by them, turned every which way, as they checked my eyes, nose, and mouth. They seemed especially perplexed by my facial hair; I was an enigma that needed to be fixed. That's when two of them grabbed my head while another placed something over my nose and mouth—I passed out.

How much time passed, I had no idea. I awoke hours, days, maybe a week or more later in a new location. I now rested on a soft bed of sorts and I was in extreme pain. My head throbbed and I ached all over, from my ears all the way down to my neck, throat, and chest. I was heavily bandaged, and I had tubes protruding from my nose and mouth, with one running down my throat and into my chest. My arms and legs were restrained. I was held motionless by some kind of elastic rope and there tubes feeding fluids to my body. Some were clear, others of an odd color—a pinkish green, a dark yellow, one a dark-mud brown that I believe pierced my stomach or bowels. It was obvious that I was in the hands of an intelligent people, though I didn't have a clue as to what was going on and I was not amused at being a lab rat.

As I lay in the bed powerless, I studied the people who had taken me hostage. My impressions quickly led me to believe that I had fallen into a society based on a military or class structure. Some of the fish-men who stopped by to observe me were obviously people of power. They were decorated and wore colored uniforms, tunics comprised of a soft material that draped from one shoulder to the waist. Their lower bodies were covered by a stiff coarse material that wrapped their waists all the way down to their thighs. These men were also armed. They sported knives carved of onyx or some other shiny dark stone. Others carried long thin harpoons ridged with nasty looking hooks on their end, and still others carried small crossbows that dangled from their waists. The ones who cared for me carried no weapons—they appeared to be of another caste and were dressed more informally with simple colored or white tunics that fell from their shoulders to floor.

It was in this hospital setting that I met my first female Aquella. Like the men, she was scaly skinned, a bluish-green in hue, but her features were more refined. Her dark eyes had coal black pupils and her face was smaller than her male counterparts. The major difference was her breasts. They were large and uncovered. I was curious as to why this was, but never did find an answer. However, thanks to her, my recovery was endurable. She changed my bandages daily, kept my beard trimmed, and was at least, gentler than the males—a blessing after all I'd been through. She also tried to talk to me on numerous occasions, but I was unable to respond with the tube running down my throat and I had no understanding of what she was saying anyway.

I realized later that I was being fed through the tubes in my arms and given pain medication. This was to combat the feverish bouts that would sometimes rack my body for days. Slowly, through all of this, I improved. This was evident from the Aquellian doctors who came in to look at my wounds. I was healing. I learned later that my head had been shaved and that surgery was performed on me—some type of genetic assimilation. Little did I know it then, but the procedure would have a drastic impact on my life. A week or two later, the bandages came off, and the tubes were pulled from my nose and mouth— a very nasty experience. I was given solid food for the first time. I'm not sure what it was, but it tasted like fish and seaweed. Not a great combination, though it did rebuild my stamina.

After what may have been months of recovery, I got the surprise of my life when I discovered what my surgery was all about. I was awoken from a deep sleep by several military types. These fish-men were heavily armed and the doctor alongside them seemed almost fearful of their presence. They spoke to him harshly and in quick tones, and he bowed and acquiesced to their demands immediately. Though my observations were still limited, I was beginning to see that Aquellian society was brutal and tyrannical in nature.

My beliefs were confirmed by what happened next. Without warning I was dragged from my bed and my hands tied behind me. The military men led me outside, where we walked the streets of the city heading toward the water. I saw bare breasted females and children along with male workers and soldiers— they lined the streets gawking and pointing at me. My ears hurt from their loud squeals and clicks and I glared with hostility at their stupid faces and wide open mouths. I was dragged to the landing where I originally entered the city and forced to my knees. It was at this point that I thought I was going to be executed, but that was not the case. I was pushed down and forced to lay flat upon the stones overlooking the water. Harpoons were placed sharply at my back and head to prevent me from moving and a sack of rocks was tied to my feet. I was in a state of shock, not knowing what to expect. Suddenly, orders were given and I was grabbed by three or four of the fish creatures and hoisted into the air. I squirmed helplessly as I was thrown into the water.

I hit the brackish pool like a rock and sank like a lead weight to the bottom of the lagoon. There, I prayed for mercy, holding my breath as the cold, dark water chilled my soul. Finally, I had no choice—I needed to breathe. I shut my eyes, prepared to meet my maker, and took a gasp, sucking in the water. To my amazement, my lungs did not fill. Something new was happening—my throat and chest felt odd, as if swollen—like something was blocking the water from my lungs. Still, I could feel air jetting through my nose and mouth, exiting behind my ears. It was like a natural reflex. I opened my eyes, and my ears popped. I could see air bubbles rising up on either side of my head. I was aghast—I was breathing underwater. How? How could I open my mouth and take in water and not have it fill my lungs? I never did learn the answer, but obviously these people had a science that far exceeded mine.

I looked around in the darkened pool. I could only see a few feet in front of me, but it was immediately apparent that I had an audience—there were a number of fish-men watching me—evidently quite pleased by the fact that I could now breathe underwater. What happened next was my introduction to life with the Aquella. I learned later that I was considered a misfit, a genetic throwback, a retarded species of mammal that fell to the lowest realms of society. I was made a slave, and relegated to a life of hard labor, working the ore mines at the bottom of the Urlena Sea.

☆ ☆ ☆

As ludicrous as it might sound, a slave is sometimes privi-
leged—privy in an odd sort of way to learn and witness the true
nature of a species by experiencing the fear and subjugation
inflicted by others. Such was the case with me. My life became
a regulated existence from dusk to dawn, going from confine-
ment to hard labor every day. Little was expected of me except
to work and produce for those in power. The only thing that
made matters worse was that as an alien in this race of fish-
men, I was considered the lowest of lowest even amongst the
slaves.

I couldn't communicate with anyone and I was exceedingly
slow in the water. My hands and feet lacked the Aquella's thin,
flexible duck-like webbing, so Dolla were used to help me keep
up, but in the mines the story was different—there I was at an
advantage. The caverns, caves and tunnels we worked were
free of water. And even though the air inside was hot and thick,
and heavy with humidity, I was stronger and far more adept
than the others in my ability to mine the rock ore that we were
forced to produce.

For hours on end we would pick the cave walls using crude
axes of stone and wood, following veins of rich silver ore. The
tunnels were long and dark, lit only by glow orbs that illuminated our personal hell. Sometimes we'd work in groups, at
other times; hours would pass where we'd work alone on the
various ore veins. When we weren't digging we were hauling
ore and rock out of the caves into the larger caverns. There,
shadowed in the dim light and surrounded by mounds of oxygen giving, purple seaweed pulp; we hammered the rock ore
into smaller fragments. The ore was then loaded into membrane bags which were then dropped into the water for transport by the Dolla.

Most of my days were spent in the caves themselves. Each
morning I would carry a bundle of seaweed pulp on my back and
a glow orb in my hands along with an ax pick, a wooden bucket,

and several membrane bags. I was constantly impressed with how strong the membrane bags were. Once inside the mine I was shown where to dig. I would then set my orb to one side, break off a piece of purple seaweed pulp to chew and begin to work. The pulp weed aided my breathing by slowly releasing oxygen into my mouth—much like breathing underwater. This became the total realm of my existence and I hated it with every fiber of my being. But I realized if I was ever going to escape I would need a plan—and a plan required that I have knowledge of my surroundings and my captors.

As I endured the ritual of my work day after day I was taken by the contrast I found in the Aquella society. Some things seemed so advanced, like my surgery, while other aspects seemed so tedious and menial—a throwback to a primitive pre-industrial culture. It was hard to comprehend. We would toil for hours in dank, wet caves, with our hands and crudely honed picks and buckets. The mines themselves were of primitive construction, very shallow by mining standards, penetrating only several hundred feet into the ocean floor. Trees taken from the islands above were used for supports so we could dig safely into the rock bed—the whole affair seemed haphazard and ill conceived.

In contrast, our light was supplied by glowing orbs that kept our work areas brightly lit. These lights were large and round, about the size of ploth's head and were never turned off. They burned continuously. I found all of this to be extremely puzzling: Why were we mining metal ore? What need did these people have for it? The Aquella lived in the ocean. And why were our picks and buckets constructed of stone, rock, and wood. It didn't make sense. To my observation, the Aquella did not use metal in any of their structures or furnishings. Their weapons and tools were made from non metallic substances as was their jewelry—what little they wore. It seemed odd that so much energy and manpower would be wasted on procuring an item that was not used in their culture. I knew there must be a reason and I had to learn it.

In the meantime there were other pressing matters. It seems that I had somehow stirred the ire of natural order with the other slaves. There was resentment of the increasing rations of food I was getting. That's how the master Aquella enforced, manipulated and maintained their power. The more you produced the more food and water you got, and I was at an advantage when it came to working in the mines. Consequently, I was rewarded handsomely with seaweed paste and water—more than I really needed.

I first became aware of this problem as we swam to the mines one morning. Two Aquella slaves swam alongside me; one butted my head with a hard crack while the other cut my arm with some sort of bone knife—it was their warning. Later, when we broke for food and water, out of sight of the guards, they approached and tried to take my rations. It was a mistake—and they learned the hard way.

As a military man, I'd had much in the way of combat training—weapons, hand to hand, knives, pistols—you name it. And when they threatened me and tried to take my rations I reacted. It wasn't that I had any resentment or anger toward these two, they were just slaves trying to survive, but I wasn't going to be walked over. When the first one waved his knife in my face I grabbed his wrist, gave it a quick twist. He screamed a shrill whistle as I forced him down—my foot slamming into his mid-section. The knife he held clattered onto the ground. When the other one jumped in to help, he too, found himself meeting a back fist to his nasal cavities. He reeled backwards and dark green blood flowed from his nose. He collapsed in a heap, a dazed look in his eyes. I quickly learned that these people weren't really built for hand to hand combat—they crumbled with the first couple of blows and it was all over. The two fish-men crawled away in far more pain than I—and now, I had a knife. It was a tool I would use many times to cut my hair and beard, and prepare my escape. I hid it away in the folds of my work tunic, anchored by the thin rope belt I now wore.

After the fight was over and things settled down, I gathered my extra food reserves and passed them out to the other slaves—I didn't need it to survive but they did. The men who tried to take my food were the most surprised when I tossed them each a packet of food. I wasn't here to make enemies.

First, and foremost I wanted to escape—I wanted out of here and I knew full well that I needed to learn more about what made these people tick. My communication with them was almost impossible until I found I could use the Dolla. It was these gentle aquatic beasts who held the key to my education.

The Dolla were the beasts of burden for the fish-men. They held a measure of intelligence probably equal to that of a child, but they were telepathic. They understood the mental commands of the Aquella and they could communicate with me over short distances, so it was only natural that they became my tutors and translators.

I learned slowly over time some of the history of the Aquella. Sharing my food with my fellow slaves had opened a lot of doors. They came to tolerate me and I needed every trick I knew to build their trust. Every day when we swam to the mines, the Dolla helped me to communicate with my fellow slaves. Through their efforts I came to understand the Aquella. I learned that they had not always lived under the sea, but had come from the surface. The ocean was their protection from the Cloud God.

"Who is the Cloud God?" I asked, half suspecting the answer.

"Cloud ... lives ... above ... sky," was the reply from the Dolla.

"Why do the Aquella fear the cloud?" I queried.

"Anger ... violent ... storms ... destroy," another answered.

"They hide under water," I noted, half-thinking to myself.

"Mine ... rock ... feed ... cloud," was the next revelation.

I was astonished. Now the pieces fit. Now I understood what had happened on the beach. My clothes, my sword—the ugly pinkish-purple cloud I'd witnessed on the island ate metal—all metal. This was beyond belief.

"How long has this been going on?" I questioned.

"No ... remember ... time ... before," was their answer.

Unbelievable, I thought. No wonder these people were living in such a confused state. They'd been attacked by something that was decimating their culture and they were losing the battle. I swam in silence with the others back to where we were confined. I had much to reflect on.

☆ ☆ ☆

Living underwater and under artificial light brought me to the point where I soon had no idea of time any longer. Days ran into weeks–weeks into months–soon a year or more had past. I had no idea anymore. I only knew one thing–I was a filthy mess, with long, stringy hair, my face and skin molting from the water and mud. I needed to escape. I knew if I didn't find a way out I would die as a slave under the oceans of Urlena. So every day, with each swing of my pick, every moment I forced more pasty seafood down my throat, I became obsessed with thoughts of escaping–how could I get away from these fish-people? Slowly an idea began to form–then a plan. First, I needed help–perhaps one or two others.

To begin, I started cultivating personal friendships with some of my fellow slaves. I found two in particular–an older fish-man I called Jazokee and a younger one I called Raktila. They seemed receptive to my overtures. When we worked together I would add ore to their sacks, which increased their food bounty. I also helped the elder Jazokee carry his bags so he could show more to the masters. In addition, I began hoarding my food and water, hiding portions in a muddy hole I'd dug in the cave we were working. My plan was contingent on so many things; I had to be ready for anything. I even stole extra rock sacks and hid them in the hole, as well as the knife I'd taken so many months before. Slowly, things began to take shape.

My original plan was to hide in one of the rock sacks and be taken out to sea astride a Dolla. I felt it would offer me the best chance of getting away, though I was concerned that my thoughts would reveal my presence—that being in such close proximity to the Dolla—they would expose me through innocent misunderstanding. The aquatic beasts were so childlike, they wouldn't understand my plight or mission, but I was becoming so desperate I felt I had no other choice—and that's where fate stepped in.

It was late in one of our work shifts, and I was working in a mine with a dozen other slaves including Jazokee and Raktila. We were spaced out about thirty feet or more, each of us picking and clawing at a vein of ore that ran through a type of hard clay. The clay was peppered with rocks and stones, some as large as a man's head, and the work was arduous. Suddenly, from the deepest part of the cave I heard a low rumble, followed by a number of clackish screams. After the cries there was a violent blast of air—an explosion. Before I knew what was happening I saw Aquella bolting for the cave's entrance. I followed their lead, running for safety as I realized there had been a cave-in. None of us stopped until we were safely outside. Once there, we sank to our knees in the mud, breathing heavily, each one of us appreciative of our good fortune. I looked around, noting who had survived. There were eight of us including Raktila and Jazokee—I was glad to see that they had made it. But four were missing. Were they hurt or dead? Was anyone going back inside to see? It appeared not. It was obvious that the Aquella were a callous lot when it came to their slaves and no one was going to chance re-entering the cave—especially the guards. They never went inside the mines unless it was absolutely necessary and now was no exception. In this case, we were simply rounded up and bound together for our trip back to the city.

As I waited in line for our journey to begin, I took the opportunity to quietly query Raktila and Jazokee. I make a number of gestures toward them in sign language, trying to find out what happened. It took a minute, but they soon came to understand my inquiry. Raktila picked up a small rock. He pointed to a light globe that lay nearby and made a striking motion, smacking the stone against the palm of his hand. In turn, Jazokee made a gesture, mimicking an explosion. I nodded my head in understanding. This was incredible. The light globes were the source of the explosion and cave in. I had no idea they were so volatile.

The next morning I got another surprise. I learned upon returning to the mines that we would never re-enter that shaft again even though most of it was still intact. In fact, most of our morning was spent blocking the entrance with rocks. The bodies inside were never recovered–there was no attempt. It appeared that the Aquella feared death and avoided it; it was a bad omen–though more than likely, the explosion and cave-in simply made work there too unsafe. To my amazement, however, the Aquella had no problem starting a new dig just twenty feet over from the old shaft. I found this logic to be skewed at best, but what really had me was the realization that my knife, water, and the food supplies I'd been hoarding for weeks were now lost in the sealed mineshaft. The reality was I would have to start over, but then a revelation hit–a really beautiful revelation. This was possibly my ticket out.

Every day I returned to the mine with a renewed vigor. And as we dug into the clay soil, creating a new shaft I paid more and more attention to my surroundings. Like the cave we'd been working before, the digging was relatively easy, and as a group of ten to twelve workers we made at least thirty feet a day. Secretly, I began hoarding more food, seaweed and water– hiding it away in shallow holes. When we reached a depth of a hundred feet or so into the seabed, I began to look for silver ore veins that led in the direction of our first mineshaft–the one we closed following the explosion. Finding a vein, I angled my digging in that direction. Over time I knew my digging was getting close, but I had to be very careful–I didn't want anyone to suspect what I was up to. For the most part I kept my light orb distant so I could work alone in the shadows.

Finally, I was ready. I estimated that I was probably within five feet of the first mineshaft–it was now or never. My heart raced as I dragged a load of ore toward the entrance of the cave. The day's digging was done and everyone was tired. The last sacks were being filled and made ready for hauling out of the cave. I stayed behind and worked slowly making sure that I was one of the last ones out. As I made my way to the mouth of the cave I found Jazokee and Raktila waiting for me–I suspected they'd be there.

Feigning sudden illness, I grabbed my stomach and bent over. My knees hit the ground and I started coughing. I motioned to them for help, my face nearly kissing the mud as I hacked away. Immediately the two rushed to my side, milling about, not sure what to do. They chattered at one another incessantly, the noise drawing the attention of one of the guards who stood at the cave's entrance. He entered to see what the commotion was all about.

Seeing his approach; I made ready. I grabbed my chest and coughed harder, rolling to one side. Concerned over my well being, Jazokee and Raktila stooped down to examine me; their whistles and clicks echoing in the cold, dank air. They grabbed me by the arms, and with their assistance, I was able to stand while the guard jabbered at us angrily. He waved his crossbow forcibly to spur us on. My ploy was working, and though I hated tricking Jazokee and Raktila, I had no other choice. Together we moved toward the cave's entrance.

Seeing me helpless in my companion's arms, the guard relaxed. He shouldered his weapon and moved out of our way, which is when I sprang into action. I quickly brought my two friends' heads together with a sharp crack. They collapsed on the floor giving me direct access to our overseer. With a sharp kick to his mid section I knocked the wind out of him. My second blow was a hard shoving kick to his chest, the force catapulting him back against the cave wall. I heard his head strike the rocks. He sank like a rock, his dark green blood staining the wall behind. I was pretty sure he was dead, but I took no chances. I hit him again, and stripped him of his weapons. Once they were in my hands I returned to my two fish friends who were sitting dazed on the cave floor. I gave them a couple of slaps and motioned for them to get up.

When I thought about it later, it occurred to me that in all the history of the Aquella I don't think anyone ever tried to escape. It seemed that these people underwent a cultural

indoctrination so strong that just the thought of doing something radical, like rebelling or escaping, seemed completely out
of their realm of thought. Jazokee and Raktila were befuddled–
they stared at me lost and dumbfounded. I waved the crossbow
at them and I pushed them harshly to the back of the cave. They
obeyed, giving me no grief. Fifty feet down we came across half
a dozen glow orbs lying on the cave floor. I stopped and gave
the two an order. It seemed strange hearing my voice echo in
the cave; I didn't use it much down here.

"Pick up the orbs!" I commanded

The two looked at me with bewilderment–I motioned with
the crossbow and pointed to the glass-like globes. They nodded in understanding and each picked up an orb. I motioned
for them to pick up more. They nodded again and gathered up
another orb. I picked up one myself for a total of five. I just
didn't know how many it would take to achieve a measurable
explosion, but I was about to find out. We headed back toward
the cave entrance.

As we neared the lifeless body of the guard I heard a commotion coming from the cave's entrance–a series of loud clicks
and whistles. Someone was calling to us–probably another
guard. Undoubtedly they wanted to know what was delaying
us, why we hadn't come out.

Anxious, I yelled to Jazokee and Raktila. "Stop!"

The two Aquella paused. They turned and looked at me. I
motioned for them to set the globes down.

"Now get out of here." I ordered, thrusting my head toward
the cave's entrance.

The two hesitated.

"Go on!" I yelled, pushing both of them roughly.

Still, addled by my actions, the two moved drunkenly
toward the front of the cave. I was anxious to see them go–
there was so little time. As they left my line of sight, I rolled the
light globes together. I then darted back to what I thought was
a safe distance and huddled next to the cave wall where I took
aim at the globes with the crossbow. There was noise coming
from the cave's entrance and I saw shadows heading my way.

With no time left, I fired my bolt and ran for my life, heading deeper into the cave.

As I ran, I was thankful that I had paid close attention to my captors. For two long years I had watched them, studying their every move—learning their fishy habits. Through patient observation I came to acquire an understanding on how things worked with the Aquella, especially regarding the use of their weapons. That knowledge had proved invaluable today, though at the moment I had other things to contend with.

The explosion of the orbs reverberated through the cave, blasting my eardrums, and knocking me down into the mud. I lay there praying, hoping against the odds that the cave wouldn't collapse around me; to my intense relief, it didn't. I got up from the floor and wiped off the black muck that covered me from head to toe and checked the mouth of the cave. It was sealed tight; my plan had worked. I turned and headed for the rear of the cave feeling confident in my plan even though I was entombed under a ton of rock, mud, and clay. I just had to dig my way out. Retrieving several glowing orbs, I headed for my secret tunnel—the one I'd been working on for the past week, and I began to dig.

I worked like a madman for more than seven hours, stopping only to catch my breath and listen for Aquella. I was paranoid, fearful of being discovered, but I heard nothing except my own panting. No one was coming after me. It was obvious I'd gone mad, so they left me to die. Finally, the air in the cave petered out and I had to chew on my supply of seaweed pulp for oxygen—another hour passed. I was now ankle deep in sticky, black mud, running low on pulp, and hoping for a miracle. It was then that my pick penetrated the wall.

Madness overtook me. I tore at the wall blindly, knocking a hole in it large enough to stick my face in. I then pressed my nose and mouth into the opening sucking up the cool, wet oxygen that greeted me on the other side. I filled my burning lungs, giving thanks knowing I wouldn't die in the black darkness of this tomb. I then widened the hole so I could squeeze through. Exhausted, thirsty and elated by my success I took an orb and made my way to the front of the cave. Along the way I found my original stash of food, water, seaweed, along with my knife. I ripped open several packs of food and a container of water, eating and drinking until full. My stomach satisfied, I sat in the mud and rested. Tears streamed down my face. I was nearly mad, and the only thing that kept me sane was realizing how close I was—that only a small wall of mud and stone blocked my freedom. I could break out at any time. I was delirious with anticipation: Should I dig now or rest?

Weary with fatigue and a fear of running into Aquella, I decided to rest, but not before exploring my options. I pulled a few rocks from the pile at the front of the cave and opened a small hole so I could see outside. Everything was dark. There were no glowing orbs or guards in the cavern. I sighed with relief. I was alone—for the first time in years I was truly alone. I blocked the hole, and moved deeper into the cave tunnel, where I made a bed of seaweed pulp and went to sleep. I slept long and hard, only to be awoken hours later by a faint noise coming from outside the cave. The Aquella had returned.

I left my orb in the dark recesses and made my way back to the cave's entrance. There I removed some of the rubble and peeked out. I could see both Aquella guards and slaves working in the cavern. All appeared to be normal. They were filling sacks of silver ore, and casting them into the water. It seemed I'd slept through the entire day; they were making ready to leave. This was good—as I had hoped, the Aquella figured I was dead. I closed the hole and returned to where I'd been sleeping. It was time to eat and drink. A new journey was about to begin and I knew I would need all the strength I could muster if I was going to survive.

CHAPTER FIVE

Escape

The cavern was pitch-black. The light I carried was swallowed by the darkness that surrounded me—it was eerily quiet. I looked out over the dark waters that filled the interior of the cavern and pondered my next move. I realized now that I hadn't given much thought as to what I would do if I did escape. My trips to and from the mines had always taken place during the daylight hours with a measure of visibility in the water. Now everything was jet black, and I was filled with apprehension. How was I going to navigate out of here and avoid the mysterious things that lurked in the depths? I stepped into the cold, black water and a chill ran down my spine.

I started swimming toward the underwater tunnel that connected the cavern with the open sea. The light orb I carried strapped to my back in a membrane bag scarcely illuminated the water around me—perhaps a foot or two at best. Still, it was better than no light at all. I swam mostly by instinct, heading down into the blackness, looking for the barrier seals that kept the cavern waters sealed from the ocean.

It took a little time, but I found the first inner seal stretched over the tunnel, blocking my exit. I ran my hand over the thin membrane, probing the tension behind it. It moved in response to my touch, undulating slowly back and forth like a beating heart in concert to the water's currents. I pulled out my knife and made a small incision; a hole big enough for me to look through. With trepidation I stuck my head through the membrane and glanced around. I was sure that the Aquella would be waiting for me—but there was nothing. I sliced the hole further and slipped through. Thirty feet later I reached the second membrane. I ran my hand across it. There was more tension here, the pressure stronger as the seal held back the ocean and the incoming tide.

I swam over to the edge of the membrane where it joined the rocks of the tunnel. I never did learn how they sealed the membrane to the rocks, but it was watertight. Carefully, I slit the membrane next to the rocks with my knife—water rushed in. Its force buffeted me. I grasped the rocks alongside for support and continued to cut. The slit was now several feet long and the water pressure diminished as a balance was struck between the two barrier seals—enough for me to slip through. I was finally free.

On instinct I wanted to head to the surface, but I had no idea what to expect up there, so I turned left, away from the path that led to my Aquella prison. I swam forever. I swam until my limbs ached, and I thought I could do no more. My eyes burned from the salt water—even my gills hurt—but still I pushed on. Finally, when my legs began to cramp I stopped and headed up. My head broke the water and I was greeted by a night sky that shimmered with a million stars. Overhead, three moons orbited in the sky, casting their reflections onto the water along with the red gas giant that hung low on the horizon. Tears filled my eyes as I wept. I had been held by the Aquella for so long it was almost more than I could bear. I looked back and forth in all directions taking in the magnificent scenery of the night. I sobbed in relief; I would never go back to that hell again.

I started swimming again, not knowing where I was going, only that I was free to choose any direction. I did not get far. Unexpectedly there was a sharp pain in my foot, making me scream. I felt a strong tug. Something was coiling itself around my leg. This was followed by a prickly feeling of needle-like barbs stinging me. Instantly, my leg was on fire. I tried to pull away, but I had no chance. Whatever held me was far too big, and not about to let its dinner escape. It started to wrap itself around my other leg, injecting me with its fiery poison. The pain was unbearable and I quickly felt both my legs going numb.

Grabbing my knife from my belt, I stabbed at the snake like thing that was slithering around my waist and chest. It was pure sinewed muscle, thick and slimy, and my blows against it were almost laughable. As it squeezed me tighter I began to thrash like a madman, stabbing at it over and over with my tiny, bone knife blade. I must have hit a nerve or a vein, for suddenly another tentacle shot out of the water; it slapped me hard alongside the head almost breaking my neck. The force knocked me to one side and I felt it strike again, this time, the blow glanced off my back, tearing the membrane bag I carried from me. The orb inside the bag slid out, and sank into the water, falling to unseen depths, and as it did, the creature released me. I felt it leave. To my disbelief I was now free, though severely paralyzed as I floated helplessly in the water.

No longer able to swim, my arms flailed in an effort to keep me afloat. I was terrified. What lay waiting below in the cold, dark depths, horrified me. The sting of this creature had almost completely immobilized me, and if it were not for the ability to breathe underwater I would have already drowned. Still, I knew it would only be moments before it would return to devour me. I looked to the heavens again and took in the stars. I wanted to die with their light in my eyes.

I waited for what seemed to be an eternity, my body bobbing up and down in the water, the waves pushing me back and forth, but nothing happened. Then, without warning, I felt a sudden surge in the water, a violent swell that momentarily pushed me half way out of the ocean. I was bewildered by the effect, but the momentum passed quickly, and I sank back into the water wondering what had happened. It then registered with me—right along with the pieces of tentacle that floated to the surface all around me. I began to laugh—the creature had gone after the orb and bit into it. Oh, how I wish I could have seen the explosion. It must have been magnificent, but seeing the floating pieces of the creature was enough. The damn thing got what it deserved. Then I realized floating food was an open invitation to others, and I was in the middle of it. Eventually someone would want me for a meal and I was unable to swim. I decided to use the only option I had left. I called out to the Dolla.

Things became a blur after that. The poison injected into my legs was beginning to take effect. Aside from paralysis, my head was burning—I was becoming delirious. I pleaded for help. I cried. I was only vaguely aware of the two Dolla who came to my rescue. They were wild creatures, not yet controlled by the Aquella. They read my delirious mind and somehow realized that I needed help—that I needed to get to land. They pushed me along in the water, half carrying, half floating me toward a body of land some distance away. By dawn's light I was shoved onto a beach where somehow I managed to belly crawl into a thicket of trees and bushes where I collapsed.

Several days passed—at least I think it was several days. I was horrendously sick and under siege from an assault of hallucinations and agonizing pain. I finally awoke, my fever diminished, my limbs stiff and sore, but again moving under my command. To my horror, I found that I looked like hell. My skin was shriveled and pasty, a ghastly white in color; I looked like something dead. It made my skin crawl. I could only imagine what my bearded face looked like—too long had I lived without proper nutrition and sunlight on my body. To make matters worse, I could see that under my tattered tunic my legs and torso had countless wounds, a conglomeration of cuts, welts and bruises, some looking infected. They ran the length of my body. I limped out onto the beach. I needed to wash my wounds and see where I was.

Emerging from the shade of the trees I walked into the sunlight, not prepared for the pain of being greeted by a blazing hot, yellow sun and sand that burned my feet like simmering coals. My white, unseasoned skin sizzled like fat in a fire, and I was forced to move hastily back into the shade where cooler temperatures prevailed. I studied the terrain around me. The view was disheartening at best. This beach, this island, it looked like the island I had been on before. The trees and bushes were the same. Still, it didn't matter. I was free—all I needed was water. I was dying of thirst. I went searching, keeping my body under the shelter of the trees and foliage. It would be a while before I would venture out into the sun again.

Hobbling along for an hour or so, I stumbled onto a small patch of damp ground. It was barely wet, but I scraped down into the sand to find wet mud. I placed the cool muck to my parched lips, relieved to know that water was near. I followed the dampness inland. Another hour's meandering brought me to a small trickling stream and an inland pool of fresh water. Face down, I drank my fill and rested. As luck would have it, growing nearby were some large brown berries—shriveled, dry looking things, but edible. I stuffed them into my mouth, chewing them with gulps of water to soften their texture. They didn't agree with me, but I was able to keep them down—they were better than nothing. I finally moved on, traversing the island, seeking someplace where I could live out the remainder of my days as a free man.

After walking most of the day, I quickly came to the conclusion that I was not on an island after all—or if I was, it was really big. I climbed a hill and looked around for as far as I could see, noting that the land stretched out forever. I saw no signs of life, just vegetation, but I was more relieved by the fact that there were no signs of the Aquella.

When the sun started to set I ventured down to the water. It was time to seek out real food. I had no tools, but I needed to eat. I walked the water's edge looking for shellfish, mollusks and mussels—I found some a few feet out. Smashing them open with a rock, I slurped the wet goo into my mouth. It was food, and it got me through the night. The next day I found a long, knotted piece of wood. I fashioned it into a spear using some broken shells to hone a point. It was a crude, and gnarled looking thing, but it got me a small fish which I ate raw. My cuisine was improving—did I dare build a fire?

Days passed as I walked the land investigating my new surroundings. I climbed more hills, heading inland from time to time, but still keeping within the protection of the trees. It felt odd not to see or hear any signs of life. In my wanderings I did find better wood for making a new spear and shells for sharpening it to a honed point. Mostly I walked with the sea to my right so I wouldn't get lost or retrace my steps. I kept my eye on various rock formations, making note of landmarks, which I thought was ironic as I had no clue as to where I was anyway—but it was my training.

The land stretched for leagues. I began to doubt that any Aquella would venture here—why would they? That afternoon, when I made ready my camp for the night, I gathered together wood and dry grass. That evening I speared two fish. I filleted them with a piece of broken shell, and for the first time since leaving Melela, I built a fire. It took forever, but I finally coaxed two pieces of wood into giving off sparks that ignited into flame. That night I ate my first cooked meal in years, and it was delicious.

Later that night I lay upon the beach and studied the night sky. I watched as the moons overhead traversed the night firmament, their marvelous splendor looming so close I wanted to touch them. They reminded me of the time before my arrival here, when I sailed the starlit reefs of space in service to the Emperor. That thought gave me pause. I wondered what was happening now on Melela. Was it fully controlled by the Relcor? Had the Emperor and his wife somehow survived? And Leanna—what had become of her? Did she forgive me for failing in my duty to protect her? I could only hope that she was at peace in some safe harbor and not like me, lost in a forsaken land with little hope for the future. My thoughts became muddled and drowsy, and I fell asleep, lying in the warm comfort of the sand. As I slumbered, the red-gas giant known as Tiiana rose in the night sky. Her glow bathed the terrain around me, and though I didn't actually know her name yet, it was just a matter of time.

The morning sun awoke me at dawn. I felt rested and ready to continue my journey searching the land I was now beginning to call home. Most of the day was spent walking. I was bored, there was nothing eventful, just the same dreary landscape of trees, sandy shores and bluffs that lined the coast for as far as the eye could see. My only real wish was my desire to find a way to carry water with me—I felt I was spending an inordinate amount of time every day searching for drinking water—I knew there had to be a better way. I headed into the foliage to search again.

I walked for perhaps a league making my way through the trees and brush following a trail of wet sand when I came across a most important find. It was camouflaged by the trees and an overgrowth of bushes and small plants, and if it hadn't been for the pool of water at its base I might have missed it altogether. At first I thought it was a hill with water flowing down its side, but when I moved the brush away to get a drink, I discovered blocks of stone underneath. I was stunned. I ran my hand over the smooth surface. This was definitely man-made—was it built by the Aquella? Perhaps when they lived on the surface? That seemed very likely, though I couldn't rule out the possibility that it had been built by some other beings. I hastily cleared away more brush—there were more stones, each set atop the other. I stepped back and looked the mound over—I realized now that it rose too steeply, the pitch was too abrupt. It had a pyramid shape. I began to walk around the mound looking for an access when I discovered a series of large stone steps leading up. I needed no further invitation—I ascended the structure.

I counted at least forty steps to the top where I reached a plateau of sorts—actually it was more of a lookout point or watch tower—and for good reason. In one direction I had a clear view of the sea behind me, and in the other, my view took in an enormously wide valley enclosed by massive sheer cliffs. I was standing on the edge of a steep precipice that took my breath away. A feeling that was compounded by my next discovery—a white-stoned city nestled against the terrain deep within the protective womb of the valley. My eyes swept back and forth taking it all in. It was a real city with structures built by an unknown people. My mind reeled with the implication and I studied the place in detail. Mostly what I saw was ruins— great swaths of rubble and rock strewn about in huge piles. The city appeared deserted, destroyed by the ravages of time and environment. The only structures seemingly untouched were the larger, massive ones. One being a pyramid shaped edifice, another some kind of cathedral, two of its spiral towers demolished, an arena or coliseum, and several others whose purpose I could not fathom at this distance.

I looked for a way to get down the cliff and access the city. In the process I caught sight of a river several hundred feet below. It was running alongside the face of the cliff where I stood. It paralleled the bluff, coursing through the valley, churning its way to the ocean somewhere downstream. I was ecstatic. The sight of an abundant source of fresh water was more than I could bear. And there was an array of new vegetation with more color and density—perhaps edible food grew down there as well. I had to find a way down into the valley. I leapt down the steps of the mound to look for a way to traverse the cliff—there had to be a way to access the city below. As I jumped to the ground my mind raced with an unbridled curiosity. Who had lived here? Who had built this great metropolis?

At the back of the mound near the edge of the cliff I found what I was looking for—a path cut into the side of the cliff that led down to the valley. I pushed aside the overgrowth of bushes that blocked my access and looked it over—it hadn't been used in years—a lot of years. Loose rock and gravel peppered the trail making any descent treacherous. Worse yet, the path was only wide enough for one person. One slip and I'd be over the edge—a drop that would easily kill me. I looked over the rest of the cliff and the valley below pondering if it would be easier to access this valley by way of the ocean, perhaps where the river met the sea. I knew that might take days so I decided to take the trail.

I pulled up a couple of bushes near the watering hole and used them as a broom to sweep the rocks and pebbles over the

edge of the cliff as I descended. Walking barefoot helped too–
my feet were less apt to slip. Step by step I carefully moved
down the trail heading deeper into the valley, keeping my back
against the cliff wall. It was an arduous, painstaking journey.
The sun was intense and its heat radiated off the white rock,
burning me. My skin was soon sunburned and by the time I
reach the bottom my feet had blisters. The tattered rags I wore
were useless and I knew now more than ever that if I was going
to survive here things had to change–I couldn't go on like this.

It was dusk by the time I reached the bottom. I was
exhausted and sore, my skin practically cooked. Fortunately,
the air near the base of the cliff was cooler; there was a breeze
and shade. The grass I stepped onto was ever so soft and invit-
ing. I sank to my knees and crawled to the water's edge a few
feet away. On my belly I sank my face into the river and drank–
it was cold and refreshing. I rolled onto my back and listened
as the river raced by. It was getting dark now, stars were beginning to appear, and I was tired. Even though I craved food, I
needed rest more. There was nothing more I could do tonight–
food would have to wait.

I planted my body against the rocks near the base of the
cliff where the grass grew like a thick carpet. I was slowly sinking into sleep when something startled me–it brought me
round to full awareness. Somewhere, just across the river I
heard a guttural cry. The wail was followed by several howls
further distant. I nearly fainted. In all my recent explorations,
I hadn't seen or heard any surface life–and now–now I wasn't
sure. Making matters worse, I was in the open and exposed—
not a good idea. Hastily, I grabbed my spear and stood, keeping
my eye on the terrain along the river's far side. I saw nothing,
but that did not calm me. Even though the water was moving
well and its banks were wide, I felt vulnerable. I could not trust
these waters to protect me from anything that might lurk on
the other side, especially if they could swim.

Forced now into retracing my steps I climbed back up the
cliff, picking a spot where I could sit in safety with my back
pressed against the canyon wall. And though it was both
uncomfortable and difficult, I was safer on the pebbly, narrow

trail as opposed to the soft grass that lay within reach of sharp teeth. So, there I remained for the night, nervously perched thirty feet above the grass, my spear in hand, watching as the moons crossed the sky. It grew cold and I shivered while struggling to stay warm. Periodically, wild sounds would reach my ears, but nothing that caused me immediately alarm—though I could have sworn I saw a glower frolicking along the tree line. That may have been my imagination—or possibly the eyes of some wild beast looking in my direction. Either way, I was glad to see the morning's sunrise.

Awakening stiff and sore, I was bothered by a new annoyance—insects—gnats or flies or something similar buzzing all around me. They bit my skin and stung my flesh, forcing me up. Brushing them away, I stood and surveyed the terrain that lay below. The river was churning noisily, and the sky was getting lighter—my stomach grumbled from hunger. Eager to find food, I walked down the trail and headed toward the water's edge. There I drank and looked for fish. I didn't see any, but I did see something else. Across the river was a grouping of trees. One of them held a rich bounty of fruit—the sight of it raised my spirits. It then dawned on me: This valley was the perfect place for life to flourish in some form or another. There was shelter here, water and probably all kinds of food. It also made sense that since people had lived here they would have farmed the land—perhaps there were still remnants of their crops. To find out I just needed to cross the river.

I walked the bank studying the water's flow. It was ten to fifteen feet wide and it was moving well, though it only looked to be a foot or so deep. At one point I found a series of pilings where a bridge once ran, but it was gone now, having been swept away. Still, this looked to be the best place to cross. Gingerly, I put my feet into the water and with slow, calculated steps I began to walk across. I didn't get far before falling. The rocks were slick and covered with moss and my bare feet held no footing. I soon found that the best way to navigate was by crawling on all fours. It was undignified, but I managed to make it.

Climbing the far bank, I pulled myself onto a grassy knoll where I sat and looked around. Not far from me was the tree with the fruit I had seen earlier—a bounty of dark red gems about the size of my hand with thin, yellow markings. I walked to it and plucked one. It smelled okay—I took a small bite. The taste was sweet and pleasant, the center filled with small seeds. I couldn't believe my good fortune and I piggishly devoured four or five until my stomach was full and bloated. I was now ready to explore the valley.

CHAPTER SIX

The Dead City

wiped my chin and eyed the trees and brush before me. The vegetation, while not overly dense, was dark, shadowed and a little forbidding. After hearing the cries from the night before I was not eager to run into some creature unprepared, so I took another route. I walked the bank of the river, following the water downstream until I found a clearing where I felt I could cross inland in relative safety. Beyond the meadow I could see the ruins of the city stretched out before me. My heart raced with excitement as I stepped forward into tall grass.

The fact that someone or some race of people had lived here at one time was exhilarating and I hoped that I could find something—tools, weapons, anything that would help me survive. I desperately needed help—I was naked prey in this wilderness. Cautiously, I approached the first buildings I came across, most of which were nothing more than rubble. I climbed over and around them, searching for anything that could be put to good use. I found nothing so I moved further into the city.

The path I walked was now wide. Was it a street? It appeared to be tightly packed gravel; great care had been taken in laying its foundation, though the grass and plants were slowly taking over. I knew from my personal travels and observations, that this city had once held culture and promise. The larger structures had been well built, the columns supporting the roofs were classic in design, their workmanship evident, even though the city had fallen from some catastrophe. I was also beginning to see signs of artwork, broken sculptures—a marble arm with two fingers still intact, bits of pottery, an occasional polished stone—all strewn within the rubble.

I wondered if the people who had lived here were humanoid like me—the marble arm gave me reason to think so, but I needed more. I stopped and peered into several buildings. Some had multiple rooms though they were dark and littered with debris. I was leery of entering without a sufficient light source—who knew what might be lurking in the dark? I continued walking.

Near to the entrance of a smaller building or domicile, I found a clay vase half buried in the dirt. I dug it out and looked it over. It was a plain looking thing, whole, though filled with dirt which I emptied out. I was elated. Now I had something in which I could carry water. It would allow me to explore in greater depth without suffering from thirst. Pondering my options, and which direction to take, I sat and rested in the shade of a building alongside the street. I needed a plan. Fortunately, there seemed to be numerous places where I could find shelter and protection from the elements—but what about wild animals? I needed to find something I could defend, if necessary. It was then that my musings were interrupted. There was a noise coming from somewhere up ahead, deep within the city. It sounded like a mixture of growls and yelps. I got to my feet and with spear in hand I moved carefully forward to investigate. I walked for a fair distance with the sounds growing louder and more hostile. I kept my back to the walls of the buildings for protection and crept on.

Finally, I reached a point where two streets intersected. I could tell from the sounds I was hearing that something was happening just around the corner—I took a glance, and caught sight of a pack of large gray-black rodents. There were about ten in number some forty feet away with their backs to me. I took them in. They were not ordinary rats, but creatures about the size of a small dog with snout faces, beady red eyes, and pink noses. They appeared savage and deadly with drool dripping from sharp, long teeth. Unaware of my presence, they scurried back and forth, trying to encircle the prey they had cornered–a cat-like creature with a baby cub. The cat was beautiful, with mostly white fur and rings of black encircling her eyes.

I studied the scene unfolding before me. The pack was working cohesively, trying to separate the cub from its mother– the two had been backed into a dead-end alley with no escape. I watched the mother growl and spit, her long, fang-teeth and claws bared in a fighting stance. I had no doubt that she could defend herself–she was large, well muscled and more than a match for the puny rat-dogs. Still, they outnumbered her and the real prey was the young cub she was trying to protect. The poor thing looked pathetic cowering behind its mother.

I waited until I could take the drama no longer. And with sheer stupidity ruling my brain, I think because of my weak-ened condition, I made a decision that held no logic at all, except that I like cats better than rats. I picked up a large rock and rounded the corner yelling and screaming like a crazed madman at the top of my lungs while charging the pack. For a split second, my appearance stunned the animals. They froze in their steps and looked at me like a banshee from hell. I took the moment and threw my rock with all my might, watching it clatter across the street toward the rat-dogs. The attack sent them scattering and chaos ensued. The rodents bolted for safety, darting into the dark recesses of the rubble that lay on either side of the street, while the cat grabbed her cub by the scruff of the neck. I saw her leap to the roof of a nearby build-ing, safely out of reach. She paused for a second, looking at me, then bounded away out of sight.

I looked to where the rodents had run. From the dark holes and recesses of the rubble I could see their gleaming eyes watching me–I was not prepared for this. My skin crawled at the nasty, guttural sounds now emanating in my direction. Spear in hand, I slowly backed away as they wormed their way from their lairs and quickly regrouped. I was now their prey. I rounded the corner of the building behind me quickly realizing that I would be dinner if I didn't find a place of safety, and quick. I needed to follow the cat's move, and get up high, out of reach—but where? I ran out into the street with my bare feet striking the stone and rocks. They hurt like hell, but I couldn't think about it. A glance over my shoulder told me the pack was gaining and they'd soon be on my heels—this spurred me on faster.

I ran down the street looking for a place where I could defend myself—the rat-dogs were gaining on me. Ahead, I saw a building with a narrow single doorway—it was my only chance. I bolted inside, stumbling into the darkened interior—suddenly a light flashed, like a picture bulb. It didn't register—I was too busy bracing for the attack of the rodents behind me. Two of the dogs flew into the room after me, their teeth and jaws snapping madly. I raised my spear, but before I could move, two laser bolts suddenly flashed down from the ceiling. Their force knocked me back, and I reeled uncontrollably, falling on my butt. The two dogs were gone, both vaporized, and the smell of their fried flesh was disconcerting at best. Two more entered the room leaping toward me. The beam fired again, and I watched in disbelief as the rodents were cooked into nonexistence. Outside, the rest of the pack came to an abrupt halt. They milled about, just outside the doorway, growling at me—a final blast from the overhead light sent them flying away in fear.

I lay dazed on the floor. What had just happened? I peered up at the small, lighted dome that now illuminated the room. The beams had come from there. I kept still; uncertain if it would think me an intruder. How was it powered? Could it tell friend from foe? I didn't want to be vaporized, so I moved with slow caution, but nothing happened. Then unexpectedly, a man wearing a hooded robe appeared before me—an Aquella. It was a holograph, and it sputtered sporadically as if its power supply was low. It started to speak, giving off a series of clicks and whistles, none of which I understood. I got up from the floor, noting that it watched me as I moved. I came close, studying the image. It was definitely an Aquella, but he looked different. The skin was not the bluish-green color I was used to, but tan, and he didn't seem to look so much like a fish. His features were broader—more human, like someone who lived outdoors all his life.

"Can you help me?" I asked, hoping for a miracle.

I wanted to talk with someone badly, but my hopes were quickly dashed. He spoke again in a language I could not understand, though his open-handed gestures were welcoming in appearance. I thought I even saw a smile waxing upon his face. But then, without warning he faded from view, leaving me alone with the overhead light starting to dim. I took advantage of the waning light, and began to search the home.

The room in which I stood was in total disarray. Sand covered the floor, the walls were cracked and falling apart, the furniture was smashed and broken, with dust and debris laying everywhere. Time mixed with the forces of nature was bringing everything down. I noticed several pictures lying nearby on the floor. I walked over and picked them up, blowing the dust and dirt off their surfaces. They were family portraits of an Aquella family—quite faded, and subtly different from the beings that had held me hostage and prisoner under the sea. Whatever had happened here had changed life drastically for these people. Was it because of the cloud?

I turned and looked to see if the holograph had returned—it hadn't, so I began searching the rest of the house. As I entered the next room, another small light came on revealing the dark interior of a bedroom. The bed had collapsed, and the material covering its surface had rotted away. I found a closet. Inside, was a pile of clothes, mostly rags, but a few were in decent shape. I also found several pairs of sandals. They were too small, but better than nothing, so I sat down and strapped them to my tired, aching, and blistered feet.

For the first time in several years I had clothing to cover my body, and footwear upon my feet. I immediately began to hope that there were other items here I could use. I began to ransack everything—I moved from room to room seeking anything that would aid my survival. In the end, I found several more pieces of clothing, a beautiful handcrafted knife of flint stone, and a crossbow with a litter of bolts. Things were beginning to look up. I took my bounty and headed toward the front doorway. Peeking outside I saw the pack of rat-dogs lurking down the street. They hadn't given up, which was good. I needed food.

From the safety of the doorway I pulled back the sinewed string on the crossbow, the material was still resilient, and the tension adequate. I loaded a bolt into the firing groove. As I stepped from the doorway I watched the rodents come together. They moved stealthily in my direction, eager to sink their teeth into me. As they closed, I fired the weapon. The lead rat-dog caught a bolt mid-chest. It yelped in terror, turned, and fell to the ground. The others were upon its carcass instantly, tearing it apart. Their hunger yielded no loyalty. I yanked the bow string back again and loaded another bolt–and while the pack was busy fighting over the spoils, I walked quietly toward them. I fired again, my projectile catching another rodent in the flank. It yelped in pain and began to run–the others followed, nipping savagely at its heels. A moment later I was alone in the street with my kill. I pulled out my new knife.

I was starved, literally famished. My body looked anorexic and sickly from two years of hard labor, lack of food and proper nutrition. The animal that lay before me was my salvation and I immediately set to work. I dragged its carcass closer to the buildings where I had better protection and began gutting it using the knife I had found in the Aquella home. The knife performed beautifully, making my task of skinning the rat-dog easier. I carved off several thick chunks of meat. Then, using dry grass and pieces of wood from inside the home, I built a fire to roast my kill. I cooked it well, for I had no desire to fall ill. Tears of joy filled my eyes that afternoon as I savored my first solid meal in years. I gorged myself silly.

With my stomach fat and content, I sat against the outside wall of the house watching as the day's shadows grew–night was coming. The fire I'd built was beginning to die, and I had no more fuel to keep it going. I needed shelter for the night, and hopefully the house with its overhead lasers would provide me safe haven.

Just in case, I planned to prop the bed across the doorway. That would keep the rodents at bay and allow me a solid night's sleep. I was just beginning to get up to move inside when I noticed something up the street—a moving shadow. I stared intently, not sure if the rat-dogs were returning, but I soon realized it was the cat creature and her cub. They were headed in my direction—no doubt they smelled the aroma of my cooking. I waited as they approached—I had no quarrel with these two and I was somehow engaged by their presence. When they got about twenty feet away they stopped. We eyed one another for a few minutes—the cub seemed a little nervous, it paced back and forth behind its mother.

I spoke aloud. It was the first time in many a day. "Easy, little one," I said, softly.

The sound of my voice caused the mother to jerk her head up—she cocked it to one side, studying me.

"Are you hungry?" I asked.

I took a slow step forward and pulled a piece of rat-dog's intestines from the ground. I chucked it in their direction. The mother hesitated; making sure all was safe. She then edged close to the offering and took a sniff. The cub behind her growled and leapt for the food, but the mother knocked him back and gulped the piece for herself.

"There's more," I noted, sending another piece of the remains in their direction.

The cub did not hesitate this time. It lunged for the raw carrion, seizing it and running off to one side where it chewed noisily, pawing the meal with relish.

I chuckled. "It's not very good, but it does fill you up, doesn't it?"

I threw a third, larger piece to the mother. She quickly grabbed it and the two darted off into the darkness with the bounty.

Alone, I reentered the house. The light came on, but it was fainter. I'm sure my presence had taxed the power source. Who could say? I still had no idea how long this city had been deserted or how long the power would remain operable. I only knew I had a safe place for the night. I moved to the bedroom, propped the bed so it blocked the doorway and fell asleep in the closet, atop a bedding of clothes. It wasn't perfect, but I slept well.

When morning came I made my way down to the river where I washed myself in cold running water—my crossbow nearby, armed and ready in case the rat-dogs showed. I was relieved that I had no issues with the rodents that morning, though at one point I did catch a glimpse of the cat watching me from afar. The rest of my day was spent exploring. With my water jug and crossbow, knife and a few morsels of foods wrapped in a cloth, I moved toward the center of the dead city. Here, the buildings became larger and more ornate—their darkened interiors harboring the ghosts of a forgotten people.

My journey across the city was arduous and taxing—mounds of rock and rubble blocked many of the streets, impeding my steps repeatedly. On numerous occasions I had to crawl on all fours over the debris and at other times I was forced to find another way around. The day's exertion was tiring—it was getting hot and I had to maintain a constant vigilance against any attack by the rat-dogs.

By late afternoon I reached the pyramid that lay in the center of it all. Once there, I climbed the steps, several hundred at least, until I reached the top. The vista above the city was magnificent. I turned in all directions admiring the views. I watched as heat waves danced over the terrain, obscuring the valley and cliffs, while in another direction I saw the ocean, its white-capped waves lapping against a beach. From this vantage point I could also see the city's far edge and the harbor that merged the city and ocean together. It was breathtaking, but at the same time lonely—the only sound falling on my ears was that of the wind and the faint howling of wild beasts somewhere in the distance. Their calls reminded me that I would need a safe place to rest for the night.

As I walked the edge of the pyramid's plateau I mulled my next move. It was obvious that there was an advantage to remaining here atop the pyramid. It offered protection—you could see everything all around for leagues. I just needed a secure place to sleep and keep out of the wind—it would be cold tonight. I looked at the array of large, marble urns that ringed the perimeter of the plateau. Perhaps I could sleep in one of them? I meandered past the artifacts and peered inside several. The bowls would easily support a man of my size, though most were black and dirty from ash and heat. Others contained shallow pools of rainwater, while a few lay tipped and broken on their sides. My thoughts were that the urns were used to illuminate the pyramid at night, or for some mystical, religious, or sacrificial offerings. I would probably never know.

In the center of the plateau was a solitary building. It was a square, nondescript cube, about ten feet by ten feet, with a large arched doorway facing me. If my reasoning was correct, the building was an altar room, perhaps used by Aquellians for their rituals. Did it provide an access to the pyramid's interior? Curious, I took a look inside, peering into a nearly pitch-black hole of untold depth. It was impossible to see anything except for a few steps leading downward. Hesitantly, I stepped inside. Nothing happened—no lights came on to illuminate the darkness. I pulled back. It made no sense to break my neck falling into some blackened cavern. Exploration would have to wait until I could find something to light my way.

I sighed with resignation. With such limited resources at my disposal, I decided to spend the night sleeping in one of the marble urns. I found a relatively clean one, dry at least, near the front corner of the pyramid. I crawled inside, padded it with the extra clothes I carried and settled in for the night. As the stars winked into existence overhead, I ate my last few morsels of food and drank what little water remained. It was getting cold and I huddled against my meager bedding. Upon the horizon; the moons of Tiiana were rising. The night sky was exceedingly clear, and the moons seemed brighter than ever, sporting an unusual display of color and definition. I watched as they flew past, their multi-colored surfaces turning slowly, revealing what appeared to be oceans and continents obscured by cloud cover. Perhaps it was all an illusion. I was so lonely and homesick for Melela, it was possible that I might see anything. I wondered. Would I ever see my beloved Melela again? I had my doubts.

I closed my eyes and began to dream, a fantasy of silly thoughts. In the morning I would make my way to the city's harbor. There I would find everything I was seeking—people to greet me, pageantry, beauty, and an abundance of food and drink. It would all be there, everything to make my life better again—including a boat that would take me away. Upon it I would sail away from this horrible place and back to Melela. A smile crossed my face as I fell into a deep sleep comforted by my dreams of hope.

The morning light aroused me; it was chilly. I could see my breath in the air and my muscles were stiff and sore from spending the night in the urn. I sat up and stretched, peering over the edge of the bowl and caught sight of something unexpected. The cat creature I had fed the night before was asleep next to the entrance of the altar room. It was a pleasant surprise seeing it there, and I wondered if it had been there all night. Was it protecting me from the rat-dogs? I liked that idea even if was a bit unrealistic. My movement awakened it. Glancing in my direction, it gave me a good long stare, followed by a wide yawn. It then got up and stretched, finally bounding off toward the rear of the pyramid where it disappeared from sight.

With the sun rising steadily higher, I headed down the steps of the pyramid and began my journey toward the ocean. My dreams had left me in reasonably good spirits and I was cautiously optimistic over what I might find at the docks. I wanted to learn more about Aquellian technology. Utilizing it would make my existence here easier, and far more productive. My hopes were that the buildings along the seafront would provide me with trade goods, tools, or materials that would aid my survival. In any regard, my stomach was growling and as much as I enjoyed having fresh meat to eat, the rat-dogs were not that tasty and there were fish in the ocean. I was eager to shoot a big one with the crossbow I carried.

It took most of the morning to cross the city. I again had to meander through the streets making my way over and around the rubble, but by midday I had reached my destination. At long last, I stood atop the smooth cut stones that comprised the street and dock, separating the city from the water. The breeze coming off the bay was brisk, it whipped my hair and beard—I took in a deep breath of salt laden air.

Like the rest of the city, the dock was eerily quiet. Rotting ropes hung from the piers while small, multi-hued cloths—remnants of flags or other decorations flapped in the breeze. I walked alongside the waterfront, noting its height, a good ten feet above the water. In several places there were stairs that led down to the piers. These piers ran out into the water and held the mooring rings for the boats. Of course, the moorings were empty. I saw no boats or anything else except water, so I turned my investigation to the warehouses and storefronts that lined the street.

It was in these structures that I saw what I perceived to be glass windows. I hadn't seen real windows anywhere else in the city. Perhaps most had been destroyed or broken when the city was under siege. I tried to peer inside several, but the glass was dirty and pitted—good only for letting light inside. I was forced, instead, to push open a few doors to look inside the stores and warehouses. Most were empty, stripped clean of anything worthwhile, though I did manage to find a fishing net that had been left to rot in one of the warehouses.

I was thoroughly delighted with my find. I pulled the net outside, shook it out and spread it across the dock. It had a couple of holes, but was still usable. I sank to my knees and with my knife, began to repair the net, at which point I became aware that I was not alone. The hair on the back of my neck stood up. Looking to either side, I saw movement from a dozen rat-dogs. They stood about fifteen feet back, slavering with drool and growling low. I glanced up—there were more on the roof overhead. I was in a quandary.

Instinctively, I made a move for my crossbow, but there was no time. There were too many facing me; it was pointless. Running was a much better option—if I could. Slowly, I edged myself back toward the water while keeping my eyes locked on them. Time was suspended as I watched their noses twitch and their tongues drool. As I crept back, I pulled out my knife, waiting for their charge as they followed my retreat. I reached the edge of the dock. There was no place to go now; they had me trapped or so they thought. It was now or never. I dove into the water barely escaping their attack. Still, it wasn't enough. Two of them followed me off the dock snapping and biting at me savagely as we hit the cold water. The others immediately scrambled for the stairs that led to the boat moorings. Their plan was simple, encircle me and attack on all sides.

The water was cold and dark as I swam for my life. I was desperate to get away, and I knew my best chance was to get in the deepest water possible. Unfortunately, the tide was out and the water level was low, and even though my gills were open, it was not enough. I felt one of the rodents sink its teeth into my leg, ripping my flesh open, the pain excruciating. I reacted immediately and began to plunge my knife into it, catching it along its side when suddenly, another one struck. This one bit me on the lower part of my arm with a bite that was vicious and deep. With a flurry of jabbing thrusts I responded to my new attacker, stabbing it repeatedly until it let go. I then returned to the first rat-dog slicing away at it until it too was dead. I pried its teeth from my leg.

With both animals dead I pushed away, heading for deeper water; I didn't get far. I was bleeding heavily, and the water around me was dark from all the blood. I couldn't really see, so I swam to the surface. I needed to tend my wounds and see how things lay, but as my head broke the water I saw more trouble brewing. The remaining rat-dogs on the dock went crazy. Seeing me alive, they began to jump into the water and come after me, forcing me to dive again. I thought it was the end.

Suddenly, there was movement alongside me—two dark shadows. At first I thought it was the rat-dogs, but the shadows were too fast. They sped by me with incredible speed, not stopping. I was bewildered. What was going on? I sank to a depth where I knew the rat-dogs couldn't reach me—where I was safe. I needed to tend the gash in my leg before I bled to death. I pulled my rope belt from my waist and tied it around my leg. It was all I could do until I could get to the surface and look at it. I swam up.

As my head broke the water, I saw immediately what had happened. Six or seven rat-dogs were floating lifeless in the water. The others were paddling for safety as two Dolla bore down upon them. I watched as the Dolla rammed the rat-dogs with their noses–the impact crushing their ribs, killing them instantly. I was thoroughly elated with my rescue–once again, I'd been saved from death by my aquatic angels. I turned in the water, grateful for their coming only to see my joy turn to panic–the Dolla were not alone.

In the distance and bearing down on me was what I could only call an armada–an armada of Aquella riding atop Dolla. They filled the ocean before me as far as I could see and I was overtaken with fear. Visions of being held prisoner again as a slave froze my heart. I started to swim for the dock, thankful that my approach was clear of the rodents.

I pulled myself from the water, climbing atop the pier, the pain in my leg and arm causing me to stumble. The pain was excruciating–blood was seeping through my rope tourniquet and puncture wounds in my arm. I needed to take care of this before I bled to death, but the Aquella were coming. I could hear their excited clicks and whistles growing louder–they were moving with great haste to recapture me. I was their prey. I limped quickly down the streets heading back into the darker recesses of the city. I knew I had to find someplace where I could hide and tend my wounds.

Hobbling down street after street, I was finally forced to stop and look at my leg–I was leaving a trail of blood and I knew I would be found if I didn't do something quick. I sat upon the ground–took out my knife and cut a piece of cloth from my tunic. I wrapped it tightly around my leg wound and knotted it. I did the same for my arm, and it seemed to help. I pulled myself up and continued on, but where was I to go? My thoughts turned to the pyramid. I would be able to see the entire city from there and keep an eye on the Aquella. I headed off in that direction limping worse than before.

It was dusk by the time I made it back to the pyramid and the coming shadows helped hide my movement. My bandage was soaked and my leg throbbed. I moved to the rear of the pyramid, keeping out of sight, and began to climb. When I got to the top I crawled across the plateau on all fours; I looked down onto the city. In the distance I could see the Aquella disembarking from the harbor. They carried hundreds of light globes illuminating the entire bay. It looked like daylight down there and I watched as they busied themselves hauling something from the water. I couldn't tell what it was from this distance, but whatever it was; they were very intent on their work.

On the streets closer to me, I caught sight of patrols moving in my direction. They were canvassing the city searching for me, but were still a good distance away. Thankfully, I had the night for cover. I looked again toward the harbor. What was going on? Why were the Aquella here in such great numbers? I edged myself back from the rim of the plateau. The situation was not good. I was seriously hampered by my wounds and I wasn't feeling well. This was compounded by my sense of impending doom—the realization that I would undoubtedly be captured again. I vowed at that moment that that would not happen. I would die fighting first.

It was fully dark now, and the Aquella were settled in for the night. I estimated there must be at least several thousand in the city. What was I going to do? I had until morning to figure it out. I picked myself up and stumbled over one of the urns. My head was reeling as I leaned against it; I felt dizzy. I sank to the ground, coddling my swollen leg which hurt like hell. Suddenly I vomited—my face was pouring with sweat. I think the rat-dogs had infected me with something. With my head spinning I managed to crawl to the rear of the pyramid, where I climbed into one of the marble urns and hid.

The night grew very cold and I shivered as sweat and fever took me. Nightmares beset me and I slept fitfully. At one point I even thought I saw one of the glowers from the beach hovering around me. It came to the edge of the urn bobbing and weaving near my head. I took a swat at it. I didn't need one of those damn things drawing the Aquella to me. I think it flew away, but I wasn't sure. It was, however, at that point that I fell into a deep trance-like sleep.

When morning came I felt a little better, that is, until I looked over the edge of the urn, and saw that I was surrounded by Aquella. There were dozens of them and it was only by sheer luck that they hadn't found me. They were too engrossed in their work, hauling their membrane bags up the steps of the plateau. I watched them, curious as to what they were doing, and I saw them cut one of the bags open. It was filled with silver ore, and they poured the entire bag into one of the urns. Why? Why were they filling these urns with the ore we had mined in the caves?

Whatever the reason, the Aquella were very intent on their project, and were quite diligent in their efforts, overfilling each urn—one after another. I was surprised at how methodic they were, but then I realized: It wouldn't be long before they reached me. I had to make a plan. As the minutes passed I watched the Aquella work, noting the brief seconds when their attention was drawn away from me—that would be the time to make my break. With my fever returning, I looked over the wounds on my arm and leg. Both were infected; there was pus in each, but my leg was worse. I hoped that it would support my weight as I would need both my strength and endurance to be successful. I waited for the right moment.

When the Aquella turned away from me I jumped from my hiding place, hitting the stoned surface of the plateau with a thud. My leg gave out as I winced in agony; I could barely walk and my head was spinning. Making matters worse, the Aquella saw me. Surprised by my sudden appearance they moved in unison toward me, unaware that I was ready to fight to the death. I backed away toward the rear of the pyramid while waving my knife. I vowed not to be taken, and as they closed around me, I saw a sense of apprehension in their faces. They knew I was not going to be a pushover, especially with this blade in my hand—some were going to die.

Our standoff was very brief, for unbeknown to all of us, there were larger forces at play, and it came upon us without warning. Faster than a cloud blotting out the sun, so it was with the virulent cloud that swept over the dead city. Instantly, the sky above us grew dark and nasty, taking us all by surprise. We looked up, and there it was, screaming down upon us like a living monster—Urlena's living wrath, the pink-purple cloud of hell. What hit us next was beyond belief.

Two years earlier I had witnessed this cloud with its vortex fingers laying waste to everything it touched, but what I witnessed today paled in comparison. Everywhere I looked there were tornadoes—hundreds of them, covering the entire city. They were seeking the ore the Aquella had graciously mined from the sea. At that moment, the words of the Dolla hit me with prophetic insight: '*Mine ... rock ... feed ... cloud.*'

Now I understood. The cloud smelled the ore, and it came for it like a starving dog, as ferocious and directed as any living being, tearing apart everything in its path. There were bolts of lightning, violent winds and noxious gases, and of course the vortex fingers that sucked up everything they touched. Ironically, I was of no concern to the Aquella now. They had their own fates to be concerned with. Most of them ran at the first sight of the cloud, while others waited until the tornadoes hit. For me, I stood in stony silence, in total awe of what I was seeing. I was in the middle of a living furnace complete with lightning, fire, and sparks. I watched as one of the vortexes moved across the ore, melting and sucking it up into the cloud, all in one fluid motion. It was unbelievable. I then came to. I realized that this chaos was my opportunity to escape. I needed to get out of here—but how?

Through the haze of my fever, I saw my chance. I bolted for the rear of the altar building, and made my way around it toward the front. There I found three Aquella huddling in fear—they were in my path. Without thinking I charged them, knocking them back, and as I did, a bolt of lightning struck the plateau. The ensuing explosion sent debris flying everywhere, its force knocking us down. When I picked myself up I found I was standing in front of the altar room's doorway with three Aquella facing me on the other side. That's when a vortex struck and they came at me.

Had it not been for my fever, I would have realized that the Aquella weren't attacking me, but were instead trying to reach safety. Unfortunately, I was in no position to analyze anything, and I panicked, taking the only option I saw open. I dove for the entryway that led down to the interior of the altar room. Into the darkness I plunged, crashing down the stairs, and landing in a heap on the floor.

Dazed and bruised, I tried to get up only to have my body slammed into a wall by an unknown assailant. It was the cat, and it tore past me effortlessly as if I was a gnat. I was lucky, the three Aquella who followed me down were not as fortunate. In its bid for freedom, the cat pounced on them, ripping and tearing them apart. They died quickly on the stairwell. It was then that I saw the cat bolt for freedom, exiting the altar room and heading into the storm that raged outside. I was now alone, left to myself, my head throbbing, my wounds seeping pus and a fever wracking me. I barely knew where I was much less what to do. I stood there wavering back and forth, my head spinning—I needed to sit down. I moved forward, taking a few steps and tripped on something—a landing, a platform, or something. Whatever it was, it caused me to fall forward, and I landed on the floor face first. Motionless, I lay there stunned.

Suddenly, there was a blazing light overhead. It filled the room, blinding me to everything, but for one fleeting second I caught sight of an immense amount of machinery lining the wall before me. I raised my hand, shielding my eyes, trying to catch a better look when someone appeared. It was a holograph, similar to the one I saw in the house. It was an Aquella, dressed in a long robe—he bowed before me. I tried to move and give a response, but before I could do anything, there was an explosion overhead. It was followed by a violent jolt. My head reeled in reaction to it and I sank into unconsciousness.

Hours passed—at least it felt like hours. I rose from my stupor and crawled—to where I do not know. My head was burning with fever and I had little understanding of what was happening to me. I know I saw some stairs and made my way up on my hands and knees. It seemed to take forever. At the top, I smelled wet dirt, and I noticed a small faint light highlighting a dark corridor. My thoughts went to the glowers—for the light seemed to move about, illuminating my direction. I entered a long, muddy tunnel and crawled my way through it. I exited the darkness and came out through some brush, only to be greeted by a blinding light that stabbed at me from overhead. Had I been more cognizant, I would have recognized it as the sun. I rose to my feet and began to walk, wandering about like a drunk, making my way through unknown terrain, my head spinning like a top. How far I went was impossible to say. I just know that I eventually fell to the ground and lost consciousness, unaware that I was no longer on the moon of Urlena.

CHAPTER SEVEN

Boutal

'm not certain how long I lay on the ground; I was very sick. My body was burning with fever; my leg and arm infected from the bites I had sustained from the rat-dogs. And I had a concussion from my fall in the altar room of the pyramid. Still, I was alive.

At some point I heard voices—I did not understand them. The language spoken was alien, but one sounded feminine, the other male, for it carried a deep and guttural tone. I did not care. I was far too weak; death would have been a blessing. Whatever the matter, someone picked me up, and I was carried like a sack of grain atop a smelly rug.

I awoke later—several weeks to be exact—lying in the deep recesses of a darkened tent. It was raining and the air felt heavy with moisture, and for a brief second I thought I was back in the mines of the Aquella. The feeling passed quickly; the air was too sweet. I gazed across the tent, my eyes taking in my new surroundings. A small fire burnt nearby illuminating an array of colored artifacts, dangling bones, animal skins and primitive weapons. Where was I?

I pulled myself up on one elbow, my head spinning as I oriented myself. My stirring caused a movement from the other side of the tent—an old woman with long, gray hair and dark skin drew near. She looked at me, spoke, and felt my forehead.

"Grith, Grith, sa-vey gorith," she said, with a toothless grin.

"I'm sorry," I mumbled. "I do not understand?"

She raised her finger to her lips motioning for me not to speak. She then went to the fire where she retrieved a bowl. She filled it with a hot soup which she bought over and began to spoon feed me. I was famished and I took the spoonfuls from her in great haste, my stomach rumbling in appreciation as I sucked up the broth filled with delectable chunks of meat and vegetables. It was the best meal I could remember and definitely nothing like the food on Urlena.

Finishing the soup I suddenly felt quite full. I lay back, overcome with a sense of contentment. I studied my benefactor, the gray haired angel tending me. Who was she? And how had I come to be here? I found it difficult to speak so I just looked at her, noting her dark leathery skin, high-boned cheeks and weathered brow. Her face was etched with a thousand deep wrinkles. She could have been a hundred or more, and yet, her eyes told another story. They were uncharacteristically youthful in appearance—and hypnotic. I felt confused looking into them so I averted my gaze. It was then that she left my side, taking the empty bowl with her. At this reprieve I looked down at my bandaged arm, the one that had been bitten by the rat-dogs. It was wrapped with a leafy poultice. I gently squeezed it—there was no pain. I sat up and looked at my leg. It was also wrapped, and the pain was minimal. I seemed to be healing quite well.

Unexpectedly, I felt a hand on my shoulder—it was the old woman. "Naka, naka," she commanded sternly, pushing me back down.

I chuckled to myself as I succumbed to her bidding. Either I was exceedingly weak or she was very strong for an old woman. Whatever the case, it seemed I had little energy to question her authority. I sank back down in my bedding of furs and blankets while she dressed my wounds, puffing on all things, a dark and twisted-looking cigar. The smoke from it swirled around me, carrying with it a pungent aroma of vanilla and mint. Oddly, she seemed to be purposely blowing it in my face. Suddenly, my vision became hazy, and my senses began to reel. I succumbed to the smoke and fell back asleep.

I dreamt—an odd dream, one with a reoccurring theme. I'd had it for the past few nights. Only this time I seemed to gain a deeper understanding. In the dream a bird appeared before me. It was a large brown and white creature with large claws and a bright red beak. It flew down and landed next to me. I was barefoot, sitting on the grass next to a stream, fishing. The bird spoke.

"There are no fish in the stream."

"Yes," I answered, casting out my line again. "You've told me that before."

"You must find the fish," it replied.

"And where do I find the fish?" I queried.

"Upstream," was its answer. "Upstream."

The bird flapped its wings and leapt into the air where it faded from view. As it disappeared, I lay back on the grass and fell asleep. I slept soundly, pondering the vision.

It was daylight when I awoke. This time I felt measurably stronger—the best I'd felt in months. I wanted to rise as I needed to go to the bathroom. My movement once again brought the attention of the old woman—she seemed to understand my need. She moved over toward a blanket that covered the entrance of the tent, pulled it back and made a command. The light from outside nearly blinded me. I raised my hands to shield my eyes, but what I saw next startled me beyond reason.

An enormous creature entered the tent—a dark brown, redheaded, furry thing covered with thick coarse hair. It must have stood at least eight feet tall, its form filling the tent. Fearfully, I pulled back, only to hear the beast produce a deep, guttural guffaw. It wasn't an evil laugh, but I was unnerved by the sight of its large canine teeth. For a brief moment I thought this might be my end, but then, without warning, the woman struck the beast on the back side—she chastised it as a mother would as a son. To my surprise, the look on the beast changed. It lowered its head and nodded in acquiescence, approaching me with an advance that was demure and gentle. The sight of this reassured me. I knew I was safe, that this creature meant me no harm. I raised my hand for assistance and with unbelievable ease the creature pulled me up and off the bed like a straw from a haystack. It lifted me into its arms like a child and carried me to the doorway. The old woman threw me a blanket just before the creature took me outside.

Outside the tent, my mind was ablaze with wonder as I took in my new surroundings. I had no idea where I was, but this was definitely unlike anything I had seen on my journey to the dead city. Before me was a small meadow surrounded by huge trees; an entire forest filled with massive evergreens that soared skyward. At their base was a mist of swirling, cool-white fog. It languished like smoldering smoke, hovering just inches above the ground. The creature set me down. My knees bowed weakly, but he steadied me with a gentle hand, and I felt my bare feet sink into the moist grassy soil. It felt good. Gingerly, I walked with the aid of the hairy beast toward a patch of thick, green foliage. Overhead, bright sunlight peeked through the trees—and the sky—it was so blue. I never thought I'd be so happy to see a really blue sky again.

Standing next to a tree for support, I relieved myself in the bushes, wondering about my whereabouts. Was I on the same planet or somewhere else entirely new? Things were so different here. I looked over the creature that had brought me outdoors. He was a curious looking thing—some sort of cross between an ape and a wolf, with a humanoid face. He had his back to me, giving me a measure of privacy, but I couldn't help but stare. His ears were long and dog like—they twitched and jerked as if they were catching distant sounds from deep within the forest. When he turned, I was able to see his face better. It was definitely humanoid, tan and leathered, though much was obscured by his mane—a band of reddish orange fur that encircled his face. From the neck down he was covered with thick, dark fur–his chest a lighter shade than the rest. I surmised from the small amount of clothing he wore around his waist, and the thickness of his fur coat, he spent a lot of time out in the elements. I then noticed his legs and feet. He wore thin sandals with leather straps that ran halfway up his large, sinewed legs—legs built for climbing and running over long distances.

I heard him grunt. I think he wanted to know if I was finished. I nodded my head and he helped me to return to the tent. I couldn't believe how weak I was. As we walked back across the meadow I took in the encampment. There were several dwellings, two seemed permanent. They were built of logs and sealed with mud, both had thatched grass roofs. The other structures were more tent-like, appearing to be constructed of tanned animal hides or canvas. The one where I'd been recuperating was the largest domicile. It was built of canvas and hide, and was situated next to a hill covered by dense vegetation. I was amazed at how lush and green everything was. Water was in abundance here. I could hear a babbling gurgle; evidence that a stream ran somewhere close to the camp. There were also campfires dotting the meadow, and I wondered if there were others who lived here. Most of the sites were cold, but several were smoldering with smoke that rose hazily into the air. One small fire held a boiling pot of water, and another crackled and spit, as fat from a roasting animal dripped down onto the flames—the aroma made my stomach growl. It smelled fantastic, and I felt like I hadn't eaten in days.

Engrossed by all the scents and smells that assaulted my senses, I grew careless, stumbling, and nearly falling on my face. The creature that walked with me caught me before I hit the ground. I was taken by his quickness, but also terribly embarrassed and perplexed by my apparent weakness. My wounds appeared to be healed, and yet, I was having trouble standing and walking. It was awkward; I didn't like depending on others.

The next few months were a radical change for me. I had undergone two years of starvation and torture as a slave with the Aquella and my mind and body were in sad disrepair.

Ahska, my caregiver, spent her days nursing me back to health. She fed me medicines and potions which slowly brought back my health. She also saw to my physical rehabilitation. As the days and nights passed, she and Oolat, her adopted son, took me outside where I was able to walk and breathe fresh air. They also spent hours during my convalescence teaching me the ways of Boutal. I learned that it was not a planet as I originally thought, but a moon—one of five orbiting Tiiana, the red gas giant that filled the sky. The other moons were Aura, Urlena, Vashia and Zin, and they filled Boutal's night sky like wondrous gems. I was most curious about them, and quite eager to know how I had traveled from the water-moon of Urlena to Boutal. I queried Ahska about this, but her response was some mumbo-jumbo about this being my destiny, which I found odd. She was an enigma, often providing me a wealth of information, while at other times coy and evasive. It often felt like she was hiding something.

Eventually, with time and exercise my body rebuilt itself though it took nearly a year. The length of time was, in part, due to Boutal's gravity. It was the largest moon in orbit around Tiiana and I suspect its gravity was even stronger than that of Melela. Consequently, my body needed time to acclimate itself, which it did exceeding well. Soon I was back to my original form, though heavier and more muscled in appearance.

It was during this transitional period that I experienced the range of Boutal's seasons, also becoming well-versed in the languages of the Motula and Solula; the two dominate races living on the moon. The Motula were Ahska's race, a dark-skinned people that inhabited the plains and coastal areas. While Oolat's race, the Solula, lived in the colder regions, making their homes in the forests, the mountains, and northern glaciers. The separation of their habitats was a good thing according to Oolat as the two races did not always see eye to eye.

Over time Oolat and I became close. We spent a good deal of time working alongside one another, planting, hunting, and fishing. I think he liked having another man around, one who shared his passion for life, even if my skin color was a bit unusual. Through him, I learned how to keep my wits and survive on Boutal. I also learned how he had come to live with Ahska. That she found him as an infant in the forest, his parents slain by the Brata; a race of gargoyle-looking creatures that lived in the southern hemisphere. Ever since that fateful day, Ahska had provided for him, raising him like a son. It was a good trade. He enjoyed being known as the Son of the Seer.

I chuckled at this, for as I came to learn, the very idea of these two living together only bolstered the air of mystery that surrounded them. This became more apparent the longer I stayed with them. I soon realized that few people came here. And the ones that did did not stay long. Part of the reason was the talismans and jujus that hung in various parts of the forest around our camp. The phylactery of bones, wood, and beads were there to warn travelers that they were nearing the village of the witch. From my observations it seemed that the few who did come were individuals desperate for medicinal cures and they believed that Ahska could help. It was usually during these times that Ahska would leave our camp for a while, or send me on a mission with Oolat, or hide me away so I wouldn't be seen. I often questioned her about this, but was told it was not time, that I wasn't ready. So, I was very surprised when one day she took me aside.

"You and Oolat need to train," she said.

"Train ... Train for what?" I responded.

"For the coming," she answered.

I wanted to know more, but in her usual way she evaded my questions and told me nothing. Instead, she brought forth the weapons that she had stored—swords and knives—weapons of battle that had been used on Boutal for eons. It was with these that Oolat and I began to train, and it felt good.

As the months passed Oolat and I trained like zealots. We ran every day, we lifted rocks and small trees as weights, and we climbed rope and hills to improve our endurance. It was during this time, oddly enough, that I learned something interesting about Oolat. As skilled a hunter and tracker as he was, he lacked any real training in battle skills and tactics. His life with Ahska had followed a more harmonious path and it became my duty to show him everything I knew about fencing and the martial arts. He was an excellent student, and his abilities quickly outshone mine. In size and strength alone he outmatched me easily, for he was a creature natural to his environment, and I spent many an evening nursing bruises and welts on my body. By the end of our training we were in the best of shape. Once again, I was tan, honed, and chiseled—my muscles taut and sleek. I never felt better and I looked forward to what lay in the future. I just didn't realize it was coming so soon or what would be demanded of me.

That fateful moment came when Ahska entered my personal abode, a tent she had given me as my own. She told me that she needed to talk with me, that the time had come. She then produced a small, ceramic jar—a flowered vase about four inches in height. It was filled with a liquid, the lid sealed with wax. She handed it to me and with dark, hypnotic eyes, instructed me.

"You have been under my watchful eye for many seasons now, Light-skin. It is time for you to seek out the fish upstream."

Her words nearly bowled me over. How could she know about my dreams? I looked at her intently—she was indeed a seer. Perhaps she had even instigated the dream.

I questioned her. "There is much I still do not understand," I said. "How did I come here? You know I am not of this place. You said so yourself. Will I ever return to my homeland? Tell me—what am I supposed to do?"

She smiled her toothless grin and answered me in her usual elusive way.

"Your life is a mystery for you to solve, Light-skin. This potion will help. When you bathe on the morrow you must mix it with the water. You must then sink your body as a rock and let the waters flow over you—all of you—especially your hair and face. Your breath must be held until your chest aches—this must be done three full times. But be forewarned—breathe as a fish and you will be silent forever, look into the waters and you will see light no more. Do you understand?"

I nodded my head. "I must submerge myself under water three times, with my eyes shut and my breath held for as long as possible."

She nodded her head.

"But why ... What is this for?"

"For your protection," she answered.

She then gave me an affirmative nod, turned, and began to walk away, while mumbling in a low, gravelly tone. "You have grown much since coming into my fold, Light-skin."

She glanced over her shoulder. "I am pleased."

She shuffled toward the doorway. Then, pausing for a second, she looked back at me. I watched as she tapped her lips with her crooked forefinger, as if pondering some thought.

"Perhaps now would be the time to rename you, second son." She waved her gnarled finger in my direction. "I shall no longer call you Light-skin. That time has passed. You will be known now as Roolka."

"Roolka ..." I repeated. It was a curious sobriquet. "Does it have meaning?" I asked.

"Black Bull," was her reply.

With that, she exited my tent, leaving me to wonder again about my mysterious life as she called it. Did she really think of me as her second son? How did she know I could breathe underwater? Of course! She'd seen the gill flaps behind my ears when I was ill. Still, how could she know what they were for? It was a curious thing to have more questions pestering me after each time we spoke. It made me tired, so I retired for the night.

The next day passed by uneventfully–Oolat and I gathered food and firewood, and again we trained. Our fighting practices were now held with broadswords–a weapon I was told was the chief weapon of choice by the Motula. I enjoyed the feel of the sword in my hands–it was much like the ones I had used in competitions on Melela though heavier. I told Oolat of my new name–he said little, except that it was a good name and that I should be proud.

That evening when our day's exercise was done I headed back to my tent, where I filled a large wooden tub with tepid water. I climbed in and rinsed off my sweat, after which I cracked the seal on the vase, and poured the potion into the water. The liquid was thick and greasy like an oily tar. It sank into the water, producing a multitude of colors which ebbed and flowed around me. I pushed the water around with my hands, forcing the fluid to dissolve and dissipate. When I thought it was ready I took a deep breath and went under. I closed my eyes tightly and held my breath, placing two fingers on my gills to keep them from opening. I counted out the seconds, holding my breath for as long as possible before rising from the water—three times I performed the ritual.

When I finished, I climbed out, dried myself off and dressed in light attire. I felt nothing unusual other than a slight burning sensation around my nostrils and ears. Before I retired, Oolat came to my tent. He handed me a carafe of warm tea—a brew that Ahska made. He told me it would help me sleep. A short time later I understood the need for the tea. My skin was reacting to the bath potion. It felt like a mild sunburn at first, but it grew more and more intense with each passing hour. I drank the carafe until empty and fell soundly asleep on my bed of furs and blankets.

Two days later I awoke with a throbbing headache. I was hung over and disoriented. What had been in that tea? I sat up holding my head in my hands. Rolling out of bed, I struggled to stand, and that's when I realized I had changed. My scream became the loudest vocal cry I think I've ever made; it probably woke the dead. I looked at my arms, my legs, and my chest. I was black—completely black from head to toe. I couldn't believe my eyes. I jumped up and looked into the water bowl where I washed my face every morning. I didn't recognize the man who stared back. I was someone else. What had Ahska done to me? What had happened? This had to be a mistake. I grabbed some soap and began scrubbing myself, but nothing happened. I remained black. I flew from my tent in a rage.

Oolat greeted me at Ahska's tent—he was standing guard. He would not let me enter. I was furious. I yelled at him.

"What has the witch done to me?"

He said nothing. I took a swing at him. He deflected my blow easily. I was now beyond reason, absolutely livid. This was rape–it was the Aquella all over again. I'd been altered against my will for no good reason, and I wanted answers. I charged at Oolat again. He pushed me back hard, letting me know under no uncertain terms that he was there to defend Ahska–to the death if necessary. Still, I was not rational. I lunged at him again. He grabbed me with his hands, spun me around and pinned me to his chest in a choke hold. I felt his hot, canine breath on my ear and cheek—he warned me.

"There are things beyond your knowledge, Light-skin. Cold winds are beginning to blow on Boutal. If you are to survive you must become one with us. Now go!"

With that, he shoved me hard. I stumbled and fell to the dirt, watching as he drew out his blade.

"Vent your anger on the trees," he warned.

He grabbed another sword from nearby and threw it toward me. It landed in the dirt next to my feet. I glared at him. He raised his blade in a fighting stance and I realized he was dead serious. Challenging him would only get me killed. I picked up the sword and stomped off into the forest.

I spent the next three days wandering the forest alone. I had much to reflect on. When the blackness of night came I gazed into the heavens and watched as the moons of Tiiana raced across the sky. I caught sight of the water-world, Urlena, and I thought about my time there as their slave. I was better off here on Boutal, but the memory of what happened there still angered me. I then began to think about my home, Melela. How were things there? Had Corin survived the invasion of the Relcor? And Princess Leanna–what had become of her? Where was she? Was she stranded like me on one of Tiiana's moons, or was she dead? I looked at my hands and scoffed. Would she even recognize me now?

I built a fire and pondered where my life was headed. In many ways it seemed that I was no longer in control, too many things were happening. I was being buffeted by unseen forces seeking to control my purpose and destiny. This most recent change was only the latest example. I studied my hands and arms in the firelight. This new color definitely changed me, and

I knew there had to be a reason–a good one. Ahska didn't do things on a whim.

Several days later Oolat found me; he brought food. He told me that Ahska was sorry for having to do what she did. I didn't believe him. Ahska was not one who second guessed her motives. What she had done was a necessity in her eyes and whether I liked it or not was of little consequence. Oolat did, however, convince me to return to the camp–nothing would be solved with me wandering in the forest for the rest of my days. Besides, what was done was done–though it would be many days before my anger would subside.

Slowly, with mundane repetition, Oolat and I fell back into our routine and I saw little of Ahska. The Solula and I worked as we always did, hunting regularly. And it was on one of our sojourns in search of fresh meat that we encountered the first coming of change on Boutal. We were stalking a darta. Hidden behind a stand of trees we peered through the foliage, our bows and arrows drawn; I could hear Oolat's measured breathing. The darta grazed in a field just ahead at about three hundred feet. I pulled my bowstring back and let loose my arrow. It flew straight, but fell short, clattering on the rocks just a few feet short of the animal. The darta jumped. Oolat loosed his arrow and caught the animal in midair as it bolted for the trees. It fell mortally wounded.

"Roolka" he laughed, "are you not tired of vegetable stew?"

I nodded my head as he handed me his knife.

"Your turn–"

I could tell he was laughing, but this was our agreement.

"You know," I complained, stepping forward. "On my world we have weapons that shoot projectiles that do not require strength alone,"

Oolat snickered. "Of what sport is that?"

I chuckled. "Point made."

I started out of the trees heading for the darta, when suddenly I was jerked off my feet and pulled back into the shadows. Taken by surprise, I started to say something, but Oolat clasped my mouth with his hand. I couldn't breathe, much less say anything.

I heard him hiss in my ear. "Brata—"

I froze—my eyes searching overhead for a sign. Oolat released me and we both edged back into the shadows. A moment later we saw them land—a group of twenty.

I had never seen a Brata before. I only knew of them through Ahska and Oolat, but their descriptions were deficient at best. I can best describe the Brata as a kind of flying monkey or a gargoyle type of creature. Their skin was coarse and leathery looking; a blackish gray and layered with short, stubbly hair. The creatures appeared to be somewhere between three and four feet tall, with small bat-like heads that boasted long and pointy ears. Several glanced in our direction. Their eyes were shiny, but pitch-black and they darted back and forth taking in the terrain around them. I noted their small, flat noses and two wide nostrils, offset by mouths that were filled with long sharp teeth. As the Brata bobbed and weaved over the dead darta I heard them cry out shrilly to one another. The sound was piercing, and as their leathery wings snapped crisply in the air I was reminded of birds of prey, jostling for the kill. Oolat and I watched in silence as the creatures feasted. They tore into the dead animal with their sharp, clawed hands, blood and fur flying everywhere.

I was held spellbound by the sight before me. These creatures were brutally savage and vile, but what really raised the hair on my neck was that some of them were armed. I caught sight of a few wearing leather harnesses with short swords attached to their waists. This meant only one thing—these demons had a measure of intelligence. I felt Oolat's hand on my shoulder.

He whispered. "We go—now!"

The two of us moved deeper into the trees. We tried to make as little noise as possible and neither of us spoke. Unfortunately, fate had something else in store. We had traveled only a short distance when the trees began to thin. The light was waning with perhaps an hour or so of sunlight left. Suddenly there were shadows overhead. The Brata had spotted us and were zeroing in for the attack.

Oolat heard them first and his bow was ready with an arrow instantly. I followed his lead. The huge, bird-like creatures rained down upon us through the trees and we countered their attack with our arrows. Oolat caught two, I missed. They were quick little demons. Soon we were surrounded and our bows and arrows were useless. We dropped them and pulled out our swords, standing back to back. The creatures came at us from both the air and on the ground and the fight of our lives began. Short sword in one hand, a wooden fighting club in the other, Oolat and I fought like madmen; the Brata were not going to take us with ease. I beheaded one after another and crushed the skull of others with my mace. Oolat, in turn, cleaved them into pieces, his sword slicing back and forth. The stench of the Brata's blood was foul.

For the first few minutes, things seemed to be on our side. We were driving them back, but more kept arriving, darkening the sky about us. Like the rat-dogs I'd faced on Aquella, I felt I was in for my final breath. Everywhere I turned I faced a tight-knit throng of the vicious little beasts. They lunged at us, darting back and forth, biting and snapping savagely like a pack of rabid birds. It was all we could do to keep their shriveled bat faces at bay. Those Brata that carried weapons carved at us with their swords, making our fight even more intense, and soon our blades were dripping with their rotten smelling blood. With unrelenting motion, I kept whipping my blade back and forth, cutting and slashing at the creatures, but it soon became evident we had little chance. There were too many. It was then that we got the surprise of our lives. Without warning the Brata suddenly broke off. They took to the air, screaming madly, just as a volley of arrows arced over the trees. I saw the gargoyles being struck in midflight, falling and hitting the ground. Many lay in the dirt writhing in agony, their wails, dismal and haunting—I had little remorse putting them out of their misery.

The day fell silent, leaving Oolat and I standing back to back, breathing heavily. We were lucky. Around us were countless dead Brata, but somehow Oolat and I only sustained minor bites and scratches—wounds that could be stitched or made well with Ahska's medicine. Exhausted, we surveyed the scene, pondering who had saved us, when a thunderous noise came in our direction—Oolat spat out one word.

"Motula!"

I turned my head in the direction of the noise and from across a field I saw men approaching. They were riding on some type of animal that I was unfamiliar with. The creatures were large and quick and we were overtaken and surrounded almost immediately. I observed the men sitting atop the beasts. They were dark skinned, sinewed, and armed to the teeth with swords, knives, and bows and arrows—a war party to be sure. I was not sure if we had been saved or not. The group meandered nervously around us. There was a conflagration of commands and orders. I wasn't sure yet who was in charge. It reminded me of my encounter with the Aquella years earlier, only this time I understood what was being said. Ahska had taught me well.

I took command and set myself out into the open with Oolat standing behind me.

"My friend and I are grateful for your company," I announced. "We were getting bored having to kill so many Brata. These lazy creatures are pitiful fighters and no match for ones like us."

The silence that followed my bragging allowed for an uneasy respite. I surveyed the men before us, taking in their faces while they stared back at us. For seconds, the only sound heard was the heavy coughs and snorts of the riding beasts. Suddenly a ripple of laughter caught hold. I watched as it spread from man to man. Soon they were all laughing aloud. One of the men, the leader, slid from the back of his beast. He dropped to the ground and approached, sword blade in hand.

I took in his demeanor—he carried himself well. I estimated his height to be about five-six, a good six inches shorter than me. His body was solid, his muscles lean and well defined—a warrior for sure, as his arms and legs were scarred from battle. He was of equitable appearance—his face round, but slightly squat, his hair, long like mine, jet black, pulled back into a pony tail and trimmed with colored sticks and leather braids.

"You are a man of powerful words," he said, moving cautiously about us.

I turned as he moved. I knew that he found it strange that a Motula would be traveling with a Solula. I spoke again.

"This beast is my friend." I acknowledge Oolat with a nod of the head. "He and I hunt, fight and kill like brothers. He comes from a powerful tribe in the mountains and he lives with me under the spell of Ahska!"

Those words brought the attention of the entire war party. The leader stopped dead in his tracks. He rested the point of his blade on the ground—a gesture I took as one of truce. I rested my blade as well. I heard Oolat whisper in his own tongue.

"Well done, Dark-skin."

It was at this point that our situation with the Motula changed. Oolat and I now held a specific purpose for these men. The leader, who called himself Wakula, was seeking Ahska. Her presence was sought by their Sovereign. They had orders to bring her to Casita, where a King called Hazadek ruled. When I inquired as to why Ahska was needed, Wakula explained that there was a brewing astir, and Hazadek needed the guidance of a seer. Oolat and I were consigned to lead the war party to our camp.

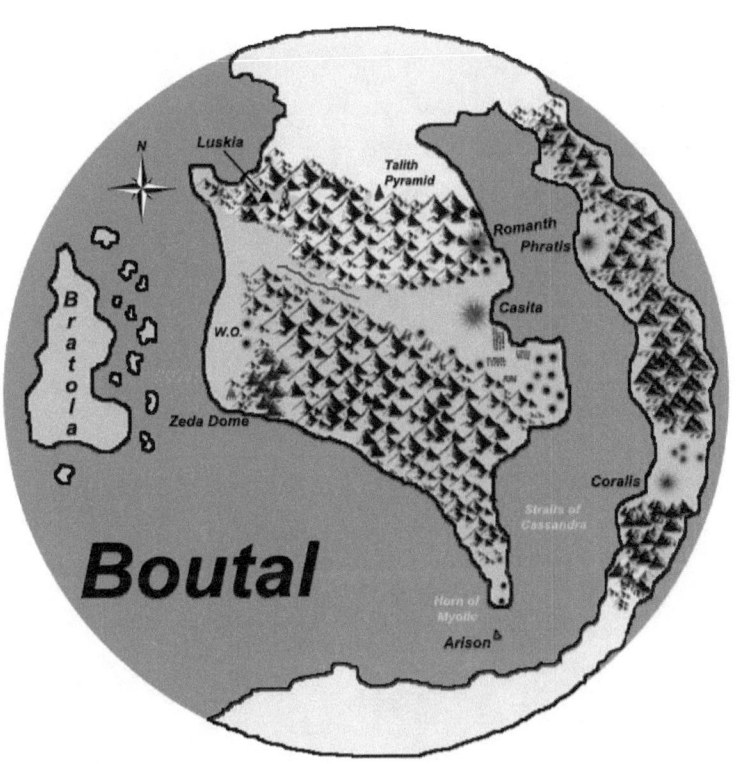

e camped for the night at the edge of the meadow, a measurable distance upwind from the dead Brata. Their stench was unbelievable. Wakula placed us in his inner circle supposedly as his guests, but both Oolat and I knew better–he wanted to keep us close. We had yet to be judged as friend or foe and Wakula had his orders. I was very curious about the brewing he mentioned, but as a stranger in his camp I had to be careful about asking too many questions.

Oolat and I sat alongside several armed men tending our wounds while the rest of Wakula's men prepared camp. Wood was gathered, fires built, and soon several large, bonfires were illuminating the deepening night. Guards were then posted around the encampment in case the Brata were to return. Oolat chuckled at their foolishness.

He whispered to me, speaking in Solula. "The Brata will not return this night. Their eyesight is poor; they do not hunt at night. When they fly in the daylight, it is their keen hearing and the scents on the wind that lead them to their prey. That's why they fled our battle today. They smelled the sweat of the Motula and heard their riding beasts drawing near."

I nodded my head and said nothing. I could see from the looks of the armed men guarding us that Oolat's guttural tongue was making them nervous. I tried to ease their tension by translating Oolat's words.

"My friend says it is good that you build large fires to keep the Brata away. The Brata enjoy finding men alone in the dark. They can carry them away without a fight and eat them alive. We should stay close."

The men murmured nervously amongst themselves and searched the night sky with their apprehensive eyes. As intended, my words did nothing to calm their fears. They were a superstitious lot and did not relish being out here in the forest with the Brata on the loose. Wakula returned. He sat across from Oolat and I while another brought food—wooden bowls filled with a dried meat and a soft rice grain; we ate with our fingers. Wakula glanced at us between mouthfuls of food. I could feel the burning stare of his inquisitive eyes. When he could no longer hold his curiosity he questioned me.

"Roolka," he commented. "I do not see your tribe's colors. From where do you come?"

Oolat scratched his head. I caught his gesture and followed his cue, noting the ornate colored sticks and knotted leather wrappings that Wakula's men wore.

"I come from the desert lands beyond the far mountains," I replied, dryly. "My people—we are wanderers. We keep no colors for our own. We hunt and fight for tribes in need. We work for food, a woman's comfort, or a place to lay our head. Only then do we wear tribal colors."

Whether Wakula believed me or not was difficult to say. He stared at me for a moment, chewing his food. Finally, he nodded his head. "I have heard of such a thing, but I have never met one such as you."

He clapped his hands together and the same man who brought the food earlier returned with several leather bota pouches filled with refreshment. He passed them out to the various circles of men sitting at the fires. Wakula uncapped the leather pouch and took a long swig. He passed it around. When it came to me I took a drink. It was sweet and acidic, a mead of some sort. I could taste the alcohol. I smiled. These people understood fermentation—all was not lost.

The bota bag came around again and I knew what Wakula was up too. He wanted to loosen my tongue with the mead. I couldn't afford to take the bait. I took the pouch and passed it on—Oolat glanced at me with apprehension. I knew that I had probably insulted Wakula, so I spoke quickly.

"Forgive me, leader Wakula. I ask that you understand—I cannot drink with you and your men this night while the Brata roost so close in the trees. They wait for us to sleep in stupor. I must be alert to save our throats should the Brata come to suck our blood."

I had to say no more. Wakula issued orders immediately that the mead be put away. No one drank that night and the fires stayed lit until morning.

At the first sign of light we broke camp and headed into the forest. The journey took several hours as we had to travel along a path the Motula could handle. The mountain trails that Oolat and I usually walked were far too steep for the riding beasts they called polono, though to my good fortune, Wakula provided me with a beast of my own. It made my journey easier, though the riding took a little getting used to. These polono did not have the soft rolls of fat atop their backs like a ploth, and the saddle chafed the butt. Of course, Oolat did not have to worry about riding. He was too large in size and he had no need—his powerful legs easily matched our gait.

While our journey to our camp was uneventful—we saw or heard no Brata—our arrival home was another story. As we cleared the trees and our camp came into sight we saw four or five Brata taking to the air—there were thirty or more in flight now distant upon the horizon. The camp itself was completely destroyed, everything had been torn apart, our tents ripped and shredded, our goods strewn and littered everywhere. Without a sound, Oolat broke from the group—sword out he bolted into a run that caught everyone by surprise. I'd never seen him move so fast. We followed immediately, pushing our polono into a gallop.

Oolat reached Ahska's tent first—it was collapsed in a heap on the ground. He ripped the leather siding open and tore away the wood poles that lay in his way. He threw aside furs, barrels, and blankets, anything that lay in his path. I realized that Ahska must be in there somewhere. I flew from the back of my polono and joined him, tearing through the debris that lay on the ground. I gave a shout to Wakula to help. Together with his men we searched the camp, but we found nothing.

With no sign of Ahska, Oolat and I feared the worst—she must have been carried off. Suddenly I heard Oolat yell. He pointed to the vegetable root cellar dug into the hillside, and we raced for it. The door to the cellar was broken open—fruits and vegetables lay strewn on the ground. Oolat entered first, his sword drawn. The light inside was dim, but we could see several bodies lying in the dirt—Brata! One moved—Oolat cut its head off. We both saw Ahska at the same time. She was bleeding, a dead gargoyle lying across her, the knife she'd killed it with still in her hand. We took her from the root cellar.

Outside, we laid her down on a pile of blankets where we tried to stop her bleeding, but it was of no use. She was dying. She asked for water which we gave her. She then spoke to Oolat in a low dry whisper.

"Oolat ... my son ..." She touched him gently on the face. "I will miss you ..."

Tears filled his eyes. Ahska then glanced at me and the men who stood in the background.

"Roolka ... fish ... a good start ..."

She gasped for breath and motioned for me to come closer. I bent my ear low to catch her last words. "... save Boutal."

She began to cough and spit up blood. Oolat lifted her body up and cradled her like a baby, rocking her gently. I left the two of them alone.

From a distance I watched as Oolat held Ahska for the last time. She died minutes later. What happened next, however, threw me. I had expected that Oolat and I would bury Ahska, giving her the memorial service she deserved, but instead Oolat laid her body upon the grass and then bolted from the camp.

On a dead run he raced across the meadow and into the forest with his sword in hand, following in the direction the Brata had taken. His speed was unbelievable and I was caught unprepared. I quickly saw that no one was going after him—I think Wakula and his men had little interest in the Solula, but that was not the case for me. I ran for the closest polono, and leapt atop its back—I tore away and rode hard, jabbing the beast in the side with my heels. My measure brought Wakula and his men into play. They mounted and followed in great haste after me.

It took a good ten minutes of hard riding, but my polono slowly overtook Oolat. As we exited the forest and hit open ground I pressed my animal on faster, closing in on him. I pulled alongside, the two of us racing neck and neck—there was so little time, but I knew I had to bring this to an end. My friend was out of his mind, running full bore after the demons who had murdered his mother. I turned the polono into him, knocking him to one side while I threw myself atop his shoulders. The force sent us both crashing into the dirt where we rolled over and over before dislodging from one another. Covered in dirt and separated by only a few feet we stood and faced one another—Oolat raised his blade and I pulled mine. He swung and our broadswords clashed with the sound of smashing metal. It was all I could do to hold my own against this powerful giant, my friend.

I darted and ducked with each thrust he made, and I countered and deflected each of his swings. I could only thank the stars above that he was winded from his run and his mind was not focused, otherwise I'd have already been dead. I began yelling at him.

"Is this how you show your love for your mother? By being stupid?"

Our blades clashed and we locked arms hilt to hilt—my face looking up to him. He pushed me hard and I stumbled back across the meadow. He then came at me swinging.

"What do you care, Light-skin. You yourself called her a witch. You said you hated her."

His remarks cut deep. The anger inside me swelled. I met his blade attack with equal force and I pushed back hard. Our blades collided over and over, smashing against each other with disharmonious reverberations. I yelled to him.

"I called her a witch because I didn't understand." Our blades met again. "And I said I hated what she did to me. You forget my friend—she saved my life too!"

We were both out of breath now and totally out of control. He swung at me and I swung back—I nearly took his nose off. He retreated. I started to press, when suddenly, out of the blue, a calmness overtook me. I think it might have been Ahska's spirit. Something seemed to placate me. I no longer had the urge to fight. I threw my sword to the ground, my heart and chest pounding from the exertion. I opened my arms wide, exposing my chest.

"You want to kill me, Oolat? Come on, then—do it! Or would you like help killing all the Brata who took your mother's life?"

I pointed angrily to the horizon.

"Do you know where they are? Where they are going? Can you kill them all by yourself?"

Oolat said nothing and the two of us stood staring at one another, panting like out of breath dogs. I shook my head in disgust and walked away, retrieving my sword from the ground. I then offered one last bit of advice.

"Personally, if it was me, I'd get help. I'd make sure every last one of the pricworms was dead."

As I grabbed the reins of my polono, I saw from the corner of my eye that Oolat's sword had fallen to the dirt.

"Wait!" he pleaded. I turned. He was now bent over, breathing heavily, his hands on his thighs, tears flowing. I walked toward him.

"Can we kill them all?" he asked.

I nodded my head. "We will, my friend, we will—of that you can be sure."

I gave him a hard reassuring pat on the back then hopped atop my riding beast. Oolat sheathed his sword and the two of us turned in the direction from whence we came. On a rise about a hundred feet back we saw Wakula and his men. They'd been watching us silently. I did not know it at the time, but they were in awe of our battle. A sword fight between a Motula and a Solula was almost unheard of, and I had survived unscathed–a measurable feat for sure.

Later that day we buried Ahska deep in the ground along with enough food and water for her journey into the land of the spirits. We then abandoned our camp and began our journey to the city of Casita where Oolat and I were to meet Hazadek, the King of the Motula.

☆ ☆ ☆

It took six full days to cross the lands leading to Casita on a heading from the mountains to the sea. As we rode I took the opportunity to study the topography and the people who populated Boutal. In the upper elevations I saw mining operations where metal and ore were mined along with salts and minerals. At the lower elevations farming became more prevalent and the number of people greater. In these areas we ran into more villages filled with families. Our party was greeted warmly, I suspect because the rumors of the Brata attacks were bringing people together out of necessity. I learned that every home was built with a cellar or safe room, and lookouts were in charge of studying the skies in case of an attack. They rang large bells, which carried warning to the workers in the field and to the women with children playing outside. These people were accustomed to living with danger.

As we drew closer to Casita the roads became wider, smoother and well-traveled. Caravans of wagons and beasts similar to the polono were bringing trade goods to market. Through the low hills and grasslands we made our way to the sea. When we came over the last rise I was taken aback by the magnificent city that lay nestled next to the blue glistening waters of an inland bay—this was Casita.

I noted the ships in the bay, there were perhaps thirty or more. Some sat anchored; others were docked next to the city. They ranged in all sizes, from frigates to brigantines to small cutters all powered by sail and oar. I was curious as to what goods they carried—what technologies did these people of Casita have? My eyes turned to the city itself. It was a sprawling metropolis of multicolored brick, mud and rock buildings—some as high as three stories, built around a huge castle that bordered the bay. The castle stood like a mountain of ebony crystal, its black stones glinting in the sunlight. It towered over the city, offering protection to all sides including the sea. I could see why many Motula considered Casita the center of their civilization.

We arrived late in the afternoon and were immediately given residence in the city not far from the castle. We were given attendants, a hot bath, and food. I could see where life in Casita could be productive and I relished the thought of sleeping in a soft, warm bed. True to Wakula's word, I fell asleep that night bathed, massaged, and oiled, under the influence of sweet mead and a soft pillow. The night passed well with dreams dancing in my brain—I almost felt as if I was home again on Melela.

When morning came, Wakula informed us that we would meet with King Hazadek in the afternoon. I was still at a loss as to what we were going to tell him. Neither Oolat nor I were seers. We were men—fighters—what did we know about the future? I barely knew anything about this moon or its people. Still, we were faced with an audience.

To kill time, Oolat and I walked the city. Of course, we did not travel alone—there were three armed guards and two females in attendance. They were there to entertain and guide us, protect us from the staring eyes, and more importantly, keep us from escaping. Without a doubt Oolat caused more of an issue than I—the Motula were in awe and fear of my giant friend, and who could say that their fears were not warranted? We walked the streets unimpeded.

I found the docks the most interesting. It was here that the heart of the city beat. I marveled at the sea vessels, their riggings of rope and canvas—the sailors sitting atop their decks shouting orders. This place was alive. We watched the ships being loaded and unloaded, tons of trade goods being made ready, raw materials coming and going. We meandered through piles of goods, canvas and burlap bags filled with grains and vegetables, clay and ceramic jars filled with oil, ale and mead. Some ships were laden with fresh cut lumber, holding boxes filled with hammers, nails, and saws. It seemed everything under the sun was being sent in and out of the city. I poked and prodded, asking questions and learning as much as I could about Casita and its citizens.

At one point I found a ship carrying minerals and ore—it was being unloaded on the dock. I noticed several bags split open—one contained a small, yellow crystalline rock. I picked a fragment, sniffed it and put it to my tongue—I queried the dock hands of its use and learned it was for medicine. I found another ship with similar wares. This one carried a white, coarse powder used for making bricks, mortar, and cement for building. I realized immediately this city had much that a man of my knowledge could use. Perhaps I could offer the King some insight after all.

The rest of the day was pleasant, but for the most part, uneventful. We toured Casita and ate a meal, paid for by the grace of the King. Afterward we entered Casita's marketplace, finding it filled with vendors—hundreds of them, all peddling their wares of fine cloths, carvings, paintings, and food. The place was alive with energy and the variety of goods was immense. The scents and tastes were pleasing to the senses. I could tell immediately that the women who accompanied us were much more eager to be here than out on the docks— they were far more cheerful and delighted in showing off their city's assets and resources. They pranced before us bragging how Casita was unlike any other city on Boutal—only the finest, most intelligent and resourceful of entrepreneurs were allowed to sell here. At this point they appeared to be right.

We were nearly through the market place and ready to head for our appointment with the King when suddenly the day became overcast, the light muted—I thought it to be clouds rolling in from the sea, but then I heard the gasps and cries. I looked up. Overhead the sky was filled with blackness—the darkness indiscernible. It appeared solid, and then individualized, the clouds holding a movement that ebbed and flowed as if alive. I realized at that moment it was the Brata—tens of thousands of them flying in unison. They blotted out the light from the sun and Tiiana, covering the city in darkness. Panic spread as everyone in the marketplace began to flee. There were screams as women grabbed their children and men armed themselves. Everyone ran, either for safety or for taking their place at some defensive point along the city's walls and rooftops. The two guards with us grabbed Oolat and I by the arm and issued quick commands for us to follow them to safety. We headed for the castle.

As I moved with the men I watched the air above. The Brata were circling overhead like a black funnel of clouds, remaining high, and out of reach of arrows or catapults. I wondered their purpose, when suddenly I saw something being dropped from their midst. I couldn't tell what it was at first, but it quickly became apparent—it was a man. I watched his body fall. It hit the castle somewhere near the upper levels out of my view. In disbelief, I watched as the Brata began to dissipate. They broke formation and headed out to sea, their departure allowing the sunlight to return. What had happened? I was perplexed and dying with curiosity. Why had they not attacked? We entered the castle and were led upstairs.

The corridors leading to the King's audience hall were packed and it took great effort to make our way through. There was a great deal of panic and fear. Everyone wanted to know what had just happened. We finally gained entrance, and I stood with Oolat in the back of the hall listening to the voices around me. The rumors were flying: *The Brata had sent a message ... They seek our surrender ... They want children to feast* on ... *The King was ready to fight ... The King was ready to surrender ... The council of the cities was ready to secede ... Casita was on its own ... The city was to be evacuated ...*

Suddenly I heard a horn blast. It cut through the air and brought silence. Someone then shouted out an order: The hall was to be cleared by all except for the King and his council. Armed men approached. They forced everyone back and the people began to dissipate. Oolat and I were unsure of what to do, but Wakula appeared. He pulled us aside and led us to a small alcove at the side of the room where we waited.

From our vantage point I watched as order befell the hall. I observed the men. Most were dressed in fine robes and silken shirts, some armed with short swords–the royalty and states-men of Motula. Though I knew little of the governing factions here, I had knowledge of other worlds, other governments, and my own experience with the Emperor of Melela–it was all much the same in many instances. I saw immediately how certain groups came together, the silent contracts and pacts linking them to one another. I took note of small things like the silent nod of the head or a glance in someone's direction–though, in truth, I did not know the basis of things yet–that would come later.

There was another horn blast and the King entered, fol-lowed by his entourage. He was a middle aged Motula with long, black hair pulled back into a bun. I noted his graying temples and the wrinkles that lined his face and forehead. His dress was a style befitting that of monarch. Draping from his shoulders was a dark, green cape that fell to his waist–a royal look that coordinated well with his brown leather pants, wide black belt, and knee-high black boots. As he turned in my direction, I noticed a golden armor breast plate cover-ing his chest–my guess to establish to his subjects that he was their military leader as well. At his immediate rear was a small group of ministers and servants and just behind them a young woman with long, flowing black hair; a maiden with oval shaped eyes and dusky-brown skin. Her appearance caught me by surprise. I had not expected to see a woman in the King's entourage—especially one so beautiful. I gazed in disbelief as she entered the hall in a plush, flaxen robe of deep red color. She walked with confidence and I noted her disciplined eye—the cordial nod that she gave to each minister and statesmen as she walked past. It was evident she knew her role well. I queried Wakula as to who she was.

"The Queen," he whispered.

I immediately thought the King to be a very lucky man. For his Queen was indeed the finest looking woman I had seen so far on Boutal, and I wondered: Were there others like her?

The King took his chair at the head of a long oblong table, with the Queen and his ministers behind. As he sat, the rest of the men in the hall took their places—I observed the order they took, knowing full well that the most important would have the closest ear of the King. I waited and watched. The room was soon filled with voices speaking simultaneously, the din quickly turning into an uproar. Everyone wanted to know what was happening and they plagued the King with questions. Unable to address the issue, the King sat forward and began pounding the hilt of his sword on the table until the room fell silent. He then made a motion to one of his ministers who quickly stepped forward. The minister carried a parchment which he unfurled and placed on the table. Wine goblets were used to keep it spread open. The King looked it over as he spoke.

"Ministers and city leaders of Boutal, I'm afraid the news is grave. We have received an ultimatum from the Brata. The vermin have laid waste to our western outposts along the Aritonian deserts—every man, woman and child has been slain. The man dropped atop the castle was the last victim—forced, I might add, to pen this decree before given death."

A murmur of anger rippled through the crowd.

"They are demanding retribution for the attack on their birthing fields. They are calling for five thousand polono, ten thousand head of krata, and the heads of the soldiers who laid waste to their unborn young."

The King's words were followed by silence, then pandemonium. There was yelling:

"No, No, No!" a number cried out.

This was followed by finger pointing and accusations. The various ministers and city leaders shook their fists and with heated ire blamed each other for the incursions and attacks on the Brata's territory. This was their fault and now Casita would pay the price—the hall was degenerating into chaos. Again, the King pounded on the table.

"Silence!" he yelled. "Or I will give them all your heads as they have requested."

The room fell quiet. The King threw his sword atop the table. He was exasperated and his words heated.

"We have been at war with the Brata for untold generations. My great, great-grandfather was the first leader of many who tried to find peace with the demons, but now they come too often seeking our flesh. I am not pleased by the actions of those of you, who foolishly sought to gain their lands, but this is a river that has been crossed by both sides many times. It is time to end it, once and for all."

"My Lord," someone spoke. "Their numbers are great—like none I have ever seen."

The King nodded. "This will be a battle unlike any before—but it comes to us like the night and we must not crouch in fear, but meet it with valor." He raised his voice so all could hear. "Seven days hence, the Brata will return for payment—we must be ready!"

"Seven days," someone remarked.

"There's no time," another commented.

"May I make a suggestion?" I spoke aloud; my voice cutting across the hall.

The eyes of the room fell toward me. I fell to one knee and bowed my head. The King looked toward me and then his ministers.

I then heard someone ask: "Who is this Citizen?"

Wakula stepped forward, his face paling.

"Forgive me, my great King. This man … he is Roolka, the seer … with Ahska. He comes from the outland tribes. He … he … does not know our ways."

The voices of the crowd rose in a flurry of anger and hostility. My brazenness was unacceptable. I rose, taking my full height of six feet. I surveyed the room with an attitude of assured superiority—challenging their weakness.

"I take it then, that you have no desire to empty the skies of the Brata demons that prey upon your women and children?" The voices fell silent. I then added. "And I was told that the ministers of Casita had the wisdom to listen when a prophet spoke."

My insult was not wasted. A number of them reached for their swords. I responded in kind—Oolat stepped forward to back me up. His size brought things to a standstill. The King sat back in his throne and studied me—he stroked his chin.

"And what say you, prophet? Can you stop the flying demons?"

I looked about the room. "Yes," I answered firmly. "But I will only give my knowledge to you, great King. I will not waste it on rabble."

I had just made a lot of enemies, but it didn't matter. I knew I would never truly fit in here. I would always be an outsider, but if I saved their hides, most would forgive me. The King looked about the room. He picked up his sword from the table and sheathed it.

"Clear the hall," he ordered. His soldiers moved forward.

A few minutes later the hall was empty except for the King and his immediate circle. I stood facing him at the far end of the table with Oolat by my side. The King leaned forward and spoke.

"Your words are filled with great bluster, seer. But you have my ear. Have you a vision for me, or hot air to warm my cold feet?"

I smiled with tight lips. "I am not a seer, my King. But I have a knowledge that will rid you of the Brata and make you the most powerful man on this moon."

The King laughed arrogantly. "I am already the most powerful man on this moon, seer. Now give me something of substance or you shall spend the rest of your days in my dungeon, begging to see the light of Tiiana."

I reached into my pocket and pulled out the yellow crystal I found on the docks—then from a small leather pouch I carried upon my waist I poured out the white power I'd found as well. The King looked at me in a curious fashion. I gave him instruction.

"Great King of Casita, if you will humor me for a short interlude. Have your men bring me more of these substances, along with black charcoal from your fires and I will show you how you can strike the Brata from the skies."

✵ ✵ ✵

The city of Casita had a population of around twenty thousand men, women, and children, and they were given to my disposal. I knew that time was limited and much had to be made ready for the coming attack of the Brata. Everyone was given a duty. Children old enough were sent to the forest's edge to gather wood, pine cones and reeds from the waterways. The wood and pine cones were burnt to make charcoal, the reeds sharpened into arrows. Women and old men were put to work crushing and mixing the different chemicals I required—the sulphur and nitrates I had discovered aboard the ships in the harbor. These were added to the charcoal to make gunpowder. Some of the gunpowder was then mixed with honey, mead, and sugar then rolled into thin pieces of parchment paper, rope and cloth and dried in the sun. These were the fuses for the rockets and bombs we were building.

Catapults were poised atop the lower tier of the castle and on the decks of the ships in the harbor. Nails and rocks were gathered and packed into cement castings, vases, jars and barrels, anything we could use to make bombs. There was no resting. Time had given us no quarter. Each day more rockets, bombs and fire candles were made ready. By day five we were nearly set. The sight of several Brata flying in the distant skies spurred everyone harder. And by the morning of the sixth day we were as ready as we were ever going to be.

In the predawn hours the King and I walked the lower fortress tier surveying our defenses. The catapults were armed and ready and our rockets stood like tin soldiers ringing the entire perimeter of the castle. Alongside the base of the interior walls were the archers, ready with hundreds of arrows. We walked past men resting within the arches and stairwells that led down into the castle. Some slept briefly on the cold stones, exhausted from their labors. These men were consigned to bring up more bombs, arrows and rockets from the lower levels of the castle when needed. Each side had its own access and only a coordinated effort would keep the Brata from breeching our ranks.

At the very top of the castle was the lookout tier, an area too small to adequately defend and keep supplied. We needed to keep the Brata from landing there so we filled it with fire candles, grease and mounds of wood. Once ablaze it would be far too hot for the Brata to land and use to their advantage. The King and I moved to the walls that overlooked the city below—it was pitch-black—all fires had been banned to prevent any accidents. I slapped the fortress wall with the flat of my hand, the rock was solid, the castle well built. Originally designed to repel an attack from any direction—it would again be tested today.

For many, there was not much sleep that night. Every able bodied person able to pull a bowstring or carry a sword was pressed into service. I knew that there was going to be a lot of deaths this day, but hopefully Casita would survive and the Brata would come to an understanding that they had no business here. At dawn's light it began.

The morning light brought hundreds of thousands of Brata across the sea toward Casita. I stood atop the castle with King Hazadek, prompting him to wait until the Brata attacked before we retaliated. The creatures had to be low enough for us to inflict damage if we were to be successful. Our archers stood ready, lining the walls of the castle, and the rooftops of the city. In addition there were pockets of soldiers armed with rockets ready for launching throughout the city. The Brata circled overhead, perhaps looking for an opening, or the nonexistent herds of animals they had demanded, but they saw none. Livid with anger, they screeched in rage and tore down upon us, their swarm blackening the morning sky.

Being that the castle was the highest point in Casita we were the first to greet the gargoyles as they came at us full speed, thousands upon thousands of them. Armed with their short swords and clawed hands, their mouths agape with razor sharp teeth, they screamed a haunting wail that shook the very air around us. I had to admit I'd never faced a foe like this and it was unnerving, but I held, biding my time. I uncovered the smoldering coals that lay in a basin at my feet and lit the oiled torch I carried. It blazed into flame while Oolat covered my back—the beasts were almost upon us. With seconds remaining I lit the trail of gunpowder near my feet. It ignited with a whoosh and a white-hot flame snaked its way across the stone visage to the rockets that stood ready. I threw my torch into the air where it landed on the upper tier, striking the piles of wood that were greased with oil and gunpowder. The thunderous roar that followed was exhilarating and awe inspiring. Flame and gunpowder flare shot upward into the sky, pumping out a white-hot blaze of pyrotechnics that annihilated everything within its reach.

Our rockets followed. They shot up skyward in a blaze of red, white, and orange color, delivering their payload of death. I watched in delight as the rockets burst open, sending out explosions of white-hot flame, followed by the nails, rocks and chunks of metal that were packed inside. The shrapnel tore the Brata open and knocked them from the sky. Adding to the vermin's disorientation was the dense gray-black smoke and putrid odor of sulfur. It took away their sight and smell. Deafening explosions added to their confusion, blowing away their ability to hear. They quickly became drunken birds, colliding into one another, tumbling chaotically—easy targets for the bowmen atop the rooftops. Arrows were loosed and the Brata wailed in agony. Thousands fell to their death or lay wounded upon the streets below—those that survived the fall were bludgeoned to death by the townspeople.

Overhead, the Brata who escaped the first attack retreated.
I watched with interest as they regrouped and tried a new
tactic—I marveled at their level of adaptation. They broke into
three groups and attacked the city from three different directions. One body flew low just above the waters of the sea, the
other two attempted to encircle us. With a wave of a flag the
King gave his order to the ships in the bay. They sent their cata-
pult bombs flying—wooden barrels filled with nails and gunpowder, some filled with gunpowder, sugar and honey—a sticky
mixture of hot syrup that seared and burnt when it exploded
and congealed upon the Brata's flesh.

Our fight with the Brata was not without mishap or death.
There were those that made it through our barrage and soon
hand to hand combat was raging everywhere. Even I had to
slice my way through many of the creatures to help others
under attack. We brought out more rockets and bombs from
inside the castle, aimed them into the air and unleashed them.
The armaments in the city followed—rockets were blazing skyward from all quarters. It became hard to breathe. Our eyes
watered and our sight was dimmed by the thick black smoke
that blanketed the sky; we fought as blind men. In the distance,
I could barely make out the ships in the harbor. Several were
on fire. There were explosions aboard their decks with flames
shooting skyward. They burnt to ashes upon the sea and men
swam for their lives.

Casita was a blackened, smoke-filled war zone and it was
hours before the sounds of battle fell distant. Finally, with
the light of day waning on the horizon, a light breeze took
hold, pushing away the smoke and the smell of death. From
atop the castle walls I surveyed the city below. Portions were
gone, destroyed by fire and explosion, and a few small fires
still smoldered, but for the most part Casita had survived the
battle well. The same could not be said for the Brata, for as
far as I could see their dead were everywhere. They lay atop
the rooftops, in the streets and in the trees—their bodies too
numerous to count. It would take days to clear them away and
dispose of them, but at least it was over, and we had won. No
one knew how many of the gargoyle creatures had survived,

but they did not return for another battle—that day, or the next, or the next after that—they had been vanquished. We knew now that it was over and at some point everyone hoped there would be a victory celebration.

It took weeks to clean up the city. The dead Brata were either buried in pits or burned in huge pyres. The Motula, of course, had their own dead to bury and mourn, but overall the mood in Casita was one of relief. The city had survived; they would rebuild and move on. Even the King was happy, though his joy was tempered by the knowledge that a Pandora's box had been opened. While my ingenuity had saved him and the city, the knowledge of gunpowder was spreading. Casita had repelled the Brata, but they were not eradicated—if Boutal were to be truly free of their deadly intent then something needed to be done permanently.

Six weeks after the battle a celebration finally took place. The castle was scrubbed from top to bottom and the smell of Brata, burnt gunpowder and sulfur washed away. The city was made anew, rebuilt and rejuvenated, fresh fruits and vegetables harvested, grains reaped, bread baked along with biscuits, pies and cakes. Domestic animals were butchered. Darta and other wild beasts were hunted and dressed, mead, wine, and ale distilled—all in preparation for the thousands who were coming to celebrate our defeat of the Brata. The city was literally aglow with the festivities—ablaze with colored flags and regalia. The scent of fresh baked goods permeated the air, as did the smell of cooked meat roasting on open pits. It was a celebration of victory that would last for days, fueled by the heady consumption of hundreds of barrels of mead and ale.

Atop the castle, the mood and celebration were as the city itself. I was a guest of the King and Queen—their guest of honor as it were, and I was placed at their table along with Oolat to enjoy the fruits of our victory. Our festivities took place outdoors for the weather was warm, and we were celebrating our victory with the citizens of Casita. It was a grand event, colorful and joyous, and I watched as the King took advantage of his newfound popularity. Periodically, he would move to the fortress walls and wave at the crowds celebrating below. They cheered his every appearance—even Oolat and I were swept up into the occasion. The merriment and music were contagious and there was more food than I had seen since my days with the Emperor. It made me a little homesick.

As I meandered amongst the invited guests that day, I felt reasonably comfortable for the first time—I was a hero, and I was dressed as they were. They seemed to accept me for the first time, thanks in great part to the King. He had sent his personal tailor to me, instructing him to sew clothes tailored for my frame, including new boots and a newly forged sword. It was part of a transformation that made me look the part of a well-heeled Motula. It was nearly perfect—well, almost. There was just the little matter of my attraction to the King's wife.

The Queen looked especially radiant for the festivities and I found it hard to keep my eyes off her. I wondered to myself how such a woman, surrounded by the plainness of ordinary Motula women, could look so luminous, and so refined. Addled by her beauty, I found myself stealing glances in her direction, all the while trying to be nonchalant and cool-headed—she was, after all, the King's wife. Still, it was hard. I found her a refreshing change against the coarseness of these people. Though she appeared like them she was different. How was it that this woman with dark-chocolate skin, so smooth and satiny, radiated such grace? And her face, it was so uncharacteristic of other Motula women. It was thin and refined, her nose slender and delicate—and her eyes—they were so blue. I knew of no other Motula woman who held this bright a color in their eyes. I was at a loss to explain it and I couldn't help but desire her.

To keep my indiscretion from getting the better of me I withdrew from the crowd, isolating myself at the castle's armament wall. There I stood looking out over the bay, and the ships that lay in anchor. With a goblet of mead in hand I took solace. I was better off here. I knew my lack of discretion would only lead to trouble and it had to be my loneliness speaking. She *was* married—she bore the King's only son, a child of three years who played some thirty feet away from where I stood. I took a sip of drink and put my fantasy to rest—or so I thought.

Fate can be an unkind tutor. She can sneak up on you and crush you with a lesson in life and love, all with a simple wave of her hand, and never blink twice. I stood sipping my mead, nursing my loneliness when fate struck in the guise of a small earth tremor. It shook the castle for only a brief second or two, but that's all it took. The wall facing the ocean, weakened by time and possibly the gunpowder used in the battle, gave way, and the King's son fell screaming to the ocean waters below.

There are times when I do not think—I react, as I did when the rat-dogs cornered the cat in the dead city. Why? I do not know. Sometimes this has gotten me into trouble. And though my next move was impetuous, foolish, and downright stupid, I wasn't about to let this child die. I cast aside my sword and ripped my boots from my feet. Then with no reservation I raced to the wall where the child had fallen and leapt over the edge, diving down toward the ocean waters that pounded below. Halfway down, it occurred to me that my neck would probably be broken when I hit the water, so I tried to flip over in midair. I was only halfway successful, and I hit at an angle with tremendous force, my left knee buckling on impact.

Under the water my Aquella gills popped open, allowing water to pass freely through my nose and mouth. I swam hard ignoring the pain in my leg, for somewhere in these cold waters was a child in need. My adrenaline was pumping, and I forced myself further down into the cold, dark waters, fighting against the currents.

A minute or two later I found the child lying at the bottom of the bay in about twenty feet of water. His face was ashen, and his body cold and still. I had no idea if I was in time or not. I grabbed him and took him up to the surface where I began to blow air into his lungs. I squeezed his chest as I swam, fighting the waves as I made my way to shore. Reaching the beach, I carried him from the water and laid him down on the sand. I then started to give him resuscitation. To my relief he responded. Water spurted from his mouth—he was alive. I pulled him into my arms, but I was unable to rise, my knee wouldn't support me. I looked up. There were people pouring out of the castle–the Queen was in the lead. She reached us ahead of the others and fell to her knees on the sand at my side. She whisked the boy from my arms, hugging him while crying and praying at the same time. Her words knocked me back.

"Oh my little baby, my little darling, please do not die. Your mother needs you here in my arms. My sweet, little baby, open your eyes. . ."

My eyes grew wide, my heart pounded–I could barely breathe. Her speech was Melelan. How could this be? Choking with anticipation, I queried her.

"My lady ... How is it that you come to know the language of my home, Melela?"

She looked at me, her blue eyes wide with surprise. Her son began to cough again. He spit up more water–then started crying. She laughed with joy; tears trickling down her face as she hugged and caressed him. She then looked at me in wonder. The others reached us. The King grabbed the boy and hoisted him into the air. His fear was evident, and his joy just as equal when he realized his son had been saved. His orders were so quick and so fluent that I could only catch a phrase here and there–but I knew I was in good standing.

Oolat reached my side. "I thought you dead for sure, Roolka."

"I might still be," I answered. "My knee's wrenched."

Oolat grabbed my arm and helped me up. And with his support we crossed the sand, heading back to the castle. As I hobbled along, I watched the King and his entourage up ahead. I saw the Queen looking back–she blew a kiss, thanking me. I waved back, my stomach tightening into a knot. Was what I suspected really possible?

CHAPTER NINE

Princess Leanna

laid in one of the castle guest chambers atop a soft down bed, pillows piled high around me, my leg elevated under orders of the King's doctor. I was to stay in bed for the next week—and judging from the swollen knee I nursed, that was not going to be hard to do. Of course, I had Oolat there to give me a hard time and several Motula attendants to help me with all my needs. Considering all I had done over the past several months, rest was definitely appreciated. Still, the only thoughts on my mind were of the Princess. I had a million questions, and yet, the situation was delicate. I was unsure of what to do—Oolat was my only confidant in this matter. I could at least talk to him in Solula with no one else understanding.

I pressed my friend for answers. Did he know anything? Had Ahska ever mentioned anything about a young girl? I told him again of my story—how we had fled Corin during our battle with the Relcor.

"The Princess would have been sixteen at the time—smaller back then, fair skinned, like I used to be—with long, blonde hair."

He looked at me funny. "What is blonde hair?"

"Her hair was white, like this ..." I pointed to my cream-white pillow top. That seemed to jog something. He began to talk.

"There was something—ten or twelve cycles past," he said. "I was outside, gathering firewood—it was night and there was a bright flash in the sky. I got Ahska and showed her—we watched and saw little sparks shooting off in the night. One grew large and came toward Boutal—I saw it fall to the ground in the nearby mountains. The next day Ahska went looking for it while I stayed in camp. She returned two days later dragging a litter piled high with blankets behind her. She told me not to come close or I would get sick."

"I did not think anything more about it, Roolka. Hunters came into our village seeking a guide to take them into the high mountains—Ahska sent me with them. When I returned, all was as it had been before. When I asked her what she had found, she said a sick animal, but it died. She told me she buried it so no one else would get sick. I did not think of it any further."

"Curious," I commented. "And you think this light from the sky might have been a vessel of some sort?"

Oolat shrugged. "It was a bright light—like a meteor. I only remember that when I saw the litter behind Ahska—there was something sticking out from under the blankets. It was wispy like hair and it had the color you mention. I saw nothing more."

I nodded my head and went into deep thought. It made sense. Our ship undoubtedly broke apart in space, but not before escape pods were launched—that would explain how I got to Urlena—and how Leanna got here. Something struck me.

"You said you saw little sparks shooting off—how many did you see?"

Oolat nodded his head. "Five or six."

I sat up. That meant there might be other survivors. If so, where were they? And were they alive? I could only hope.

Night fell and I slept fitfully. So much was playing on my mind and the mead I consumed could not kill the pain in my leg or the excitement in my heart. My keepsake—the daughter of the Emperor was alive and well and living in Casita as their Queen.

How did it happen? How had my sixteen-year-old charge come to find herself in this place? I realized now that a good deal of time had passed since our arrival on the moons of Tiiana, perhaps four or five years at least. The child I had watched over was now a woman, full grown, and quite beautiful.

I then thought about the others we had escaped with. Had any of them survived, and if so, how would I find them—especially if they were on the other moons? Then of course, there was the question that burned at me the hardest. Through all of this—was there a possibility that we could return to Melela, and if so, how?

The morning's light brought me a few answers. As Oolat slumbered on the floor, I lay in bed mulling over the situation when I heard a light rap upon our door. I responded with an invitation to enter, expecting it to be my Motula chambermaids bringing our morning meal. When the door opened, I saw to my surprise, it was the Queen and her personal entourage. I tried to rise.

"Please, don't ..." she commanded, hastily, "... the doctor told us of his orders."

She approached my bed with her four female attendants following close behind—the youngest, a girl of about ten years. With nary a sound, the four servants took their places at the end of my bed—they stood silent, awaiting the wishes of the Queen. I looked to her highness—she smiled at me, studying me. I understood the need. After all, it had been years since we'd seen one another, and Leanna had never seen me with facial hair, much less a full beard. And both of us were now a different color—it added to the mystery. I waited politely and said nothing.

"I want to thank you for saving my son's life yesterday," she began finally. "Your deed was incredibly brave—it has become the talk of the city."

"Thank you," I answered, politely. "How is your son doing?"

"Well, thanks to you. Have you had breakfast?"

I shook my head, no. "I am waiting for it now."

She smiled broadly, exposing a dimple in her cheek. It was a smile that lit my heart like an exploding sun. I wanted to leap from the bed, grab her up in my arms and hug her. I wanted to tell her how much I missed her and how often I wondered what had happened to her. But I was forced to still my tongue and glance away.

Oolat was my saving grace—he made a loud, great snore which drew everyone's attention. He rolled over to face us, yawned, and showed off his mouth full of large, yellow-tinted teeth. The young girl, who stood closest to the Queen, became very nervous. She hid fearfully behind the Queen's dress drawing her attention. The Queen laughed, and put her arm around the girl to calm her.

"You need not fear our giant guest, my child," she stated reassuringly. "I don't think he's eaten any children in quite some time."

She glanced back at me with a twinkle in her eye, and I was overcome. My charge still carried the look of the young, free-spirited, girl I had known so many years before. Oh, how I wanted to leap from the bed and tell her everything, but that was impossible. Neither one of us could risk exposure. Without any further ado, the Queen clapped her hands, and three men entered the room. They carried trays of food and drink.

"I took the liberty of having our personal chef prepare a morning breakfast for you and your friend. It is the least that I can do and I hope you enjoy it."

She motioned to her attendants. "Ladies—"

Upon her bidding, the Queen's attendants surrounded my bed and began to fluff my pillows—they helped me to sit up while the Queen took a tray from one of the men and placed it across my lap. It was piled high with mounds of food atop large plates—fresh fruit, breads and cakes, a mixture of meats and a carafe of drink set to one side. The Queen gestured to one of the plates filled with a dark meat, cut into thin slices.

"This is a delicacy of rare tastes" she said. I caught the nervous glance of her eye.

"Thank you." I responded. "I'm sure I will enjoy it. You and the King are most kind."

As I sampled the thin slices of meat, I nodded in appreciation—it was good. I watched as the other two male servants set their trays near to where Oolat's rested. My giant friend was slumbering through all of this.

The Queen clapped her hands again and everyone in her party fell into place. She turned to leave. I thanked her again.

"Your highness, your graciousness and generosity are most appreciated. Oolat and I are pleased that we have been able to offer our services to you and the King.

"Enjoy," she replied. "We shall take our leave now."

With that, the Queen, her entourage and food servers left the room. I waited for the door to close. I yelled to Oolat.

"Wake up! Wake up, you hairy beast!"

I threw a pillow at him, hitting him atop the head. He opened his eyes, bewilderment written upon his face.

"Roolka ... what ... I was chasing a darta in the forest."

I waved my hand anxiously for him to come to the bed. "Get up, my friend. Come here."

Oolat got up. He saw the trays of food on the floor. "Where'd this come from?" he asked, making his way to my bed.

"The Queen sent it to us—a gift for saving her son." I spoke now in his tongue. "Make sure we're alone—search the room and hallway."

I could tell Oolat thought I was crazy, but he did as I asked. He found no one. I was relieved.

"Please," I asked. "Sit by the door and let no one enter."

He looked at me as if I had lost my mind, but I think he sensed that something was up. He shrugged his shoulders and sat with his back against the door—no one would get through it without permission. I lifted my plate off the tray and looked underneath. As I suspected, there, folded neatly was a handwritten note. I opened it and an aroma of delicate perfume touched my senses. My hands shook as I began to read.

My Dearest Captain,

Words alone cannot adequately express my feelings of joy at seeing you alive and well. I am so overcome that my hand

153

shakes just writing you. To relay the events I have experienced since our journey from Melela would fill a book, but there is no time to address these issues now. I need you to know that you and your friend are in great danger. The King has come to fear you and your abilities. Your knowledge and popularity amongst the people are a threat to him. You must leave as soon as possible. I so wish I could go with you, but I cannot. Please, destroy this note immediately and know that I will remember you always and forever.

Leanna

I was dismayed by the note from the Princess—how could I leave her now, just after finding her? Still, precautions had to be taken. I motioned to Oolat.

"Bring me a candle, my friend."

Oolat complied. I took the note and passed it through the flame, igniting it, but not before taking one last whiff of her perfume. I watched the note burn and fall in ashes to the floor. Oolat ground out the embers as he looked at me curiously.

"We are in danger, my friend. We need to think about leaving here."

Oolat nodded his head. "Can we eat first?"

I nodded affirmatively. He returned to his tray and began to eat. For me, I had little stomach.

☆ ☆ ☆

It was later that day when Oolat and I had an unexpected visit from the King and his ministers. He entered our chamber to see how I was progressing, but he paid little heed to my swollen knee—worse, he was remiss in acknowledging the fact that I had saved his son's life. Still, I was cordial. I told him I was slowly getting better and that I would be up and about soon.

"As you know, Roolka," he began, posturing himself with grandiose movements about my bed. "The defeat of the Brata came from your invaluable guidance. Your counsel was wise and of great service to both myself and Casita. But now that the creatures have fled to their own dominion, my ministers and I are growing concerned. We know they will return—they always have." He stopped and gave me serious warning. "And we will not have the element of surprise as we did before—unless ..."

He bent over the end of the bed, making his offer quick and to the point—I felt the added weight of his words with his heavy grip on my leg.

"... Roolka, I would like to press you and your friend, Oolat into my service. I want you to take command of my fleet." He stood back, adding. "I will pay you in gold, forty rills a month to rid us of the Brata forever."

To a degree I was surprised by the monetary offer, but not fooled—in truth, I knew he was handing Oolat and me a death sentence. His smile was thin and slick, the greasy look of a snake seeking an opening. I smiled smugly and countered his offer.

"Fifty rills a month."

I caught him off guard. His eyebrows arched—I continued.

"I also want a bonus of five thousand rills contingent upon the success of our ridding the Motula of the Brata forever."

The King stood back, stunned—his ministers glanced at one another nervously. I raised the stakes.

"And, of course, I will provide you and your city with far more substantial means for defending yourself against any future invaders."

The King was intrigued—he liked the game. "Go on—"

"I will build you a new weapon—a weapon that will make you invincible. They're called cannons. They're maneuverable and can be mounted anywhere, on your castle walls, aboard ships, even atop the hills surrounding the city. They can be used repeatedly, almost anywhere. I think when you see them in action you'll be quite pleased."

The King nodded his head, finally acquiescing to my idea—after all, what did he have to lose? He glanced at his ministers, then to me. With a laugh, he pulled a leather pouch from his belt and flung it onto the bed. I heard the jingle of coins.

"You did not disappoint me the first time, Roolka. I will be anxious to see what you give me next. And if you can destroy the Brata forever, five thousand rills will gladly be paid."

✼ ✼ ✼

A week passed and my knee had healed sufficiently for me to move again. There was so much to do. I was in charge of building new weapons for the King, taking command of his fleet, destroying the Brata, and I needed to learn more regarding the Princess; all required preparation and I needed educating. I had only been on Boutal for two years and much of that time had been spent under the care and tutorage of Ahska. There was much I still did not know. And I knew if I was to achieve success I needed more information about this moon and her people. My first request was for maps detailing Boutal's seas and continents. I also called for artisans, blacksmiths, and carpenters. They were needed for building the cannons and fitting the ships with the armament. I also requested the assistance of a star guide—an astrologer who could help foretell the success of our mission.

Over the next five months I spent my time learning in depth the history and workings of Boutal and the Motula. I learned more about their pre-industrial culture, their feudal system of government and their religion—a pagan worship revolving around Tiiana and the other moons. At times, a number of the ministers thought it odd that I knew so much about technology and science and yet, so little regarding Boutal and its people. Pressed for answers, I explained that my ignorance was due to my life as a nomad living on the desert plains and later being secluded alone in the mountains of Cylanth with monks and the Solula–those answers seemed to suffice. In actuality, I don't think the King really cared. As long as I supplied him with superior weapons, I could do no wrong. Besides, I knew he was planning on having me killed; I just needed a plan in place to keep that from happening.

With the help of the King's servants, and the common workers of the city, I quickly came to an understanding regarding the daily life of the Motula. As with all planets and moons, there were seasons of the year, religious observations, fertility rites, celebrations, and holidays. The lives of the people revolved around these events and I hoped this knowledge would come in handy.

As the cannons were built and placed on the ships I took the time to talk with the sailors, fishermen and deck hands. These men understood the sea and were eager to share their knowledge. They told me of the fish and other creatures that swam within the deep waters, as well as their lore and superstition about the ocean; a common thread that seems to run through all seafaring people. I was eager to know how they navigated upon open water and what the currents and prevailing winds were. From them I learned the sailing and trade routes to Phratis, and Coralis and the other Motula cities along the Isle of Colas, Boutal's second largest continent. I even managed to find a few sailors who had survived the previous campaigns with the Brata and I picked their brains on what they had seen and experienced. They told me of the narrow straits and rocky reefs that linked Bratola's outer islands. These volcanic atolls were the birthing fields of the gargoyles, the same ones others had tried to destroy before. After hearing the tales and studying the maps I knew now why the eradication of the Brata had failed. The Bratola islands were a formidable barrier, difficult to navigate, much less conquer. In fact, even with the use of the cannons, I was not entirely certain that *our* plan would succeed.

It was nearly year's end now and I was under pressure to complete my task for Hazadek. He wanted both Oolat and I gone, and he voiced his opinion ardently on how and when we should begin our war with the Brata. To buy time I told him we weren't ready, that a number of ships still needed to be outfitted. He was angry, but I softened his stance with a demonstration of cannon fire. The presentation took place atop the castle. From this vantage point we targeted an old ship sitting in the bay, blowing it out of the water with our first two volleys. The King was ecstatic, relishing the newfound power I was placing at his feet, and he accepted my argument and request for more time. He coyly acknowledged that the weather around the Horn of Myolic was extremely abhorrent this time of year, and if outfitting a few more ships meant eradicating the Brata, then so be it.

As the next few weeks passed, I tried to focus on my work, but there was a constant gnawing in my stomach. It was the realization I was giving Hazadek unlimited power. The more I was near to him the more I came to hate him. He was a small-minded, greedy little dictator that cared for no one other than himself. To insure his power he instructed me that only Casita's ships were to carry full armament in this campaign. He wanted no other Motula city to pose him any threat. I saw this attitude even more when it came to the Princess. Though she performed her role as Queen well he treated her like a lowly servant. His actions were an abomination, and there was no opportunity where I wasn't plotting against him. I despised the power he held over her, and how he mistreated her. My favorite thoughts were of running him through with my blade and stealing her away. Unfortunately, both of us were under surveillance, she by her servants and staff, and I, by the soldiers who were always in my company. Still, there had to be a way to free her from this despot.

Finally, after racking my brain, an idea struck. The celebration of the year's end was about to begin, and I knew there would be festivities throughout the city, including a great feast at the castle. In attendance would be dignitaries and royalty from all the cities contributing to our armada. Oolat and I were, of course, invited which presented me with the opportunity I needed. I begged the King the honor of opening the festivities with a prayer—to give grace to our endeavor. To my delight, he granted his permission.

On the evening of the great feast I rose to speak to a multitude of Motula dignitaries and statesmen. I told them that I was giving thanks to Systaka, our mother Goddess, and I would speak in the language of the mountain monks who lived high above the deserts in the snow covered hills of Cylanth. No one questioned me or my intentions, so I began my blessing in the language of Gernaic, a language I knew the Queen understood, but no one else. I had to be certain that the voice I chose was nowhere close to Melelan, just in case the King had heard her speak it on occasion.

"My beloved Princess ... I speak to you in the tongue of Gernaic ... I pray tonight that my words will allay your fears and give you hope. I plan in the days hence to flee the King's armada, and take rest in the arms of the sea where I might swim to safety. From there I plan to rescue you. I know how we might flee this world and return home. I just need your blessing. Pray tell me how to storm this castle and kill this King who holds you prisoner. Give me the word, my Princess. Your will is my command. Amen."

My prayer passed with no one having a hint of its true meaning. Even the Queen gave no hint—I didn't expect her to, and I purposely avoided making eye contact with her for fear of giving myself away. I simply let the festivities take their course and soon everyone was drinking and eating, their heads becoming sloppy with food, ale, and mead. The hall soon became loud and boisterous with unruly celebration. Midway through the festivities I saw the Queen take her leave, the King dismissing her with a bored, dispassionate wave. He was too busy flirting with two young ladies who sat afar, the pair giggling like silly lambs at his drunken antics. It was sad to see. As the Queen retired, I noted her look of weariness. I wanted to follow; it was a foolish urge, and I had a problem of my own to contend with.

I sat with Oolat at a table piled high with food and drink—across from us sat several statesmen from Arinth—two fat brothers who'd been commissioned by the King to captain vessels of their own. For hours Oolat and I were forced to listen to the dribble and bluster of two slobs who couldn't find the sharp end of a sword. I laughed aloud several times as Oolat insulted them in Solula, his keen wit forcing me to bite my tongue repeatedly. Finally, the fools fell into a stupor, blind drunk, leaving us in peace. Still, we had protocol to follow. We waited until the King took his leave—he finally sauntered off with the two young women he'd been flirting with. Left to ourselves, Oolat and I retired to our chamber.

Alone in our room, our conversation turned to the events at hand. The armada was scheduled to leave in two days and I was concerned about how my message was received by the Queen. I wanted desperately to hear from her for time was running out. In the meantime I informed Oolat that he needed to flee Casita.

"You are not built for water, my friend—and your life is very important to me."

"I think I should stay," he countered. "I could hide and wait for you in the hills outside Casita. Then together we can free the Princess."

I shook my head, no. "It would be too dangerous my friend. My journey back will take time and it will be perilous. I can pass for a Motula, you cannot. Should the King's men find you, or see us together—we will be killed instantly. My friend this is a mission I must undertake alone. You can best help me by taking safe harbor with your people. I will find you later."

"Where?" he asked.

"Tell me of a Solula village that is safe—a place where the King cannot follow our trail."

"The ruins of Luskia," he replied thoughtfully.

"Luskia?"

"It is a secret place some forty leagues west of Ahska's camp. Only ghosts live there. No one knows of it—we will be safe."

"Luskia, it is then." I affirmed.

With our plans finalized Oolat headed for the window, but not before we shared a warm embrace. It was time to part ways, much was about to happen—suddenly there was a light rap upon our door. We both turned and caught sight of someone sliding a piece of paper under the threshold. I raced over and picked up the note. Inside was a message.

My Dearest Captain,

Your message was most welcome and brilliant. My heart has so longed to hear the words that might grant me exit from this miserable place. However, I must first tell you of the King's plans. You will never be allowed to return to Casita—your death will be imminent should you try to return from Bratola. The King also plans to use your cannons against the Solula. After Bratola he plans to take their lands and steal their precious metals and minerals. Please advise your friend, Oolat. His people are in grave trouble.

I must also tell you of the King's plans regarding myself. I am forced to leave this very week for a pilgrimage to Romanth, a city some ninety leagues north of Casita. I am to be confined there in the Temple of Solis for a period of not less than forty days, as a lady in waiting. It is the requirement of Systaka for creating a second heir to the throne. This King wishes his heirs to be betrothed to the city-states of Coralis and Phratis. Please, my Captain, if you can—rescue me from this unkind fate, as I can no longer bear sharing this man's bed. On the northeast side of the temple there are three hills, go there and wait. I will watch the hillside each evening in search of your lantern. And I will pray for your safety.

Leanna

I was furious over the note sent by Leanna and I was bound by honor to rectify the wrongs *I* had set in motion. This King would not be allowed to wage a war upon an innocent people if I had anything to do with it. I would see to that. I reread the note, burned it, then passed the information on to Oolat—his anger was evident. I told him I would never allow his people to be harmed, but first I needed to reach Romanth and rescue the Princess. We agreed once more to meet again as we planned earlier, but now we gave allowance—additional time might be required for our rendezvous.

A short time later, under the dim light of the stars, I watched as Oolat slipped out our window high in the castle. Barefoot and using only his hands and the claws upon his feet he scaled down the very side of the castle. At the bottom, he glanced up and gave me a wave; he then took off into the night. I was impressed—for a creature so large in stature his stealth was amazing.

t was the morning of our departure and I faced the King of Casita on bended knee, asking his forgiveness–my companion, my trusted aide, Oolat, had deserted our ranks.

"I will seek out the traitor upon my return," I told him. "After we eradicate the Brata from Boutal."

He stared at me silently with bloodshot eyes as I continued with my appeasement.

"I will personally lay his hide at your feet, Sire. So you may warm your feet on cold mornings."

The King mumbled something unintelligible. He was hung over from two days of drunken debauchery, and his mood was foul. Still, he had little recourse. The armada was ready to sail and he needed me to guide the fleet in the extermination of the Brata. He finally gave his command.

"I will await your return, Roolka. We will attend to the Solula's desertion then. Now sail! Rid us of the Brata forever."

"Yes, my liege."

I rose to my feet and quickly left the King's chamber hall. From there, almost at a run I hurried to my ship. I wanted to be on board and out to sea as quickly as possible. I was anxious to begin my mission, and I had no desire to brook further interference from the King. Unfortunately, things went slower than I anticipated. Coordinating our sixty-three ships, making ready to sail, and leaving Casita was a measurable task and it took most of the day to do just that. Further complicating our departure were the people. The docks and beaches were literally packed with thousands of people—I wholeheartedly believe that the entire city of Casita had turned out to bid us goodbye. Everywhere I looked there were men, women, and children animated in their celebration. They lined the streets and the coastline and even reveled atop the buildings. They waved and cheered, bidding us farewell—it was a grand sight and I realized that for many, this was the biggest event of their lives. I even looked to the castle, hoping to catch a glimpse of Leanna. I saw someone in one of the upper windows waving a white scarf. Was it her? I couldn't be sure, but I hoped it was.

It was late afternoon by the time our ship reached the deeper depths of open water. Once there, the Captain began bellowing out orders. I watched as the men scurried across the deck and shinnied up the masts and yardarms, unfolding the rigging and main sails. For some reason, seeing the huge sails fill with air elated me. I finally felt free again, unencumbered by civilization. I looked to the sky. Tiiana was a huge, bright red ball darting in and out of the clouds. I took in a cool, salty breath, refreshed by the air tempered with wind and sea spray. This was a day for adventure.

I walked the deck inspecting the cannons that lined each side of the ship—we carried fourteen—seven per side. Below, in the hull, we carried our payload of gunpowder, paper wad, and cannonballs along with enough food and water to last the three month journey to Bratola. We were ready to engage the Brata. I only wished in my heart that this was a mission I was intent on carrying out. It would be a glorious battle, fraught with danger, and I had no love for the rapacious gargoyles. I found them to be frightful and treacherous creatures, but this was not my battle—even with my promise to Oolat. I had other priorities.

I made my way to my cabin—quarters I shared with the ship's Captain.

Inside the cabin, I studied the charts the Captain had spread out across his escritoire. My fingers traced our route. We were presently journeying east, but we'd be heading south soon. Our journey would parallel land for several hundred leagues until we reached the Horn of Myolic. Once there, we would round the horn and turn north, follow the coastline again for another two hundred leagues, at which point the armada would turn west on a heading toward open sea and Bratola. I studied the map detailing the topography of the Horn—it was here that I needed to jump ship. The area was a tumultuous violent mix of dreadful weather, a merging point where the warm waters from the equatorial currents collided with the southern arctic winds. It was the ideal place for me to fall overboard, as many a sailor had met this same fate crossing the Horn.

I checked my personal belongs. I carried a flask of squid oil, a set of leather unders, oiled with darta emulsion to repel water, and a leather sea cap. Strapped to my inside thigh was an eight inch blade and upon my other a thin leather purse, filled with fifty gold rill—enough to purchase polono and weapons. Everything was ready and my heart skipped as I fantasized about rescuing the Princess. I hoped all would be successful.

The next few days that passed were torture for me. My legs were used to land, and the deck rolled and pitched against the sea. The sailors laughed at us landlubbers while the Captain consoled me. I would get accustomed to it, he said. I knew I would. At least I was not leaning over the edge heaving up my meals like some of the others. It took several days, but my sea legs finally grew.

Nine days after leaving Casita we sailed through the straits of Cassandra with little problem, but then, things began to change. We were drawing closer to the Horn of Myolic. From atop the deck we could see banks of dark clouds obscuring the distant horizon, and I felt a chill just looking at them. The land to our immediate west changed in appearance too. Trees and brush gave way to rock and grass as things got colder. Finally, there was nothing left, but dismal windswept land. A terrain covered by ice encrusted rock, sand, and the daily deluge regurgitated by the sea. The Captain navigated our ship, giving a wide berth to the shoreline. Too many ships had met with the sharp, craggy rocks—rocks that gutted those who ventured too close.

Pelted by freezing, wind-swept spray, I studied the shoreline from the deck as the sailors secured the rigging and sails. Their mood was solemn. It would take a good six days to round the horn, for it was a watery hell, and the perfect place for me to make my escape. As night approached, I noted the lack of stars. They were hidden by the thick, dark clouds that boiled angrily over our heads.

On our third day a huge storm struck. The thunder clapped and lightning rippled almost within hands reach, as the rain came down in torrents—there was no visibility. To keep in sight of the other ships we kept oil fires burning on the decks, but they offered only a meager light. It was almost impossible to see them. Our only hope was to keep our heading into the wind, and stay clear of the rocks.

After our dinner, I retired to my cabin, leaving the Captain to navigate the first watch. I tried to sleep, but there was too much on my mind; this was my night to escape. I stripped down to my bare skin and coated my body with squid oil. The sailors used it to ward off shakas, a carnivorous fish that swam in these waters. Slathered in oil, I slipped into my leather unders—they fit me like a second skin. Afterwards, I strapped on my knife and gold pouch, followed by my leather breeches, coat, boots, and water cap—if all went well I would not freeze in the ocean waters or once I reached land. I heard the bell ringing for the second watch.

Outside, on deck, the weather was brutal—the sea was raging in a blind fury. Waves whipped by wind crashed and buffeted the ship—darkness was everywhere. I pulled my way to the wheelhouse, using the guide ropes strung across the deck. I found the Captain and the second mate there—they were fighting the wind and sea to control our direction, the muscles in their face and necks taut as they maintained control. I nodded to the Captain.

"Keep her heading true—on this sighting," he yelled over the wind, pointing to the heading mark with his finger.

I nodded my head and took his place at the wheel. It was stiff and hard, difficult to handle even with the help of the second mate. I understood now why these sailors had such well developed arms and legs; the ship seemed to have a mind of its own. For the next hour I stood my ground as the Captain went below to get a hot meal and drink—a man could only take this abuse for so long. Half an hour passed and another sailor took the place of the second mate. A half hour later the Captain returned, which was fortunate as the storm was worsening. He took control giving me time to rest. My arms ached and throbbed from the strain. Gingerly, as waves crashed over the deck I followed the guide rope back to our quarters. Suddenly, a huge wave hit, pouring ten feet or more of water atop the deck. I knew that this was the moment. I let go of the guide rope and allowed the wave to take me. In one massive sweep I was carried over the edge of the ship and tumbling down, headlong into the cold, icy water—I even managed to scream.

Under the water, the force of the waves rolled me over and over. I sank, sucking water through my nose and mouth, feeling the familiar pop of my ears. With each breath, I took more water through my sinuses, past my ears, and out through my gills. I was breathing with little effort. I let the weight of the gold and the water filling my boots to drag me down. My feet came to rest in the silt at the bottom of the sea—I stood in about thirty feet of water. I had no idea what was happening above, but down here the currents were relatively calm. I waited, allowing my body to acclimate—I couldn't see anything.

Several minutes passed. I had no light to guide me and my direction was unsure—I forced myself back to the surface. Near the top, I felt the currents and waves sweep me—I was pushed back and forth like a cork. My head finally broke the surface and I felt the sting of the wind upon my face. I saw no ships anywhere near. I took a moment and looked around—I saw and heard nothing except the wind. I noted its direction—it was blowing toward land. I allowed myself to sink again and I made my way in that direction.

I made good time with the wind and water behind me, until I reached the last thirty feet. It was here, at a depth of six feet that the water surged violently back and forth, forcing me in every direction as I fought the undertow, rip tides, and eddies. I was like a cork bobber, battered and pummeled, struggling for each step. I literally had to crawl upon the ocean's floor, picking my way from rock to rock, losing my grip on numerous occasions. In the end, my outer clothing was torn and ripped, my muscles beat. I grew tired, and even though I couldn't drown, I knew I could still die from exhaustion. The thought of the Princess kept me going—she was depending on me.

It was barely dawn when I finally crawled out of the water and onto land. I was exhausted and I lay exposed. It was still raining, hard and cold. I forced myself up and onto my knees—somewhere there had to be shelter. I stumbled forward; hypothermia numbing my body to senselessness. It was only the oiled under-leathers that kept me warm enough to keep from freezing. There were moments where I lost sight, but I just kept going—I crawled, I staggered, I muddled my way deeper inland. Somehow, I found an area sparsely covered with wind-swept, leafless trees—a winter dead grouping that granted a measure of shelter from the storm. I lay there, huddling against the frozen stalks, eventually falling into unconsciousness.

How long I lay there I will never know, but when I awoke the sun was out, the storm had passed. It was still cold and bleak and I was very hungry. My muscles stiff, I struggled to pull myself up. A quick look around told me the direction I needed to take. There was a small fishing village about forty leagues up the coast. I had seen it three days earlier upon our passing. I needed to make it there if I was to survive. I started walking, and though it took me two long days and nights, I made it.

The fishing village was nothing to speak of—a few rock structures, a tavern, and a small port for the fishermen who eked out their lives in this desolate area called the Horn of Myolic. I couldn't imagine anyone wanting to live here—it was far too bleak to suit me. My arrival, however, was another matter. No one had ever survived falling overboard in these waters before and I was treated well by the denizens. I was given food, a warm fire, and rest, everything necessary to make me ready for the next portion of my journey. Of course, there were no polono here—for that I needed to walk another twenty leagues to the next village. My sojourn began two days later.

The next village was bigger—mainly fishermen, but also a few farmers who had polono. I purchased one out of its prime, and for twice the money, along with rations. I was thankful that things had gone as well as they had, but I still had several hundred leagues to cross. And I knew that the closer I drew to Casita, the wider the berth I would have to make. This caused me concern, as time was pressing down on me. I had to reach Romanth as soon as possible.

My progress went well. I made it to a third village where I purchased more rations and another, younger polono. I now had to cross a series of mountains, and was told that the trail was well marked, though occasionally plagued by thieves who waylaid those who traveled alone. With that advice I purchased a good sword and made haste into the wilderness. I intended to cross this area as quickly as possible, and if the moons held enough light I would cross even then.

The first day brought me no problems; I saw no one. At night I rested my beast in the shadows of the trees and let it graze on fresh grass, while I slept lightly with no fire. The second day was as the first, uneventful, until I caught sight of something unusual. It was nearing dusk, and the light was waning, but up in the sky I saw what I believed to be a grouping of Brata. They were heading north and flying quite fast as they headed deeper into the mountains. I was perplexed by their appearance. What were they doing here? Had they spotted the armada sailing up the east side of the coastline? I counted my blessings; at least they hadn't seen me.

My third day was altogether different. I was slower in my advent through the mountains. My polono was tired from being pushed so hard and I was more cautious. Seeing the Brata the day before told me something was going on, *but what* was the question. At midday I approached a meadow with a stream flowing through it. My riding beast and I both needed rest and a drink of cool water. I pulled my saddle from its back so it could cool down, setting it atop the grass. Suddenly, I caught sight of six men heading toward me from across the field. They began to yell, prodding their beast into a gallop, and I knew their intentions were not good. I hopped atop my barebacked beast, jabbed it hard in the sides with my boots and took off. I took to the trail and raced down it hoping to avoid a situation—that was not my luck.

The beasts these men rode were fresh—mine was not. They slowly gained on me and I knew I couldn't outrun them. Changing my direction, I drew my polono into an open meadow and pulled out my sword. If these bandits wanted a fight, I was happy to oblige them. I bellowed out a war scream and charged at them while waving my sword high. The tactic seemed to catch them by surprise.

Riding into their midst, I swung hard, giving solid resolve to my blade—meeting their drawn weapons like a mad wasp stinging relentlessly. Our blades crashed, the sounds resounding through the air. I cut one's belly, his innards pouring onto the ground. Another caught my blade with his wrist—he fled minus one hand, his blade lying in the grass, hand and fingers still wrapped around the hilt. The four that remained were better at their evil trade and we sparred back and forth. Our polono snorted and coughed as we jostled, pushing back and forth, our blades wickedly slicing the air. I was knocked from my beast. I rolled over onto the ground, the wind knocked out of me, my blade fallen from my hand. I scurried across the grass for it as the men charged. I found it just in time. I raised it, ready to face the onslaught coming toward me. What greeted me was unexpected.

The men charging me suddenly showed a great look of panic upon their faces. They struggled to rein in their polono, their eyes wide with terror. They yelled in horror and tried to turn their beasts, but they were too slow to avoid the shadows that raced past me at breakneck speed. I was dumbstruck. The three blurs who sped by were black giants, all wielding blades, and they attacked the Motula accosting me with an incredible fury—they were Solula.

In less time than I could think, the four remaining bandits lay dead—their bodies on the grass, their blood saturating the ground. I looked at the hairy giants that had just saved me—who were they? I threw my blade to the grass. I wanted no fight with these three. They paused and looked at me.

"He is ugly," said one.

The other two laughed in guttural tones—then one added.

"Oolat's words were true—he can wield a sword."

My mouth fell open. How? How did these three know Oolat? I dropped to one knee.

"Great Solula warriors," I spoke, my eyes averted to the ground in respect. "Your assistance in saving my life is a blessing—I am in your debt."

"Rise," said the first one. "We are in your debt. Come, we have much land to cover and time is waning."

So began my next sojourn. I recovered my saddle and rode with my three saviors into the mountains. The journey granted me an insight into the Solula as a race—something which, until now, I had been lacking. Other than Oolat, I had never met any other Solula, and I was impressed with their abilities. They were ferocious creatures, and yet they moved gracefully. I was in awe. I studied them, noting the differences and similarities to Oolat. My friend's face held a ring of bright orange color; these three were more a yellow or a golden in hue. Were they of a different tribe? I was unsure, but it didn't matter, there were more important issues. We needed to reach Romanth. They took me across the lower lands of the Motula avoiding any contact with the populace.

Along our travels, I questioned the three as to how they knew Oolat, and I was informed that all Solula knew Oolat. He was the son of Ahska–the seer. I asked how they found me. Their answer was obscure, but I gathered that they had methods of communication of which I was not aware. I was just happy to have guides who knew the land and who were there to see that I made it to where I needed to go.

We journeyed for days, keeping to the edge of the mountains. We moved steadfastly, skirting the Motula villages and mining operations. No one saw us pass. On the way we ate well–a diet of fresh darta and vegetables provided by my traveling companions. It was good to travel with resourceful individuals, though my days were plagued by rumination about the Princess; would I reach her in time?

It took a little over three weeks to finally reach our destination—far longer than I expected, and I was concerned. I'd lost so much time on board ship, escaping, making it back to civilization, and then here—nearly five weeks in total. The Princess' letter had stated she would be sequestered for forty days. My time was running thin, and I was consumed by the fear that she'd be gone before I arrived. What would I do then?

The next day we stood in a forested area bordering the western edge of Romanth. From my vantage point I studied the layout of the city with my companions. It was a quiet, picturesque farming community with a small seaport. To the north, and somewhat separate from the city, was a gray-stoned structure with two towers about three stories high–I surmised this was the temple. It was a fortified structure–perhaps originally designed to protect the seaport and city. It had a perimeter wall that stood a good ten feet in height, surrounded by open fields, and it was guarded. I wished I had a looking glass to get a closer look. From this distance I couldn't gather enough detail–we needed to move closer.

True to Leanna's note, there were a series of three tree-topped hills that bound the northeastern side of the temple; we made our way there. The area was pristine—covered with heavy brush and shrub, and we had little trouble making our way unseen. An hour later we were on the other side of the temple hidden within the landscape. While the Solula made camp, I crawled up to the top of the tallest hill and studied the compound that lay below.

Peering through the brush I garnered a good view of the temple which lay less than a league away. It was a distance from where I could watch the soldiers, but draw no interest if seen. The activity below seemed calm and tranquil, nothing out of the ordinary, and I found it impossible to ascertain if the Princess was even there. I returned to our camp and told my companions that I needed to journey down into Romanth. We needed supplies and I had to find out if the Princess was still here.

It was late afternoon as I made my way toward the city. There wasn't much movement, but enough to cause me concern. I feared running into someone from Casita who might recognize me, so I kept my face bent low as I walked the streets. I entered a small square filled with a number of shops selling meat, textiles, and dry goods. One was selling lanterns and candles, items I needed, and there were several people inside. As I looked over the store's wares I listened in on the conversations, hoping to garner information on the Princess, but what I heard was of little use. With little recourse, I was left to questioning the store owner.

"Romanth seems quiet this afternoon," I noted casually, as I made my purchase. "I would have expected more activity with the Queen of Casita visiting."

The store owner shot me a disgusted look. "They're probably at the dock sobering up."

I know he wanted to say more, but didn't know me. I might be a spy. I threw in my own barb.

"Can't be too soon before the louts leave—eh?"

He nodded his head. "Not soon enough—her ship should arrive in a day or two. Maybe then we can get our village back."

With that, I bid him goodbye and gathered up my purchase—a lantern and half a dozen candles. I returned to the hillside where the Solula awaited me.

That evening, as darkness approached, I stood on the hill-side overlooking the temple and lit the lantern. I had enough candles to keep it lit for two nights. If my stay was longer I would need to purchase more, as I wasn't sure how all of this was going to work out. I had no real plan, and I lacked any real resources, including diagrams or maps of the temple or its grounds. As much as I disliked it, I was relying on Leanna to provide me with a lead to follow. Perhaps she would find a way to get a message to me; I wasn't sure. It didn't seem real-istic that she'd be able to simply walk up the hill and meet us. I just hoped that I wouldn't have to storm the temple to take her. That would mean engaging a lot of men, and our numbers were few, and it would endanger her as well. I did not like my options—so I waited.

The next morning came and nothing happened, so we took turns watching the temple throughout the day. There was periodic activity as guards rotated their positions around the perimeter—other than that we saw nothing of benefit. We waited. Again, on the second night, I lit the lantern. This time there was a response, obscure as it may have been. In one of the upper windows on the tower closest to us was a light. It swung briefly for a moment then disappeared. Was this the sign I was seeking? We took turns watching the temple through the rest of the night, but saw nothing more. There were no other signals or signs of movement within.

The dawn came early; I watched the sun rise in the east. Out on the sea I noted a vessel approaching—a rather large ship. It docked out in the bay and several row boats made their way to shore. I had to assume this was the ship from Casita, the one sent to bring Leanna back. I was now on edge.

In the shadows of the trees, I waited with my three Solula companions—it was nearly noon and there was movement below. I climbed atop my polono—my height was now equal to that of the three Solula who stood on either side of me. Nothing was said, we just watched the gate of the temple as it opened, a group of riders exiting. There were about twenty in total; all male except one—a lone rider, gaily dressed in feminine attire. She rode near the center of the column.

As the group cleared the temple they turned toward the bay, when suddenly they stopped. There was some sort of problem; I was too far away to see it clearly. I did see Leanna dismount her polono along with several of the soldiers. They seemed to be looking at the hoof of her animal. Suddenly things became chaotic. In the breath of an instant I saw Leanna grab another polono. She leapt atop its back and charged in our direction, her move catching the King's men off guard. There was an outburst of yelling and orders were given, sending several of the men after her; the rest soon followed.

In a blaze of heated fury I saw Leanna slapping her polono madly with her reins—she yelled and kicked at it, spurring it into a full gallop. The race was on. Instinctively, I started to move forward, but I was stopped by a blade of steel that crossed my chest. The Solula, whom I had come to know as Mooka, held me back. He glanced at me.

"Wait for the woman, Roolka. We'll take care of the rest. Take to the forest—others will lead you to safety."

I looked at him. "You understand that when they see Solula, it will mean war with the Motula?"

He snarled back, "They already declared war."

With that, my three Solula friends bolted from my side. They ran at full speed, their swords glinting in the light as they brandished them back and forth. I pulled forward so Leanna could see me—I waved to her. She was already across the field and starting up the hill. I watched as she put her head down, slapping her polono even harder. The three Solula separated so she could pass between them. They blocked the soldiers following behind. I heard yells and screams and I held my breath as the three took on the twenty soldiers. Leanna continued her way up unimpeded—as she neared the top I galloped forward to meet her. She bought her polono to a stop, her animal heaving from the exertion. We turned and looked below. A violent battle was raging between the Solula and the King's guards. There were dead, at least six or more, but no one was coming after us.

"Come on!" I yelled, motioning to Leanna.

We turned our animals and rode over the hilltop and into the trees, then down the backside of the hill. Behind us, the battle continued to rage. I could hear the sounds of metal blades clashing with yelling and screaming. We pressed on heading deeper into the forest. Leanna and I did not talk—there was no time. We needed as much distance between us and the King's men as possible and the ride was becoming harder as we ascended into the mountains.

We probably traveled for an hour; perhaps longer—her polono could not take anymore. Its breathing was labored. We were climbing steeply and it could no longer carry Leanna and move with any great speed. When we reached the crest of the hill we stopped; a valley loomed before us. We could see farms with pastures where polono and krata were grazing. I stopped and dropped from the back of my polono. Leanna bought her animal toward me, and I helped her down. We said nothing, but it was the most gratifying embrace I've ever felt. I held her tightly in my arms, as her eyes filled with tears. She kissed me on the cheek.

"Thank you, thank you, thank you," she breathed heavily in my ear.

"I can't tell you how much I've thought of you," I said.

"And I, you," she replied.

Our embrace ended and the two of us stood like fools gazing into each other's eyes. We both had so much to say, neither one of us knew where to begin. It was awkward, and yet, exhilarating at the same time. I took her hand and gave it a squeeze.

"We need to get you another polono—and some other clothes."

She nodded her head and began ripping off her outer skirt, exposing a long pant-like undergarment beneath her dress—it freed her legs for riding. She cast the dress aside. I immediately picked it up.

"We can't leave a trail for them," I warned. "Take it with us. We'll get rid of it later."

She smiled. "I'm glad you are here, Rez. I prayed for it. Things were coming to a point where I couldn't take it anymore. My life ..." She began to stutter—her eyes watering, "... was becoming unbearable."

I took her in my arms and held her close. "My dear Princess, you must never fear. I will never let them take you again. I will defend you with my very life."

I felt her breakdown and sob in my arms. It reminded me of our embrace in the palace years earlier when I rescued her from the Relcor, only this time I gave her a few minutes to cry.

Finally, I said. "We must go. We need to put as much territory between us and them as possible. They'll be searching for us."

She pulled back and we began to walk our polono down the hill toward the farms that dotted the valley. I walked hand in hand with her.

"How did you come to get here?" I asked.

She gave a shrug. "I don't remember much," she recounted. "I was on the ship with you and the others when we escaped from the Relcor. I was banged up and still groggy from etheral, but I remember a lot of noise and explosions, then nothing. The next thing I remember was this old woman, black with scraggly hair—she put me on a litter and dragged me somewhere. I couldn't understand anything she said, but she cared for me. She kept feeding me this disgusting stuff—it made me sleep a lot. And then she gave me to this family—an older couple. I learned later that they were some sort of Motula royalty. They raised me."

I chuckled. "Ahska."

"Who?"

"Ahska ... She's the old woman who found you. She found me when I arrived here as well—turned me black as night, too."

I raised both our hands. "I guess she did the same for you."

"I'm not sure when this happened" Leanna responded, stroking her arm. "I was a mess back then—both my parents dead, you gone, my skin a different color. At times I felt like a prisoner being held against my will. It took a lot of getting used to. I had a very difficult time, but things got easier each time she visited.

"Visited? Who?"

"The old woman—she would come and look in on me, talk gibberish for hours and give me medicine. I remember having the strangest dreams when she visited."

I was stunned by Leanna's words. "What happened then?" I asked.

"I made the best of the situation," she answered frankly. I lived with this family. I learned their ways, their language, and their customs. Then I met the King. The next thing I know I was bartered away—given to him like a piece of furniture. There was a ceremony, if you could call it that, but I was never really asked or given a choice."

She shuddered. "I was forced into his bed. My only joy in the union came from our little boy." She stopped and looked at me. "But he's gone now."

"Do we need to find a way to rescue him?" I queried.

"No ..." she replied.

We began to walk downhill again.

"You see, in Motula society once males reach a certain age, they are raised exclusively by their fathers. Harazz—that's his name. He's almost at that age. And I was already out of favor with Hazadek—he only kept me for his needs."

"You have no idea how many times I wanted to run my sword through him," I said. "He was a contemptible boar. And I saw how he treated you. My Princess, I humbly apologize for my taking so long to rescue you. I will understand if you look upon me with disfavor."

Leanna began to laugh, but I took no offense. The sound of her joyous mirth made me smile. She placed her head on my shoulder and held my arm as we walked.

"My Captain, you are so chivalrous, you make me giggle like a silly girl. You arrive in Casita with a Solula as your friend—most unusual in itself—then you save the city from the Brata. You rescue me from a thankless King and give me back my freedom. And now you expect me to look at you with disfavor because you weren't quick enough. I don't think any man could have done more than you."

She looked up at me. "You are my hero." Her voice dropped to a whisper, "ever since I was ten."

My mouth fell open. Her blue eyes sparkled.

"You never knew?" she queried.

I shook my head, no. "You were a child. I was–"

"... older ..." she finished, "... and in the service of my father."

"Yes."

The forest was beginning to thin; we were near the valley floor. I looked through the trees and saw no activity.

"We need to get you a fresh polono."

Leanna nodded her head. I took the saddle from her mount and laid it on the ground.

"I'm going to see if I can purchase one from the farmer who lives here. I want you to stay here out of sight. We can't afford anyone seeing you. But if you see or hear anything–ride after me."

"I will."

With that, I left Leanna hidden in the trees. I took the saddle from her mount, carried it over my back, and approached the closest farmhouse. The process didn't take long, I found the farmer eating his evening meal. I told him my polono had broken its leg and I needed another. At the sight of my gold he was eager to sell me a beast and he even threw in some hot food to seal the deal–hot beans and biscuits. I thanked him and returned to where I left Leanna. We were famished and ate quickly. We then picked our way through the trees and brush, staying out of sight. It was dusk by the time we reached the other side of the valley, and it was getting cool.

We rode up the mountainside until we could go no further. Night was falling and it was getting harder to navigate the terrain. It made no sense to risk us injuring ourselves climbing over mountain tops and ridges in the dark so we stopped and made camp. I was angry with myself at my lack of preparedness, for there was little to shelter ourselves with. I tethered our mounts and cut the branches off several small trees. I built a small lean-to and we huddled under its shelter for the night. Neither Leanna nor I slept well, but neither of us complained. I think I had the better part of the arrangement. I was overcome with my feelings for this young woman—she was soft and she carried upon her body the scent of an angel. I was not near as fresh. I hadn't had a bath since swimming in the ocean three weeks before, and I must have smelled horrible. Still, she didn't say a word, but slept with her head upon my chest.

At morning's light we began our journey again. We ascended to the top of the mountain at which point I caught sight of a dozen or more men combing the valley floor below. They were quite distant, but they were on our trail. We increased our gait and headed down the mountain's far side. I still had no real idea where we were headed, but if we were to escape we needed to get further into the mountains. Halfway down the mountain side, fortune granted us a reprieve—two Solula warriors armed with large blades suddenly barred our path. I climbed from my polono's back and knelt before them. I spoke in their tongue.

"It is with great honor that I meet the Solula warriors of these mountains. Mooka told me that you would be watching. May I count on your help in finding my friend, the great warrior, Oolat?"

"Rise Roolka," spoke the bigger of the two. "There are many Motula coming. We must flee this area and hide your trail."

The two turned and we followed. As we did, I saw numerous other Solula appear from behind the trees and bushes. Some were armed, while others carried brush—they beat the ground upon which we rode, covering our trail. We left the area, following the two warriors who had met us, heading higher and higher into the mountains. It began to snow.

Leanna began to shiver. I gave her my ragged coat for warmth, but our teeth still chattered. Neither of us was prepared for the weather we were experiencing and we suffered because of it. I informed our guides, letting them know that we would freeze if we didn't find warmth. The big one nodded his head. Suddenly, he raised his face to the mountain, his voice

180

calling out one of the eeriest of calls I've ever heard. It was a wail, a cry and a song all in one. It was pitched in tone and intensity and it varied in pattern. When he finished he looked at me.

"Help will be here soon."

A short time later several more Solula arrived. These creatures were smaller in stature. I noticed breasts partially hidden by their fur—they were female. I whispered to Leanna in our native tongue that I'd never encountered a female Solula before. The females approached. In their arms they carried furs which they draped over us, making the difficult journey at least warmer.

We left the tree line and entered the snow-covered high country. The wind whipped around us, snow and ice stinging our faces. Evening was falling, and the temperature was dropping further—we approached a village. It was a Solula grouping of homes nestled right into the side of a mountain. With the snow and rocks covering the terrain I would never have seen it had I not been brought here. We were met outside by a Solula couple—they invited us inside while our mounts were led away. Both Leanna and I were extremely grateful for the reprieve.

The home we entered was uncharacteristic of anything I had seen so far on Boutal. The interior was warm, sealed from the wind and cold, and heated by a small fire. There were candled lanterns burning to give light, their reflection amplified by small sheets polished gold and silver—metallic mirrors that adorned the home's interior. Whoever lived here was a master craftsman; the decorative work was magnificent. I understood now why Hazadek wanted to invade, and I added avarice to his list of demerits.

Our hosts were cordial and as refined a couple as I have met anywhere on any planet. The male was an older Solula, called Oreis. His fur was coarse, with a tinge of gray—his wife or mate, a younger creature who called herself Myiata. Both seemed quite curious about Leanna and me.

Their first measure of hospitality was to ask us if we wished to bathe. I'm not sure if this was purely out of kindness or a sign of self preservation. I'm sure I was quite rank; I could barely stand myself, and I don't know how Leanna handled me the evening before.

"I would love a bath," I informed them, "but I have no fresh clothes."

I heard a quiet, chuckling noise—quite mirthful in sound. Myiata turned away. I think she was laughing at me—after all; the Solula had no real need for clothes.

"I think I can find something for the two of you," she said finally, leading Leanna and I to another area of their home.

A few minutes later I was alone in a bathing room with soap and cloth in hand while Myiata took Leanna to find some suitable dress wear. I was most appreciative of the privacy and more than happy to strip out of my filthy clothes. I then sank my body into the hot pool of water that lay serene within a large room that had been carved from the mountainside. I began to wash the grime from my body.

The tub in which I bathed was virtually a small pool built for someone the size of Oreis and his mate—it was warm and relaxing with a hint of steam rising from its surface. Dug into the rock, it was faced with smooth dark stone and I reveled in its warmth as I was chilled to the bone. I learned later that the heated water came from deep within the mountain and actually had to be cooled before being used for bathing. However, that was not the only surprise I got that night. I was deep in thought scrubbing myself with a heavy lather, when Leanna entered the room. She stood looking at me, a wicked smile crossing her face. I then watched in disbelief as she disrobed in front of me. I turned and averted my eyes. I then heard the splash of water, followed by a hand touching me on the arm.

"Captain?" a soft voice sighed.

I turned, and with my heart in my throat, I met Leanna's gaze. She stood barely a foot away, fully naked to my view with her long, dark hair cascading down around her shoulders. I swallowed hard taking her in. Her breasts were firm and full, about the size of small melons, both buoyed by the water; her nipples taut and firm. And her eyes, there was something in them calling to me. I felt like a moth drawn to the flame as a million voices screamed in my head. This was the Emperor's daughter; she's sixteen. No, that wasn't true. Not anymore. I could see that quite well. This was no child. This was a well developed and attractive woman with nothing out of place, and I couldn't help myself. I was aroused. In all my imagination I had never thought of Leanna in this manner. But ever since finding her in Casita I'd felt something growing, an attraction, a desire—a need. And here she was, naked and willing, and so damn alluring. I hadn't been with anyone since leaving Melela. Still, even with all that, I was hesitant and unsure.

Leanna sensed my indecision. She pulled close, laughing softly as she placed her hands on my shoulders, her fingers caressing my neck. I caught the faint scent of perfume as she embraced me, our bodies pressing together. The scent of her nearly drove me mad. I turned my head and averted my eyes; this was wrong. She was the Queen now.

A voice whispered in my ear, soft and low in its resonance.

"My Captain." Her breath was hot against my skin. "My sweet, sweet, Captain. Listen to me. My mother and father are gone. The Empire is gone. Your obligation to the Imperial service is complete. It is only you and me now—just you and me. I'm a grown woman. A woman who's already given birth. You and I are the only two Melelan in God knows how many light years, and we only have each other. Now unless you find me unattractive, I want your attention."

With that, she bit me gently on the neck, and I was overcome with madness. I wanted her more than any other woman I'd ever known, and I couldn't help but take her. She was young, vibrant, and exciting, and our lips met with unbridled lust and passion. I began to kiss her fervently upon the mouth, cheek, and neck, and then back again. I was insane with desire and I felt my fingers pulling at her like a greedy dog wanting to eat her up entirely.

"I am all yours, Rez," she whispered heatedly, as I took her to the edge of the pool. "This has been my fantasy for as long as I can remember—to have you make love to me."

With that, I lifted her from the water and set her atop the smooth rock. I climbed out after her. Our bodies were hot with steam rising from our skin. She lay back and I felt myself lying atop her. We kissed again and our bodies joined together as one. It was a moment I will never forget—making love for the first time to my Princess of Melela.

☆   ☆   ☆

The next few days that passed were as close to a honeymoon as I've ever known. Just being alone with Leanna was the most precious experience of my lifetime. Never in a million years had I dreamt that I would lie with the fairest of creatures from my home planet, Melela—my Princess, Leanna. The words of her mother now took on new meaning as this young woman carried my heart.

Our days together also allowed us to come to know the full details of our arrival upon Boutal. I spoke of becoming a slave to the Aquella, their operation on me, and my escape. I told her that my sole purpose for survival was the hope that I would one day find her, that she was the link to my sanity. Little did I know until then, she felt the same way. Ahska had told her caregivers that she was the key to a great puzzle; that a man would come for her and that man would save Boutal, and their duty was to protect her. Leanna's words gave me pause: Was I this man? And if so, why was I so important?

I also learned from Oreis during this period that Mooka and his two companions had died helping us escape, but Oolat was well and awaiting our arrival in Luskia. I was saddened by the news of Mooka and angry. I told Oreis that Mooka was a great warrior, and I swore that his death would not be in vain, that Hazadek would pay. For some reason Oreis did not seem concerned. He explained that Hazadek was only one of many who had tried to take their land and gold–the others had all failed. However, he was concerned over something else. There were Solula missing.

"Missing?" I inquired.

"From villages further north. Solula have been disappearing, leaving no trace, and no bodies. It is a strange occurrence, one we do not understand."

"Then you do not suspect the Motula?" I asked.

He shook his head. "This is something new. The Motula are savage, but they are not clever enough to hide men in this fashion."

I agreed. This was very strange.

Two days later a Solula warrior came to Oreis' home. He told us that Hazadek's men had given up the search and were returning to Romanth, and that it was safe for us to go. I was curious as to why the King's men would have given up so easily, as Hazadek would have their heads if he knew they had just quit. I pressed the Solula for answers, and I learned that they created a ruse by slaying Leanna's mount. They threw her animal off a cliff, next to a raging river, and placed her blood-soaked dress there as evidence. To the King's men it appeared that she had fallen over the cliff, her body either swept away or devoured by wild animals. It was a savage, deceitful tactic, but it evidently worked. We were free to go.

CHAPTER ELEVEN

Our *journey to Luskia was* uneventful. We were no longer under the pressure of hiding from the King's men, though I knew there would be some sort of retribution against the Solula. It only seemed logical that they would be blamed for Leanna's death. My main concern was that the King would be looking for Oolat, and our journey was taking us past Ahska's camp—his former home. I trusted my Solula guides to keep us posted on the whereabouts of any soldiers. Along the way, I relayed to Leanna the story of how Ahska had found me, sick and wounded. Explaining how the old woman had nursed me back to health, and blackened my skin to hide me amongst the Motula.

"I owe her the greatest of apologies," I said. "I was so upset when she turned me into a black Motula warrior—I didn't understand. And yet, because of it—I found you."

Leanna smiled. "She could have told you about me."

I nodded. "True, but what would that have led to? If I had known you were alive and in Casita, my whole approach would have been different. More than likely, I would have charged in and tried to rescue you, and gotten us both killed. No ... things went as they were supposed to."

She drew her mount next to mine, leaned over and gave me a quick kiss.

"Yes, they did. Now, my dear Captain. I have a royal order for you."

I looked into her mirthful, dancing eyes. "And what is that, my Princess?"

"I want you to train me in Motula weaponry."

I started to say something, but she cut me off.

"Did you know that for two years I took fencing and blade from three different instructors on Melela?"

I shook my head, no.

"It was my goal to impress you. There's nothing more serious than a thirteen-year-old girl in love."

I looked at her—she was serious. Reluctantly, I acquiesced.

"We'll begin after we make camp."

We passed through the mountains to Ahska's camp without hindrance. I was glad to rest there for a day—it brought back many good memories. It also gave me a chance to pay my respects. Kneeling beside the old woman's grave I asked for her forgiveness, and I requested her guidance for the coming journey. I kept hearing her prophetic words ringing in my ear, "save Boutal". I still had no clue what she was talking about. What was I to save Boutal from? And how would I accomplish it? If anything, I had made things worse here. I'd already started a war between the Motula and the Brata, and now the Solula were involved—these were not events conducive to saving this moon or its people.

Four days later we met up with Oolat in Luskia. Actually, he found us, as I really didn't know where Luskia was—the name referred to an entire valley. We were just traveling west, meandering through the mountains which were heavily forested with trees and brush when he appeared. I was overjoyed at seeing him, and he was pleased with my success in rescuing the Princess. He was happy to see that even an ugly Motula like me could find a mate.

We set up camp near a running stream and that night, over a fire, Oolat informed us of what he knew regarding Luskia.

"This place—I will take you there tomorrow—is old. Ahska told me that there were ghosts from the past living here—that I should be wary. She said many lived here at one time, but a plague came—it took all the lives and left the place barren."

I looked at Leanna—this was indeed intriguing.

"Why were you here then, when you found me? I asked.

Oolat shrugged. "Ahska had a vision. We walked for days to this place—we found you on the ground sick. I picked you up and carried you back to our camp."

"So, you've never lived here then?" Leanna inquired.

Oolat shook his head.

We talked for a while longer and watched the moons cross the night sky. Soon the hour became late and we headed for bed. Tomorrow would be a busy day.

I didn't sleep well that night. I had dreams—perhaps it was the excitement of learning how we got here, or perhaps, something more ominous, but whatever it was—I was up at first light. After a quick meal Leanna and I mounted our polono and we traveled with Oolat to Luskia—the journey was shorter than I expected. We left the others at the camp. I think they were a little leery of journeying into the forbidden zone, and we did need our supplies replenished, so they went off to hunt for fresh food.

Luskia was, as Oolat foretold, a dead place. In fact, there didn't seem to be much to see. The vegetation of trees and brush were quite dense, thick and overgrown—it was difficult to tell what had been before, but I saw evidence that a small city had existed here at one time. There were rock foundations, and I thought I could make out marble columns lying in the dirt—they were just crumbled bits and pieces now. Seeing them reminded me of the dead city on Urlena—had this place been built by the Aquella? After all, I had come from there to here, perhaps they had too? The concept made sense, but how did it happen?

Oolat took me to the place where he thought he and Ahska had found me.

"I think this is the place. You were lying right about here."

I stooped down and felt the ground—it was relatively level, covered with dirt, grass and rock. I didn't see much in the way of clues. I stood and brushed off my hands.

"Let's look around. I vaguely remember being in darkness—there was a light, and I crawled toward it—it was as if I was in some sort of tunnel."

"What about that hill over there?" Leanna commented. "Perhaps there's a cave?"

We walked toward the hill, then around it. It was large and rather steep looking, covered with brush and small trees—mostly thin, tall saplings. I grabbed one of the trees to pull myself up—it ripped from the ground and I fell, landing on my back, the entire tree in my hand. Leanna rushed to my side.

"Are you okay?"

"Yeah," I answered, somewhat embarrassed.

I tossed the tree to one side and picked myself up. I looked at the hole left by the roots. The soil was dark and rich—very loamy with worms in abundance. I scooped up the dirt in my hand—there was grass, twigs, leaves, and small rocks, but mostly a compost of decaying materials.

"This is odd," I commented.

"What?" quizzed Oolat.

"This dirt is very rich, but the trees here are thin and weak. They should be huge with deep roots—as large as the ones over there." I pointed to another area of forest. "But this sapling came right out of the ground—as if it couldn't penetrate the soil."

I began to scoop the dirt away, making the hole larger. A foot down I discovered a large, flat gray stone. Eagerly, I scooped away more dirt—the gray stone became bigger and bigger until I saw it to be mammoth in size. It had to be four feet in depth and six feet in length. Underneath the stone was another, perhaps the same size or larger. I glanced at Leanna.

"I think we found it."

She looked at me curiously as I widened the hole, scraping away more dirt. I reached a third stone. I could see now that the structure was both stepped and angled—my hunch was correct.

"Yes!" I cried with excitement.

"What?" asked Leanna, not comprehending.

"This isn't a hill," I said. "It's a pyramid!"

With the help of the Solula, we spent the next several days prodding and digging away at the hill, revealing the edifice that lay hidden underneath. I was ecstatic—this place had lain undiscovered for an eon and I knew it would explain much. I just needed to gain entrance. Three days later we found something, but it was inconclusive. Our discovery was a shallow cave-like hole in the side of a hill about a quarter of a league from the pyramid. We began to dig. It seemed the best place to begin and I thought it might be the tunnel I originally crawled through. That thought quickened my pace—I was eager to find out.

Unfortunately, our efforts at accessing the tunnel were quickly stymied. We had only dug a short distance when it began to rain—and it was no light shower. The skies opened up with a deluge of water that was torrential and unrelenting. Soon the entire terrain surrounding us was soaked and the tunnel we were excavating filling with water. We tried to dam it with dirt and place a tent covering over it, but it was to no avail. The whole hillside around us turned into a quagmire of sludge—a rocky, muddy soup that kept sliding down and collapsing upon us. The more we tried to remove, the more unstable it became, and I feared we'd be buried alive. Making matters worse, I learned from those familiar with the area that this was the beginning of the monsoons—a rainy season extending a month or longer. I was thoroughly dejected.

Back in our camp I found myself depressed. We were so close, and it would be months before the ground would be dry enough to dig again. It was unfair and I cursed our bad luck. How was I to discover if this pyramid was built by the Aquella and what lay inside? That thought plagued me. I feared that

Leanna and I might be exiled on Boutal forever, living out the remainder of our days as castaways.

Leanna tried her best to console me, she understood my unhappiness, but her words did little to raise my spirits. I was sorely tired from all that had transpired over the last several months and I needed rest. Later that evening, we sat under a tarp next to a fire, eating a cold meal and conversing. We weighed our options, trying to decide what to do.

"If only there were another pyramid like this one," I said, wistfully. "One without a sea of mud and water swallowing it. That would give us a direction to go in and perhaps hope."

That's when I heard one of the other Solula speak—his name was Rixxca.

"There is a village called Talith, in the mountains not far from the Northland ice plains," he said. "I visited there when I was young. In the summer, when the snows are gone, you can see a mountain of stone—bigger than this one."

My heart raced.

"Could you find it again?" I asked.

He nodded.

"The village of Talith is still there. And the Solula there would know the way across the mountains to where it lies."

"How long a journey?" I inquired.

"It will take ten days," he replied. "But before we go you should be forewarned. This is also the place where many of my people have disappeared."

I thought that to be a very strange coincidence.

☆　☆　☆

Our travels began immediately and I was never so happy to leave the rains behind. We headed back taking an easterly direction, covering again a portion of the same territory we had traveled on our way to Luskia. Along the way we stopped at several Solula villages, as we had to prepare ourselves for the journey ahead. It was getting colder, and would so from here on out. We were now headed toward the Northland plains where nothing existed except ice. For the Solula, this was not a problem, they were well adapted to this climate, but for Leanna and me it was a different story. We needed clothing befitting the freezing temperatures.

Our problem was solved by a number of generous Solula who donated their efforts to our cause. They sewed us tight fitting leather britches overlaid with thick, dense chaka fur along with face masks and gloves to protect our skin from the winds and snow. Polaca were rounded up to carry our supplies. They were surefooted creatures well adapted for this snow-covered region, and highly prized by the Solula for their climbing abilities. This was an important attribute if we were to reach Talith and the ice plains safely.

Our sojourn began and we had little trouble in the beginning. It was still warm by Solula standards, though the nights were exceedingly cold and clear. The monsoon rains we'd left behind us had not yet reached this far north, but it was only a matter of time. When they did, this area would be buried in snow for months on end. Still, even with the slightly warmer temperatures it was still freezing by my standards, and it forced Leanna and I to spend many a night huddled together under piles of furs which was not an entirely bad thing.

It took two weeks for us to reach the Solula village of Talith; longer than we anticipated. The village was a small hamlet of twenty homes nestled against a granite rock mountainside. Our arrival was greeted warmly, but there was an air of mystery as well, for the locals were on guard and suspicious—half their kind was missing. Oolat explained why we had come, we broke bread with our hosts and I urged them to tell me what was going on. I wanted to help.

I learned that the disappearances were oddly random and sporadic—with the most occurring three months past, during the warmer weather. The disappearances involved Solula who were out by themselves—alone—either tending their herds or hunting—they simply disappeared without a trace. Sometimes their herding sticks or swords would be found, but there was never a sign of struggle, blood or any other indication of foul play. It was very unnerving for these unassuming people. Their only recourse was to alter their daily habits and move together in groups or pairs—which seemed to have stopped the disappearances. And with the arrival of the winter snows, the Solula were indoors more, and no longer subject to the vagary of this strange fate. With more pressing matters on my mind, I let the oddity of this matter slip—something I would regret later.

We rested for two days in Talith, restocking our supplies and acquiring a guide for the next part of our journey. I was happy for the reprieve, as Leanna seemed to be experiencing some difficulty; she complained of being tired. I didn't think much about it at first, only that our constant movement had taxed her; she wasn't used to the thin air. I assumed rest was the answer and I was glad that we were given quarters with a young Solula couple—Markeea and Lakona. I think the two were newlyweds. They seemed to spend much time caressing one another, much like Leanna and myself.

After two days of rest and our supplies replenished I was ready to begin the next leg of our journey, though I still had concern regarding Leanna. Her exhaustion had not abated and I was worried she was becoming ill. Making matters worse, Toska, our Solula guide informed me that the next part of our journey would be extremely perilous. The mountain trails upon which we would be treading were narrow, slick with ice, and in some places barely etched into the face of the cliffs. Our undertaking was unsafe even by Solula standards, and I was unsure if Leanna was well enough to make it. I thought it best that she stay behind.

I entered the abode in which we were staying and found Leanna resting in bed, eating a light breakfast. It had been provided by our female host, Lakona, who was most kind and dutiful toward us. Approaching the bed, I sat next to Leanna and took her hand. She smiled weakly and I noted how drawn her face looked. I lied and told her how beautiful she was, but soon our conversation turned, at which point I suggested she remain behind. My comments on her health were not well taken and we argued.

"You're tired," I said. "You should stay here and rest."

"No," she countered, setting aside her bowl of meal. "I want to go. Suppose you find an access that will get us home?"

I laughed. "Do you honestly think I would leave you here alone?" I placed my hand on her to reassure her. "If we find something, I will return, by then you'll have your strength back."

"But I want to go. I don't want to be all alone here. I'll go crazy."

"Look," I insisted. "Toska says the path is treacherous, slick with ice. We're not even sure that we can make it across. Look at you—you're exhausted. It's simply not worth the risk. Why take the chance?"

"I'm not that tired—not all the time. Let me come with you. I'll be fine."

Unexpectedly, Lakona came to the bed, concern written on her face.

"No!" she stated emphatically. "You are with child."

"What!" I exclaimed, looking up.

Lakona reiterated her words. "She carries in her an unborn."

I looked at Leanna; the grin on my face reaching ear to ear. Leanna gave me a perplexing look.

"What did she say?"

"You're pregnant!" I exclaimed, grabbing her by the arm.

Leanna's mouth dropped. She stuttered. "How? How does she know?"

I looked at Lakona and asked.

Lakona smiled. She then gently wafted the air under her nose with her long, furry fingers. "Her scent tells all."

I was beside myself with joy, and I grabbed Leanna, hugging her tightly.

"Thank you my sweet love. Thank you!"

All of a sudden, and much to my surprise, Leanna began to cry, her tears turning into a sob. I was taken aback.

"What?" I asked. "What is it? Are you not happy?"

Leanna looked at me with reddened, tear-stained eyes. "Rez, so much is happening. I just don't know what to make of it all."

"I know," I responded. "Things have moved too fast. And I've overstepped my station, haven't I? I expect too much and I must apologize. There are things that need to be addressed. I'm sorry, my Princess.

"Stop," she replied, irritably. "That's what I'm talking about. I'm not a Princess, not anymore. In fact I'm not the person you think I am."

I was confused by her outburst, but I gave her a moment.

"Rez I have a confession to make. I haven't been totally honest with you on a number of things."

"About what?" I asked.

She wiped her face on one of the furs. "I told you I was bartered away to Hazadek. That he took me unwillingly." Her voice fell very low. "That isn't entirely true."

"I'm listening."

"Rez, I'm sorry. You look at me with this adoration, like I'm some young virgin—a Princess you've placed on this pedestal, but I'm far from it. He didn't have to barter for me. I solicited his attention. I wanted it."

"Did you love him?" I asked.

She shook her head. "No. I just didn't know what else to do. I was so depressed living with that old couple. Everything I ever knew or loved was gone. The longer I remained there the more hopeless things became. I didn't know you were alive. Then Hazadek came for a visit. He was a King and I saw an opportunity. I was used to being waited on and having things my way. I thought if I was his Queen I might be happy, but I was wrong."

I began to laugh, my response catching her off guard.

"Why is that funny?"

"My Princess—I mean Leanna. If I were you I would have done no different. We've all done things here in order to survive. And my crimes are far worse than yours."

"I thought about taking my life," she interjected.

"But you didn't," I countered. "And what now? How do you feel now?"

"I feel a measure of peace—that with you I might have a chance for happiness, but I'm afraid. If you leave me now, something might happen, and then what would I do?"

"Leanna, what would you have me say. I cannot guarantee anything except for what I feel in my heart. I have known you since you were four years of age. I have seen you grow and develop, and were it not for our circumstances, I would watch you marry some other man as it would be your duty to the Empire. But instead, I face you as a man to a woman with our child developing within your belly and I will not pretend to be unhappy."

"You would take me as your wife then?"

'Yes, a million times over. Leanna, I love you. You are the light of my life. Will you be my wife?"

She nodded her head and the tears filled her eyes as we embraced. I think Lakona thought us mad, but I saw her smile ever so slightly as Leanna and I kissed.

Later that morning I left with Oolat, Toska, Rixxca, and two other Solula for our trek over the mountains. I hated leaving Leanna behind, especially after learning that she carried my child. I wanted her at my side, but it was imperative that we reach the pyramid that Rixxca had told us about as soon as possible. And at the rate the snows were coming, the passes would soon be impassable—it was now or never.

The first part of our journey was easy and I was floating along like a cloud. I was going to be a father. Plans had to be made. When I returned, I needed to make Leanna my wife—the proper thing to do for our soon-to-be son or daughter. I was beside myself with joyous optimism. In a million light years, I could never have foreseen this happening. I was living a story straight out of a fairy tale and I was eager to be a father and a husband.

As the snow crunched under our feet and our climb took us higher and higher into the cloud-covered peaks, I made secret plans for our future. I fantasized that after we found the pyramid I would somehow find a way to get us home; there had to be a way. I think Oolat thought me mad. He kept telling me that I was turning into a lovesick mikatoo, a fatuous bird that lived in the southern hillside forests. I told him he was right and I tried to concentrate harder on our passage through the terrain. This place did not forgive mistakes.

The weather was mild over the next three days, though I saw little of the terrain. We were surrounded by heavy clouds which forced us to keep our eyes peeled on the trail. The journey was arduous to say the least, made worse by the elevation. Fortunately, the heavy cloud cover kept me from seeing over the edge of the cliffs. Though not prone to acrophobia I did experience some dizziness from the thinness of the air; I was still acclimating to the altitude. In order to ensure my safety, ropes were tied to my waist connecting me to Oolat and Rixxca. The two warriors helped me immeasurably as we crossed the divide, where in some places the ground fell for a league or more down the mountainside.

When night fell we had no fires. We simply ate our evening meal and slept until morning. I was wedged in between Oolat and Rixxca for warmth and security, my backside pressed against the mountain. These two kept me from freezing as the nighttime temperatures sank into sub-zeros. I was ever so thankful that Leanna wasn't here experiencing this. She was safe in Talith, basking I hoped, next to a warm hearth.

On the fourth morning we rose to weather intermittent with snow and sunlight and we made good time. It felt warmer now with Tiiana glowing dimly overhead, her red form greeting us as she peeked through the thinning clouds. Rixxca informed me that our journey was nearing its end; we were almost to the valley of the pyramid—I was ecstatic. Suddenly, the joy of his words turned sour. We caught sight of something dreadful–something so unexpected it took our breath away. In the distance, a good stretch from our sight was a flock of ten Brata. Oolat saw them first, and his hand instinctively pushed me back against the mountainside. We all stood there rigid, frozen as they flew past, our bodies cloaked by the rock and ice. It was hard to tell, but the Brata seemed intent in their direction; their flight was labored as they carried something in their midst and they paid us no heed.

The appearance of such creatures so far out of their element stunned even the Solula. We were at a loss to explain any of this, and it immediately raised the specter of the missing villagers. I cut the ropes that bound me to Oolat and Rixxca.

"Wait here," I ordered the others as Oolat and I headed up the mountain trail alone.

We followed in the direction of the Brata. It took only a few minutes, and we quickly crested the peak we were traversing, the trail broadening as we entered a large valley. I was amazed at what greeted me, but there was little time to gawk. The Brata were in our line of sight and we were open to being spotted. Ducking behind the rocks and boulders Oolat and I picked our way down the mountainside, my eyes wide with wonder, for there, just across the valley was the pyramid we'd been searching for.

The sight of the edifice was a mystery in itself, and one totally out of character with what was anticipated. It stood less than a league away, but it wasn't buried under snow and ice as we expected. Instead, the pyramid's walls seemed to be radiating heat, a shimmering the color of warm amber. It seemed to be affecting the entire valley as the pyramid was surrounded by fields of newly sprouted grass, a green, velvet carpet that stretched for nearly a quarter of a league, stopping only when it met with the ice. It was here that the Brata had landed. Oolat and I crouched behind a pile of boulders alongside the trail, and we watched as the Brata laid their bounty on the ground next to the snow line.

What happened next was beyond all expectations. For as soon as the Brata landed something gave rise within the pyramid. From an opening in its side a bunch of spider-like creatures began pouring forth, crawling across the grass. There were perhaps a dozen or more, a dark fire-red in color, and they moved helter-skelter, very erratically, almost as if they were robotic in nature. I was stunned. What were these things?

Peeking out over the rocks I studied the creatures, noting their eight appendages—four arms and four oddly jointed legs—legs that seemed to be struggling against the terrain.

Oolat looked at me. "What are they?" he whispered.

I had no answer.

I kept my eyes glued on the aliens, trying to understand what they were. They appeared to be about four feet in height, and to my utter amazement seemed to have heads and torsos that were humanoid. The rest of their appearance seemed insect-like, for their bodies were squat and muscular and they held fat, bulbous posteriors similar to that of an ant or wasp. These things were an amazing conglomeration of arthropod life, and I was transfixed by the sight of them. They were definitely bizarre and frightful looking, worse even than the Brata. One thing was for certain—they had a measure of intelligence. Each one was wearing a warming device. There were heat emanations rippling off their bodies, and they carried armament—they were fighters.

"What in Ahska's name is going on?" Oolat muttered, under his breath.

I shook my head. "I have no idea, my friend, but it can't be good."

Together we watched as the spider creatures approached the Brata—almost instinctively the gargoyles took a defensive stance. They pulled out their weapons guarding the bounty that lay on the grass behind them. One of the spider-men strode forth alone—it was met by one of the Brata. There seemed to be a dialogue. The spider creature then handed something to the Brata, who took it in hand. He examined the item while the spider pointed and made hand gestures. Suddenly, the Brata turned and pointed the item toward an ice cliff that rose up half a league back on the ice pack. He fired the weapon he held, the white-electric proton blast that ensued knocking me to the ground. From behind the rocks I peered out fearfully to see the damage created. The ice cliff lay shattered with a gaping hole in it, chunks of ice and rock falling to the ground, the explosion reverberating throughout the mountains around us.

Oolat looked at me, his eyes wide with terror.

"It's a photon blaster!" I whispered in disbelief. I couldn't believe what I was seeing.

Oolat and I glanced up fearfully, taking another look over the rocks. The Brata were leaving, taking flight. They had what they needed and were on their way. I could now see what they had left behind. There were two bodies lying in the grass. The spider creatures were gathering them up. One was a Solula—the other a smaller black female. It was Leanna, of that I was sure. I jumped up only to be instantly knocked down by Oolat. He held me, clasping his hand over my mouth as I struggled. I was insane with rage—they had my love.

Oolat pulled me close, whispering in my ear.

"If she is dead, then it is. But if she is not, then we must take her back with stealth. I see in their hands, weapons that will kill over a long distance. Are these not like the weapons you told me about when we hunted darta?"

I nodded and he removed his hand. I pulled myself up carefully looking over the rocks. He was right; the creatures were heavily armed.

"This is bad ..." I said, studying the aliens as they moved back toward the pyramid, "... really bad. If the Brata use that weapon against the armada, the Motula will be wiped out."

Oolat shot me a look. "We must not allow that to happen."

"I agree," I replied. "But if we're going to stop them we'll need more than sword and cannon."

"What do you suggest then?"

I peeked again over the rocks. The spider-men were halfway back to the pyramid with the bodies of Leanna, and I assumed, Lakona. I never felt so helpless. I fingered my sword nervously, pondering some kind of plan. I then noticed a dark bank of clouds spilling across the ice plain toward us, a storm front carrying wind and snow. Its approach did not enhance my mood until I realized it would give us cover, allowing for unseen movement across the valley. I looked at Oolat.

"There's a storm coming. We need to get down there, if we're going to rescue Leanna and Lakona. This may be our only chance."

"I'll get the others," responded Oolat, slipping away.

In less than a minute he was gone from my sight, leaving me alone to watch the aliens as they disappeared into the pyramid. Oddly, the aliens posted no guards or sentries outside the edifice; this raised my concern. Were these creatures that self assured? Or were they leaving? I didn't like that idea, and I hoped the lack of guards was simply due to the approaching storm; it looked like a nasty one. Oolat arrived with Rixxca and the others and we huddled together discussing our approach. The storm had already buried the pyramid from our view, and was heading our way. We moved into it, our swords drawn.

With the wind blowing and ice pellets stinging our flesh, we crossed the green grass that lay underfoot. It was soft and squishy, a muddy mixture softened by thaw and melting snow. The oddity of it had the wheels in my head turning. It suddenly dawned on me; these creatures, whatever they were—they didn't like the cold. They were wearing body heaters when they met with the Brata. Was their natural environment a place warmer than here? That would explain the pyramid being so radiant; they were using it to heat the valley and melt the snow. Were they the builders of these edifices and not the Aquella? My mind swam with the implications. I realized now that there was much I did not understand regarding the moons of Tiiana or the races that lived here. This put me at a serious disadvantage.

It was very dark now as we made our way though the swirling, black clouds of the storm. The wind was biting, the snow and hail painful as it pelted our bodies—still we were unobserved in our approach. Making our way to the side of the edifice, we paused for a moment, using its side for shelter. We then moved stealthily forward, heading toward the opening that lay in front. We reached the hole and I peered inside. It was a large, black cavern, barely holding off the weather that was trying to enter. I removed my leather mask so I could catch a better look. Before me were steps that led up–a design to keep water and snow out. I stared into the orifice and saw nothing–no lights, no guards, no movement. It seemed deserted. With our blades ready we cautiously penetrated the pyramid, Oolat and I on one side, Rixxca and the other Solula on the other.

I soon came to suspect that no one was here. We found no guards or sentries, nor did we hear any sound to give us trepidation. It seemed the aliens were gone, taking whatever they needed and fleeing. We lit some torches for light and continued to explore, but still, we saw nothing. I was beset by worry over what had happened to Leanna, my mood darkened by the cold wind that moaned through the cavern, chilling my soul. Where was she? What kind of creatures would kidnap people in this fashion? Was my love being eaten by them? They had the look of carnivores. I was crestfallen. What was I going to do now? Oolat seemed to read my thoughts.

"You must not give up," he said. "They took her for a reason."

His words gave me hope and we pressed on. Finally, we reached a large room near the center of the pyramid. It was vaulted and open, the cold breeze behind us dissipating within, though my breath still puffed like a steam engine. We held up our torches and spread out to cover more space. To one side I came across a series of panels–they were covered with tiny colored gems which glistened under the glow of my light. I ran my hand over the inlaid display, my fingers rippling across the miniature gem stones. Suddenly a bright burst of white light overtook the room. We all jumped back expecting an attack by the aliens–but there was nothing.

My eyes swept the room. I was not entirely certain if I triggered the light or someone else, but I was glad it was on. The room was now fully illuminated, exposing a vast array of scientific apparatus. I had not seen anything like this since my days on Melela. Most of it was well beyond my means, but what lay at the center of the room was undeniably the most strange of all. There, lying atop a round dais was one of the alien creatures we'd seen earlier. It was either dead, dormant, or in hibernation. We approached it with the utmost of reservation, our swords poised high.

Oolat and I circled the alien, scrutinizing it, taking in its bizarre mixture of insect and hominid complexities. It was a freakish looking thing, its red skin covered with a protective armor of tough, leathery scales. About four feet in length, it was supported by four thin, spindly legs that were jointed in two places, each ending with hoofs that were padded and callused. The head and face were a bizarre combination of human and arthropod attributes. It bore an almost human looking face with two eyes, a nose, a furrowed brow and brown, silk-like hair, though the resemblance ended there. Its jaw was entirely insect-like, featuring a menacing pair of truculent mandibles—clasping pinchers that seemed welded to the lower jawbone with a small mouth set in between. I touched the mandibles with my sword blade. They were hard and brittle, and the clackish sound my blade made against it sent a shiver up my spine.

I bent down and peered closer at its face and torso. It lay with eyes closed, its head turned to one side. I examined the four arms that extended out from the torso—all were curled up and limp. From what I could see they were similar to human arms in form and function, except for the dermal armored skin. The upper two limbs extended down from the shoulders and yielded hands with three fingers and an opposing thumb. The other two arms protruded from the creature's midsection, but instead of displaying hands, they terminated into long, shovel-like appendages, each one showing definite signs of wear. I wondered if they were used for defense or perhaps for digging. Though puissant as weapons, I felt the two appendages were better designed for toiling in the soil, leading me to believe that these creatures were burrowers, living at least in part, underground.

Lastly, we examined the creature's bulb-like posterior which displayed a rather formidable looking stinger. It protruded from its hind end by a good eight inches, was serrated and held a needle sharp point. There was a clear fluid oozing from it, perhaps a toxin. Oolat and I glanced at one another. Neither one of us knew what to make of this alien thing, except that it raised the hair on our necks. Oolat snarled in disgust and wrinkled his nose, and before anyone could say anything he raised his sword and smashed it down, cutting off the stinger with a quick swipe of his blade. The creature did not flinch. He then moved to the front of the thing and brought his blade down on the creature's face, striking the pinchers attached to its jaw. The red mandibles splintered into several pieces and fell to the floor. Oolat kicked them away with his feet. Through all of this the creature lay stationary, a dark syrupy liquid dripping from its wounds. The smell was not pleasant, but it told us the creature was dead.

We continued to look around the room seeking clues on how the pyramid worked. I knew this was the place where the creatures had come through. It made sense, and I relayed my theory to Oolat and the others. These pyramids held some method of transferring matter from one place to another. If I had come to Boutal from Urlena, via a pyramid, then they too, must have come through from somewhere else—but from where? How would we figure this out? We continued to search the room looking for answers—an hour or more passed.

I was beginning to give up hope. I stood in front of the panel where the lights had gone on. I studied them, running my fingers over the gems. They were of all kinds of colors and patterns, but I couldn't get anything else to happen; it was maddening. We finally came to the realization that we were going to be here a while, so Oolat and the others went to get the polaca. We needed our supplies; it was going to be a long night.

While the Solula set up camp at the pyramid's entrance, I continued to look around, and my carelessness almost cost me my life. I was so intent on studying the colored crystals on the panel I was unaware of the half-dead creature slinking up behind me. The overhead light must have warmed it sufficiently to animate it and it was only the hairs on the back of my neck that gave me pause to turn. I gasped in horror as the human spider that had lain dormant on the dais leapt upon me. It grabbed me around the neck with its two hands, and tried to impale me with its missing stinger, its fat, bulb-ended body pummeling my stomach. I struck back with my fists, catching it in the torso and chest. I felt its grip tighten.

Unable to immobilize me with its venom, the creature flailed me with its two shovel-hands and tried to bring my head into its snapping jaws, fortunately shattered by Oolat's blade. I saw firsthand its teeth—saliva dripping, yellow fangs. I struck harder as the creature pinned me against the panel, its splintered jaw snapping angrily in my face. I suddenly felt a sharp pain in my side. One of its shovel appendages had stabbed me. I was bleeding. The thought of this disgusting creature killing and eating me threw me into a frenzy. With my adrenaline pumping, I kneed it in the midsection with all my might. The creature winced, and I continued to hit it with a barrage of blows to the head and stomach. I was lucky the cold had slowed the beast. It collapsed under my attack, allowing me to break free—I pulled out my blade.

Pulling to one side, I made ready my swing to end the fight, but the pain in my side cut me short. I glanced down. The gash in my side was ugly and bleeding profusely. I had to stop and apply pressure. Suddenly the creature lunged at me, catching me off guard. It caught my leg and I fell back, my sword flying from my hand as I hit the dais behind us. The thing was upon me immediately, stomping me with its feet as it crawled atop my body. In desperation I struggled to get away, but it was useless—it had me. Our faces were soon inches apart, and the look of its black, soulless eyes made me shudder with revulsion. I strained with one hand on its throat, keeping it at bay while kicking and kneeing it as hard as I could. My blows were of little use. Though weakened by the cold, and with wounds of its own, the creature continued to flail at me unmercifully. Fortunately, fate was on my side. In our struggle atop the dais,

I came to feel the hilt of my sword pressing against my leg—it lay just within reach. Hitting the creature in the face as hard as I could, I gained a momentary reprieve. A few seconds that granted me the opening I needed. I grabbed my sword, and with every ounce of strength remaining in my body, I plunged my blade savagely into the creature's midsection, twisting it forcefully as I did. I felt the blade pass through the spider's body, exiting its back. The look on the creature's face was one of total disbelief. It froze instantly, then began to convulse, giving off a grievous, ear-shattering wail. Blood flowed from its nose and mouth, whereupon it collapsed atop me, lifeless.

Filled with fear and loathing, my body shaking from the exertion, I tried to move, but I was pinned down. This was grave; I was bleeding heavily and there was no one near to help. I struggled to push the creature off, knowing if I didn't I would die. Suddenly, the light over the dais flared. It seemed like an explosion with everything going black—the room about me disappearing from view.

CHAPTER TWELVE

Philip Golan

think I knew that I was no longer on Boutal, but I couldn't
be sure. The spider-wasp creature still lay atop me and I was
hurt badly. The pain in my side was incredible, though that
probably didn't matter. If I'd landed on their world, I knew I'd
soon be dead. I prepared myself for the worst. Looking around,
I tried to see where I was, and if anyone was coming—I saw no
one. In fact, I couldn't see much of anything. The light overhead was blazing like a miniature sun, obscuring everything in
view. Unexpectedly, there came a sound—a mechanical shuf-
fling of sorts. I turned to see where it was coming from and
caught sight of two robots approaching.

They were tall, mechanical beings, about seven feet in
height, humanoid in form with smooth, silvery skin. They said
nothing, but I sensed they were studying me as they stared at
me with their fixed, cobalt-blue eyes. Almost effortlessly, and
with incredible speed, one pulled the spider-wasp off of me.
He snapped its neck with a deliberate, quick twist, and threw
it aside. The sound sent a shiver down my spine, my fear rising
as I saw the other one reaching for me. He lifted me up from

the ground nearly crushing my arm in the process. I began to plead.

"Please, I'm not one of them. You need to understand ..."

There was no response from the robot that held me; I was only a rag doll in its hands, dangling there.

"Who are you?" a voice suddenly spoke.

"Rez Cantor," I cried out in agony, tears filling my eyes, "of the planet Melela."

The voice began to laugh. I struggled to look at the robots— were they talking? Or was the voice coming from somewhere else? I heard the voice again—there was something strikingly familiar in its sound ...

"My friend, your words are quite humorous. But Rez Cantor is not black. Kill him!"

I realized then that the speech was Melelan.

The robot holding me grabbed my head, and I began to thrash and twist with all my might. I didn't want to die and I fought as hard as I could, struggling to stop him from twisting my head off. I began to scream.

"Wait ... Wait!!! They turned me this color on Boutal. I commanded the Shadow Guard for the Emperor's daughter. Philip! Wait!!!"

I don't know why I said his name—it just popped out. Had I recognized his voice? Or was it that he spoke my tongue? I would probably never know. I was just thankful for his next command.

"STOP!" he yelled.

The robot obeyed.

"Put him down!"

The robot released me and I fell to the floor in a heap. I held my side—I was still bleeding heavily, and on the verge of passing out. Suddenly, I heard a whirring noise and I saw a man in a wheelchair enter the light. He was half human and half machine, but I still recognized him—it was Philip Golan.

"Philip ..." I managed to sputter, as I passed out on the floor.

I awoke later—how much later, I didn't know. I was getting to hate these moments, moving from one place to another, losing time and memory. And now I couldn't see. It was dark wherever I was, but warm. It felt like I was lying in a warm bath of some sort, floating comfortably, but unable to move, or open my eyes. It was then that I heard Philip's voice.

"My dear Rez, you don't know what a joy it is to have you here. It's been so long—so, so, long."

His voice cracked—I could feel his emotions coursing through me. I realized then that I wasn't just hearing him. I could actually feel his words, and understand his mindset.

"Yes," he responded. *"We can both hear and feel one another. Welcome to Aura, my friend—my virtual world of science and magic. Are you ready?"*

I felt something being placed over my eyes—glasses, I think. I felt a slight pinch on my temples followed by an ever so light electrical discharge. Philip appeared before me—I was perplexed. He looked normal—fully human and no longer confined to a wheelchair. He approached and threw his arms around me, giving me an enthusiastic hug.

"It's so good to see you," he said.

I was floored. This was not the Philip I knew. I looked around. Everything was dark except for him and me.

"What is this?" I asked.

"A world where you and I can converse and make ready," came his reply. "You see, I know of your plight. I know you are trying once again to save the Princess."

"How?"

"I probed your mind while you were in stasis."

I think he caught my hint of confusion.

"I'm sorry. Let me start at the beginning. You were wounded by a Zecla—a nasty wound if I say so myself."

I looked at my side and saw nothing.

"You can't see it here ... but let me continue. For the past three days you have lain in my laboratory—I had to perform surgery before infection set in. I injected you with a nanovirus and antibiotics—you are healing nicely. Another day and you will be good as new."

"What of the Princess?" I queried

"I think there is still time to save her," he responded. "She is being made ready for the birthing."

I was utterly confused—birthing? My child—so soon? So much was happening and I understood so little. I felt Philip's voice in my head.

"Not your child, my friend," he sighed, heavily. "Rez ... I wish I had more time to explain—there is so much you do not understand and time is against us. Suffice to say, the Zecla have entered the first phase of their migration and I'm afraid the moons of Tiiana are in great trouble."

I felt the seriousness of Philip's words weighing down on me. And with them came an image—a million Zecla pouring forth like angry ants from the side of a pyramid. The sight took my breath away and from somewhere in the back of my mind I heard another voice speaking to me—Ahska.

"Save Boutal," came her thought. I was nonplussed. Was this her real warning—the true meaning of her words?

My mind seethed with turmoil. I felt the need to move, to get up and do something. Unexpectedly, I felt a reassuring hand on my shoulder. It was Philip trying to calm me—I don't think he heard Ahska. It didn't seem so. Instead, I felt a wave of tranquility overtaking me, along with his mandate.

"Do not worry, my friend. I know you are overwhelmed right now, but everything will be revealed with time. Right now, you need to rest. I have much to prepare."

Suddenly, I grew very tired.

CHAPTER THIRTEEN

"Rez ... *Rez!!!*"

A voice called to me.

"Yes?" I muttered, still hazy, and lost in a dream.

"It's time to wake up."

"Yes," I responded again. "I'm awake."

I opened my eyes. Everything was dark around me, my vision muted. It seemed I was looking through thick, dark glass. Sitting up, I put my feet over the side of the bed. My movement felt heavy and constricted; like weight had been added to my frame—it was all very strange. I looked at my hands. They were coated entirely with a silver metallic alloy—as were my arms and legs. I thought to myself—*this is unusual,* but for some reason, it was of little concern. I put my hands to my face. There was nothing to feel. My head and face were completely featureless, as if covered by a helmet, my face encased behind a dark viewing plate. It seemed my body bore a sleek, smooth armor that covered me entirely from head to toe.

"What is all of this?" I muttered, softly.

"There is no need to worry."

I looked up to see Philip standing before me.

"What's going on?" I asked.

"You're going to Zin," was his reply. "It's where they've taken the Princess."

"What?" I stood and faced him. "Philip! I don't understand. What is happening?"

Philip smiled. "My friend, you are about to embark on a daring rescue."

☆ ☆ ☆

I stood at the opening of a pyramid looking out onto a great sea of frozen azure-blue ice. It was dawn, and the light from Tiiana was just barely visible on the horizon. Though I couldn't feel it, I knew it was cold. The sensors in my head were registering two hundred below and the air, what little of it there was, was thick, and nearly liquid in form. I stepped out onto the ice. It was bone dry and brittle, cracking under my weight like eggshells—a very strange sensation. Of course, I did not actually hear, see, or feel these things directly. That was impossible, for my entire body was sealed within a special suit, including a helmet with a blackened visor designed to protect me from all that I was about to encounter.

This was Philip's gift to me. He had endowed me with a variety of new attributes, some technical in nature, others more basic. I'd been altered down to my very core, fused with nano-virals and nanites—microscopic machines. They coursed through my blood, insulating and protecting my body, repairing any damage that came my way. As I surveyed the terrain before me I felt a sense of irony with all of this—once again, I'd been refashioned to meet the needs of others. I was now a living, breathing machine–a cyborg.

Encased inside a flexible alloy of metal and darkened, nano-sheeted plastic, I was impervious to cold and heat, and the radiation that bombarded Zin continually. Only this way could I make this journey; a journey that would take me through extremes no human could endure, except me—like this. This was a mission, Philip informed me, where I would lead six others—robots—all linked to my brain. Together we were going to travel five hundred leagues across the moon of Zin. A crusade that would take us through inhospitable terrain, across an acorn-shaped moon covered with dry, crystallized ice, airless mountains, sweltering tropics, and a radioactive desert—and it was all under the control of a locust, warrior-race known as the Zecla. This was our route and my destiny—to reach the hive, the lair of the Zecla Queen, where I would rescue my fair love, the Princess Leanna, if I could.

Though I knew little more at the moment, I felt everything was as it should be—that Philip had my back. He was feeding me everything I needed and I felt duly confident as I climbed into one of the ATRs to begin our journey. We moved quickly, and with the exception of the ice crunching under our feet, there was no sound coming from our all-terrain rovers. Their speed and maneuverability were without par for a mechanical transport. They were spider-like in their design, built to mimic the appearance of the Zecla, duplicating their ability to crawl and climb over any type of terrain. Their design was also our disguise as we forayed into their territory. Our mission needed to be quick and decisive, but stealth came first and foremost.

We made distance in our rovers, picking our way across the ice, skirting the deep lying crevices and ravines that plagued our path, our heading taking us south toward the inhabitable zones of Zin. I said a prayer. Philip had informed me that I had twelve days to accomplish this mission before the armor I wore suffocated me from within. He said it would not be a pleasant death, and I had no desire to find out.

Our first two days passed without incident. The area we crossed was literally a frozen wasteland of bone-dry ice—nothing lived here—which is why Philip chose this entry point. It was far too cold for the Zecla, and the pyramid we came through was unknown to them. It had lain buried for centuries under a glacier of ice. Even our own transport there had been difficult; we had to melt our way out, which took an entire day unto itself.

Riding in the company of robots for hours on end was maddening and somewhat disconcerting. My companions did not converse; they had nothing to say, except for what fell within their parameters. They kept me apprised of our progress, our running time, and the necessary course adjustments we needed to make, but nothing more. I sorely missed Oolat and Leanna—his banter, her affection. The only positive note was I was able to sleep while the ATRs and robots marched on unrelentingly.

On the third morning I noticed a change in the terrain. Up ahead in the distance the ice abruptly ended. In its stead was an enormous range of mountains—herculean peaks that cast deep shadows across the terrain for leagues. It was this range that divided the moon's hemispheres—where the tectonic plates of Zin's moon collided—the northern half frozen ice, the southern half superheated mantle.

We reached these mountains by midday and began to ascend. And for two days we climbed upward, surrounded entirely by frozen black granite. Upon reaching the pinnacle I looked behind, and saw the curvature to the moon. The air here was nonexistent—the sky so cold and clear, the stars seemed to just barely dance over my head. I had no time to enjoy the view. My supply of oxygen was limited and we had our mission to complete.

Cresting the final summit I finally saw what lay ahead, and it was daunting. Tiiana loomed before us in all her radiant glory. She was huge—filling the entire sky as Zin was the closest moon orbiting her. I looked down on the cloud cover that stretched as far as the eye could see—it completely masked the terrain below. I was appreciative that my eyes were shielded from its reflection. We began our descent entering the cloud cover, and I quickly found normal vision to be useless in the dense soup. Still, I had no trouble. Philip had enhanced my eyes' electromagnetic spectrum and my cyborg components had radar and infrared.

Our worst dilemma was the wind—the lower we went, the more violent it became. Ice and snow began to pelt us like rock-hard missiles and the winds became hurricane in force. The metallic spider feet of the ATRs were drill-bit sharp, and they burrowed and twisted, digging into the rock as we picked our way down the mountainsides. At times our descent was almost vertical, and yet we remained glued to the mountain walls—it was an eerie feeling. For the most part, I had little to do except wait and watch as the winds ripped and tore around us. It was like nothing I've ever experienced, my internal sensors registering gusts and gales at nearly two hundred leagues per hour. It would have been impossible for me to navigate alone in this environment. I gave Philip Golan and his robots their due; he was a true genius and I was impressed at the technological wizardry getting me through all of this.

Up and down the snow-covered mountains we climbed, hugging the terrain like ants on a trail. As our elevation slowly fell, the snow eventually turned to hail, then slush, then rain—a torrential downpour still driven by near hurricane winds. The deluge was so thick I would not have been able to breathe had it not been for the armor and the osmosis process Philip had developed for my survival. Our descent became more hazardous—we were plagued now with raging torrents of water that carved and sliced the very terrain around us, stripping the land down to bare rock. At times our ATRs leapt like frogs over narrow mountain ravines—channels filled with water that raged so fast they could power a jet engine. Some, however, were so wide and dangerous we had to alter our route. And at other times we took more drastic steps. We rappelled down sheer cliffs and zip-lined across the canyons that stymied our path. I was ever so appreciative upon reaching level terrain once more.

The ground we now entered was a quagmire of quicksand. The rains had abated slightly, but we were faced with a run-off of fine silt and mud, much of it sticky, soggy, and treacherous beyond means. To prevent our sinking we had to buoy the ATRs with broad mud shoes. It took hours to cross, but finally, we came across vegetation—a kind of blackish moss that gave some stability to the soil. Eventually this moss gave way to small, stubby bushes—a pale gray-white in color. How the plants thrived here I did not know. We pressed on.

With each passing hour the soil became drier, more packed and solid, and our gait increased. We made good time. Trees began to appear—large, freakishly twisted things with a green and pink moss covering their bark. They towered over us, their tops penetrating the clouds that hung overhead. The air was becoming warmer, and I began to register small life forms on my sensors—mostly insects—small, tiny things that crawled or flew within this wet, damp land. I also noticed the color of my metallic skin changing. The warmer it got the more we went from silver to pink to red. I surmised the purpose was part of our disguise; we needed to look more like the Zecla.

Hours passed. The clouds above were thinning, and I was reading an opaque signature of heat and light coming from Tiiana. She was still beaming overhead, but down here in the gloom, it was still quite dim. The land began to change again. The vegetation became thick, and our path blocked by a dense briar; a prickly, thorn-laden ivy that was difficult to cut and traverse. To make matters worse we were encountering some type of radioactive mist or fog. It rose from the ground impeding our sensors. It was then that Philip's voice popped into my head. He told us to find the river one league east and enter it. I knew that this was one of his pre-recorded messages; we had reached some sort of strategic point. We backtracked slightly and found the river; it was a murky waterway filled with silt and debris, and moving quite fast. We entered the water and floated like half-submerged submarines downstream, acutely aware we were entering land occupied by the Zecla.

Unlike the other moons of Tiiana, there was no day or night on Zin, though there was a rotation in play. This moon was acorn-shaped, like a top, with one end always facing Tiiana, the other facing the cold reaches of space. That's why the equatorial band that ringed the planet was so important to the Zecla. This was their farmland, their breadbasket. We entered an area where the trees were thin and lofty, their branches covered with white wispy webbing. I could not fathom the purpose of the silk-like substance at first, but it became thicker as we headed downstream and soon covered everything. I then noticed a number of large, white sacks hanging from many of the trees—my sensors told me they held the bodies of decaying flesh. How or what the Zecla farmed or trapped here I did not know, nor did I care. This place was a hell hole and I had little interest in learning more about the personal peculiarities of the creatures that had abducted my love.

A short time later the terrain began to change. There was additional light now, and the river began to broaden and slow. It was treeless on either side of us, grass and flowers covering both sides of the bank. I noted the vegetation. The grass was a carpet of thick, reddish-brown, accented with flowers—star shaped petals of deep red and green, sitting atop white, wispy stems. They were the only thing of beauty I had seen so far on this moon.

For the next several hours we floated downstream see-ing nothing, but slowly that started to change. Signs of Zecla industrialization were beginning to appear. There were elec-trical towers and power lines running near to the water and I noted a number of flying ships aloft in the sky. The appearance of these things forced us to be more cautious and we sank lower into the water to keep from being seen or detected. Shortly thereafter, we came across a number of Zecla working along-side the banks. They were carrying the white silk sacks I'd seen hanging in the trees earlier, but this time they were being used to hold something else—what, I was unable to assess. I was just thankful that the river was dirty and we floated by unnoticed.

Eventually we reached a point where the river meandered toward a city of some sort. It was here that I began to see signs of Zecla technology. Our first contact was a series of square cubicles seemingly stacked haphazardly on top of one another. Each had an antenna sticking from its highest point though I had no idea of their purpose. There was no data, radio, or electromagnetic energy being transmitted or received. Next we came across a series of large siphoning tubes. They were sucking up massive quantities of water and we had to steer clear of the intake manifolds. Then further downstream we ran into the reverse process, a series of tubes dumping sewage and industrial waste back into the river. As we floated downstream the river seethed and boiled as the caustic waste swirled around us; I became concerned over the resistance of my metal skin. The robots allayed my fear. I then realized that the industrial brew was a blessing in disguise, for the thick muck hid us well, and we could easily spy on the Zecla without notice.

Using small sensors and micro-cameras, the robots and I studied the Zecla and their technology, picking up indications of steam, smoke, and carbon particles from oil and fuel. The pollution became thicker as we entered the industrial portion of the city. Here we came across thousands of Zecla at work. They were everywhere, pouring back and forth from tunnels that ran deep into the ground. They reminded me of ants on a carcass, working diligently to strip meat from a bone. What were they doing? I had no idea, only that the noise level I was registering was off the charts.

A little further downstream I began to garner the answer. On either side of the river we came across large, cumbersome ships—spaceships and rockets, literally hundreds of them packed into rows. They sat stoically atop concrete airstrips and extended back as far as the eye could see. The smell of liquid rocket fuel permeated the air. How many of these ships were they building? I couldn't guess; I just saw them pointing skyward like twisted spirals—black needles sticking up from a pin cushion. It was beyond belief, and it didn't take much to fathom what the Zecla were up to. This was no migration— these creatures were building an armada. They were readying for an invasion—an invasion of Boutal and the other moons.

Moving past the launch field we entered a metropolitan area—a Spartan city of little color. It was here that the robots and I had to submerge again to keep from being seen. There were Zecla all around us, most occupied with their daily tasks, some walking, others riding on different modes of transportation. It was here that I caught a few minute glimpses of their environment—a city filled with small, knurly domiciles, bizarre lattice-shaped towers and misshapen humps that looked like squashed beehives with a thousand holes poking throughout. I could not fathom the minds that had created such a bizarre architecture. And yet, all of this had been built by an intelligence—an intelligence that was readying an attack on the other moons of Tiiana. Would we be able to stop them?

The river finally terminated into a small ocean, or a lake of gigantic proportions. We could not see the other side and the bottom fell to unseen depths. I was sure that there were life-crushing creatures swimming in its depths. We had already seen fish in the river, and I was not eager to meet any new monsters. My experience on Urlena had been enough for me. Still, we had to cross and since Philip had provided no data on any underwater life forms, we were on our own. The only thing I knew for sure was our direction; we needed to head south.

Propelling ourselves through the ocean, we kept our heads low. I was surprised by the fact that we saw no vessels traversing the water, and I wondered why. Did the Zecla have a fear of water? I did see a number of flying craft. They flew at various altitudes and there were enough of them that we were forced to submerge often. As I studied the crafts with my instruments I tried to see what propelled them, for they were quite diverse in size, make, and speed, but my attempts were futile. I did find, however, that they were headed in our same direction—a disturbing coincidence.

For two days we swam the ocean, discovering midway that the water was getting warmer the further south we got; I surmised this was due to Zin's proximity to Tiiana. The gas giant was baking the moon's southern hemisphere with an unrelenting barrage of electromagnetic and ionic energy—the bulk being absorbed by the water. It was becoming inordinately hot, too hot to support aquatic life, and before long we were swimming in a cauldron of boiling brine.

To hasten our journey we rose to the surface and increased our speed. We were fortunate now to have ample cover, provided by a bank of thick, hot steam. It layered the sea like smoke, and we crossed with no hindrance until we reached a series of concrete towers that mired our path. We slowed our speed, analyzing the pilings that stood before us. They were massive things, iconic in structure, protruding a good thirty feet above the water. The problem, however, was not their size, but the bevy of violent currents churning around them—including a violent undertow. To safeguard our approach we fired nano cables toward the towers, penetrating the concrete. We were now secure and could approach safely—we then sent probes down to see what was happening in the water below.

The mystery ended rather quickly. We found that we were not bound to concrete pilings, but penstocks—gigantic intake towers that ran all the way down to the seabed floor. These intakes were sucking in water in a massive volume to feed hydroelectric generators. This find told me for certain that the ocean we were navigating was artificial. It had been created by a dam in order to generate electricity for the Zecla. I found that extraordinary and almost incomprehensible. A structure capable of holding back an ocean of water—it had to be staggering. And if we were at the intake towers that meant the dam couldn't be that much further ahead.

To escape the undertow currents produced by the intake towers we had to utilize the same techniques we had used when crossing the ravines in Zin's northern hemisphere. We jumped like frogs, hitting the water some fifty feet out and with the use of thrusters made good our escape. A league later, we reached the dam, finding it hidden behind a thick, rolling cloud of steam. Floating next to it we began our ascent, drilling through the slick, black algae that covered the outer side of the dam and into the concrete. Our progress was slow and measured as we had no idea of what lay above, and utmost care had to be taken. For a hundred feet the steam easily covered our climb, but then it weakened to a mist. We were now under the threat of being exposed and we still had another hundred feet to climb. To make sure the way was clear we sent out small rover drones. They carried tiny cameras within their frame—electric eyes that could see what we could not.

Scurrying up the sides of the dam, the drones took their place on top giving us another firsthand look at Zecla technology—and it was astounding. The dam itself was a broad curved structure, built of steel and concrete over a quarter of a league in width. I knew it would have to be this wide just to hold back the water. The ocean of pressure behind us was beyond calculation, and yet, this was but a mere glimpse of what lie ahead. In either direction, the top of the dam was populated with gigantic electrical towers. The metal monsters stood at least ten abreast, too many to count, their rows disappearing from view in either direction. Upon them were massive electrical cables, some as big as my leg, pulsating with electrical current—the output was staggering. It was so strong that the interference generated quickly overcame our drones; one by one they succumbed to power failure and died.

The loss of the drones caused me great concern. It was imperative that we learn what was on the other side of the dam. But with such unbridled power surging overhead, zapping our small spies, we were handicapped in determining our course of action. What were we going to do?

In answer to my ruminations, I received a message from one of the robots telling me to release an air drone, which I did—three of them. They took off from the water's surface and sailed high into the sky, heading across the dam. Only one made it. The other two were fried in mid-flight—cooked into a blackened, jellied mass of plastic and circuit board. The lone survivor told another story. Through its field of vision I caught sight of what awaited us, and it sent a ripple of dread down my spine.

First, there was Tiiana; her gigantic, fiery form loomed over everything, filling the entire sky. There was no escaping her here, and her fiery glow made the terrain dance and shimmer with the heated look of Hell itself. I wondered how anyone could live here, but they did. My second bout with dread came at the sight of the chasm that yawned wide on the dam's far side. From our drone's measurements, the valley below was at least three leagues wide and held a depth of nearly two leagues.

It made me wonder how the Zecla had mastered building a dam of this size. It was beyond my comprehension and I was filled with trepidation knowing we needed to traverse it to reach the bottom without being seen.

I flew the drone low, noting the bottom of the dam. There was a small lake at its base, fed by water passing through the dam's overflow conduits. These conduits were a safety feature. They kept the bulk of the water from overwhelming the physical structure. I watched as the overflow jetted through the canals, falling to the ground and the lake below. From there a river formed; it ran toward a small city and the desert beyond. This was our destination.

Turning the drone toward the city I surveyed its layout, noting the movement of the Zecla. It was more like a military base than anything else, with perhaps fifty thousand inhabitants. In its center, adjacent to the river, was a large black dome—the Queen's hive; the place where the Queen produced her progeny. I felt my stomach tighten knowing that Leanna was almost within reach. Just up from the dome I took in the pyramid; the transport facility they were using to move between moons. I scanned the rest of the base. There wasn't much to see—mostly surface structures, an air terminal, tarmac, heavy machinery, and air carriers ferrying personnel back and forth. I suspected that most of the base's facilities lay underground. In this heat it would almost have to, but that didn't ease my mind. The reason: behind the base was a huge launching tarmac filled with rocket ships. I couldn't count their number as the heat from Tiiana obscured my sensors, but I somehow knew there were a thousand or more.

My mind was reeling—did anyone realize how advanced the Zecla were with their plans? Between the ships I'd seen earlier and the ones being made ready here, they could attack every moon simultaneously and no one would be able to stop them. How in the name of Melela had this come to be? And how could it be stopped?

Suddenly, I heard Ahska's words ringing in my head. "Save Boutal," she said.

I laughed aloud. If she could see this, she'd know it was impossible. How could I, a single man, stop an armada like this? How many Zecla were on Zin? A hundred thousand? Two? Perhaps a million or more? My heart began to race—I was vexed—sweating. What was I going to do? I wanted to rescue my Princess and somehow save Boutal, but how? This was impossible.

Suddenly, I heard Philip's voice in my ear. He spoke softly.

"My dear, Captain. I have to surmise by the triggering of my voice and the rate of your blood pressure you are in some sort of dilemma."

"Yes," I answered.

"Your coordinates suggest that you are still leagues away from the hive dome. Is this so?

"Yes."

"Explain your situation."

"The dome is surrounded by an army of Zecla—they are loading their spaceships. I think we might be too late."

Philip's voice remained even. "Is the top of the dome open?"

"I'm not sure. Let me check."

I focused my eyes on the view through the air drone. The top of the dome seemed solid.

"I think the dome is still closed."

"Good," came his reply. "We still have time. But you must hurry, it is imperative that you get inside as quickly as possible. If the dome opens and the Queen's eggs are bathed in Tiiana's light, the Princess will be lost. Do you understand?"

"Yes."

Philip's voice fell silent and I got a grip on myself. I took a deep breath and ordered the drone to return. If we were to succeed in this attempt, we needed a better analysis of the dam. We had to get past it to reach the dome and rescue Leanna. As the drone came near I took it underneath the overflow conduits that channeled the excess water from the dam. There were at least a dozen of them—huge, gaping holes in the concrete— each one spaced a couple hundred feet from the other, and they allowed the ocean's water to pour forth unimpeded, hiding everything behind it. It was this spewing, raucous waterfall that would be our salvation, for it was a jet stream powerhouse, as loud as a thunderclap, shooting out hundreds of feet as it descended to the desert floor. It was the perfect cover.

With our plan set we began to move, edging our way alongside the interior of the dam. Unfortunately, the closer we got to the overflow channels the stronger the pull of the water became. It was like a drain in a tub and the suction was overwhelming, becoming exponentially stronger with each step. I began to wonder if we could actually survive our passage through in this manner, but there seemed little recourse. It was then that I received another message from my companions. They proposed an alternative method of passing through the conduits—two of them volunteered to act as base anchors. They suggested attaching themselves to the inside wall of the dam, a measurable distance below the overflow conduits. From there, the rest of us would use our nano cables to pass though the overflows.

I liked the idea—I thought it brilliant, though it gave me pause to wonder how much of this trip had been preplanned by Philip. At every turn we always seemed to have the right tools on hand. I could only thank heaven that he had planned for every contingency. We immediately put our newest strategy into play, dropping to a level underneath the overflows where the water was pitch-black. Once there, the seven of us linked our cables to one another. The five of us then waited while the two anchor robots dropped further down into the water. Their descent seemed to take forever, but eventually we received a signal informing us that they were secure on the wall. The five of us began to ascend—three of us taking one channel, the other two, another. I was in the middle of the three.

As we edged our way up to the overflow channels, the pull of the water grew more and more intense. It swirled in fury and velocity, threatening to dislodge us from our perch. We could not allow that to happen. Every step had to be planned and perfectly executed. The process was painstakingly slow as each footstep had to be drilled and anchored before taking another.

Any misstep had the potential of dislodging us, whereupon we'd become a missile shooting to our death.

We entered the overflow concaves and things got worse. The interior was slick with moss and algae–every step more treacherous than the last. The force of the water exceeded a hundred thousand gallons a second. We were, but a hair's breath away from death, or worse yet, exposure to the Zecla– we could ill afford either. Overall, the process took hours, but one by one we passed through to the other side.

In the end, we sat resting like spiders on the outside wall until it was confirmed that all of us were safely through. From there, we began our slow descent, picking our way to the bottom of the dam, our forms hidden by the massive overflow that fell to the lake below. As we descended, I feared that the Zecla would somehow spot us, but the water's roar and the spread of the overflow covered our movement completely.

I slept a bit on the way down–leaving my descent to the ATR. I had no choice. I was exhausted. Though I had the body armor of a cyborg, I was still human inside and this mission had been fraught with more danger than I cared to admit. I needed rest, especially with what was coming.

When I awoke we were near the bottom of the dam. The spray and steam were everywhere and our forms were hidden nicely as we crawled over the rocks and into the lake. On the lake's bottom we rested again, secure from view by the bubbles and white foam above us. I then heard Philip's voice.

"Congratulations, Captain. You made it."

"How? How do you know?" I inquired.

"I've been tracking your position through a satellite hidden in the ionosphere of Tiiana. It sends me data on you and the robots, though no direct communication. It allows me to provide you with direction. Are you ready for the next step?"

"Yes," I answered, not knowing if he heard me or not.

Without warning I felt a slight jolt and a burning sensation in my brain. Philip was uploading more information on the hive dome, the inner workings of the pyramid, and the Zecla

Queen. It hurt like hell, but it was something I needed if I was going to save my love and get us out of here alive.

My head ached as we crawled along the riverbed, picking our way through the mud toward our destination. The water was moving steadily, though slowing, but the steam was still strong. I hoped it was enough. I felt vulnerable, for I knew in my heart, if ever there was a place where our mission might be compromised, it was now—and we were already one robot short. It seemed one had developed a malfunction, and was stuck back at the waterfall, which I thought odd. Why there of all places, and after everything we'd been through. It didn't make sense. Still, I had no time to dwell on it. There wasn't anything I could do anyway. I just hoped the robot wouldn't be needed.

Closing in on the hive, I reviewed the information Philip had given me. It was rattling around inside my head like a pebble. I knew the Zecla Queen was really nothing more than an egg layer. She was so fat and heavy that she needed to be buoyed by water and kept warm. That's why the dome was here next to the river—she floated inside; supported by a large, warm pool of water, where she was waited on by workers as she laid her eggs. This was her entire existence, eating and producing offspring. The workers who tended her were blind females. They pulled her eggs from the water and packed them next to one another inside the dome. Food for the soon-to-be-born was supplied by male workers and soldiers—they brought whatever the Zecla harvested in their farmlands and the bodies of beings from the other worlds. This food was immobilized by their venom, wrapped in webbing, and kept alive until the time came when the overhead windows of the dome would open. When the light and heat struck the eggs they would awaken and the feeding frenzy would begin. The Queen and the female workers would also die at this point, becoming food for the young.

According to Philip's information, once the food supply in the dome was exhausted, the young would be herded together and placed on spaceships. They would be launched from Zin and sent out to the other moons. Landing in virgin territory, the young would spread like a disease on the unsuspecting populations. They would feed ravenously, stripping life and substance from the moons until everything was gone. They would then begin to build new hives and the process would start anew—it happened every two thousand years.

I was stunned by the knowledge I suddenly had rolling around in my brain. This had happened before? How? What had happened? There were no Zecla on Urlena or Boutal—at least that I was aware of. Why hadn't the other moons been devastated previously—or had they? Philip gave me no answers; perhaps he did not know. I was a little upset and I really wanted an answer to all of this.

We swam past the pyramid and on toward the dome. The underwater openings to the Queen's lair were wide and dark—feces material floated out toward us in large chunks. It was being carried downstream. I knew somewhere inside this piece of hell, Leanna lay wrapped in a cocoon, food for these despicable creatures and I needed to rescue her. The robots and I swam inside ever so carefully, and I raised my head above the water. The interior was dark and foreboding—utterly pitch-black. I switched to infrared vision, picking up the signatures of the female workers at the edge of the pool. They were scurrying back and forth plucking the Queen's eggs from the water and carrying them off to another area of the dome.

I felt a movement in the water. It was the Queen. She floated nearby, her form stirring up the water, but with the pool being so warm it was hard to differentiate her from the heat of the water. The three robots who accompanied me came to my side. Together we released a payload of insect drones—tiny, little creatures each about the size of a butterfly. The array of insects took flight, flitting into the darkness as they searched for Leanna. I hoped for the best—that Philip had found the key. On Aura, he had taken blood samples from the two of us, extracting the genetic markers that made up our Melelan DNA. With it, he correlated the data, giving the insect drones the secret to finding Leanna. They would seek out my Melelan love and lead me to her–if all went well. I waited.

It seemed to take forever–the dome was vast. I couldn't even begin to estimate how many eggs might lie in here–perhaps a million–maybe more? I kept my eyes on my sensors looking for the light signature telling me they'd found her. I was alone now with one robot. The other two had left to cover our escape. If I was successful in locating Leanna and retrieving her, I still had to get us out of the dome and into the pyramid. And that's where the other robots were headed–they were our backup.

I saw a small light flash–it was the signal I'd been waiting for. I commanded my ATR to move. No longer did I have any regard for anything in my path. My robot companion backed me up following me from behind. I pulled my sword from its sheath–a touch I'm glad Philip had allowed me to retain and I held it high. It was time to reclaim my love, and I was not going to approach it quietly.

Cutting across the water we headed in the direction of the light, knowing full well we were attracting the attention of the Queen's female attendants. They might have been blind, but they could still smell and hear, and they knew the moment we broke the water's surface and pulled onto dry land. With quick and decisive movement they came at us screeching madly, giving off an eerie wail of a cry–their sole purpose to protect the Queen and her eggs. I wanted to use my blaster and take them out immediately, but it was far too dangerous–this was a rescue mission. Instead, the robot and I met them head on, slicing at them with our swords while moving in the direction of Leanna. Our progress was quick, and I gave no quarter as I crushed and smashed everything in my path.

Our trespass in the dome was now raising quite a stir. The screeching was getting louder, in part I'm sure, to warn the soldier Zecla that something was wrong. Suddenly I felt a great slap on my side. It hit me hard and quick, knocking me back–my ATR rolled. I saw a huge, dark, snake-like appendage whipping back and forth; it was the ovipositor of the Queen lashing down on me, striking hard and fast. I was taken aback—somehow I thought she'd be slow and sloppy, but then, *she* was protecting her young.

I scrambled up swinging my blade, cutting at the snake-like tail that whipped toward me. I saw the robot behind me leap with its ATR. It landed atop the Queen's organ, its sharp, pointed feet sinking into her flesh. There was a horrendous scream as the robot cut her with his blade. He lashed down at her savagely, and with blazing speed, peeled off her flesh in huge chunks. As he violated her, I bolted to his side, sinking my own sword into the Queen's body. A message suddenly flashed before my eyes, ordering me to leave.

"Find the woman!" it demanded.

I turned my attention back to looking for Leanna, and I saw the drone's lights flashing madly. They were beaming their location with a furious intensity. I raced toward them, slicing at the female Zecla slaves who were converging again to attack. They fell quickly to my sword, their hands and limbs thrashed by my blade, their heads rolling. I reached Leanna's body. She was wrapped head to toe in a white filament, covered by the butterfly drones as they winked and flashed letting me know it was her. I wanted to rip her cocoon open, to cut the veil covering her, to see her fair face again, but there was no time, and Philip had warned me not to.

"She's in stasis," he had informed me. "Do not revive her. The toxins in her blood have slowed her metabolism—that is why she's alive. If you wake her, she will die. Wrap her in the zelcan bag you carry, and bring her to me so I can awaken her safely."

I put all my faith in his words. I pulled out a small packet. It was the silver zelcan bag I carried for this purpose. I unfolded it and snapped it open. I pulled the bag over Leanna's head and worked it down over her entire body, sealing it at the bottom. I picked her up and slung her over my shoulders just in time; a number of female slave workers had rallied for another attack. They came at me in a unit, biting and stinging—their venom dripping off the ATR and my metal body. I swung my blade again to clear a path. I was impervious to their stings and bites, but I had to defend Leanna. If she were bit or stung again, there was no telling what might happen—I couldn't allow it.

I became a madman. I needed to get the hell out of this place. I pounced over my attackers and with the greatest of haste headed toward the water. On my side, I could see my companion robot still swinging his blade. He was facing an avalanche of Zecla females attacking him. I leapt over the egg laying ovipositor of the Queen. The appendage had been severed from her body and was now lying in a pool of blood. With the Queen mortally wounded the Zecla females had no other purpose except to destroy her oppressors. More and more kept coming and I could hear new sounds—soldiers were approaching with weapons. I leapt into the water and swam for the openings leading to the river. I barely made it.

Though the water was not moving rapidly, I still had to get upstream to the pyramid and there was already trouble brewing. My communication with the other two robots informed me that action was being taken. One had swum the river downstream to the rocket launching area; he was our decoy, drawing the Zecla away to give us cover. The other one was waiting for me under the cover of the water in front of the pyramid. Just as I reached him, he climbed up the riverbank and onto land; he raced ahead toward the pyramid's opening. There was laser and blaster fire. It was coming in all directions, and through the water I could see the flashes of light everywhere. I waited for his word, which came quickly. I pulled from the water with Leanna in my arms, and I moved quickly, trying to shield her as best I could.

My sword was of no use here; I cast it aside and pulled out a photon blaster. Zecla soldiers were scrambling toward us from every direction. I was amazed at how quickly they moved on four legs. As I ran, the robot laid down cover fire—I flew past him. Suddenly, the ground began to shake; I thought it an earthquake at first, but it was followed by an explosion, and the decibel reading in my visor went off the chart. It literally brought everything to a standstill. I looked toward the dam, catching sight of a brilliant white flash so bright I had to turn away—from it a mushroom cloud formed. I needed no further incentive. Someone had just detonated a thermonuclear bomb. I moved into the pyramid with my companion robot behind me. We stood for a second; firing into the pyramid's interior, clearing any opposition. I then moved further inside while the robot began firing at the ceiling. The roof behind us collapsed, sealing the pyramid's entrance—no one was coming in.

I no longer needed to know what was happening outside. I knew we were dead if we didn't get out of here quick. The dam had been blown with a thermonuclear weapon and I couldn't begin to imagine how much water was on its way toward us. The robot and I raced up several stairwells to where the transport dais lay inside—we encountered two Zecla—they died quickly. I separated myself from my ATR and carried Leanna to the dais. I stood with her in my arms while the robot worked the gem stones. I felt the light overhead grow bright and just as we faded from the room I saw the robot beginning to glow. I knew what was coming; Philip had planned this very well. No one would ever use this pyramid or transport dais again, that was for sure.

eanna and I arrived back on Aura, safely and in one piece—but not without major issues facing us, the first being our health. Philip had his robot assistants take Leanna from my arms. She was the closest to death and he needed to immediately unravel the damage done by the Zecla. She would lay hospitalized for weeks, though her outcome would not be as optimistic as I would have wished. For myself, I had to have my silver skin literally peeled from me. The process left me stripped raw, right down to bare muscle, as Philip grafted a new lamina to my body. The pain was unimaginable and I lay for weeks on end under the fog of pain medication as my body healed.

Sometime later I regained consciousness in a room filled with an array of medical equipment. There were monitors and IV drips—I had wires pasted to my naked skin which was no longer black, but my natural, light brown, skin tone. I looked over and saw Leanna. She lay bedridden with wires running to monitors and an IV feeding her body. Her beautiful dark-skinned face was ashen, and I was gravely concerned. I heard the whirl of Philip's wheelchair. He approached my bed, look-ing quite tired.

"How is she?" I asked.

He shook his head. "It's not good. Their venom damaged her heart and part of her brain. She's in a coma."

"What about our baby?"

Philip looked at me with regret. "There was nothing I could do. The baby expired when she was stung. I'm sorry."

I wanted to scream—tears welled in my eyes. "Will she live?"

He couldn't answer.

"Those bastards," I muttered. "How could they?"

Philip squeezed my hand. "If it's any consolation, we dealt them a serious blow. They won't be able to attack the other moons. You saved hundreds of thousands of lives."

I wasn't so sure. "Philip, have you reviewed all the data we took of Zin?"

"Not entirely. Nursing both of you back to health has been a full-time job."

"Are you aware of the airfield further upstream near the city? There were hundreds of rockets there."

Philip shot me a disturbed look. I could see his brain work-ing. I think the robot part of him was connecting to some com-puter interface—he was downloading material as we spoke.

"I was afraid of this," he said, finally. "They've adapted—I may have underestimated them."

I studied Philip. I watched as his face went blank again—his mind was occupied somewhere else. He was a man of my own race, but he was also different now. Aside from being confined to a wheelchair, half his face and head were covered in metal and I think part of his brain as well. I wasn't sure if he was completely human anymore. Somehow he was intrinsically linked with the robots of Aura. Were they the natural race of this moon? Had they evolved here? I couldn't fathom how that might be. I had so many questions and I needed some answers. I had been to four moons now and I still had no understanding of what was going on. I pressed Philip for an explanation.

"What happened, Philip? How did we get here?'

His human eye focused on me. He laid his hand upon mine like a father to a son.

"I guess you'd like some answers, Captain. I can only imagine your confusion about everything that's happened since our arrival in this part of the universe."

I was in agreement.

"As you probably remember, we were fleeing Melela from the Relcor. I had just linked to the computer on the ship and I was preparing us for a warp jump to get us into deep space when several nukes exploded around us. Their combined force virtually tore open the threshold of space, so when we jumped we jumped into a rip–an actual tear in the very fabric of the universe. That anomaly placed us here, on the far side of the galaxy, a hundred and twenty thousand light years from home. Unfortunately, we didn't come alone, an unexploded nuke trailed us and when it detonated it destroyed our ship. It shattered the drive engines and broke us into pieces, forcing us to abandon ship. You and the Princess were unconscious as were numerous others. It was complete chaos; people were screaming, there was blood everywhere, and so many dead. It was every man for himself."

He choked. "I'm sorry, I was never a soldier ..." His voice trailed off.

"Philip," I said. "None of this was your fault. We lived, that's what's important. Now, please–tell me more."

"Your men–they were very brave. They grabbed us. They took you and the Princess one way and me another. There was so much confusion; half the ship was in flames and things were exploding everywhere. We were thrown into escape pods and launched into space. I had no idea who went where. Right after we left, the ship exploded and we shot off into space in a dozen different directions. I think my pod was damaged–we seemed to have little control over its flight and I passed out. It was only later that I learned we had crash-landed here on Aura, that I had been injured during the impact and that the others with me were dead. It was the Aurian robots that found me. They brought the pod inside the dome and repaired me as best they could. And now, here I am—half Melelan, half Aurian robot."

I think Philip tried to smile. And I could only imagine the hell he must have been through joining with a race of robots. I remember my assimilation with the Aquella—it wasn't a pleasant experience. I recounted my tale—giving him some solace that things had been difficult for all of us. Still, I needed more information.

"Can you explain to me what you know about this place?"

"Aura?"

"Aura, Boutal, the war with the Zecla—all of it."

"You do understand—my knowledge is one sided, coming from the Aurian's records."

That made sense. I nodded and he continued.

"It would seem that all of this started about four thousand years ago. The Aurians, according to their own words, were an advancing civilization deeply in love with science and technology. They had a thirst for learning and were eager to meet and develop relationships with other species—many of whom they had watched develop from afar, through telescopes and telecommunications. They were eager to meet other explorers like themselves, so eventually they built primitive spaceships, propelled by simple means, and they sailed off toward the other moons to meet the beings who lived there. It was their grand adventure and eventually they traveled to all the moons surrounding Tiiana."

"On each moon they met new races—the Aquella, Visi, Motula, Brata, and of course the Zecla. These initial contacts were peaceful and mutually welcomed, though very exclusive—limited greatly by the difficulty involved with space travel and the environmental conditions on each moon. For the longest time, it was only the Aurians who moved between the moons, then the Aquella and finally the Visi. The Motula and Zecla never achieved that high a level. Still, these different races were drawn together by a purpose. Each sensed a destiny in their developing relationships with one another. After all, their worlds were so close to one another—it seemed right. So, they continued to exchange information, science, medicine, and philosophy by whatever means possible. They even traded a little and over time their knowledge began to grow."

"With the passage of a thousand years the Aurians realized that there had to be a better way to move between the moons. They worked in great detail with the Aquella and the Visi. These two races were more advanced and closer to the Aurian's own intellectual level. I think, from what I've seen, that the Visi may have actually been even more advanced than the Aurians, at least on certain levels, but they were not as driven in their purpose. At any rate, the three races developed the transports you've been using. They built the pyramids maximizing each moon's magnetic field and soon they had a linked transport system that bound the five moons together. Now for the first time in their history anyone on any moon could travel to another instantly. In a sense this was a technological revolution unlike any other and it overwhelmed everyone and everything. Suddenly, rules had to be made. Each moon needed treaties, pacts and agreements to protect their sovereignty."

"The best laid plans," I interjected.

"Precisely," he replied. "But the one thing everyone missed was the psychological mindset of the Zecla. You see, for thousands of years they appear normal—if you can call any race normal. And while most races build, grow, and develop their civilization, fighting and squabbling along the way, the Zecla are different. Their race has a birthing cycle, unique to their own kind, which repeats every two thousand years. As you saw in the hive dome, a Queen will lay hundreds of thousands of eggs to sustain their species. But what the Aurians, Aquella, and Visi did not understand at the time was that just before the birthing season begins, a massive psychological change overtakes all the Zecla. They become driven by a genetic impulse so strong it literally overpowers their rational. Single-minded in their need to survive and propagate, they are driven to spread like locusts. Ordinarily the Brata kept them in check—"

"What!" I interrupted. "The Brata? The Brata live on Boutal. I don't ..."

"Understand? No, I'm sure you don't. You see, Captain, at one time the Brata and Zecla cohabited together on Zin— they were natural enemies. And they held each other in check for untold eons, but something happened. Perhaps there was some change in the planet or its ecosystem, or as I have come to hypothesize, it was the Aurians themselves who changed the game by giving the Zecla unearned knowledge and power. Whatever it was, the Brata were no longer able to contain the Zecla and when the birthing season arrived the Zecla were unconstrained in their efforts to spread and feed. They'd been given access to transports that led to each of the moons and they seized the moment. They secretly started building small hive domes on the different moons and sending their eggs through. No one suspected and it had deadly repercussions for all concerned."

"When the Aurians and the other races found out about the Zecla and their plans they felt betrayed. They destroyed the hives and the eggs and incapacitated the transports. The Zecla were enraged—they no longer held logic or understanding— they felt the other moons, by destroying their offspring had, in effect, declared war on them and they responded in kind. They launched rockets with warheads and the moon wars began."

"How did the Brata get on Boutal?"

"There was a meeting between the Aurians, the Aquella and the Visi. They knew that the Zecla had activated the transports to Boutal, which of all the moons was the most underdeveloped and vulnerable. But it was too big to easily search and these races were now engaged in a war with the Zecla. So, a deal was struck with the Brata. If they would go to Boutal and seek out the hives and kill the Zecla, the Aurians would give them the necessary means to destroy the Zecla and retake Zin."

My mouth fell open. I could not believe the tale I was hearing from Philip's lips. This was incredible and it explained so much.

"I guess the Brata never made it back."

Philip shrugged. "I would have to assume that was the case. The war turned very nasty and lasted for a number of years. The

Zecla were bombed with photon and electromagnetic weapons until almost nothing remained. The Aurians even sent robots in to finish the job, but they failed. They found out firsthand that the Zecla had developed their own variety of chemical and viral weapons specifically designed to cripple and eliminate their enemies. One was a viral-gas cloud that ate metal ..."

I sat up in bed. "The cloud—it's a weapon? My God, that's what destroyed the Aquella! How did the Aurians and the Visi survive?"

Philip looked at me with a silent stare. His human eye became wet, he blinked.

"They unleashed their weapon here on Aura," he said, softly. "And it wiped out millions. They had to vent the planet's atmosphere to kill it. Those that survived gathered all things together, seeds, animals, as many life forms as they were able— they then surrendered their essence to a life of suspended animation, until the robots they built could build protective domes over the cities. Their plan was to pump air back in and reanimate themselves. It just never happened. I would have to surmise from what you have told me that the same has become true for the Aquella."

"Yes," I answered somberly. "But what of the Visi?"

Philip shrugged again. "I have no real knowledge. The war tore everything apart. Each moon was fighting for its own survival, contact was sparse and it eventually faded into nothing."

"Have you ever tried to contact them?"

"No, not really."

"What can you tell me about them? You said earlier that you felt that they were more advanced than the Aurians?"

I watched as Philip retrieved data from someplace or someone—whomever he was in contact with. He came back to me.

"They call their moon, Vashia. It's a small moon about the same size as Urlena, but it doesn't have the water Urlena does. It was a beautiful place—the farthest from Tiiana, but closer to the sun—very temperate—no real mountains. I see a lot of trees and flowers ..."

"What about the people—the Visi?"

"The data shows that they're a quite pale in color, tall and slender, and very graceful—almost fluid in motion. Oh, and they like to meditate. According to what I am seeing from Aurian records, they were instrumental in aiding communication between the races and developing a number of medical advances."

Those words lit up my heart and spirit. I looked over to see the love of my life lying in a coma, her beautiful spirit damaged by creatures that held no appreciation for the lives of others. I sat up and ripped off the wires that were stuck to me. Though I felt pain, I ignored it, and I threw my legs over the side of the bed.

Philip tried to stop me, but he backed away when he saw how determined I was. I stood, completely naked and took a tentative step toward Leanna. My head swam; I was stiff, I had lain too long, but no more. I waited until the dizziness passed and I took another step. Two more and I was by her bedside, looking down upon her sweet, young face. She was too young to die. I wouldn't allow it—not without a fight. I turned to Philip.

"We need to try and contact the Visi. Perhaps they survived. Maybe they can help."

He nodded his head in agreement and turned to roll away.

"I'll see what I can do, along with some clothes, Captain."

✳ ✳ ✳

Three days passed—then five—then two weeks, and we heard nothing. Philip was trying everything he could to see if he could reach the Visi, but it seemed we were wasting our time. For me, my days were occupied sitting alongside Leanna's bed, robed in Aurian dress, talking to her endlessly. She hadn't changed since the rescue, her consciousness was still lost deep within the dark recesses of a coma. I wasn't even sure if she could hear me, but I needed to be there—I wanted her well. Occasionally, I would feel her hand twitch when I touched her, it gave rise to my optimism, but there was nothing more. This was the toughest assignment of my career, watching her lay there barely breathing, seeing her slowly waste away. I prayed hard on many a day for her to just wake up.

At times, when I could no longer take it, I would walk or exercise, strolling through the silent streets of Hartha—a beautiful, glass-domed city set against a background of chalky white-gray hills. This place truly looked like a moon, a ghostly looking orb with no atmosphere—the light from Tiiana radiating and reflecting off its surface in stark tones of black and reddish-white. There were even trees out there—frozen dead sticks with nary a breeze to bend them. It was sad to see. I suspect that this had been a beautiful place at one time—a place full of life.

It was on one of these walks, where I was lost in thought wishing for things to change, when something happened. I had my face pressed against the glass dome wondering how the Aurians had lived before the war. I didn't hear Philip approach. So much was running though my mind. How things were on Boutal? And Oolat—I wondered how my giant friend was doing. He probably thought me dead. It would be nice to return and let him know I was alive—I owed him that much.

"Captain?"

I jumped. Philip was parked right next to me.

"I'm sorry. I didn't mean to startle you, but I think we have something."

Philip's words lit me like a firecracker. I exploded. "You mean from Vashia! What? Tell me!"

"I'm not really sure—there were a couple of beeps on one of the communications machines. I'm not really sure what it means. Come take a look."

We headed off toward Philip's lab. I had to laugh, though I said nothing. He wanted me to look at something he didn't understand. That was like me asking a ploth to read—he was that far ahead of me intellectually. Still, what did I have to lose? We reached the lab and Philip played me the recording of the message. All I heard was static with a couple of beeps—more like pops to my ear. Still, he seemed to think it was something—he made a suggestion.

"Perhaps they think this is a trap of some sort. Why don't you relay a message to them?"

"What would I say?"

"Tell them the truth. Tell them who you are and why you're contacting them."

Truth was I was impressed with his suggestion. Why hadn't we thought of it sooner? He gave me a device to converse into and I began to speak.

"To the Visi—my name is Rez Cantor; I am not from the moons of Tiiana, but from another place, light years away. I am trapped here on Aura with my companion, Leanna. She has been hurt by a Zecla and lies in a coma. Can you help us?"

I spoke the message over and over. I tried different words and phrasing—I tried different languages. I spoke in Melelan, Motula and Solula and several others I knew, including Barsin—anything to get their attention. I spoke for hours and nothing happened—the day wore on. I was growing tired and beginning to think we had wasted more time, but I tried again. I rambled, speaking aloud to myself—more of a prayer I guess—hoping for the best. I left the speaking device on. Suddenly, for some unexpected reason, Ahska popped into my mind—the thought of the old woman made me smile. I began to speak in Motula again.

"Ahska, my old and wise mentor, are you still out there? Can you help me one more time? You told me I was going to save Boutal, but I am really lost right now. I am trapped on Aura and I need help. Can you speak to the Visi, their Gods or whomever and ask them for help? If you truly believe that I can save Boutal—then I really need your help right now."

I started to repeat my rehearsed message. "To the Visi—my name is Rez Cantor; I am not from this ..."

Suddenly, and without warning, an apparition appeared before me, its voice ringing in my ears. It was loud and quite clear.

"You speak Motula very well. It is a difficult language to master," it said.

I jumped up, knocking my chair back—the communications device I held falling onto the table. I backed away from the ghost floating before me. Its form wavered. It was the image of a man, with a white wispy figure—he studied me.

"Philip!" I said aloud. "Philip you might want to come see this."

I nodded to the figure and mumbled. "My name is Rez ..."

"Cantor, yes I know. And you would like our help?"

"Yes, yes I would. My love, my companion, a female, she was stung by a Zecla and taken for food by their species ..."

I heard Philip wheel into the room behind me, I kept on speaking.

"... I rescued her from Zin. We've been trying to help her, but she lies in a coma. This is my friend, Philip. He is Melelan too—he crash-landed here a few years ago—he's been trying to cure her with Aurian technology."

"Yes" replied the man. "It would appear he has become part Aurian himself."

"He had little choice," I explained. "He was unconscious when the Aurian robots brought him here after our ship exploded—they did it to keep him alive."

"Yes, quite so ..." the ghost noted. "... some of the wreckage landed on Vashia. Tell me, who is responsible for the recent attack on the Zecla?"

I glanced at Philip.

"I guess we're both responsible," I said. "Philip learned about the history between you and the Zecla and he's been monitoring their activities on Zin ever since. They've been building an armada ever since the birthing season began. And they started kidnapping Motula and Solula from Boutal—that's how Leanna ended up on Zin. After seeing what happened to the Aurians and seeing what the future held for the other moons—we couldn't stand by and do nothing—so we struck first, eliminating their threat."

The Visi stood silent before us. I wasn't sure if he was judging us or maybe even communicating with others like himself. I quickly added to my explanation.

"Look, can you understand? We're not from here. We never meant to get involved with all of this. But ever since arriving here, I keep getting put in the middle of your war. I don't know why. I mean we're a million light years from home. We're escaping oppression ourselves, from a race called the Relcor, and we ended up here by mistake. All I want to do is go home."

I think I began to break. I was stressed—my voice cracked. "I just want to take my Princess home. She's already lost so much."

The next words that came out of the Visi's mouth stunned me beyond measure.

"Ahska was right, you are conflicted in spirit, but not without a caring heart. Our transport will be open. Come; bring your mate to us."

With that he faded from view leaving Philip and me alone in the room.

Philip looked at me. "What was that all about?"

I sighed with relief. "They're giving us access to Vashia."

CHAPTER FIFTEEN

My arrival on Vashia was entirely uneventful, which was to say, a complete surprise. I carried Leanna in my arms– she was comatose and we were greeted by a bevy of Visi who took her from my arms. My first impression of these airy, white beings was not without complete wonder. I felt as if I had stepped into a land of fairy tales. I noted very little equipment in the transporter room and the Visi themselves seemed quite mystical in both appearance and manner. They were not what I expected.

To begin, they did not carry Leanna in their arms as I had; she seemed to float effortlessly in the air as they took her away. I wanted to follow, but one of the Visi stopped me. He handed me a silver roped necklace with a small, amber colored crystal attached. I turned it in my fingers, curious as to its use. I noted that he wore a similar necklace, though the crystal was white in color. Unexpectedly, I heard a voice ringing in my ear.

"My name is Yllis, he said. "Please, if you would, place the seti stone around your neck."

I followed his instruction, while asking its purpose.

"It is a communications device," he answered, his words filtering into my mind. "It will allow us to communicate by thought instead of by tongue. It is much faster."

"A convenient tool," I thought. "Where are they taking Leanna?"

"To a refuge where she can be examined. Our healers will listen to her spirit and they will diagnose the extent of her damage, then if possible, she will be restored."

"How long?"

"That is impossible to say—it will be her decision."

I didn't know what to think. I had never felt so lost and helpless. I could only hope that these beings could help her. Yllis seemed to understand.

"Your thoughts are noted," he said, "And we will do everything possible to save her. In the meantime, there are things that you need to see, learn, and plan for."

Yllis took me outside the pyramid and my eyes were wide with wonder. It was late afternoon and the sky was a deep bluish-purple in color. There were trees everywhere—some typical in their appearance, with dark, brown trunks and green leaves, but others were hued in light tones of blue and red, with leaves that radiated pink and gold. On the ground were flowers of every size and color, and there were insects and birds, all buzzing and chirping—most I couldn't identify. But the most wondrous of effects were the musical tones that emanated from the very ground upon which I stood; a melodic harmony that seemed to well up through my feet and into my body. It was as if the soil or the moon were humming. The effect was quite alien, a little unnerving, and yet both pleasant and exhilarating.

"It is the sound of harmony" said Yllis, noting my wonder. "Our moon sings—it helps to keep our spirits in alignment with the natural order of the universe."

I nodded, and said nothing as we continued to walk further into the countryside. Soon the trees thinned and we entered an open area—a terrain covered by grass and flowers. I could see for leagues now and at no point did I see any buildings or homes—no structures at all—I was quite curious. Where did the Visi live? How did they protect themselves from the environment?

"We have no need for protection," interjected Yllis, reading my thoughts. "The air and ground are constant to our needs. They yield and furnish all our wants."

I thought the answer was cryptic, but I felt the statement to be true. It seemed that Vashia was an Eden—at least for them.

Suddenly, something caught my eye; I looked skyward. Overhead was an asteroid belt. I saw light being reflected from it—a twinkling of color that was becoming more apparent as Tiiana sunk lower on the horizon and the sky got darker. I watched for a minute as the belt twisted and turned, arcing past our field of vision. Like some kaleidoscope, the colors waxed and waned from red, to purple, to blue and green, then back again. It was a marvel to behold.

Yllis noted my appreciation.

"At one time, before the moon war, we had no ring encircling our moon," he said. "This is a byproduct of our war with the Zecla, and though it appears now as a thing of beauty, it nearly destroyed our fragile environment."

"How?" I inquired.

"When the Zecla learned we had destroyed their eggs, they sought revenge. But Vashia was more distant and they had limited resources, so they took aim at Vas, a small sub-moon that was in orbit around us. They blew it up, causing Vashia to experience a violent upheaval. The loss of our little satellite changed our magnetic fields, and for hundreds of years we were subjected to a rain of asteroids. Our thin atmosphere could not protect us—many died."

"I'm sorry." I responded "It would seem that all of the moons of Tiiana paid dearly for the Zecla's treachery."

"Yes, and we almost had things in hand, but with your friend's preemptive strike, we'll never know.

"What do you mean?" I sensed Yllis was unhappy.

"The attack was unwarranted and unnecessary."

"I'm sorry you feel that way." I responded. "But from what I saw on Zin, it was the Zecla who were massing for an attack."

Yllis seemed to be biting his tongue. He changed the sub-ject. "It doesn't matter; we have another issue that is more pressing—something that needs to be resolved."

Suddenly, I found myself somewhere else. It was lighter—both the sun and Tiiana were higher on the horizon. I felt my body sway—it was very disconcerting.

"The feeling will pass," noted my Visi guide.

"What happened?" I asked.

"I have moved us to another location."

Teleportation—how was this possible? I wanted to ask why, but I felt it was pointless. I knew I probably wouldn't understand the answer. Instead, I focused on why we were here. I looked ahead and caught sight of an area that seemed damaged. The terrain was unhealthy looking—the grass and trees dead—there were no flowers or insect life.

"This is from your ship," said Yllis.

"What?" I exclaimed.

"There—if you look to the center, you can see the remnants of your ship."

I gazed into the distance to where he indicated and saw shards of wreckage littering the terrain—this was where our ship had crashed.

"Since falling to Vashia this area had been deemed lifeless. We are unable to remove the wreckage. It would seem that your technology, the science that drives your craft, is harmful to our species."

I knew immediately he was referring to the warp drives. For some reason they must be leaking radiation and poisoning the area.

"I would like to help," I began, "but this is beyond my abili-ties. You need to speak to Philip. He's the only one who would know how to safely remove what is harming you and your moon."

"The one who attacked Zin?"

"Yes."

It was easy to see that Yllis was not happy with that answer, but it was the truth. I didn't know enough about warp cores or how to build a proper shielding.

"Can we count on you to start a dialogue with him?" he asked.

"Of course—I'm sure he'd be willing to help."

Without warning we were back where we started. I felt the dizziness in my head again, but it passed quickly. I was unduly impressed; this was such a unique way to travel. We walked toward the pyramid which was just barely visible the evening light. I took a deep breath—the air was cool and laden with the scent of flowers—the ground humming softly. It was mesmerizing.

"I'm glad you can appreciate the beauty of our world, Captain. It's taken us over a thousand years to rebuild."

"Yes," I mumbled, in slow reply. My thoughts were becoming jumbled. I rambled. "It reminds me of my travels with the Emperor ... visiting many unique worlds. I miss that."

"You'd like to return to Melela—wouldn't you?"

I wanted to answer, but Yllis stopped me. His tone became more serious.

"Captain, allow me to be blunt. We are extremely disheartened by the recent turn of events regarding the Zecla. Your attack upon their moon wiped out nearly three hundred years of hard work by the Visi. We nearly had the Zecla under control, but because you killed their Queen we'll never know."

I wanted to apologize, but Yllis continued unabated.

"Consequently, we're forced to change strategies—adopt a new plan, just in case."

"In case of what?"

"Captain, while we can appreciate the magnitude and force of your weapons, they don't necessarily provide a solution to everything."

"I don't understand. Are you saying the Zecla are still alive—that they could still attack?"

"We're not sure. We do know that the Zecla are resilient and resourceful. If they have survived it would be better to be prepared."

"Prepared? For what?"

"Captain, the arrival of your people here upon the moons of Tiiana has altered things dramatically. We would like nothing better than to help you return to Melela. But first, we need your assistance."

"Yes, of course ... anything."

I had no idea what Yllis was talking about at this point, but unexpectedly I was caught by a barrage of thoughts running though my head. They were odd rambling fragments—broken ideas and thoughts: *invite Philip to Vashia ... repair his body ... robots come, repair Vashia ... reform Aura ... construct a ship ... go home.*

I grew drowsy from it all and I sank like a stone to the grass, where I fell into a dreamlike slumber. I lay there semiconscious as a group of Visi floated out from behind a grouping of trees. Hovering over my body, they gently stroked me with their hands head to toe. They raised me up and I floated back toward the pyramid. I don't think I've ever felt so euphoric.

✵ ✵ ✵

I arrived back on Aura unsure of what happened on Vashia, or how much time had passed, if any. For some reason it didn't matter. I just knew I needed to find Philip, but he was nowhere to be found. I walked the halls looking for him, finally locating him in a small telecommunications room watching a series of monitors. He waved me in.

"Rez, you're just in time to see our handiwork. Come take a look at this." He pointed to the monitors. "I've reconstructed the data we gathered three months ago when you were on

Zin–a lot of it was damaged by EMP waves, but I've salvaged quite a bit."

I glanced at the screens, peering from one to the next. Each screen was showing a different perspective of Zin. Some showed views taken by the robots on the ground, but several were taken from space. The digital resolution was a little spotty, grainy and uneven, but watchable. Suddenly, there was a brilliant flash–the monitors went white from the glare. I listened as Philip narrated.

"It took three nukes to blow that dam. I knew it would– that was one massive piece of concrete. I planned this attack for two years, you know. And finally, I nailed those red-scum bastards."

His wicked grin was retort enough for me to read the pleasure of his success.

I looked to the screens–the monitors had returned to normal and the images were beyond belief. I watched as the dam burst. It played almost in slow motion, the cracks in the concrete turning into fissures, widening with each passing second, until finally the dam burst apart. Huge chunks of concrete exploded outward from the force of the water as the ocean punched its way through. As the dam weakened, the effect cascaded, more and more fell, until it all gave way. The deluge of water rolled onto the desert floor, a wave half as high as the dam itself. There was nothing in its path that could stop it.

I caught another flash–the pyramid exploded into a nuclear cloud, the force of the explosion taking half the military installation with it, including the dome. The buildings outside the immediate blast zone literally melted from the heat, while everything else was torn asunder by the wind blast that followed. I saw machines and vehicles tumbling like toys. But that was not the worst–the final death knell was still coming. The water from the dam rumbled across the moon of Zin with an earth-shattering resonance–the weight alone must have been immeasurable. It surged across the desert floor, crushing and sweeping away all that lay in its path. The rocket ships that stood ready on their launch pads were the last to go, but the water took them as well, knocking them down and swallowing them as if they were puny sticks. It looked as if everything had been obliterated, but there was more to come.

Philip clapped his hands like a gleeful imp as he watched the annihilation of the Zecla. He played with the buttons on the console speeding up the footage.

I was a little bewildered. "Haven't you seen enough?" I asked.

"Oh, my dear Rez." You haven't seen anything yet. It gets better, so much better. Just watch."

The film he played for me now showed a view from outer space–the picture was better. I observed as the wall of water from the dam headed into the most southern desert lands of Zin. It was leagues wide now and it rolled unrelenting–half a league high, a tsunami unlike anything I'd ever witnessed. Still, I was not ready for what came next. The picture shifted in view, focusing directly on the southern pole of Zin. Here, the desert was so hot the sand was nearly molten—it flowed like melted wax. There was no water here. Water never made it this far south–it evaporated long before reaching this latitude–but not this time. There was so much water held back by the dam that it couldn't evaporate in time as it rolled across the desert and it hit the molten sands with a force equal to that of a thousand nuclear bombs. On the image shot from space I thought I saw the entire moon convulse–it was cataclysmic.

Philip clapped again–his heady smirk mixed with a wild, crazy look of joy.

"I was worried at first when you told me about the other rockets, upstream near the city, but not anymore. Look, see for yourself."

I glanced back to the screen depicting Zin from space. There was a thick, dark band ringing the moon–a circle of death. It was moving steadily north giving off flashes of light in its wake.

"What is that?" I asked.

"The end of the Zecla," he responded, proudly.

"Could you be more specific?"

"It's a storm front of unprecedented magnitude. I imagine there's never been anything like it on Zin before—at least on the south side of the equator. It's virtually a steam-driven hurricane so large it encircles the entire moon. Nothing will escape its reach or force. It's a hot gaseous mixture that should put an end to everything the Zecla ever built or produced. And when it hits the ice front on the north side—Kaboom! Goodbye Zecla! I can hardly wait to see the results when Zin rounds Tiiana again. I want to savor her destruction with my one good eye."

Philip was beside himself and I had to give him credit. When he went after something he didn't do it halfway—it was all or nothing. In spite of what Yllis said, from what I was seeing, this probably did spell the end for the Zecla. How could any species survive such an onslaught? Their entire moon was being ravaged down to the core—perhaps the Visi were just overreacting.

I watched the black ring steadily heading north, and I realized this was a recording. Whatever had occurred on Zin—it had happened weeks ago. This storm was probably now at its apex covering the entire moon. I knew from experience, the winds had to be torrential, traveling at several hundred leagues per hour. There would be lightning, tornados, floods and radioactivity—not to mention the tonnage of rock and dirt that would fall from the upper atmosphere all over the moon. It would fall for days, weeks—possibly months. This was indeed a ring of death and I gave little hope to the Zecla. So, why was I concerned?

Philip laughed again and slapped his hand down on the console. He rewound the tape and began to play it again. I had little stomach for it—the look in his eye was disconcerting, and admittedly, I was a little repulsed. While it was true, I hated the Zecla for what they had done—I did not revel in seeing the demise of their entire species or their moon. I left the room; I had other things on my mind.

I wandered the halls, alone, passing several robots here and there. There were no greetings—no responses at all from the metal giants. They were cold and artificial; though I got the

255

feeling they were watching me, sensing that I was somehow different. Admittedly, they had helped me rescue Leanna, but we had no bond further than that. They were tools–a means to an end, and nothing more. It made me wonder if Aura had always been this way. Had the Aurians always been austere and reserved? One thing was for certain, I really wanted to leave.

Perhaps it was this longing that drew me back to the transporter room. Whatever the reason, I found myself inside staring at the gemstones, pondering their purpose. I gazed at the colors–red, blue, white–suddenly a light went on in my head. The panel made sense. It was so simple. These colors represented the various moons. How I knew this, I was not certain, but I sensed the reasoning behind it. Red represented Zin, Vashia was white, Urlena–green, Boutal–amber–and Aura was blue. I also garnered the reasoning, that if the gems were pressed in a particular manner, the transport process would begin.

Unexpectedly, Philip rolled into the room. "Captain, what are you doing?"

I jumped and turned. "Philip, sorry–I didn't hear you. I was just thinking about things–missing Leanna and all."

I saw Philip's features relax. He nodded his head in understanding.

"Will the Visi be able to help her?"

I was pleased to see his demeanor normal again.

"It will take time," I answered. "All we can do is hope."

"Yes, yes, her injuries were extensive–it will take time, I'm sure. I wish I could have done more—but what of Vashia? How did she fare from the war?"

"She survived, barely–perhaps you should see for yourself."

He patted the arm of his wheelchair. "No, I don't think I could leave Aura. It wouldn't be right–there's too much work to be done."

"Philip, we may not have a choice."

"What do you mean?"

"The Visi asked me to talk to you. You see part of our ship crashed on their moon. The aft section with the warp drives, and they're leaking radiation. The Visi need our help in removing the debris."

I saw Philip's good eye light up. "The drives are there?"

"Yes, but they're leaking. And I can't do it alone. I don't have the knowledge–I need you."

Philip sighed. I could see his mind turning. I interjected the offer made by the Visi.

"The Visi have suggested that with their help your essence could be transferred over to an Aurian robot. They could give you the use of your legs again. You could rebuild our ship–take us home. You might even help the Aurians rebuild their civilization. After all, one power cell could generate enough power to light up this entire city."

Philip nodded his head, and his face went blank. He seemed locked in conversation with someone. I wasn't sure. He finally looked at me and gave his answer.

"This is a matter requiring some thought and discussion. I need to see if there are materials here that would allow for construction of a ship. And I would need a special body. Would I be able to transfer back?"

I shrugged. "I can check for you."

"No matter—I'm tired of this chair anyway."

Without any further discussion, Philip rolled away. He became quite animated; talking to himself and gesturing–it sent a chill up my spine.

I didn't see Philip for quite a while after that. He kept to himself, holed up in his laboratory doing who knew what. For myself, I found a renewed interest in learning more about the Aurians and their technology. I poked my head into different labs and new areas of the city. I wanted to know how everything worked here. I thought my newfound curiosity odd on one hand, but also completely natural. Still, something told me to avoid the prying eyes of the robots.

Over the next several weeks I conversed with the Visi through holographic communication. They kept me abreast of Leanna's condition–she was still in reformation, whatever that was, and there was little change. I missed her dearly. I also conveyed to the Visi that I had spoken with Philip, informing them that he was very busy. I thought he was willing to help with the wreckage, but I still had no firm answer. I would contact them when I knew something.

A week later I had his answer. It was early morning, and I was sound asleep when Philip approached my bed, awakening me.

"I'm ready," he said, a very pleased look upon his face. "I've finished my robot—we can begin at any time, but the transfer must take place here on Aura."

I rubbed my eyes and sat up. "I guess," I answered, "but it's not up to me."

Philip rolled away and with a smug response said. "If they want the debris removed from Vashia, then the transfer will take place here."

I sat dumbfounded, not sure what to make of this. It was obvious that Philip did not completely trust the Visi. At any rate, I got dressed and made my way to the recording room where I contacted Vashia. Yllis appeared. I told him that Philip was ready, but there was a condition, and I explained. I could tell Yllis was not happy. He said he would need to speak with others, and he disappeared. I was perplexed—as a Visi, why was he sour? It seemed, oddly enough, that there was a level of intrigue taking place that I didn't care for. The Visi were aloof, Philip was acting strange—and here I was, in the middle, and in the dark.

Another week passed, during which Philip and the Visi conversed extensively. Though I was not privy to the details, the final plans were laid out, and the Visi finally arrived. They passed through the transport effortlessly, though I sensed they didn't like being off-moon. They wanted to accomplish their task and head home as quickly as possible. I understood their reasoning. I had walked their moon and I felt the connection they held with Vashia. It was a powerful narcotic.

What happened next occurred exclusively between the Visi and Philip. I was left to my own devices as they entered an Aurian medical facility. My only glimpse of things came as they placed Philip on a bed, alongside another holding the robot he had built. It was covered by a long, white sheet hiding its features, so I had no idea what to expect. Needless to say, I was extremely curious to see how all of this would work out. My wait was not long.

By the end of the day I met the new Philip Golan. He stood almost nine feet in height with a large, well built, muscular frame. I was surprised at how he had mimicked the human physique in his design. For some reason, he felt the need for a body that conveyed power—perhaps compensating for his disability and time in a wheelchair. Now he was a giant, towering over everyone. The real difference was his face. Philip had opted for a totally new look—a new design. His head was proportionate to the body, but the face was missing, replaced instead, by a smooth, dark facade—a thick, translucent sheet of black glass. What gave Philip his physical appearance was the human face he projected from within—like someone looking at you through a window. His facial attributes appeared a deep blue in color, a pixel generation of light and dark shadows that gave detail and depth to his face—a full range of human characteristics. The effect was quite eerie, but it did grant Philip more expression than the other robots of Aura. His voice, however, was another matter. It was inhuman sounding, synthesized and cold, which took a little getting used to. Philip promised it would improve with time.

Philip spent the next several weeks tweaking his new body. He was ever so proud of his accomplishment. And even though it took the miraculous talents of the Visi to handle the actual transfer of his mind into his new facility—he took full credit for its brilliant design. He strutted around acquainting himself with his new attributes and abilities. I was surprised he didn't hurt himself patting his own back, though I had to admit his new body was a robotic wonder. I even helped him with some of his development. After he mastered learning to walk, run and keep himself from crushing things, we went on to more difficult tasks. I gave him lessons in sword play to further develop his coordination, which he practiced religiously.

Oddly enough, Philip required no sleep, though he did give himself down time, as old habits die hard. And after mastering his physical abilities he began working on a plan for moving the warp drives off of Vashia. The idea of building a new ship and returning to our homeland was an incredible motivation. He visited Vashia and looked over the site where the drives lay—his new body suffered no ill effects as he was impervious to the radiation. When he returned to Aura he assembled the Aurian robots and they began building holding containers for the warp cores. The entire process took about a month, and not long after Philip and a task force of robots returned to Vashia to recoup the damaged drives.

I traveled with Philip this time, though I had to stay away from the contaminated area as the radiation was quite deadly even to me. I'm not quite sure how long it took for the Aurians to secure the drives—time on Vashia seemed to run contrary to my internal clock. Things here seemed to move at a standstill. I found it disconcerting and hard to get used to, but my interest in being here was for a different reason. I needed to know how Leanna was doing—was she getting better? I pressed Yllis very hard for information. Finally, my persistence paid off—he agreed to let me see her.

"You understand that if I open the window and allow you in; you cannot speak to her, touch her, or in any way disturb the harmonic vibrations being issued toward her form."

I nodded my head. I had little understanding of what Yllis was talking about. I just wanted to see Leanna once more. Yllis took my hand and we traveled by teleportation to some unknown place. My head was spinning madly when we came to a stop. I fell to my knees waiting for my thoughts to clear. Regaining my senses, I looked around. We were situated next to a pool of water sheltered by a grove of trees. It was quite serene, with the light of day fading, the scent of flowers in the air and starlight reflecting off the water. Suddenly, I caught sight of a glow forming within the pool; it became brighter in intensity. I turned my eyes away and caught sight of Yllis; his eyes were closed and his arms were outspread. He seemed to be in a trance or meditation. I looked back to the pool. The light was gone, replaced now by Leanna's sleeping body. She floated horizontally just inches above the water, her body naked to my view. Her appearance stunned me, not in the fact that she was naked, but that she looked so childlike, young and radiant. I was taken with the transformation she was undergoing. She was regenerating, her hair returning to yellow blonde, her skin a soft, milk-white. This was how I remembered her from my younger days when I guarded her life, and now she lay just inches away. I desperately wanted to reach out and touch her, but a voice cautioned me—do nothing.

I awoke sometime later outside the pyramid. Tiiana was cresting upon the horizon, her morning light bathing me. I sat up and rubbed my eyes, my mind spinning in a thousand directions. What had happened? Had this all been a dream? Did I really see Leanna or was it all in my mind? The thought pestered me for a short time, but in my heart I knew it was real. Leanna was still alive and hopefully, being cured. I yearned to kiss her sweet lips again. I would have to thank Yllis when I saw him next. I was forever grateful.

It wasn't much longer after my visit with Leanna that Philip completed his mission on Vashia. We returned to Aura with the warp drives and Philip began to build our new spaceship. He told me it would be smaller than the one that brought us here as materials were limited, and he only had three hundred robots to help him with the construction. Still, he was optimistic that he could have a ship ready to fly within several months—if all went well. That news left me with a bevy of emotions. The thought of returning home was exhilarating and yet, I had lived here for so long on the moons of Tiiana I didn't want to go—so much had happened to me here. And of course, there were other thoughts. What had happened to Melela and the Melelan Empire? Had our home world managed to survive? Or had the Relcor usurped everything? It was a mystery that begged to be solved.

CHAPTER SIXTEEN

Collision

fter returning to Aura with Philip and the warp drives, I
found myself with little to do. With Philip now fully assimi-
lated into the Aurian Robo-clan, I was totally alone and iso-
lated. None of them had any need for me. I was an extrane-
ous cog in a world of robots and machines, each bound to one
another by digital means. It was disheartening and lonely. A
number of times I tried to engage my friend, but as the days
passed, he became less inclined to spend time with me. I was,
after all, just a useless human—forced to sit back and watch, as
he and the robots built our new ship. I found the matter rather
ironic. Why did Philip want to build it? If he was now truly
more Aurian than Melelan, what was his need to return home?

Left to my own devices for entertainment, I used my energy
to continue my education on the moons of Tiiana. I found a
library within the city, where I was able to access the Aurians'
computer network. It was here that I spent hours studying the
histories of Aura and the other moons. Surprisingly, the communications stone given to me by Yllis seemed to help my comprehension and understanding of the Aurian language. I put in
many hours mastering their long-dead tongue.

Another find was the history of Urlena. The Aurians had an incredible amount of data on the Aquella and their moon, and I was most curious about what had befallen them. Through their pictographs, maps, and pictures, I learned much regarding the Aquella and their sea faring empire before and during the time of the first moon war. I saw with amazement a society that had just reached a golden age—a people who were proud and free. They were reveling in a renaissance of spiritual awareness, art, and scientific discovery. I then saw how they fell.

The Zecla took advantage—they secretly hid eggs on an island called Aquilika. It was a small Aurian transfer point in the southern hemisphere used for trade between the moons—maintained by a small Aquellian tribe. When the eggs hatched under the basking heat of a summer day, the newborn Zecla overran the island, devouring everything and everyone. The Aquella there had no chance. It was only the ocean waters surrounding the island that stopped the creatures from spreading to all of Urlena. The Aquella and Aurians were forced to sink the island, rendering it useless to the invaders. In retaliation, the Zecla launched their missiles at Urlena—aboard were warheads containing the viral seeds of the cloud that decimated Urlena and all her people. Seeing Urlena die left me depressed.

After reading and learning so much about the different moons, I journeyed to the Aurian observatory. I found it empty and filled with layers of dust and debris. I don't think anyone had been here since the Aurian people had died centuries ago. I cleaned the place up and pondered the use of the equipment, surprising myself that I knew how to turn the power on. I put the observatory into motion and turned the telescopes onto the moons surrounding Tiiana. For hours I played with the lenses studying the stars and moons, looking at their features, wondering how things were going there.

I saw the water world of Urlena whirling overhead, her green waters lapping against the islands and continents. I think I even caught sight of the cloud—a small pink form hovering over an island sucking it dry. It made me angry. I felt sorry for the Aquella, having to spend their existence hiding under the waves–it was inhumane. I turned the lens toward Boutal. She was, as I remembered, pristine–her mountains green with trees and oceans a deep rich blue–I could feel her calling to me. I wanted to know how Oolat was doing and how the war between the Brata and Motula fared. Zin was of course in oblivion. I saw nothing on her sphere except for swirling dark, black clouds. She was encased from pole to pole in a violent, atmospheric turmoil, and I had a feeling she would lay dead for centuries–a final rebuke from Philip and the Aurians. Well, at least there was one comforting fact–the other moons were safe now from the Zecla.

Finally, I took a look at Vashia. She lay the most distant, but the telescopic lens of the observatory brought her cool, blue features close to my eye. I watched as her asteroid belt twirled in display while my thoughts ran to my love, Leanna. I realized, ironically, how a part of me lay upon all the moons of Tiiana–I had history with each one of them, both good and bad. It made me wonder how I had come to be here. How different would things have been if Philip, Leanna, and I had not appeared? What would have happened? One thing was for sure, I was ready to leave.

"I have been waiting to hear those very thoughts" a voice said to me.

Caught unaware, I whirled around to find a white ghost-like form floating in the air before me. It was Yllis.

"H-h-how?" I managed to stutter, "How are you able to appear here? Are you able to teleport this far?"

"My journey is an extension through your mind. You are the conduit for my coming."

"So, I'm crazy now–seeing ghosts."

Yllis laughed, if you could call it that. "No my friend, you are not crazy. We've been preparing you for this, remember? And the time has come. Much is beginning to happen."

"What? Is it Leanna?"

"Come to Vashia," Yllis said, fading from view.

I really hated that. Why couldn't they tell me straight out what was going on? Why all the mystery?

I left the observatory hurriedly and headed for the transport. As I made my way, I could see through the dome's casing the airless moonscape surrounding the city. There, appearing in the distance were hundreds of burning welding arcs—tiny fireflies sparkling in the cold night. Aurian robots were everywhere. They dotted a huge scaffold working like ants on the construction of the spaceship. I paused for a second, watching them. It was amazing to see the speed at which the ship was being assembled, but then again they were robots, under the guidance of Philip. They never slept, there were no limits to their physical endurance, and they could work outside the dome with no atmosphere.

The transport room was dark when I entered; the only light available came from the red lights of the warning system. Philip had set it to prevent any unauthorized use. I disabled the function and brought the transport online. That brought an unexpected response. A voice began speaking—it was Philip.

"What are you doing?" his voice asked, over a speaker.

"I have to leave. I'm going to Vashia," I answered.

"I cannot allow that," he countered. "I need you here."

"No, I have unfinished business."

Philip's answer was to begin to shut the transport down. The response made me angry. I furiously began to work the controls. How I knew what to do was beyond me. It must have been the conditioning given to me by the Visi. I worked heatedly, running my fingers over the gem stones. My efforts locked the system, preventing Philip from taking over. I shouted to him.

"I will return when I have finished my work, my friend. Remember, your allegiance is to the Emperor and his daughter first and foremost. As your superior officer in the Emperor's service I am giving you a direct order—complete our ship!"

With that, I entered the transport dais. The overhead light flashed and I was gone. I reappeared on Vashia.

I stood on the dais facing Yllis.

"Captain, I am honored with your return."

My mind was bursting with curiosity. I leapt from the dais, toward him. "You said something was about to happen. Tell me, what is it? Is it Leanna?"

"The Zecla have not been exterminated as you previously assumed," he responded flatly.

"What?"

I felt as if I'd been kicked in the stomach. I didn't know what to say.

"How? Are you sure?"

"Yes," he replied. "We have noted ships escaping Zin's atmosphere."

"But they were nuked–their entire moon is in turmoil."

"As I told you, the Zecla are extremely resilient and resourceful. They have found a way."

"Where are they headed?"

"For Boutal," was his solemn answer.

I was in shock. This was not what I wanted to hear. Yllis pulled close to me.

"Captain, I know you are overwhelmed by the news, and of the challenge to Boutal, but there is still time to prevent the Zecla from gaining a foothold. The future holds many options. Come; allow us to put your concerns in order."

Reeling from the revelation about the Zecla, I followed Yllis out of the pyramid and into the gardens. As before, the day was bright, the flowers were in bloom and everything seemed to be reverberating intensely into a melodic crescendo. It penetrated my very essence and it made my head pound–it was almost more than I could bear. I felt like I didn't belong here–not at this moment anyway. Yllis comforted me.

"I know you are overwhelmed by the magnitude of our harmonic vibrations, but it is necessary for what needs to occur. You will understand shortly–please endure as best you can."

We entered a garden grotto surrounded by tall, red-barked trees with vibrant purple leaves. It was a large, open area, imbued with bubbling fountains and small pools, multi-hued plants, and crystalline rock formations–a beautiful blending of the terrain and flora. I followed Yllis down a meandering, brown clay path, lined with tiny flowers. The air here was fresh and invigorating. We changed direction and approached the end of the grotto where I could see a broad waterfall. It flowed over a translucent, white quartz cliff about twenty feet high and its spray glistened like a rainbow in the light. Kneeling before it was perhaps a thousand Visi, oblivious to our approach. It wasn't until I walked between them that I realized that they were all in some sort of meditating trance. I understood now my feelings of being overwhelmed. It was emanating from them and I had to force myself to stay focused as Yllis took me to the water's edge.

Standing before the waterfall, I watched as the water tumbled and churned, creating an airy mist that rolled across the water toward me. It became thicker, rising in height, turning into a cloud-like fog that was soon above the level of my head. It was now so thick and dense, I could barely see through it, and to some measure it seemed alive. I felt somehow that its subsistence was linked directly to the harmonic vibrations from those who were chanting behind me. From within the cloud I caught sight of movement. A shadowy form was solidifying—it was a woman—a young female dressed in a sheer batiste covering that flowed from her shoulders to her toes. She walked from the mist atop the water in bare feet, her radiant face surrounded by long, dark hair. She was a Visi, a figure true to her physical form and quite beautiful. She approached me, stopping at the edge of the water. It took me a second, but I recognized her, and when I did I almost fainted. This woman, this Visi—it was Ahska. She was alive.

I have always considered myself to be a strong man, but I was stunned to the core, and my knees were shaking. I didn't know what to say or do. I never expected to see this woman, my mentor, alive and well in this form. I felt ashamed, maligning her, as I had. She beckoned me, calling me into the water. I took a step forward, my feet sinking in the mud.

"Roolka," she said warmly, her soft hands stroking my face. "Put to rest your doubts and fears. All that has been said and done has been done so for a reason. Your path, though at times erratic, is a true one. Still, there is much that needs to be accomplished. You must remain strong."

I was overwhelmed—there was so much emotion in the air. "I will try," I replied, choking on my words. "And I place myself at your service."

"Are you ready then?" she asked.

I nodded my head and answered. "Yes."

Smiling at me, Ahska extended her hands outward, and I watched as four silver roped necklaces materialized in her palms. Each necklace held a richly colored seti stone like the one I wore; only they were of different colors. She presented them to me, placing each one around my neck.

"Roolka I am giving you these gems to aid you on the rest of your journey. While you have learned the tongues of many, there are still a few beyond your ability. These stones are your key. They will aid you in your effort to save the people of Tiiana."

"But where am I to go? What am I supposed to do?" I asked in angst.

"Return to Boutal, my warrior son. Join with your brother, Oolat—he is waiting. But before you go, I have one more parting gift."

Again, I was surprised by what she brought forth. In her hands materialized a sword sheathed in a glistening black, leathery material. She presented it to me. I took it in my hands and pulled the blade out. The craftsmanship was magnificent, unlike anything I had ever seen. The blade gleamed with the shine of a polished mirror; I turned it in my hands, feeling its balance.

"This is a craft of the Visi," said Ahska. "It will read the needs of your mind and bend to your will—even the cloud of Urlena cannot dissolve its design. May it protect you on your journey."

Ahska's form wavered slightly. I saw she was fading away. "What of the Zecla?" I asked, quickly.

"The Zecla are migrating to Boutal," a soft, sweet voice said from behind me.

I turned to see who had interrupted my conversation and the sight greeting my eyes caused my heart to pound. There, standing just two feet away was Leanna. She looked absolutely radiant—a fully developed woman with vibrant color in her face, both pink and healthy. I stumbled from the water and closed the gap between us.

"Leanna, my love, my Princess—is it really you? Are you finally well?"

I wanted desperately to sweep her in my arms and kiss her, but I was afraid she wasn't real or that somehow she might break. I saw the twinkle of laughter in her eyes. She clasped her arms around me and placed a soft and gentle kiss on my lips.

"My Captain, my Captain. I am real and I am almost complete. I have just a small amount of mending left, and I will be here awaiting your return. Promise me you will return. I want us to journey home together."

I was confused. My emotions were running amok. My love stood before me, looking as beautiful as the day I found her on Boutal. How could I leave her now? Why must I follow my duty? I think Leanna suspected my hesitancy. She placed two fingers on my lips and whispered to me.

"Because I have been joined with the Visi, I have come to understand more than you. Our future must begin on this path my Captain—there can be no other way. Our journey here was for this reason. Now go, save the moons of Tiiana."

With that she and the other Visi disappeared, fading from my view. I stood alone now with Yllis. The grotto was empty and the intense feelings of harmony had subsided greatly, but I was still overwhelmed. I looked at Yllis, not knowing quite what to say.

"Thank you, my friend," I managed to choke out. "Thank you and Ahska for saving my Princess."

I felt a smile of warmth emanating from Yllis. "You are most welcome," he said. "But come—it's time to go."

We journeyed back to the pyramid and the transport.

✲ ✲ ✲

I arrived on Boutal instantly–amazed once more at the ease and fluidity at which one could travel between the moons of Tiiana. Now that I grasped how to work the transports I wished I understood the process of what made them work, but that would have to wait, there were more important matters to attend to. I looked around. Aside from the light blazing over my head, the interior of the pyramid was dark and quite cold. It felt like no one had been here in quite some time. I moved from the dais, my sword in hand, to the panel, where I passed my hands over the gemstones, turning on more lights. The additional lighting warmed things immediately. Now that I could see where I was going I headed toward the tunnels that led to the outside. It got colder and colder as I came closer to the pyramid's entrance.

To my dismay, the weather outside was extremely bleak. It was freezing cold with gray clouds billowing overhead and it was snowing. The green grass was no longer–it was buried under a thick casing of ice–and I quickly realized I was ill equipped to endure the freezing temperatures outside. The tunic I had worn on Aura and Vashia was far too inadequate to sustain myself here on Boutal. I needed warmer clothing if I were to survive. I stepped outside, braving the cold for a few seconds while yelling at the top of my lungs.

"Oolat! Oolat, my friend. Are you out here?"

There was no response, but that did not surprise me; the winds were too strong. I shivered with the intense cold. The wind coming off the glaciers was biting, and I felt my bare legs burning. I couldn't take it. I turned and ran into the pyramid, rubbing myself to get warm. I made my way back to the control room where the lights gave me just enough warmth to keep from freezing. I thought immediately about returning to Aura to obtain suitable clothing, but I knew Philip was probably angry at being rebuked and that was not something I wanted to deal with. There had to be another way. I began to look around the interior of the pyramid. I sensed intuitively that there was more here than what met the eye—I just needed to pay attention. My investigation soon led me to a small supply room located in a hallway just outside the dais room. There, I found an array of clothing and tools and I realized this was not without good cause—the Aurians would have prepared this place for their own people knowing full well the conditions outside.

I went through the clothing. There were jump suits, hooded jackets, gloves, boots and face masks. They were nicely padded and finished with a silver metallic coating for keeping the heat in and the cold out—the boots even had removable spikes for crossing the ice in safety. I looked though the equipment—there was rope and climbing apparatus, a variety of small ice picks, and several small pouches with folded tents inside. I also found what I believed to be a flare gun. I was overjoyed—this was an invaluable find. Without any further hesitation I dressed. I knew now that I could venture outside without fear of dying. I took a face mask down from the wall. It was properly equipped with dark eye lenses to prevent snow blindness and nose filters to protect the sinuses and lungs from prolonged exposure to sub-zero weather. I took it, along with my sword, and made my way back to the pyramid's entrance.

Fully dressed from head to toe, I exited the pyramid and stepped out onto the ice. The air about me whistled and howled—I felt its angry push. It seemed to be worsening, but I was suited well, and the freezing winds had no ill effect. I looked around; seeking a path that would lead me back into the mountains, but my visibility was obscured by the blowing snow and the waning light. This could be a problem—if the inclement weather kept up I might not be able to make it back to Talith. I had no guides this time, no polaca or even food for that matter. I wasn't even sure if I could find the Solula village on my own. I returned to the interior of the pyramid.

For two days I waited for the weather to break; I was quite starved. I melted ice to drink. Things were so dismal, I was quite ready to return to Vashia or Aura, but something prevented me.

I felt if I returned I was giving up, and I didn't want to do that. Instead, I took to searching the pyramid again. I found no food, but I did find a small cache of weapons—several photon blasters and a microwave rifle. I was overjoyed with my find, though disappointed that the charges on the weapons were weak, and I wasn't sure how to recharge them. Still, with the weapons, clothing, and survival gear now in my possession, I was ready to go no matter what the weather. I loaded myself up—making a knapsack out of one of the tents, and I set off for Talith.

My boots crunched crisply on the new snow that lay on the ground as I left the pyramid. It was intensely bright—the clouds had parted and Tiiana was shining lambently overhead. My vision would have been shot within hours had it not been for the face mask I wore. I began to climb upwards to the trail that led into the mountain passes. This would not be an easy journey. The ice covered trail was thin and dangerous and the craggy cliffs could easily tear the clothes from my back—still, there was little choice. As I made my way up the hillside I had a measure of good luck, though my inexperience could have cost me my life. I was unaware that there were fierce creatures that lived this far north, within the extremes of the glaciers. On my previous trip I had traveled in a group and we saw no wild beasts during our journey, but now I was alone and vulnerable. That was enough for the pack of animals that had stumbled upon my trail.

I'm not sure what made me turn around to look behind, perhaps a habit, glancing back to see where I'd been, but when I did, I saw movement on the snow. There were five of the things—large, bear-like creatures sporting white fur, cumbersome in size, yet quick and agile. They loped after me, quite assured that I would brook no real fight, that I was a fresh kill in the making. I smiled at my good fortune and my stomach growled as I pulled the microwave rifle from my shoulder. I looked through the scope and flicked the switch to turn the weapon on. I heard the whine as it charged, a small red light blinking just adjacent to the scope's cross hairs, readying me to its progress. It turned green and I was ready.

I sighted and fired at the beast leading the pack. It was a quiet, noiseless pulse that discharged without recoil. The results were instantaneous. The creature's head exploded as the micro burst lit its brain on fire, dropping it dead in its tracks. The other beasts were thrown into a tizzy. They skidded to a stop and began to mill about, sniffing the air and the blood-soaked snow. I fired again, this time catching a second one in the chest. The blast tore the creature apart with blood and guts going everywhere. I really hated weapons like this. They were vile, disgusting things good only for killing and not in a clean way. Still, without the rifle I would be facing an onslaught of these beasts who wanted nothing more than to chew on my bones. I watched now as they ran for their lives.

Retracing my steps, I slogged through the snow back toward the creatures I had just killed; their blood was already freezing. Using my sword I skinned one of them, cutting off a hind quarter, which I sectioned into smaller pieces. I then set my rifle to low, and gave the meat a short microwave burst, cooking it. I was seriously hungry and I filled my stomach. These bear creatures were a much better meal than the rat dogs I had eaten on Urlena. With my immediate needs met, I used my sword to fillet several more pieces of meat, which I cooked and packed into my makeshift knapsack. I now had enough meat for a week or more. I left the rest of the remains where they lay, knowing it would keep the others busy and off my trail. I started off once again for Talith.

For the next three days I traveled, making my way over the mountains—my back glued to the side of the cliffs as I edged myself along the narrow trail. It was tough going, my progress hampered by slick, icy rock and loose stone. It was especially difficult at night when I feared falling over the precipitous cliffs in my sleep—there were drop offs where I could not see the bottom. I tied myself to the rocks with rope to keep me from falling, and I slept very lightly. On the fourth day my difficulties lessened. I left the cliffs and entered an area where the path broadened and vegetation grew—evergreen trees and fresh grass. I was taken aback at first, but then I realized months had passed since I had left Boutal. It occurred to me that in the lower elevations it must be late spring or possibly even summer. My assumptions were confirmed when I found an abundance of melting snow and running water–there were also other noticeable signs of life. I pulled the hood from my head and the mask from my face and took a deep breath. It was definitely warmer and the gait of my walk increased.

As I headed toward the lower elevations I found my mood upbeat and I quite literally forgot where I was. I was so preoccupied with my mission and my desire to get to Talith, that I failed to realize that I was no longer black–that my color was a brownish white and that the Solula had never seen anyone of this color. To make things even more suspect, I was walking through their land dressed like an alien from outer space. These are things you can forget, until you realize you are looking at the end of a sword, held by a creature with a very short temper and a very suspicious mind.

I spoke very quickly.

"I am Roolka!" I stated aloud, in fluent Solula.

My speech caught him off guard. I raised my hands to show I was unarmed. I then slowly reached down and unbuckled my sword belt–it fell to the ground.

"I am looking for Oolat, my great warrior brother."

Two other Solula exited the trees nearby and joined the one with the sword. He looked at them and commented.

"This one says he's brother to Oolat."

The two creatures looked at me with suspicion.

"Oolat's brother was black," one of the others said.

"I am heading to Talith," I continued. I have come to learn about the war between the Brata and Motula. I fought the Brata who kidnapped Solula from Talith. Take me there and I will prove my words."

The third one suddenly chimed in. "I smell meat. "You carry darta meat?"

I pulled the makeshift knapsack from my shoulder, and tossed it to the Solula.

"I killed two white snow creatures that lived up in the ice. I carry their remains—it is yours. Take some."

The eyes of the Solula got very large. They shot signals of curious disbelief between themselves. The leader of the three spoke again.

"I have heard it said that Roolka was a great warrior, but two skarra? You have no wounds or scars. Even a war party of Solula would have taken some injury."

"I had help from Ahska," I answered.

That response seemed to answer everything. They lowered their weapons and ripped open the knapsack. The meat was quickly divided and we sat and ate. I was pleased to share my bounty, though I was curious as to why three such agile hunters would be in need of food—it seemed uncharacteristic. I bided my time, allowing the three to fill their stomachs. When they finished they agreed to take me to Talith.

It was good to travel with Solula again—I felt at home and we made good time. On the way my three companions filled me in on some of the events transpiring since I left Boutal. It seemed that the Brata had indeed defeated the Motula and their armada of ships. The loss had devastated the empire of King Hazadek and had thrown the Motula people into desperation. The Brata were raiding the continent at will, taking whatever they pleased. The Motula population now lived in chaos and fear. Even the Solula were affected. They too, were being attacked by the Brata. Even the darta were scarce, which explained why my three companions were hungry. I asked what weapons the Brata carried when they attacked, fearing that they had blasters, but that turned out not to be the case. Whatever weapons the Zecla had furnished the Brata had been exhausted—that was a good thing. And yet, this moon was still a mess.

We entered the village of Talith and I was excited to finally be back in a place of comfort. I was greeted warmly by Markeea, but I sensed sadness in his being. I knew he had lost his beloved, Lakona, back when she and Leanna had been kidnapped by the Brata. I cursed myself for not being able to rescue her from Zin.

I knew her death had been most unpleasant, but in truth, her spirit had been lost even before Philip had blown up the place, and nothing I could have done would have changed things. I felt guilty. Worse though, was the news of Oolat. He lay inside Markeea's home in a coma healing from wounds sustained in an engagement with the Brata. Markeea confided his worries to me as he led me to his home.

"His wounds have healed adequately, but his heart is heavy. He sleeps without waking and his body is waning. He believes you to be dead and that he is at fault for leaving you unprotected—this hinders his recovery. Perhaps your arrival now will give him solace and hope."

I nodded my head, realizing now that I should have returned earlier to let Oolat know that I was okay. Why had I waited so long? We entered Markeea's home and I was taken to a small room where I found Oolat lying on a bed of woven blankets and furs. He lay on his back recluse in a deep sleep and our entrance did not cause him to stir. I crossed to his side and knelt down. I laid my hand on his arm.

"Oolat, it is me, Roolka. I am here by your side. I am not dead and I have returned to Boutal. You need to wake up—we have work to do."

I saw a twitching movement in Oolat's closed eyes. I knew he heard my voice, but there was nothing more. I spoke again, but the results were the same. What was I going to do? I sat on my haunches and thought. I even said a quick prayer asking Ahska for her advice.

Markeea entered the room. He asked if I needed food or drink. I replied no, I was fine—it was getting hot though. I took off my coat. Now that I was inside, I no longer needed its protection. It was then that I realized that Ahska had answered my prayer, for encircling my neck were the seti necklaces she had given me. I pulled the amber colored one from over my head and placed it around Oolat's neck, setting the stone over his heart. I then placed my hand around the other stones I wore and closed my eyes—I thought hard, relaying a message to my friend.

"Oolat ... Oolat ... Can you hear me?"

I felt myself drifting. Everything became white and misty. It seemed I was entering a fog, a deep cloud that hindered my view. I walked aimlessly through the mist calling out Oolat's name. I yelled aloud that Roolka had returned. There came a response.

"Roolka is dead," a sluggish voice responded.

"Then how is it that I am here," I answered.

"I am dreaming–another nightmare," came the reply.

"Must I take my sword and challenge you again, my friend? I nearly bested you when we fought at the death of your mother."

I heard a snort. "I was distracted."

"I have been with your mother. She sent me back to help you and Boutal."

There was no response.

"She lives on Vashia," I continued. "Her mind and body are young again. She gave me a seti stone so that I might communicate with all the races on Tiiana–it is how I am talking with you now. Oolat ... it's time for you to wake up."

A large, dark figure moved toward me in the fog. I saw the mist swirl as it came close. It was Oolat–he stood like a zombie, uncertain and confused.

"Is this how you live?" I asked. "It seems rather bleak, for a warrior as great as you."

There was no response. My friend just stood, looking dumbfounded. I pulled my sword from my side.

"Ahska gave me this sword when we visited on Vashia. She said it was created by the Visi–and they are known for their healing mastery."

I pulled the blade from its sheath. It glinted here even in the fog. I stood back and swung, catching Oolat on the side of his arm with the dull side of the sword. I didn't want to cut him; I just wanted to wake him up. He flinched from the blow. I swung again catching him on the other side. He rubbed his arm–I was getting his attention. I moved back and swung, hitting him on the leg. It caused him to snarl. I moved around and hit him on the buttocks–again a growl ensued. I moved around him striking him hard enough to get his attention—each blow seemed to bring him closer to awareness. Suddenly and without warning he reached for his blade. He still seemed dazed and lazy, but he pulled it out and responded to mine and our dance began. I took it easy—but I continued to smack him and he did not like it. His anger grew.

The mist swirled around us as we fought and with each strike our blades clanged and resounded sharply. He was getting faster and more responsive—I could see the dullness fading from his eyes. I was ecstatic. It felt good to fight my old friend again. It was just like our days training in Ahska's camp when I first came to Boutal. He was there for me then, and I, for him now. The fighting became furious—I would not let him stop. I was bound to free him from this dream world. It took only a few more minutes and Oolat's power began to exceed my abilities. He pressed me hard, moving faster and faster, his bulk and the force of his blade backing me into retreat. I was losing and it felt great. Suddenly his blade smacked against mine, and my sword flew from my hand—Oolat pressed the point of his blade to my neck. I opened my eyes.

Oolat lay on the bed before me. His eyes were open—he was staring at me.

"You are out of practice," he said.

"And you are awake," I countered, the smile on my face stretching ear to ear. I called to Markeea and told him we needed food and drink.

It was two more days before Oolat was up and on his feet. He told me how the Brata had attacked him and several other Solula as they were securing provisions for a return trip to the pyramid. The attack was unprovoked and caught them by surprise. The Brata had suddenly appeared, flying overhead—they began throwing rocks at the hunting party in an effort to steal their bounty. During the engagement, a stone had struck Oolat in the head; rendering him unconscious—he had lain that way ever since. I felt bad. I apologized profusely for abandoning him and Boutal and I told him of my journey to Zin and Vashia. I told him of my visit with Ahska and I shared my vision of her through the seti stone. What I didn't expect was that he would receive his own message through the stone—one to which I wasn't privy. It was an emotional reunion for him and the event bound us together even tighter than before.

Later, as Oolat and I took a short walk, he returned the seti stone he wore.

"Here," he said, handing me the necklace. "It gives too many dreams—they hurt."

I nodded my head in understanding and placed the necklace around my neck. He then foretold his last vision.

"Ahska says to tell you that the Zecla have arrived."

"How? Where?"

Oolat shrugged. "I have no further knowledge."

I was in a quandary. If the Zecla were already here, where were they hiding? How would I stop them? Boutal was a large moon to say the least. I confided my concerns to Oolat—both of us realized that the Zecla would devastate Boutal if we didn't find a way to stop them—especially if they linked up with the Brata.

I had so many questions running through my mind, but Oolat was getting tired—he was still recovering and needed rest. We headed back to Markeea's home and I asked him no more about the Zecla or his visions. Instead, I queried him about the Brata—there were a number of things that didn't make sense.

"Why do you think the Brata attacked you with rocks? They are such fierce fighters—their attacks are usually with sword and knife."

Oolat shrugged. "I cannot answer," he replied. "The party was small—perhaps five or six. Their numbers may have been too few for a direct attack."

That made some sense, but my mind was still spinning with questions. "What can you tell me of the war between the Brata and Motula?"

Oolat rubbed his head—the spot where the stone struck him. "I have heard the Motula lost much of their fleet. Only a dozen ships returned. They lost many men."

"And the Brata?"

"Not much is known. Some say the Motula cannons destroyed their birthing fields, but I do not know for sure."

Oolat's answer had a measure of plausibility. If the Motula armada had inflicted damage on the Brata, it might explain their desperation. It also might have made matters worse. If they were hurting from the war, they would be more apt to link up with the Zecla. I knew now it was time to move; immediate measures were needed if I was going to succeed in stopping the Zecla.

"Thank you, my old friend. Now get some rest. I have much to do and I want you well when we journey from here."

He clasped me on the shoulder, and entered Markeea's home, as I left to seek the Council of Talith. I needed their help. When the three elder Solula members convened with me, I explained the situation, informing them that Boutal would soon be invaded. I spoke of my experience with the Zecla, letting them know that their arrival could spell the end of life on Boutal as they knew it. They agreed immediately to spread the word to other Solula villages.

I also needed a polono and supplies. Markeea was most helpful in organizing those needs. He even blended me a potion, allowing me to dye my skin black again. It was a temporary solution, but I knew if I was to learn anything from the Motula in the lower villages I would have to look like them. I bathed that night and darkened my skin to that of a Motula warrior.

With the dawn's light Oolat and I began our travels—I was chomping at the bit. I was dressed again as a warrior, riding a polono, though I carried the weapons I brought from the pyramid—the blasters and the microwave rifle. Our destination was the Motula mining villages in the lower mountains. I needed to speak with the Motula people and learn what had transpired on Boutal while I was gone. I was worried that I would find Zecla along the way. It was a cold thought.

CHAPTER SEVENTEEN

The Artonian Desert

olat and I made good time leaving Talith, even though it was necessary for us to stop periodically to rest. He was out of shape from lying on his back too long and I was out of shape from being away from Boutal. I was hurting. My entire body was once again unaccustomed to the heavy gravity and my legs and buttocks were sorely in need of reacquainting themselves with riding a polono. To regain our prowess Oolat and I returned to our daily timeworn ritual. Each morning upon rising, we began our day with a sword fight. It toned our muscles, honed our skills and brought our kindred spirits back into harmony. It was our therapy and our preparedness for the battle that loomed on the horizon. We both needed to be ready.

Each day we traveled through the mountains was a day of renewed strength. The exertion and fresh air were a welcome change from the sterile air of Aura and my body responded well. My only concern was the feeling that something seemed out of place. Even Oolat commented on it. We both sensed that the forest was awry. It was eerily quiet and we saw little sign of wildlife, only a few birds and no darta at all. We both sensed a negative vibration in the air–the moon of Boutal was on edge.

After journeying for four days, we came upon a small mining community. I slid from the back of my polono and observed the mine from the safety of the trees. There were only a couple of wooden buildings, a sluice and a saw mill next to a creek. As for signs of life, we saw none. I studied the mine's entrance, looking for activity, but saw nothing. The place seemed deserted. Oolat and I entered the area carefully and found that it had been deserted for quite a while. The place had been stripped clean. We made camp there that night and headed out the following morning.

Two more days passed and the terrain we traveled began to change. We moved from the high mountains to hills covered by deciduous trees, to a lower basin of grassy rolling hills. We were entering the Cassandra Pass—a large open prairie that separated the continent's two major mountain ranges. I knew that there were farming villages and hamlets located here—we just had to reach one. So, we headed east, paralleling the tree line, keeping our exposure to a minimum.

The first farming hamlet we came across was almost nonexistent. It appeared that a fire had swept the village and most of the buildings had burnt to the ground. Those few that remained were deserted. It was a dismal sight, and it left Oolat and I with little choice, but to press on. We sought out the next community, hoping to find it occupied. As luck would have it we reached the next village near nightfall. Hidden against the shadows we watched, observing a dozen or so homes in the distance. I was perplexed—much of the area surrounding the village was scorched and blackened like the first village we'd passed. Had there been a fire here too? That fact seemed oddly coincidental, especially considering how many homes had once dotted the area. As darkness fell we saw a few lanterns—at least I knew there were people here.

With the morning light I journeyed alone to the village. I was uncertain about the relationship between the Solula and the Motula, and Oolat and I wanted no trouble with the people who lived here. I approached the dwellings atop my polono, and found myself immediately unwelcome. Bows with arrows were pointed at me by two old men and several women. In the background were children. A number of them stuck their heads out trying to garner a better look at me. I raised my hands to show that I meant no harm.

"My name is Roolka." I said aloud. "I am traveling alone and in peace. Can you tell me what happened here?"

The first old man scowled at me. "You know what happened warrior. Now get away before I set loose this arrow for your heart."

I took his warning seriously and backed my polono away. I had no desire to pull an arrow from my chest. I withdrew to the trees where Oolat waited. I was almost to him when he ran from the trees pointing and yelling.

"Brata! Look! In the skies behind you."

I turned on my polono and saw the grouping in the sky. They were too far away for me to see how many there were, but they were headed straight for the village. I heard a bell ringing. The warning bell of the Motula—they were being attacked. I didn't hesitate to respond, neither did Oolat. We both headed back toward the village—he on a dead run, and I, on my polono in a heated gallop. I saw the people in the village scattering. They were trying to reach the safety of their underground shelters—I could hear children screaming and mothers yelling. It was chaos.

There were about twenty Brata and they were closing rapidly. I knew that Oolat and I would be no match for so many in a simple sword fight, so I brought my polono to an abrupt halt, yanking its neck hard. I forced it to the ground, using it for cover as I pulled the microwave rifle off my back. Oolat fell to his knees beside me.

"What are you doing?" he asked with panted breath.

"There's too many," I said, flipping the power switch on my weapon. I heard the hum of the rifle as it warmed up. I handed Oolat a blaster.

"Here take this—press the red button. When they get close, point it at them and squeeze the trigger."

Oolat nodded his head and pressed the button; the blaster gave off a high pitched whine. I took aim with the rifle, sighting the lead Brata within the cross hairs. I squeezed the trigger and heard the pulse of the rifle. The lead Brata exploded in mid-flight, his blackish blood falling like rain on the ground below. The sight of their leader exploding before their eyes immediately brought chaos to the rest of the group. They scattered like birds uncertain of what to do. I fired again repeatedly, and with each pulse, Brata fell from the skies. I was surprised by their tenacity. Outmatched by a superior weapon I would have thought they would have fled, but this was not the case. They were intent on this village and I soon saw why. There was a child sitting, exposed and unprotected in the field just ahead—they were after him.

My weapon ran out of juice and fell dead. I threw it to the ground and pulled out a blaster.

"Come on!" I yelled to Oolat.

The two of us headed toward the child, though Oolat passed me as if I was standing still. I covered his advance with my blaster, firing the weapon at the Brata who were circling overhead. He scooped the child up in his arms, but not before receiving an arrow in his arm. Someone from the village shot him, thinking he was going to harm the boy. I heard him yell out, but I was too busy taking on the Brata to render any aid.

Unlike the microwave rifle, blasters are noisy and inaccurate. They fire with a wide spread, taking out a multitude with each burst. I only got two more shots off before the weapon fell dead, but it was enough to bring down another six Brata—eight remained. I whipped out the flare gun and fired the incendiary weapon into the air at an incoming formation of the gargoyles. It exploded amidst them, searing four more. They fell to the ground writhing in pain. I heard Oolat firing his blaster. He took out another two, before his weapon went dead as well. He threw it to the ground and reached for his sword. There were two Brata left. The two of us prepared for their attack—fortunately they came after me first, for Oolat was hampered by his wound and the child he carried. I saw him put the boy under his arm and snap the arrow's shaft, leaving the head embedded in his shoulder–he moved toward me with sword in hand.

The Brata flew in between us trying to separate us. To them, I was the smaller, easier target and I was forced to roll onto the ground to miss being impaled by their initial pass–it was a close one. I heard Oolat yelling, telling me to be careful. Suddenly a woman ran toward us–the child's mother. Oolat tossed her the boy and ran toward me–we stood back to back as the Brata came back around.

As ironic as it might sound, I was bred for this–at least in my mind. Our few days of practice had helped prepare me for this battle and I felt ready. I was even eager to fight these cannibalistic creatures once again. They flew low and fast, within close proximity, their swords waving, and the fighting ensued. Admittedly, the Brata had an advantage with their ability to fly and the open sky to maneuver in, but I had the blade given me by Ahska which bolstered my confidence. It was my first real fight with my new sword and I was not disappointed.

Our battle went on for some time as we parried with the gargoyles–the two beasts were fluttering about as they sought to sever our heads. Unexpectedly we had a surprise–help from the villagers. The two old men and several women were converging toward us with bows and arrows in hand. They loosed their arrows and the Brata nearest me caught one in its side. It wailed in pain, snarled, and fell to the ground. As it tried to squirrel away I pierced its heart with my blade and it fell still.

I turned to Oolat. He was still engaged, but it wasn't for long–several more arrows flew and the gargoyle he fought fell, mortally wounded. It flopped on the ground in agony. Oolat approached the creature prepared to slay it. He raised his blade, but I stopped him.

"Wait! I want to see if I can talk to it."

He looked at me.

"With the stone." I motioned to the necklaces around my neck.

He stepped back as I approached the creature. The gargoyle watched me with hate filled eyes–its blackish blood seeping out onto the ground. It waved its blade at me, a warning to keep back as it struggled to crawl away. I wasn't sure how I was going to accomplish getting a stone around its neck, but my attempt was short lived at best. Someone shot an arrow; it pierced the beast directly in the skull. It fell back, collapsing lifeless to the ground. I looked up to see the old man who had warned me away earlier that morning.

"They're no good unless dead," he stated. I nodded my head in agreement, sheathing my sword.

I looked around the village. The few remaining Brata that lay on the ground still alive were soon dead. The women of the village saw to that. They beat them to death showing no mercy or emotion. I wiped the sweat from my brow. It had been a good and successful fight and it seemed that no one had been harmed, except for Oolat.

"How's your arm?" I asked.

"A scratch," he answered.

I took a look—it was more than a scratch, but nothing critical.

"I am sorry." I heard a female say. "I did not know you were trying to save my son."

Oolat and I turned to the Motula woman who spoke.

"May I dress the wound? I am a healer."

I looked at Oolat. This was good. This was our chance to find out what was going on.

"Please," I said. "If you would be so good as to care for my friend we would be grateful."

I turned just in time to see the old man picking up the blaster Oolat had dropped in the dirt. He handled it to me gingerly as if carrying a bomb.

"Here, this is yours," he said, adding quickly. "You're not from here are you?"

I shook my head as I tucked the blaster into my belt. We then headed after Oolat and the woman who had offered to treat him. Halfway to her home we were interrupted by a loud, distant roar coming at us from behind. Everyone stopped and looked to the horizon. There, hovering low against the distant mountains was the sight I feared most. It was a rocket ship. I could see the booster flares shooting from its back end. It was descending slowly behind the mountains, somewhere in the far reaches of the Aritonian desert. I heard the old man comment.

"Third time this month I've seen that. I wonder what it is?"

I took a deep breath and said nothing. We then entered the Motula woman's home where she began to tend Oolat.

Our visit to the Motula village provided me with a great deal of information regarding the status of Boutal. While Oolat's wound was cleaned and dressed, I learned what had transpired here. Since the loss of King Hazadek's armada, the other city states, led by Coralis and Phratis had sought to press things to their advantage—they had declared war against Casita. Consequently, Hazadek was in need of a new army to defend his throne. His edict was to conscript every able man over the age of twelve into his service and any village that refused was burnt to the ground. Many rebelled and they faced Hazadek's wrath. The loathsome tyrant needed to be dethroned.

Oolat and I spent the night in the village, where we rested and broke bread with the villagers. The following morning they provided us with dried meat and meal for our journey, enough to last us a week or better. We said our farewells and headed west toward the Aritonian desert where the Zecla rockets were landing. I realized now that it made perfect sense for the Zecla to choose the desert lands of Boutal. The terrain and weather were hot and dry—similar to Zin, and the ocean would provide a source of water. It was all that they needed.

As we traveled, I told Oolat of my worries. I told him of my mission on Zin—what I had seen. How the temperate zones on Zin were abhorrent of life, the decay I witnessed, and how the Zecla devoured everything. He was chilled by my tale and neither of us wanted to see it happen to Boutal. Our journey now was one of peril and we made haste through the Cassandra Pass toward the broad expanse of the Aritonian desert.

For five days we rode west, then south, keeping to the edge of the mountains and trees so we wouldn't be seen by the Brata or the Zecla. Even though I knew the Zecla had landed much further south, I had no idea of what their reconnaissance might be. Would they have scouts in the desert moving north to investigate and explore the area? To be sure, I wanted to remain close to the mountainous terrain, in case we had to make a sudden retreat.

The following day our journey took us past the western outposts of Hazadek. They were still deserted, decimated by the Brata the year before. The King no longer had the resources or the men to sustain his reign this far west. I looked over the structures. Some were still in pretty good shape, and might be of use to us later.

Three more days went by and still we saw nothing. I was worried that we would need to turn west and travel out into the open desert. If this became the case, our cover would be gone, and we'd be exposed and vulnerable. My concerns were unfounded. On the morning of our fourth day we found something that chilled us to the bone. We stumbled onto a number of darta carcasses along a hillside; they had been picked clean down to the bone. There were also traces of the silk-like webbing I'd seen on Zin—I knew we'd found the Zecla.

Oolat and I exercised extreme caution now, I dropped from my polono and we moved on foot. For safety, I hid my riding beast in a narrow ravine, one dense with profuse vegetation. Then, with swords drawn, Oolat and I picked our way though the rough-hewn terrain. I sorely wanted to pull out my blaster, but its charge was extremely weak, and I had no desire to use an advanced weapon that would draw our attention unless absolutely necessary. We walked for more than a league before finally coming to an area that had been cleared of trees. The sight greeting us was ghastly. The hills before us were laid barren—the entire forest cut down. Why? Why were the Zecla harvesting trees? What were they building? My heart was racing as we altered our direction.

With vegetation no longer available for cover, Oolat and I were forced to move further back and up into the hills where shelter was still to be found. This new turn forced us further away from the desert floor, but it granted us a wider vantage point. From our new height we could easily observe the desert that lay west of us–it was all stripped bare, looking raw and wanting. I was disgusted by what the Zecla had done. Already they were laying claim to Boutal's bounty.

We moved again, heading south, creeping from one hill to the next looking for their encampment. We darted between the trees and rocks, and at various points, crawled upon our knees to stay out of sight. Our efforts soon paid off. We reached the base of another hill and began to edge our way to the top. There were loud noises coming from up ahead. I peeked over the boulders near the top and cast my eyes on the scene below. I was aghast at what I saw. There were Zecla everywhere–far more than I had anticipated–well over two thousand by my estimate, and they were very busy.

As far as I could see, all the terrain to the south, right up to the sea itself was stripped clean. Timber lay strewn in huge piles; many of the logs were already skinned of their limbs and branches. It was evident that the Zecla were widening the scope of their endeavor, cutting away more vegetation, including the hills to the east of us. They were extremely efficient and moved like ants, dragging fresh cut timber and vegetation in a never ending stream toward the settlement. They worked in teams, some shearing the logs with small axes, others rolling the cropped timber toward the sea. There were also a large number of soldiers armed with blasters and swords. They guarded the perimeter of the encampment, and the Zecla who were foraging in the hills. Both Oolat and I caught sight of a number of lookouts on several nearby hills. I had no idea how good their eyesight was, and no desire to be seen. If we were spotted we wouldn't get out alive.

For what seemed an eternity, Oolat and I crouched behind the rocks studying the movements of the enemy. In the desert, two rocket ships were being dismantled. The Zecla were using their framework to construct a new hive dome–it was rising up in the center of their habitat. They were using the ship's outer skin to seal the black monolith in darkness. Seeing the black dome rise set an ominous tone—it meant that the Zecla had a new Queen. I also saw that near to the hive, they were excavating a deep channel to divert ocean water. Timber was being used to shore up the loose desert sand. This let me know that the Queen would be laying her brood soon. I wasn't sure what her gestation period was, but judging from the fortifications, the Zecla were prepared to defend her and their endeavor at all costs.

I gave Oolat a worried look. Neither one of us could believe our eyes. This was a massive undertaking by the Zecla. How were we going to stop them?

Oolat's expression was equally grim. "What should we do?" he whispered. "There are far too many for us here."

I nodded my head in agreement. "We're going to need an army."

Suddenly we heard a roar in the sky overhead. We looked up and saw a ship descending, plumes of white hot flame thundered from its rear as the ship's booster engines slowed its descent to the desert floor. I tapped Oolat on the arm–I could see that the Zecla were preoccupied with the arrival of this ship–this was our chance to get away without being seen. We withdrew from the rocks and made our way back over the hills.

Oolat and I didn't talk. Aside from not wanting to be caught by the Zecla, both of us were too overwhelmed with what we had just witnessed. How many more Zecla were arriving with this new ship? How many more ships were coming to Boutal? The thought of a hundred thousand Zecla arriving on this moon scared me to no end. How were we going to stop this invasion? To make matters worse, I now had Ahska's voice ringing in my head.

"Save Boutal," she kept saying. "Save Boutal."

How in the world was I going to do that?

We were almost back to my polono when Oolat and I were stopped dead in our tracks. Somewhere up the hill we heard a crashing sound, as if someone were thrashing through the brush–the sound was getting closer. Oolat and I pulled out our swords and separated. We took cover behind the trees and waited. Almost immediately, six Zecla came into view. I

watched as they passed through the trees, heading downhill–
their path was coming much too close for comfort. I took in
the six spider-wasps. Two were armed with sword, one soldier
leading the group, another bringing up the rear. In between
were four worker drones. They were laboring with something heavy; it was giving them great difficulty as they passed
through the brush. Almost immediately I realized they were
carrying the body of a young Solula–a slab of meat for harvest.
I was livid. The sight of a helpless Solula in their arms brought
back memories of Lakona and Leanna. I could not allow this
to happen again. I looked to Oolat, making the sign of cutting
one's throat with my finger. He nodded in understanding and
awaited my cue. Soundlessly, we moved into position.

We allowed the Zecla to pass so their backs were to us when
we pulled from the trees–we attacked from either side. I came
around my tree and swung my blade, slicing the head clean off
the rear guard before he knew what happened. His head rolled
onto the dirt like a ball bouncing downhill, while his body
dropped like a sack of flour. Oolat was immediately on top of
the Zecla carrying the body of the Solula, wielding his sword
like a machete. His blade crushed the first worker, halving its
head in two, dropping it to the ground. The other three were
panic stricken. They released the body they carried and tried
to bolt, but the body of the young Solula was heavy and bulky.
It fell to the ground atop them, trapping two underneath–the
result securing their immediate deaths. Oolat beheaded them
as they squirmed on the ground while the fourth scurried off
into the forest–Oolat hot on its trail. I, in turn, was left with
the Zecla warrior who stood in the front, ready now for my
attack. He gave a nasty hiss as I moved toward him–our blades
clashed.

This was my first real battle with a Zecla warrior. While I
had been attacked from behind in the pyramid and I had killed
many on Zin–this was my first real face to face battle with a spider warrior and it was brutal and savage. We fell to blows, our
bodies twisting and dancing amongst the trees. I was surprised
how the creature reared up so it could equal me in height, its

four arms flailing at me. Fortunately, the creature was not yet used to the heavier gravity of Boutal and I pressed this to my advantage. I fought angrily and hard against my adversary. It took all my strength to fight this red spider-wasp with its four legs, four arms and mouth full of razor- sharp teeth. I quickly learned that it spit–a vile, sticky substance that burned the skin. I felt a spattering of it on my arm–it was like fire. I think the venom was designed to blind its intended victim and I did my best to avoid being hit again. Of utmost concern to me was its poisonous stinger, a shank to be avoided at all cost.

I cannot say exactly how long we parried; my adrenaline was pumping so hard I had no recognition of time. I hacked and stabbed at the creature, sinking my blade into it as often as I could–its body was very resilient. It was fortunate that my arm and blade were longer than his, and I was a better swords-man. As we scurried back and forth across the terrain it tried to pin me against a tree so it could impede my ability to move. The maneuver failed and I severed two of its hands in response and when it reared up to flail me I countered with a deep pen-etrating thrust to the underside of its torso. I heard a deep wail and blood gushed from the wound. The Zecla stumbled back and fell, collapsing to the ground in agony. I went after it like a wolf on a wounded rabbit. I severed its stinger and hacked off two of its legs. It couldn't run now.

Oolat returned—he was breathing hard. I motioned to him to wait. He planted the tip of his sword into the ground and did not interfere. I approached the Zecla cautiously. I wanted it dead–I was severely prejudiced against these creatures, even more so than the Brata, but I needed to learn from it. The Zecla raised its blade in an attempt to fend me off and I hit it with my sword, knocking it away. It was defenseless now, but I held no confidence. It was mortally wounded and still very dangerous.

I called to Oolat. "What of the other?"

"Dead," was his reply.

I walked around the Zecla that lay on the ground in front of me. It watched me like a snake, glaring at me with its black, oval eyes. As I moved to one side it struggled to crawl away and snarled viciously when I stopped it. I took one of the seti necklaces I wore around my neck and threw it on the ground. The creature looked surprised; it glanced from me to the yellow stone. I spoke to it for the first time.

"Pick it up." I pointed to the stone with the tip of my sword.

The creature snarled at me, but complied—it picked up the stone with its one good hand. The connection between us was immediate. I felt its pain and the rush of hate-filled thoughts lashing out toward me.

"Why are you here?" I asked.

Though surprised by our telepathic link, the creature wasted little time. It immediately began assaulting me with vicious threats.

"You will soon die Aurian dog. My Queen will feed her pups on your bones and we will devour everything on your moon."

"I am not Aurian," I responded.

"It matters not. We are here now—this is our new home. We take it all."

I didn't like what I was hearing.

"How many Zecla are here?"

The creature snarled. "Millions."

I knew it was lying. I caught glimpses of chaos emanating from his mind—the exodus from Zin had been a catastrophe of epic proportions. Countless ships had attempted to fly in the face of hurricane winds—most had crashed and burned. Still, many others were being made ready for flight and there were thousands of Zecla warriors still alive. I also saw a young Queen being groomed—some sort of impregnation ritual—and the dome being made ready for the eggs she would bring forth. What was unclear was the number of weapons they carried. I risked a dangerous ploy in an effort to garner more information.

"You are a poor excuse for a warrior," I sneered. "I think the Zecla are leaving the defense of their Queen to their females." I leaned down a bit and leered at him. "No, I am mistaken—a blind female would have given me a better fight."

I sensed a heated rise in the creature, but he said nothing. I looked over to Oolat and made an offhand comment.

295

"Look Oolat, they don't even trust this pitiful minion with his own blaster."

I laughed; the insult hit its mark. I caught the creature's response—a quick rambling of conflicted images. *Weapons destroyed. Worry. Technology lost.* I then saw another image—Zecla cannibalizing ships—forging new weapons. The creature averted his mind—I lost his fleeting ruminations. I stood and moved to one side. I taunted him again, waving the point of my sword in his face.

"No matter, Zecla, I got what I needed. You've told me all I need to know. I will now destroy you and the rest of the Zecla, just as I did when I nuked Zin and gutted your fat pig of a Queen!"

I thought the creature would go berserk. Even with its mortal wounds and lack of two legs, it leapt for me, screaming and foaming at the mouth. It spat at my face. If not for Oolat, I could have been seriously wounded, but he was on top of the creature instantly, ramming his blade through its midsection, nailing it to the ground. It squirmed in agony, castigating me through our mind link, filling me with their intentions, their desire to suck the very life out of everything. I saw firsthand through its eyes how bleak the future lay for Boutal. I pulled back, raised my blade and cleaved its head from its body. The connection between us was instantly severed.

Oolat looked at me wide-eyed. I think he was hesitant to ask what I'd learned. I took the seti stone necklace from the creature's dead hand and threw it to him. The link between us was established and he quickly learned all that I knew from the Zecla. He threw the necklace back to me.

"What are we to do then" he asked. "Do we just give up?"

"No," I answered. "There's got to be a way to stop them—but it will take more than the Solula and Motula to make it work. First, we need to get out of here. More Zecla are bound to come looking for these six."

I motioned to the bodies that lay in the dirt. Oolat nodded in agreement. We then looked at the body of the Solula that was lying stiff in the dirt. There were a number of nasty looking wounds upon its body.

"He's been stung repeatedly," I noted. "He will not live."

"Is he in pain?" asked Oolat.

I shrugged my shoulders. "I don't think so, but I cannot say for sure."

"I must return him to his tribe—for proper burial."

"I understand," I responded. "It is unfortunate that the Solula have to learn of the menace they face in this manner."

I sighed. My thoughts were dark and heavy with the prospect of what lay ahead, but suddenly a thought struck. I knew that somehow, for some reason, I had to return to the pyramid at Luskia. What I needed was there. I confided my thoughts to Oolat.

"Take this young warrior to his home," I instructed him. "Allow his tribe to bury him as a warrior—then contact every tribe of Solula. Have them move north to the mountains where there is still snow—the Zecla dislike the cold, and will not venture there unless they have to. We need to prepare for the battle.

"What are we to use for weapons, Roolka? I saw the vision from the Zecla. They still have cannons, bombs and blasters. We cannot match them with swords alone."

"I will get us the weapons, my friend, along with people who can help. But we need to move quickly."

With that resolution, Oolat and I set off on our respective journeys. He went inland, carrying the body of the young Solula, and I back toward my polono. I agreed to meet him in two weeks at Luskia, if all went well.

CHAPTER EIGHTEEN

The Valley Of Ghosts

had seven days of hard riding before reaching the Luskia valley. I had forgotten how mountainous the terrain was and how dense the vegetation, not to mention the cold. These factors caused me to deviate from my path, taking precious time away from my mission. It was fortunate that two Solula came to my aid–they took me directly to their camp near the pyramid. I should not have been surprised by their appearance. They said they had been awaiting my arrival–that Oolat had called out to the wind, warning all the tribes of the invasion by the Zecla. There was now a mass migration in progress with every Solula tribe heading north. They informed me that Oolat had requested their assistance–he knew I would need help in gaining entrance to the pyramid. I was pleased. It was good to know that I had help, especially if the Brata or Zecla were to appear. I also appreciated knowing that the Solula were moving north out of harm's way, even if it was for a short time.

At morning's first light we began to look for an entrance to the pyramid. This proved easier said than done. Nearly a year had passed since my last visit to Luskia, and the snow and rains had shifted the terrain, obscuring everything around the pyramid. I couldn't even see where we had dug the earth away from the pyramid the first time. After prodding the grounds for two days, we widened our search to the sloping hills that fell away from the pyramid and I stumbled across the shallow cave I had tried to dig the year before. There was new growth obscuring it, but I had a feeling about this spot. We began to excavate and soon had a shallow tunnel carved into the hillside. Our digging was easier this time, as the soil was more cohesive. The monsoons hadn't started yet, and we weren't encountering the runny sludge like before.

With the Solula's help we dug about ten feet a day. We could have dug faster, but timber had to be cut and split in order to shore up the soft, moist soil surrounding us. The work was hard and labored. It reminded me of my years as a slave, in the mines on Urlena, sweating in my own filth. I hated those memories and it was only my purpose here that kept me going. Soon, we were sixty feet into the hillside and it was getting difficult to breath. The air had become stagnant and we had no real light to guide our efforts as the lanterns kept burning out from the lack of oxygen. It made me wish for an Aquellian light globe or purple seaweed to chew.

Fortunately, we caught a break—we reached a wall of hardened mud. It was dry and solid, with a finished look, as if built by someone. We hammered our way through it, opening a hole which led to another tunnel free of mud. I could feel the air moving now—it blew gently upward into our faces from someplace distant and unknown. I took a lantern and peered inside—it was pitch-black, but I was not to be deterred. I hoisted myself up and over the mud wall, passing though the hole we made. I dropped down on the other side and began to walk, leaving the Solula behind with the task of widening the opening.

My footsteps were muted as I descended into the darkness on a path of stone. I sensed a familiarity with this place—was this where I had come through? How I arrived on Boutal? I looked at the brick work surrounding me; much of it was worn and crumbling. This tunnel had been built a long time ago. Thank heavens, it was still passable. I followed the path not entirely certain where I would end up, but I was absolutely ecstatic knowing that it led somewhere.

At the end of the stone path I found another opening that widened into a yawning cavern of blackness. At my feet lay a new pattern of stone tile. I was standing on a plateau of some sort, its end blocked by a short wall. Beyond the wall was a vast vacuum, silent and empty–I had no idea how large it was or how far it went. The light I carried was swallowed by the darkness. I looked behind to see where I had come from. In the far reaches of the tunnel I could just make out a small pinpoint of light. This triggered a memory, a reaffirmation of my birth on Boutal. I knew now that I had reached the entrance of the pyramid.

I stepped inside and looked around. On either side of me, descending deep into the bowels of the edifice, were stairs. I chose a direction and began to descend. I was forced to walk with extreme care, keeping one hand pressed against the wall for support, the other holding the lantern. The stairs were steep and covered with loose dirt, and my footsteps echoed coldly in the void–it seemed to take forever to get to the bottom. The process made me wonder–how did I climb out of this place so long ago—with a fever yet? It was inconceivable.

Finally, I reached the bottom. I waved the lantern, seeking a direction to take, but saw nothing. I decided to follow the wall–eventually it would lead to something. My assumption was correct. Not more than twenty steps I ran into something I had never encountered before in any of the pyramids. There was writing on the walls–hieroglyphics, pictographs, words, and diagrams. Were these the written instructions on the inner workings of this place? I ran my fingers over them–noting the pictures of the moons, their people and animals–some I recognized, others were a mystery. I marveled at the color and detail, though my scope was limited to lantern light.

Excited by my find, and eager in my thirst to learn more, I decided to shift my search. I knew the transport dais was probably located in the center of the pyramid and with it would be a control panel and lights. I turned my direction to what I thought was the center of the structure and started walking. After wandering a bit I ran into the control panel near the dais. I recognized the gems that were imbedded on its surface. They were not configured quite like the ones on Aura or Vashia, but I understood their purpose. I ran my fingers over them, pressing here and there, and soon heard a quiet hum. Suddenly, a glow began to materialize overhead. The lights were coming on. I shielded my eyes as their intensity increased.

I stood for several minutes, blind as a bat, peering through the cracks between my fingers as my pupils slowly adapted. What greeted me was incredible. The pyramid was enormous—larger than any pyramid I'd been in and I realized now that ninety percent of it lay hidden deep within the terrain of Boutal. No wonder no one knew about this place.

My eyes raced to take everything in. There were paintings everywhere—a virtual history of the people who had built this place. There were also five large consoles, circling outward across the floor, and there were more panels set against the walls—it was machinery that I could only guess at. What did all of this do? Why was there more here than in other pyramids? My mind whirled at the wonder of it all and my heart pounded with excitement.

From somewhere above I heard a voice calling down to me. It was Oolat. I looked up to where I heard his voice, but the light impeded my view. I hollered to him.

"I'm down here. Take the steps, but be careful, they're steep."

Oolat was at my side within minutes—he gazed silently at the wondrous scenes that were depicted all around us. Most displayed images of the races near to their respective moons. We found Boutal with her people—the Motula and Solula. Zin with her races—the Zecla and Brata. But strangely, the others were less familiar to me. The people of Urlena, Aura and Vashia no longer appeared quite the same. Oolat pointed to them.

"Who are they?" he asked.

"Those are the Aquella," I answered, pointing to a group of men standing near Urlena, "though their skin color is now greenish blue. And those are the Aurians—they're all dead. I know of them only through the pictures I saw on Aura. And those are the Visi. Judging from these pictures this was their physical form back when the pyramid was built. It would seem that they've changed quite a bit. I wonder what happened."

Oolat and I spent the next several days working in the pyramid. There was so much to see and learn—it was overwhelming. I had a million questions and so little time. I started with what I was most familiar—the dais in the center. I knew it was used for traveling from moon to moon, and it controlled some of the physical aspects of the pyramid's inner workings, like the lights, but there was so much more here. There were the other console banks lined with gemstones set at different intervals along the floor. What was their purpose? Were they computers? Electrical relays, switches, or something else entirely?

I felt helpless in my frustration. My wonderment regarding the science before me was compounded by my fear that the Zecla were building their army; that they would be ready to move soon. And I had to be ready in order to stop them. This made me painfully aware that I needed to figure out how things worked here. I needed a plan. I needed weapons. I needed help.

I spent hours wandering the pyramid looking at everything, trying to fathom the secrets that lay within, but I seemed to be getting nowhere. The majority of the consoles were silent, unresponsive to my touch, and I realized the knowledge I'd garnered on Aura was not nearly enough to solve this gigantic puzzle. I was missing the key. I finally sat down with my back against one of the consoles, too tired to do anymore. Oolat lay nearby, snoring away in a deep slumber. I rested my chin in my hands and pondered the hieroglyphics before me. I took in the colorful moons of Tiiana looming before me on the wall—red, blue, green, yellow and white. Those colors had initiated the pyramids on other moons. Why didn't they work here? What was I missing? Surely the builders of this great pyramid would have left some sort of message? I fell asleep.

I began to dream—I was in a small air vessel, traveling through the clouds over Boutal. On the ground below I could see a pitched battle–there were Zecla and Brata–they were in violent conflict with another force. I couldn't see who–the clouds were obscuring my view.

A voice spoke to me. I turned. Yllis was seated next to me.

"Captain ... do you know why you are here?" he asked.

"No," I muttered hazily, "because I crashed ..."

"You are a man from the stars."

"Yes."

"Born to lead the moons of Tiiana?"

"Lead? How?"

"Captain ... What burns brighter than the moon or the stars in the sky?"

"I'm not sure ...

"Would you not say that love burns brighter?"

"Yes, I suppose ..."

"And where does your love reside?"

"Within my heart."

My head shot up from the console. I was wide awake. I looked around the pyramid and saw no one. Had I been dreaming? Or had Yllis really visited me? I got up and began to walk around. I looked at the paintings on the walls–there was a clue here–what? I looked at the five moons circling Tiiana. Urlena was sea green, Zin, a dark red, Boutal, a rich amber, Vashia, white and pure–suddenly something clicked–it was the color. I reached for the necklaces that dangled upon my chest–they rested just over my heart. I looked down at them, fingering each one–they were each a different color–red, blue, white–*each color matched the moons on the wall!* Of course! Why hadn't I seen this before? Each necklace the Visi had given me represented a moon. I walked to the wall of the pyramid and looked at the images depicted there. My mind spun. What was the connection?

Oolat approached me from behind. I had awoken him.

"Are you at it again?" he asked.

"I had a dream," I answered. "Yllis gave me a clue–it has something to do with the seti stones."

Oolat nodded his head and yawned.

"Good, tell me about it later. Right now I really want to sleep. This light, it's brighter than Tiiana, and it's keeping me up. I'm going outside."

I almost died. Oolat's words hit me like a tidal wave. I looked at the light overhead–it *was* beaming down on us–just like Tiiana! I looked at the consoles laid out on the floor. Why were they situated at disjoined intervals? I looked back to the artwork on the wall. The moons were orbiting Tiiana at similar intervals. I looked at the consoles. They were orbiting the light, mimicking the picture. They were positioned in the same spherical arc as the moons on the wall.

I raced over to the closest console and stood before it. Where was I? I counted out from the center. One, two, three, four–this one was Boutal. I peered at the console, studying its format. I ran my fingers across the gems, looking for—suddenly I saw it—a small, empty indentation. It was missing a gemstone. I felt for the necklaces at my neck. I pulled them off and selected the amber one.

"Wait!" I yelled to Oolat. "I think I found the answer!"

I pressed the stone into the empty spot; immediately lights began to flicker and illuminate on the console panel.

"Yes!" I screamed.

I raced to the next console–it was Urlena. I looked for the missing stone. There it was. I placed the green necklace stone against it and the console began to respond. I ran to the next– Aura. She was blue. I found her empty spot and placed the stone. I didn't wait to see what happened, I was on to Zin, then Vashia–she was the last. Every stone was now in place.

Suddenly, before my eyes, the entire pyramid sprang to life. Every console was ablaze and the world with the entire pyramid seemed to explode with unbridled power. In mid air, images began to appear–holographs of the moons, their people, diagrams of the pyramid–I had found the key. For several minutes I watched dumbstruck as the moons twirled and rotated in motion above our heads. I now saw holographs of Aurians, Visi and Aquella–they floated over their respective consoles–each looking at me. They bowed. I was speechless.

I glanced at Oolat. He was as spellbound as I. Neither one of us knew what to do next. I collected my thoughts.

"Can you understand me?" I asked, in Aurian.

The three holographs nodded to me. "Yes, we understand," they replied.

"The Zecla are invading Boutal," I said. "I need to stop them, but I need help. The Motula and Solula have no resources to stop the Zecla. Can you help us?"

My question was answered before I had the words out of my mouth. I heard a grinding noise and I turned to see a wall on the far side of the pyramid rising. Behind it lay an armory—lights blinked on and I saw an array of weapons unlike anything I've ever seen. I moved toward the arsenal room. Inside were blasters, light cannons, microwave rifles, communications devices and of all things a small flying craft—the same one I saw in my dream.

For the first time in days I thought now that we might have a chance, but there was still much to learn and coordinate. To make matters worse, I still needed to raise an army. The Solula alone would not be able to repel the Zecla. I would need the Motula also, and Aurian robots, if Philip would grant me access. And what of the Aquella? Would they join this cause? Or were they too lost under their sea of despair? Did we really need them? Or was my resentment toward the fish men coloring my judgment? I had so many questions. How would I ever find their underwater city again?

I spent the next two days training Oolat and the other Solula in the use of the weapons we found in the armory. There were more Solula arriving every day and I wanted them to have a fighting chance. I put Oolat in command of his people and had him establish a perimeter around the valley to ensure that we would not be caught by surprise. We placed microwave cannons on the hills overlooking our position, and every Solula carried a blaster. Though I wanted to keep our location a secret, things were moving quickly. We needed to be ready—just in case.

When I wasn't involved with planning our defenses for Boutal I was inside the pyramid learning. The computer generated holographs residing there were an invaluable wealth of information. They expanded my knowledge of the moons and their races and granted me access to additional resources. I was shown where other pyramids lay hidden on the different moons. Some were shrouded underwater, as with Urlena, while another lay underwater on Boutal near the horn of Myolic. Others, however, were concealed underground like Luskia, though most were no longer viable—they were either off line or had been destroyed during the war.

As we spoke, the holographs were analyzing all the transfer points and making available to me options that might make my efforts and plans more successful. In the interim, they relayed to me their account of the war, the history of the pyramids and the abandoning of Luskia. I learned that Luskia's demise was due to an unfortunate accident. The war was going badly. Boutal was the only moon free of Zecla and not under attack. The Aurians were here experimenting with a new bio-weapon designed to repel the Zecla when the weapon accidentally discharged, and the containment fields were breached. Everyone in Luskia was forced to flee Boutal and head back to their own moons. The aftermath left Luskia lost to the eons. Everything had lain dormant until now.

The bio accident on Boutal had even affected the Motula and Solula. Though the two races were never really cognizant of the moon war, the Aurian weapon had decimated the valley. No one passing through the valley ever made it out alive. And so, for over a thousand years, the races of Boutal avoided Luskia, calling it the Valley of Ghosts. I knew now why no one had discovered this pyramid—no one from Boutal had lived to tell about it.

With my knowledge of what had happened here in Luskia, I was bound and determined that it wouldn't happen again. I knew I had to find a way to keep this war clean and simple, if such terms can ever be addressed to war. There had to be a way to stop the Zecla without destroying Boutal in the process. But how would I accomplish this? Even nuclear weapons had failed on Zin.

I knew in my mind that I was spinning in a vacuum. I needed fresh data on the enemy. Over two weeks had passed since our last reconnaissance. At what stage of conquest were the Zecla now in? What was their rate of progression? How did things lie? The flyer in the armory was the answer to my prayer. It was small and agile, a craft of Aurian design, built originally for their movement upon the moons. The holographs gave me instruction on how to pilot the craft; it was a marvelous piece of technology. With it, I could spy on the Zecla, high against the clouds, even if the Brata were nearby. It was well suited for our reconnaissance.

With the help of several Solula, we carried the craft from the armory to an underground flight deck conjoined with the pyramid. There, Oolat and I removed the domed canopy from the top of the craft so he could sit inside—his frame was too large otherwise. Though my Solula brother never said anything, I don't think he was too keen on flying, but as my co-leader his help was invaluable in assessing the situation on Boutal. As we climbed in and buckled up I promised him I would take it easy. I don't think my answer assured him.

I pressed several buttons on the instrument panel, and was surprised by the power that surged through the craft. It levitated from the ground in an effortless motion. I looked over the instrument panel—a couple of lights were burned out, but the gauges were registering and I saw nothing to raise any concern.

I looked over to Oolat. He appeared tense.

"Are you okay?"

He shrugged and I tried to set him at ease. "Look, I know you've never done anything like this before, but there's nothing to worry about. I've flown dozens of ships like these, and I've never crashed. Just pretend you're on a ship, sailing. It'll be like floating on waves."

"I don't like water," he replied, sourly.

It seemed my words were falling on deaf ears and I decided there was nothing more I could say to quell his fear. I turned the control wheel and edged the power shift forward. There was a gentle hiss from the anti-grav drive, and the craft moved forward into the darkness, our heading; a runway that led off somewhere into the depths of a tunnel. We floated for almost a league, guided by the soft headlights emitting from the ship's forward section. They illuminated our journey through the runway's subterranean access.

The daylight at the end of the tunnel came at us unexpectedly and we flew out into the morning air, exiting through the mouth of a cave. I heard Oolat gasp as the ground fell away. He grabbed his seat and the side of the craft with his hands, white-knuckled. I wanted to laugh, but dared not. I understood his flying with me was a major undertaking and he deserved my respect for getting on board.

I turned our aircraft around and faced the mountain, hovering just over the treetops. I wanted to give Oolat a chance to catch his breath and I needed to see where the entrance to the cave was. It was quite ingenious. The mountain's orifice was well shadowed by trees and rock. No one would ever guess that a runway lay just inside. Knowing our return point, I took our craft high into the thinning atmosphere of Boutal. It got cold quickly and I was thankful I was prepared.

High in the sunlit sky I practiced with the ship's controls, assuring myself that I understood piloting the ship. The craft was easy to navigate, not unlike other craft I had flown while in service to the Emperor. I loved flying anyway and this craft had a simple elegance to it. It hovered and floated silently with ease and could fly at several hundred leagues per hour when pressed to full throttle. Even Oolat was coming around. His eyes were wide with wonder as the land below us fell to miniature and the clouds which he thought solid proved to be an illusion, melting at his touch.

It wasn't long before we left the mountains behind, our heading taking us over the prairie lands of the Cassandra Pass. At this point we saw nothing that gave us pause. We passed over the western outposts of Hazadek and I slowed our speed so that we might investigate them better. They were still deserted.

Moving further south we crossed into the drier desert lands. Here, I stopped the ship. We hovered near the clouds and glassed the terrain with binoculars I'd found in the armory. I knew at some point we would spot the Zecla; it was only a matter of time. An hour later and three quarters of the way into the Aritonian desert we made our first sighting.

Oolat and I watched a patrol of Zecla moving west; there were about twenty of them. I wondered what they were looking for, perhaps food, or maybe a place to establish a new outpost. I took out a writing instrument and a piece of paper, noting their position from my readings on the instrument panel. We then flew on. Soon the black, ominous hive dome appeared on the horizon. It loomed large as we approached.

At two leagues out, we passed over the Zecla's forward outposts. There appeared to be five defense towers, each one heavily fortified with laser or blaster cannon set atop the steel and wood structures. I surmised that their framework had been built from the dismantled spaceships. The fortifications were substantial. They sank into the sand, and seemed to be connected to underground bunkers. I could see Zecla moving in and out of the shadows, and I wagered that they had tunnels running all the way back to the dome. I made note of their perimeter. It ran in a semi-circle from the hills bordering their east side all the way to the ocean on the west. It was a solid formation, providing protection for the dome by anyone advancing across the desert. I drew a map of their installation.

Upon completing my map and noting their armaments, I edged our ship forward until we were directly over the dome. From our height I easily surveyed the entire encampment. The canal was finished—water filled its form, linking the ocean and the hive. The dome was nearly complete, only the opening at its top remained. With binoculars, I peered down upon the Zecla who were scrambling like ants over the structure. At the rate of their movement I knew it wouldn't be long before the opening was sealed. The Zecla were working on it furiously. Sensing their urgency, I wondered what the status of the Queen was, but even with binoculars, I was unable to see what was happening inside. The interior was too dark.

There was water inside; that was evident. This was a necessary requirement to support the Queen's heavy egg-filled body. It made me wonder how close she was to actually laying her eggs. Though I knew from Philip's comments and my own studies on Aura that her eggs had to be laid in the dark, I wondered if in this case the process was being accelerated. There were, after all, Brata flying about. Undoubtedly, they were working hand in hand with the Zecla to bring her food. Oolat drew my attention. He noted to me the various piles of white bones, darta and other creatures. It was obvious the Zecla were feeding their pig Queen and I wondered: Were there Motula bones as well? Whatever the case, this was not a good sign. It meant we didn't have much time–a matter of weeks at best.

I looked to the east. The scene there was just as grave. The low lying hills where Oolat and I had spied on the Zecla two weeks prior were barren. There were no stumps or vegetation of any kind, erosion was running rampant. The land was carved with deep chasms and crevices. It was like nothing I'd ever seen, and quite ugly. Overlooking the desolation were steel towers armed with cannon. It was obvious that the Zecla were getting ready, fortifying their entire perimeter. They wanted no surprises coming from any direction. I glanced at Oolat–I think he read my thoughts. How were we going to assault this fortress and drive these invaders from Boutal, especially with the Brata covering the air?

As I searched for an answer, I noted the white-capped waves on the water rolling in toward shore. It seemed to my eye that the Zecla defenses were weaker along this front. There were only three towers with cannon pointed toward the sea. Why? I then realized only a few cannons would be needed as approaching ships would be sitting ducks atop the water. Still, this detail gave me pause. Was this periphery their underbelly? I made a mental note of it.

Satisfied that I had the latest information on the Zecla, I turned my thoughts to another issue. This war was to be

fought against two enemies, one of whom I knew very little—
the Brata. Other than being in conflict with them from time to
time, I understood very little about the gargoyles, their habitat or their purpose. I knew that they were originally from Zin,
and were once an enemy of the Zecla. But now they lived on
Bratola, a continent I had never seen—one far too important
not to investigate.

The flight to Bratola took about five hours at high speed,
and along the way we passed over a number of small islands
dotting the ocean. I was intrigued with the fact that each island
we passed held an increasing number of Brata upon its shore.
It then occurred to me that this was how the gargoyles made
their journey from Bratola to Cassandra—island hopping. The
revelation did not comfort me, for the further west we traveled,
the more Brata I saw—they were assembling in greater multi-
tudes and moving to join the Zecla. I knew that once the two
races converged a reign of terror would ensue, and all life on
Boutal would be devoured.

I pressed our airship to its highest level and Oolat and I
raced across the sky heading to the Brata's homeland. Upon
reaching the outer edge of the continent we crossed over a
bevy of volcanic islands. They were varied in size and form, the
majority still active with huge, monstrous volcanoes spewing
lava and ash. It was on these islands that we encountered sight-
ings of the Brata. The gargoyles seemed to relish the rugged
volcanic terrain, still black and dark, with steam rising from
its surface.

As we flew overhead I marveled at the geologic wonder
that unfolded before us. Below us now was a bank of dense,
steamy clouds that stretched for leagues. They rolled over the
coastline in lofty waves, obscuring huge portions of the Bratola
continent. Still, there were hills and mountains jutting skyward through the veil, most covered with greenery. Oolat and
I flew for leagues surveying the mystical terrain, and we saw
just enough. My observations told me that the land below was
rich with abundance and quite ripe with vegetation and life.
It made me wonder—why would the Brata leave this place for

Cassandra? Why had they not settled down here? It had to be their taste for blood and battle. Why else would one leave paradise? With that revelation, I knew we had to reach Casita. The Motula people had to be warned before it was too late. I pushed our ship forward.

On the horizon ahead, nightfall was coming—we were rounding the backside of Boutal and heading into the shadows. Though we had been in the air for hours the closest route home was the most direct, and that was our flight around the girth of Boutal. It would take us across the isle of Colas and to the city of Casita. Once there, I would temper my anger and still my tongue in an effort to reach out to Hazadek. He needed to be convinced of the peril that he and his people faced. Soon, the black darkness of night swallowed us and the stars popped into view. Oolat was stunned by their beauty at this high altitude and we both watched in wonder as the moons of Tiiana whirled and danced overhead, their profuse light illuminating our way.

Neither Oolat nor I slept that night. There was no autopilot on the flyer, so we steered by the stars and compass. It didn't really matter anyway; my mind was consumed with worry. Seeing Aura and Urlena riding high in the night sky made me realize that Boutal couldn't win this war on her own. As much as I loved the Solula and Motula people, they were no match for the Zecla—they would be crushed. I needed help from the races that had started this whole thing. I needed Aurian weapons and robots. I needed the Aquella as well. They had played a part in the first war with the Zecla. If I could convince them to join in this battle we just might save Boutal. And then there were the Visi—it was time for them to do their part.

It was early morning when Oolat and I sighted the isle of Colas. We flew like a jet over her mountains and fertile fields, our stomachs growling with hunger at the sight of darta running in herds below us. Both Oolat and I were famished, but hunting would have to wait. Farms came into view, and finally, a city next to the sea—I believed it to be Phratis. We passed over water again, the straits of Cassandra which separated the two continents. Soon we would reach Casita. Unfortunately, a surprise crossed our path, an armada of ships sailing upon the ocean.

I brought our vessel to rest, hovering near the clouds, as we observed the ships on the water beneath us. There were at least thirty in number and I knew immediately they were sailing to Casita. This was the war we'd heard about in the village, and it was about to get ugly. I throttled our craft forward and headed for Casita. The flight took us three hours at high speed, and it was mid morning by the time we reached Hazadek's realm. We hovered there for a minute, high against the sky, while I glassed the city.

Casita looked dark and sad. There was little movement in the residential areas, and none of the gaiety I remembered from the open market, and certainly no vibrant activity on the docks. I only caught sight of military movements reinforcing the harbor and castle. There were sword wielding soldiers patrolling the streets and the coastline. Wooden towers had been erected with lookouts watching the sea, ready to give warning of approaching ships. Cannon were being moved and placed in strategic locations to defend the city and harbor. Casita was preparing for war. I commented to Oolat.

"We don't have time for this petty foolishness—there's too much at stake."

Oolat grunted in agreement. "How long before those ships arrive?"

"Three or four days—depends on the weather."

"You better get us some help then."

"Yes," I replied, forcing our flyer into abrupt motion. "I've had enough of this."

The city of Casita quickly fell behind us.

CHAPTER NINETEEN

The Moons

I *t was late afternoon and* raining by the time we reached Luskia, and Oolat and I were tired and hungry. Unfortunately, there was little time to rest and much to do. I took a quick meal and a bath. My skin was irritated. I needed to wash off the sweat and remnants of black dye that coated my skin in ugly blotches. The dye, given to me by Markeea, was now making my skin peel, and it itched like crazy. Still, it had served its purpose. Refreshed and oiled with a soothing potion Oolat concocted for me, I entered the pyramid where the holographs were waiting. I briefed them on our findings, informing them that I had to leave immediately. Arrangements had to be made with the other moons. Time was running out.

My first stop was Vashia, and I arrived on the moon of the Visi, finding the pyramid empty. I thought it extremely odd that there was no one in view and that no one came to greet me when I called out. Where had they gone? Why was there no one here to help me, especially in this time of great need? I exited the pyramid and walked the grounds and gardens. The flowers were still bountiful, and blooming with a profusion of color, while the sky was breathtakingly beautiful. One thing was missing, however—I sensed no harmonious music or vibrations. I was perplexed.

Expanding my search, I traveled further out into less familiar areas, seeking a sign of my esoteric friends, but it was difficult to gain my bearing. I had no idea where I was. The truth was I never really understood how the terrain surrounding the pyramid of Vashia was laid out. Every time I came here things seemed different. I think the Visi were very good at making things materialize and disappear at will and my mind was unable to fathom their wizardry. Still, I had to try.

After changing directions several times I finally stumbled onto something that seemed somewhat familiar. The trees were of red bark and their limbs held fragrant purple leaves. Was this the place where I had seen Ahska? Suddenly, I heard a voice—someone was singing a soft melody with a lilting lyric. I made my way toward the sound. Just past the trees I came to a small stream, a gentle, gurgling brook which I stepped over. I looked up to the area from where it flowed and saw a hill covered with green grass. On top of the hill was a large singular tree, its limbs spread out in a majestic form, shading the ground beneath. At its base was a lone figure—a woman. It was Leanna.

To see her sitting there alone was a miracle. I raced to her, covering the distance in seconds. She looked up at me and smiled. I stopped and knelt by her feet.

"Rez, my love. I've been waiting for you. Come, sit with me." She patted the grass next to her.

I was confused. I wanted to speak, but the words would not come. I could only stare at her. She was so beautiful. Her large eyes were so blue; they beckoned me. I obeyed her wish and sat, and as I did, she placed her arms upon me and drew me near. She kissed my forehead. I felt my head sink against her soft breasts. I was so tired, and the rhythm of her heartbeat called to me.

"Sleep, my warrior Captain, sleep," she whispered. "It is time for you to dream."

To say that I was perplexed by the Visi and their methods was an understatement. For some reason they felt there was a need to communicate with me on a subconscious level. As I lay on Leanna's lap, falling under her trance, my mind was running in a thousand directions. All of the anxiety I carried was running rampant. Plans had to be made. The war was coming. The Zecla were on Boutal. I needed the Visi's help. I needed to go to Aura and Urlena. Why was no one paying attention? Suddenly I heard music and voices, chanting in a slow rhythm. It was very calming. I stopped my incessant chatter and inquired as to what was going on.

"They are singing to you," Leanna whispered.

"Who?"

"The angels of time."

I was confused. "What?"

"Listen ... listen to their sweet voices," she instructed, "breathe in their song. Yes ... that's it. Slowly ... breathe in ... relax ... float upon their wings ..."

I felt myself sinking deeper and deeper into a gentle fog. I was floating on air. My thoughts slowed, coming to a complete stop. I heard Leanna speaking, her voice calming me further, and slowly I fell into a more complete euphoric state.

"The Visi cannot join you in this fight today, my hero, my Captain. Their will is no longer on this plane–they are one now with a higher order. All they have given has been for Tiiana, but in memory, they're willing to grant one last wish–you will have time."

I slept for days? Weeks? A year or more–I have no idea. All I know is that when I awoke on the hillside I felt the best I ever had. Totally invigorated, I sat alone thinking of Leanna. I wished the young girl who had stolen my heart was here beside me, but things were different now. Her manner had changed. I was no longer certain that she was a physical being anymore. She seemed more Visi than Melelan, and yet, that was okay. I knew I should feel resentful of this fact, but I didn't. I still had my mission. I needed to rid Boutal of the Zecla.

The walk back to the pyramid was uneventful. I saw and heard no one—the moon of Vashia was eerily quiet and vacant. The interior of the edifice was also empty so I programmed my journey to Aura and walked to the dais. The light from above consumed me and I disappeared, not realizing at the time that I would never return to Vashia again.

✳   ✳   ✳

My arrival on Aura was in direct contrast to my peaceful exit on Vashia—it was noisy, raucous and nerve biting. There were sirens wailing, red lights flashing, and three robots in combative mode moving toward me. I barely had time to step back and pull my sword. My reaction was instinctive, but it proved life-saving. I swung at the closest one, a silver giant who pulled a blaster from his side. My blade sliced down catching his wrist—his metal hand falling to the floor. I was stunned—my blade cut his hand off. I moved back and away. The three tried to encircle me. I evaded their grasp. Why were they moving so slowly? They were robots—sorely faster than me. I was bewildered, but I had no time to think. They were nearly upon me and I was in for the fight of my life.

I whipped my blade, darting between their giant bodies, ducking and flailing at them with my sword. I gasped in disbelief as white hot sparks flew, my blade passing though their metal sheathing as if they were made of butter. They began to short circuit. Within seconds the three were disemboweled, their hydraulic fluids ebbing onto the floor, their wires cut and dangling. I watched as they thrashed about, jerking in spasms, their circuit boards sputtering. They were unable to comprehend their loss of movement. Unexpectedly, I heard a voice from behind.

"What have you done? You have slain three of my Aurian brothers! Who are you?"

I turned to see Philip standing there, his blue eyes pulsating. There were more robots behind him. I placed the tip of my blade against his chest. I saw its point melt into his sheathing.

"I could ask the same of you," I answered, heatedly. "What has become of you? Are you Philip Golan? Or are you some dead Aurian living in his head?"

His answer confirmed my suspicions.

"A little of both, I'm afraid. Why are you here, Captain?"

"Because I need your help. The Zecla have invaded Boutal. They have a new Queen and they've built a dome. The Solula and Motula will never be able to defeat them on their own–I need you and your robots."

I saw Philip's consciousness waver. How I was able to sense this I did not know, but I could tell he was in contact with someone else. He began to speak.

"The Aurian council says they will give you weapons. Whatever you need, but the robots must stay. We have to finish the ship."

"No!" I shouted. "That's not good enough! How can you expect a group of primitive Solula and Motula to wage a war with weapons they don't understand? They don't have the knowledge or the experience–and I don't have the time to train them!"

"Nevertheless," he began.

I charged toward him and glared up at his face plate. I pressed the point of my sword against the underside of his chin. His metal skin buckled and yielded to my blade tip. I was ready to shove my sword directly into his robot brain. I shouted at him and the Aurians who were lurking somewhere in his head.

"Let's get one thing straight you empty-headed pricworms. You're the ones who started this mess. You cheerfully invaded the moons of Tiiana two thousand years ago thinking how grand it would be to make contact, meet new species, and learn new things. And yet you never gave any thought that you might be throwing off the balance of evolution when you established contact with these other races—that some of them weren't ready. And to make matters worse you didn't even bother to study or investigate the Zecla before you gave them full access to the transports. No! You are guilty! You are guilty of being blind and stupid. You started the moon wars through your self-inflating arrogance and the price paid has been far too high. And if you don't do everything in your power to correct this situation right now, I will make it my personal mission to rid the moons of your very existence forever."

I turned and darted back to the console that governed the dais. None of the robots flinched. My fingers flew across the gemstones. The light overhead pulsed in response, and I moved to the transport.

"Wait!" a voice shouted. It was Philip, but it wasn't. There was more than one voice resonating. "You are right. We are at fault. And we agree that we must help. What do you want?"

"I want every robot you can spare, with as many weapons as you can transport. I need hovercraft, vacuum bombs, and communications devices—everything short of nukes."

"Where?"

"Send them to Luskia."

"Luskia? You activated Luskia?"

"Yes," I answered, disappearing from view.

✳   ✳   ✳

I had no idea what to expect when I arrived on Urlena. It had been over two years since my escape from the moon, and I was near death from my encounter with the rat-dogs. My memories here were mired in fear and desperation. This time I was better prepared. With my blade ready, I surveyed my surroundings. The interior of the pyramid was in deplorable condition. Dirt, dust, and rubble lay everywhere, along with piles of bones. I remember that the cat creature was in here when I left. Was this her lair?

With extreme care, I moved from the dais to the control panel. I wasn't sure how long the light overhead would remain on. It seemed to be waning a little and I didn't want to get caught in the dark. I found the console and looked it over—it was missing a gemstone. I took the green seti necklace from my neck, relieved that Luskia no longer needed the stones to function. I placed the gem in its spot—there was a surge of power. Suddenly, the console lit up and I saw activity within the room. An Aquellian holograph sputtered to life.

The Aquella began to speak to me, but I couldn't understand what he was saying.

"Aurian! I need you to speak in Aurian."

"How may I assist you?" he asked.

"My name is Rez Cantor. I have journeyed here from Luskia. I need to speak with the leaders of your people."

"Allow me to call them for you." he said.

"You don't understand," I interjected. "There is no one here. Your city—this place you call home, was decimated two thousand years ago—by the Zecla."

"Yes, yes ... I remember now—my memory was shut down. It is sad that I have been away so long. How may I assist you?"

"Your people fled to the sea. They are living under the water—where they mine a silver ore. Do you know where this might be?"

A holographic map suddenly appeared. The Aquella pointed to it.

"I have some recollection that there were certain tribes— the Aquita and the Anoni who were researching the possibility of moving our people under the waters for safety. Perhaps they are the ones you are seeking?

"Did they mine a silver ore?"

"That is a distinct possibility. I am uncertain—our moon has many mines. At one time it was our chief export. Would you like me to show them to you?"

"No, that will not be necessary. Where did the Aquita and Anoni live? Can you show me on this map?

Several points of light illuminated on the holographic map. "Where are we?"

Another point of light illuminated—the distance between where I was and the islands that the two tribes had inhabited was quite far—almost half a moon away.

"When I was on Aura I learned of an island called Aquilika—it had a pyramid used by the Aurians. Where is it?"

A fourth light ignited on the map—it was much closer to where the tribes had lived. The question was—was the pyramid still viable? Could I transport there? I asked the holo.

"The pyramid of Aquilika lies underwater. If it still stands it would have to be activated from within using the seti stones you carry ..."

The holo reiterated what I had learned on Aura.

"... You see this is the location through which the Zecla invaded Urlena. We were afraid they might try to access our moon again. The pyramid was uncoupled from the Aurian link and sunk beneath the water after the island was destroyed. We could take no chances."

I was unhappy; this was not the answer I wanted to hear. How was I going to find the Anoni or the Aquita? Even using the maps I'd seen on Aura, the seas on this moon were vast and for me, uncharted. I could swim for years and not find any underwater cities—perhaps I should swim out and make contact with the Dolla? They could help. I didn't like the idea—swimming out into those cold, monster-laden waters again was entirely unappealing. Still, something had to be done.

"Is there something I can help you with?" the holo asked again.

"No, I'm just thinking to myself ... I'm trying to figure out how I can reach your people."

"Perhaps, I could call them ..."

"We went over this before," I responded with exasperation. "Your city was destroyed—"

He cut me off. "You Aurians think you know everything," he bristled.

I was surprised. It seems I'd struck a nerve.

"We do know how to communicate through other means," he relayed, indignantly. "Your race is not the only one with advanced technology!"

I bowed my head. "My humblest of apologies, my Aquella advisor. I meant no disrespect. I would be honored if you could contact your people. I have a very important message I need to convey."

The holo responded with what I felt was a smile.

"I will send out a message," he stated, coolly. "The Aurian ambassador is presently in Alanth requesting an audience." He then faded from view.

I was thrown by the events that had just occurred. Did these people have communications technology that still worked? From what I had experienced in the mines I had my doubts. But then, there were the light globes, and the holographs, and that electric beam thing that had killed the rat-dogs in that Aquella home long ago. Yes, I suppose there was a chance that somewhere on this godforsaken moon there might be some method of communication I was unaware of. But how would I know if the message was received? Would anyone even come? After all, two thousand years or more had passed since the first war. Was anyone still listening? I left the console and headed for the stairs. I needed to clear my head and it was time to see what lay outside.

The light from the sun and the reflection from Tiiana made things exceedingly bright outside. I had to shield my eyes as I ascended the stairs. At the top of the stairs I peered out through the open doorway with my blaster drawn. I was nervous of what might be waiting to greet me. My fears were unfounded. I was greeted by nothing—just a windswept breeze coming off the ocean. I looked over the plateau, noting the dismal looking yellow clouds floating overhead, and the roofs of the white marble city that lay beyond.

The top of the pyramid was a mess. The marble urns that had once lain in a symmetric pattern around the edge of the plateau were now broken, the pedestals on their sides—rubble everywhere. The city, what had he called it? Alanth. It was even more desolate and forlorn than before. Entire sections lay collapsed with rock and debris filling the streets. The place looked like it had been hit by a massive earthquake. I wondered if all this had been done by the cloud. It was disheartening.

With few options available, I decided to head to the docks to see if anything of use might be found there. I walked down the stepped facade of the pyramid with my blaster in hand and no real idea what I was doing, but there were three choices: return to Boutal empty handed, jump in the water and swim, or give the holograph a chance to make contact with someone. I was really hoping for the third choice. I really had no desire to swim the waters of Urlena again.

I walked the streets of Alanth for the better part of an hour. The process was a weary one as piles of rock from the fallen buildings stymied my way at every turn. In tiresome effort, I crawled and stumbled over loose piles of marble and rock. It was worse than before, and I could see the demise of this city was accelerating. The forces of nature were rapidly taking over. Plants and trees were encroaching into the city from every direction, while the rain and wind weathered the stone to dust. Things were returning to their natural state.

My hands were sore from climbing over piles of rock, but I was almost to the docks. I could hear the roar of the ocean, the waves beating against the shoreline—I wondered if I would find anything there. I was not overly optimistic. There had been nothing two years ago, why would it be different now? I ascended a hill of rubble, pulling myself up over the loose rock, hoping for a better view. Suddenly my attention was drawn to my rear. I heard an old familiar sound, a cascade of scurrying rat noise followed by low growls and yelps. I looked behind; it was like déjà vu. On the debris-laden streets below was a large pack of rodent dogs converging together into a cohesive unit. There were perhaps forty to fifty of the filthy, slathering vags following my trail. I pulled my blaster from my hip. I'd waited a long time for this.

Without wasting a second I fired, centering my aim on the densest portion of the pack. I was eager to repay the disgusting wretched creatures a hundredfold for the pain they'd inflicted on me. My first shot obliterated at least half of them, and sent the rest scattering like leaves in the wind. I looked at the smoldering, burnt carcasses that lay in the dirt. Seeing the bulk of them dead felt good. Putting my blaster back in its holster, I made my way further up the hill. I knew the others would be back. I certainly hoped so. I wanted to kill every last one of them.

I crested the hill and continued on my way without further incident. The streets ahead of me were open and free of any danger. It would be a while before the pack would have the courage to challenge me. They would be too busy eating the remains of the ones already dead. I reached the docks and as I expected, the whole area was even bleaker than my previous visit. The foundation supporting the stone stairways that led to the water and street were crumbling, half the buildings lining the wharf had already fallen. Between the storms, the sea, and the pink viral cloud, everything was falling apart and being reclaimed by the moon. I was beginning to think I was wasting my time—there was nothing here worth waiting for. It was time to return to the pyramid and forget about the Aquella. I would find another way to take on the Zecla.

I was just about to turn and leave when something from out in the bay caught my eye; a glistening flash of light. Suddenly, a number of Dolla broke the water's surface. Like speeding bullets they raced to the dock where I stood, their long snouts protruding above the water. They began to chatter rapidly, issuing a flurry of simple phrases.

"You ... Aurian ... want ... Aquella"

I rushed to the water's edge. "Yes," I said. "I am seeking the Aquella."

"You wait ... soon here" they said, disappearing under the water.

I was stunned. How did they know? I had only been here a few hours and the holo had only sent the message out a short time ago. Suddenly, there was a swell out in the sea. A large body, something about the size of a large whale was emerging from the ocean–my God, it was a submarine. I watched as an oblong, rusted, barnacle laden submersible cruised into the bay. In all my years as a slave on Urlena I had never seen anything like this.

I waited for the vessel to come to rest, wondering what was going to happen. I had my answer almost immediately. A portal along the side of the vessel fell open, its bulk resting upon the water. I saw two Aquella standing atop its surface; they were scanning the dock. I waved to them. How in the world did these people have something like this–a submersible of all things? I was beginning to realize that there was more to the Aquella than I realized.

For a moment nothing happened, but then four Dolla began to race toward me. They pulled ropes tethered to a collapsible, floating runway. I watched as the runway unfolded, it was inflating, buoying itself against the water. The Dolla brought it to the base of the stairway where I stood and held it taut.

"Come," a voice commanded.

I descended the stairs toward the floating runway. As I neared the water I recognized the material the Aquella were using for the portable jetty. It was the same membrane material they had used to take me underwater with, and haul ore from the bottom of the ocean. I stepped out onto the runway knowing that the material would hold me easily, and began to walk toward the ship, my anticipation mounting.

As I approached the ship I saw an Aquella male exit. He was young and of short stature, which surprised me somewhat. I observed his manner and dress; he looked like a priest. He moved quickly, striding toward me wearing a long, flowing purple robe laced with an intricate design of gold thread. The cloak covered his features from head to toe, but its intricacy and richness told me he was of royal lineage, perhaps a religious proctor or a government official. His hurried convergence also conveyed the feeling that it was protocol for him to meet me at least part way. When we reached a point midway on the floating jetty, he bowed, and I returned the courtesy. He then began to speak.

"Crisk-a-toc, plat-eeee, tit ro tictictic—"

His intonation of clicks and sharp whistles played harshly upon my ears. I winced.

"I'm sorry," I responded in Aurian. "I don't understand you."

He looked at me with curiosity, both of us realizing that we didn't understand one another. I took one of the seti stones from my neck. I handed it to him, motioning for him to place it around his neck. I felt the touch of his mind the instant he took it in his hand. It was an odd syntax of thought. He was afraid, yet curious, and struggling to maintain composure. He had never met an Aurian before. I spoke first.

"My intentions are peaceful," I assured him. "I have come seeking your help."

The look in his eyes was enough to tell me he was overtaken by the mind link. I caught his rambling ruminations: How? Why? Was this really possible?

"Yes," I answered. "We can now understand one another. My name is Rez Cantor and I know of your people—the sea dwellers of Urlena. I have been here before. I was held as a slave at one time. I labored under the water in one of your mines."

I turned my head and pulled back my hair, showing him the breathing flaps behind my ears.

"Your kind did this to me."

"I'm sorry," he responded. "That was not my people. Only the Aquita breathe the water. I am of the Anoni tribe."

He pulled off the hood covering his head, revealing his scalp. His head was covered with a dark, stubbly bristle of quill-like hair. Turning his face, he showed me the sides of his head. He bore no surgical scars behind his ears or upon his neck.

"We live underwater as well," he continued, "but we do not breathe it as they do. They are primitive creatures. We do not find their practices necessary."

"I see."

My mind was in a whirl. So, this was how it lay—different tribes, different changes to their evolution since the war.

"What do you know about the war?" he inquired.

"I know that the cloud sent by the Zecla drove all your people under the water. I know with it ravaging your moon that your people may never bask in the sunlight or revel under the red warmth of Tiiana."

I caught the revulsion he felt from the mention of the Zecla. It was a curious response since he was far too young to have experienced the war or even remember it.

"I am watching my people and our moon slowly die," he interjected. "It is enough."

I bowed my head. "I meant no disrespect. In fact, this is my purpose here."

Suddenly, we heard the agitated chatter from the Dolla who were floating on either side of the runway.

"Danger ... coming ... now ... disappear," their voices echoed.

I looked up, and on the horizon, moving like a tsunami, was the cloud. It was pitched and angry looking. I turned. The Aquella representative who had stood with me was already running for his ship. I heard his voice call.

"Move, if you wish to live. Giragoc approaches!"

I bolted after him. Giragoc? Was that the name for this thing?

I entered the submersible, ducking my head to make entry. It was not built for someone of my size. Two Aquella seamen cut the runway loose, raising the portal doorway behind us. The door was then sealed quickly with a gel and we began to submerge. I felt the violent torrents of weather and water bear down upon us from above. I could only surmise that the cloud was trying to rape the metal from the ship's hull.

"Do not worry." I heard the voice of the young Aquella say. "We are far enough under. Giragoc cannot hurt us now."

I nodded my head and looked about the ship. It was tightly compartmentalized and my view was limited, though I could see other Aquella nearby. They stared at me. I took a moment to look them over. They looked very similar to the Aquella who had held me years before, thin faced, black eyes, but there were subtle differences. Their color was more brownish, their skin smoother, less scaly, and their heads bore short, brown quills instead of tentacles. It was obvious the Aquita had used some type of genetic manipulation or mutation to secure their survival from Giragoc, and who could blame them? I saw the Aquella ambassador studying me; he was as curious of me as I of him.

"Where are we going?" I asked.

"We journey to my home, Atorika. There, you will meet with Iantikke, our Queen. It is only she who can give guidance and grant fulfillment to your needs.

"Thank you," I responded with a quick nod.

"I am known as Salokka-ril, of the Iantik linage," he continued, bowing his head.

"If I might be so bold, Salokka-ril of Iantik—can you tell me what happened after the sinking of Aquilika?"

The look of surprise in Salokka-ril's eyes was apparent; I had to explain.

"I am not Aurian. I come from a place far away from the moons of Tiiana. I have been sent here by the Visi to help you and your people. My mission is to help all the moons regain what they lost in the war with the Zecla."

I thought Salokka-ril was about to cry. He fell to his knees and prostrated himself in front of me. I heard a prayer of thanks running across his lips. He looked up at me.

"We have been praying for a thousand years. Our people will rejoice at your arrival."

"Please," I said, stooping down closer to his level. "I am not who you think I am. I am no savior. I'm simply a soldier following his duty—trying to get back home."

"Still," noted Salokka-ril, his eyes, wet. "We welcome your arrival."

"Please," I requested again. "Tell me what happened on Urlena."

Salokka-ril rose from the floor; he began to fill in the events following the sinking of Aquilika.

"You must understand that my knowledge comes from those who lived before me. From the songs and poems that make up our history."

"Yes." I affirmed.

"My people were besieged by Giragoc," he continued. "Many today do not realize that he is an artificial creation; a weapon sent by the Zecla. Many, like the Aquita, have come to regard him as a God which they worship and make sacrifices to."

I nodded my head. I understood this better than he knew.

"What most of our race do not understand is that Giragoc is more today than he was when he first arrived."

"How?" I asked. "Can you explain?"

"There was more than one Giragoc. The Zecla fired many rockets at our moon. They carried many weapons—many Giragocs. That was how they were able to destroy so many of our cities. Their weapons killed hundreds of thousands of Aquella. But over time, the various Giragocs met, they merged and became stronger."

"They adapted," I interjected.

"Yes," said Salokka-ril. "Soon Giragoc was so large that we had no defense against him. We had to find a way to protect ourselves, and our seas became our salvation. We found that he couldn't penetrate the density of the water, so we sought refuge there, but it was difficult. Different tribes sought different solutions. No one could agree on one approach, so each tribe took to their own methods in order to survive. The Aquita found a way to manipulate their genetic makeup and with surgical procedures they learned to breathe the sea water. They became like the Dolla. We chose a different route. We had no desire to give up our love for the sun and air so we chose a different science to help us survive."

I was just about to ask Salokka-ril what his people did. How they managed to survive, when an alarm began to sound.

Salokka-ril turned toward it, just as one of his men approached. The man said something to him.

"We are here," he said, turning back to me.

"Atorika?"

"Yes," he answered.

I was stunned. The journey here had been so short. How was this possible? The information provided me by the holo in Alanth did not indicate that Atorika lay so near. I could have swum here. Another alarm began to ring, interrupting my thoughts. Several Aquella moved past me. They approached the portal and began cutting away the gel sealing the door–the portal fell open and light flooded the interior of the sub. For a moment I thought we were on the surface.

I waited eagerly for word to disembark. I was stiff from being in such cramped quarters and anxious to see what lay outside the ship. There were a million questions running through my mind–if we were back on the surface of Urlena, where were we? If we weren't, why was there no water flooding the ship? I was vexed and impatient for answers and the Aquella working in front of me were impeding my view.

"It will only be a moment more," a voice said in my head. It was Salokka-ril.

I was embarrassed. I realized now that my emotions and the questions I had were running rampant in my head–I had betrayed myself. I apologized to my host. "As I told you earlier– I am not a savior, but a man–a soldier fulfilling his mission."

"Your honesty is a blessing," he countered. "Come; allow me to welcome you to Atorika."

Salokka-ril and I exited the ship and it was not what I expected. I could see nothing. We were in some sort of bubble connected to a white opaque tube that ran into the distance. I had trouble getting my bearings and was forced to follow Salokka-ril as he led the way. As we walked, I ran my fingers along the side of the tube–the material was intriguing. It was smooth, glass-like, cold and hard. There were minute flecks of color layered within, mostly green and red. It was then that I realized that I had seen this material before—in the city of the Aquita. They used this material in their city.

"It is a common material ..." noted Salokka-ril. "... and very abundant upon our moon. We call it marblis."

"What lies on the other side?" I asked.

"The ocean," he replied.

"How thick is it?"

"Less than two inches."

I was impressed.

We reached the end of the tube and began to ascend a series of stairs. There were more Aquella here—many more—they stopped and stared, parting the hallway to let us pass. I remember this happening the last time I was with the Aquella, but this time it was different. This time I was not a prisoner; bruised, beaten, and bewildered by fear. My stature and demeanor were completely different now, and I felt a totally divergent attitude with these beings. I was a guest, and an important one.

We continued to walk, passing several more tube entrances that led out and away from us. It seemed we were in a hub used for trade and commerce—I imagined that it was here that the Aquella imported food, supplies, and other sundries.

"Our trade routes are very limited." noted Salokka-ril, reading my thoughts. "Between the situation with Giragoc and hostilities with the Aquita, our resources are very limited. We have to be careful.

I was surprised by Salokka-ril's revelation. Here was another race with hostilities between tribes. I was unsure what to make of it.

"I'm sorry," the young diplomat interjected. "I shouldn't have said anything. These are matters for our Queen to discuss."

Before anything more could be said we exited out onto a street, and the city of Atorika opened to my view. It was breathtaking. There were Aquella moving everywhere. This place was a virtual metropolis. In every direction I saw tall, luminescent colored buildings shooting skyward. They lined wide, brown streets where purple seaweed grew in abundance. I marveled at the architecture, noting how each one glistened like mother of pearl, spiraling up thirty or more stories. At the apex of the structures, covering everything overhead was a white sky reflecting colored hues of green and brown. It was immediately apparent, it was artificial. The city of Atorika was encased within a dome. I glanced at Salokka-ril.

"We are presently on the sea floor, protected by a canopy of marblis," he noted. "It allows us to live here in safety."

I shook my head in wonder. Of all my journeys on the moons of Tiiana why hadn't I come here first? It was a stupid thought. I knew there was a reason for everything. I followed Salokka-ril down the street. We had an appointment with the Queen.

CHAPTER TWENTY

Aquitika

antikke, the Queen of Atorika, was an elderly woman of an age I was unable to determine. She looked old, and she moved gingerly as she walked to her throne, but as a former dignitary with the Emperor, I knew physical attributes could be deceiving–they often held little relevance. The key in this case would be Iantikke's mental capacity and the relationship she carried with her people. These were factors still open for exploration and it was much too soon for me to determine what kind of ruler I was facing.

As I waited for an audience with her, I studied her court and throne. The chamber hall in which I waited was large and richly decorated with colored tapestries, hand painted artwork, sea plants and flora. Nestled amidst the flora and artwork were statues of a gorgeous white silver–Aquella men and women poised in scenes depicting Anoni life. In addition, there were two large aquariums that ran the length of the throne room on either side. They were filled with colorful fish, odd-looking sea crustaceans, plants and other artifacts gathered from the ocean waters outside.

The Queen's hall was also filled with Aquella royalty, both male and female, and they seemed quite curious about me. I noticed a lot of whispering and commentary taking place just before the Queen entered. Presently the room was still and I waited quietly with Salokka-ril at my side. The two of us knelt on bended knee at the bottom of the stairs before the throne, awaiting permission to speak. As with any first contact with royalty, I took my cues from the young diplomat next to me. I hoped this approach would aid my quest by demonstrating a measure of respect toward the sovereignty of Iantikke's throne.

After a short interlude with Anoni formality, the Queen finally addressed us. Actually it was Salokka-ril, as I did not understand her. He rose to his feet and conversed with her briefly while I remained kneeling. I then felt a tap on my shoulder, whereupon I rose, and faced the Queen. She was studying me intently.

Salokka-ril turned to me and informed me of what was transpiring.

"I have graciously offered your gift of the seti stone to the Queen," he whispered. "But she feels it would be more comfortable if I translated instead, with your words passing through me."

I nodded; it was understandable. The idea of someone else's thoughts jumbling around in your mind could be unsettling, even if the reality was entirely different. Still, this made things more difficult, but it was her decision and I had to respect that.

"That will be fine." I noted in reply. "Please thank the Queen for granting us an audience."

Salokka-ril passed along my request; the Queen nodded in response. I then explained my reasons for coming to Urlena, relaying to her and the royal denizens filling the hall, the imminent threat facing the moons of Tiiana. I warned them that even as we spoke, the Zecla were birthing new young. That this impending event would lead to the demise of Boutal and that it would eventually arrive on Urlena—unless the Anoni and Aquita joined in our quest to stop it. I asked for her help, men, weapons, any technology that she might be able to spare.

Almost immediately I saw the Queen turn to her advisors who stood on either side of her throne. There was a conversation between at least three or four of them and it went on for several minutes. I realized now how shrewd the Queen had been in rejecting my offer of the seti stone. It was obvious she wanted no link granting me understanding of what was transpiring, and I sorely wanted to know what was being said up there. I hated politics. Finally, they stopped and the Queen addressed Salokka-ril. He turned to me.

"The Queen would like to know if you are the slave they heard about in the mines of Aquita."

"Tell her yes." I replied.

At that response, I saw heads bobbing and tongues wagging again. I wasn't sure how things were going. Another question was then passed through Salokka-ril, to me.

"They would like to know how you escaped."

I was floored. I had come here with news of a war that might literally wipe them out and they wanted to know how I escaped from the Aquita. It then dawned on me—perhaps they thought me a spy. After all, I had little knowledge of their political or religious standings. My life as a slave in their mines had not given me a lot of time to reflect on their personal agendas or beliefs. So, perhaps they suspected me of being a pawn of the Aquita. I could not say. I looked helplessly at Salokka-ril, and then I explained how I had faked my death and dug myself to freedom. The story seemed to placate them, but I was still stunned by their lack of concern regarding the Zecla. How was I going to convince them that my requests were dire? How was something so simple turning into something so difficult?

Suddenly, the Queen began to cough. Her chest heaved with labored breath, while one hand covered her mouth. Several Aquella moved to her side; I thought one to be a nurse. She waved them away and composed herself—then spoke. Salokka-ril translated.

"The Queen would like me to convey her sympathies regarding the situation on Boutal. But she feels additional time and discussion are required before she can grant your requests.

In the meantime she would like you to be our guest. Does that meet with your approval?"

I nodded my head. What choice did I have?

With our meeting cut off, we were whisked out of the throne room and I was left to Salokka-ril. I was concerned over what had just transpired. How was the Queen? Was her health failing? If she couldn't grant me the men and weapons, who would? Who were the others in charge of this kingdom? I wanted to ask Salokka-ril, but his mind was occupied and his gait quick as we left the palace and headed out to the streets. Once there, in the freedom of the crowd, he began to talk.

"Do not be discouraged," he consoled me, "The Queen is very thoughtful in her decisions. You may be assured she will grant you another audience."

He fell silent again and we continued walking, taking several quick turns before heading down a large, almost empty, spacious street. I was bewildered by Salokka-ril's odd behavior and extremely curious as to where we were going. I was just about to ask, when suddenly the young diplomat stopped dead in his tracks. He bent his head close to mine and spoke in a low tone, giving me the feeling that he didn't want what he was saying to be overheard.

"I have brought you here, Rez Cantor, so that I might have words with you in relative privacy. This seti stone is a wonderful link between us, but I find that I must still speak aloud to help convey my thoughts. And what I have to say needs to be said where others cannot hear."

"I understand," I said with a nod.

Salokka-ril looked around. The coast was clear.

"Perhaps you gathered this from our audience with the Queen, but my city, Atorika, this place where the Anoni reside, is a small and troubled domain. You see, the Aquita are pressing in on us from all sides—not a day goes by without them raiding us. They steal our resources and kill our people. Making matters worse, Atorika is shrinking. We have fewer births each year. All of this is bringing an unwanted change to our people, and there is political mischief in the air."

I nodded–I was not surprised by this. Atorika was a closed environment, limited physically by the dome. Whatever their means to expand, explore, and develop; it was being strangled by their circumstances. Not many societies can survive such restrictions, especially when they are engaged in skirmishes with their neighbors and have a viral cloud of death hanging over their heads. I asked Salokka-ril to explain the history between the Anoni and Aquita.

His discourse was short and to the point–I sensed his distaste for the Aquita. The strife between the two tribes had been in play for over a thousand years and many lives had been lost. Over that time the two had attempted to find common ground, but both kept drifting further and further apart and a lasting peace seemed even more distant than ever. The divide now encompassed the very social fabric of their societies. As Salokka-ril told it, the Anoni were the enlightened ones, suffering under the military aggressiveness of the Aquita. They were the statesmen, magnanimous in their willingness to share culture, science and personal freedoms, while the Aquita were dogma-driven fanatics. They considered the Aquita to be a brutal military state, even though they were the tribe who had led the battle against the Zecla at Aquilika two thousand years ago. Sadly, with the arrival of Giragoc, the Aquita had become enslaved by religious fervor. They were now consumed by appeasing the cloud God, Giragoc. I had seen that for myself.

"It would seem that I have come at a bad time, asking for men and weapons."

Salokka-ril nodded in agreement. "Yes, just this morning we lost three Anoni in a raid on one of our mines."

Salokka-ril's words hit me like a ton of bricks. "You mine silver ore, too?" I asked.

"Yes we use it in many things, our technology, our art. Our mines are the richest on Urlena. The statues in the Queen's chamber hall were made from our silver ore."

That simple statement from Salokka-ril told me just about everything I needed to know regarding the Aquella and their moon. What had I stumbled into?

I was given a room with a bed of soft seaweed for the night. The reprieve gave me time to think and plan my next move. Now that I knew that the Aquita were trying to take over the Anoni for their silver, it put things in a different light. There was more going on here than propaganda or ideological differences. It was down to survival of the fittest. And knowing firsthand the brutal, single mindedness of the Aquita I was willing to bet they had the upper hand.

I wasn't sure now how to handle the situation. Did the Anoni know why the Aquita wanted their silver? I had my doubts. And would it matter even if they did? This was definitely an ugly position to be in and I was still left with the burning question: How was I going to get these two tribes involved on Boutal? I needed these people and their unique abilities to help me stop the Zecla before the Zecla took over their moon and devoured them. My plight did not allow me to sleep well. I was pestered by bad dreams.

The morning came early with Salokka-ril awakening me. He took me out to eat—a fish paste banquet that brought back unappealing memories. Over the course of our meal he questioned me about life on the other moons and the events transpiring on Boutal. Some of his questions seemed pointed and probing—a ploy, I'm sure, to learn my plans for Urlena, which I thought was humorous as I didn't have any. After our meal, he took me on a tour of the city. I saw how the city fed itself, using trained Dolla to plant the sea bed with food crops. The creatures were also used to herd schools of fish into net traps and defend the city by forewarning the Anoni of enemies approaching their territory. Salokka-ril then took me to the pens where they raised young Dolla. The place was alive, and I felt I was in a room of children playing. I was overcome with their cheerful chatter and they were most eager to converse with me. They kept calling me "father" which seemed to surprise my young diplomatic guide.

At day's end I met with the Queen once more. She gave me the news I expected—that because the Anoni were under siege from the Aquita she could spare no men, weapons or technology. Her people's needs had to come before mine, though she did promise that if things changed she would reconsider. I knew it was fruitless to try and change her mind so I bowed politely and thanked her for her time and consideration. I asked her if she would grant me leave to return to Boutal. Her answer was quick; I was most welcome to take leave. She then ordered Salokka-ril to place a sub at my disposal and she granted me passage to Aquilika along with the few meager supplies I requested.

Late that night Salokka-ril and I boarded a submarine, and we left Atorika for Aquilika. To my disbelief we arrived in the area of the pyramid in a matter of hours. I was amazed. I hadn't figured how the Aquella did it, but it was obvious that their subs moved at tremendous speed. I really wished I had one on Boutal—it would give me a great advantage. Even so, I had to count my blessings. I had garnered much information and understanding regarding the Aquella during my visit.

Another hour passed; we were now surfaced and floating atop the water. It was a beautiful dawn. The morning sky was clear and the ocean calm, with Dolla playing freely on either side of the ship. I looked to the horizon. Tiiana was rising, her ruby red chromosphere blooming like a flower as she rose over the water. It was an incredible sight. I turned to Salokka-ril. The young diplomat seemed remorseful.

"I wish my Queen could have helped more." he said. "I would have liked to join you on your quest. I believe it has merit."

I looked the young Aquellian in the eye and put my hand upon his shoulder.

"We have a saying on my world, my friend. It's not over until the bird has flown the cage."

He looked at me inquisitively, as he handed me a light globe wrapped in netting—my request of the Queen. I looped my arms through the netting, strapping the globe to my back. I was ready. Salokka-ril handed me his seti necklace. I took it from his fingers, but before our link was entirely broken I explained the meaning of my words.

"Destiny often has her own plan, my friend. And we will meet again—perhaps on Boutal."

He smiled. And with that, I jumped into the water, plunging into the dark, unseen depths, the light on my back struggling to illuminate my way. Swimming hard, I forced myself down, my ears popping, my gills opening. I could breathe now and the water passed through me with ease. The Dolla were ecstatic. They raced to my side, rolling and swirling around me, eager to help me access the depths.

The pyramid of Aquilika lay at a depth of several hundred feet underwater. I came across its form, my hands gingerly sliding through the slick moss and seaweed that covered its sides. The feel was greasy and a little unpleasant. I was glad to have the light and the company of the Dolla. They bolstered my confidence, assuring me that the way was clear, that there were no predators near. They even led me to the opening of the pyramid. I found the access easy.

I swam through the long, dark tunnels and into the interior of the edifice. To my surprise the water did not entirely fill the giant structure—it ended in a pool not far from the dais room. I think the air pressure inside kept the water out. I pulled myself from the water and walked to the pyramid's main access panels, the light on my back pushing away the darkness. I placed my seti stone into the dais panel and waited as the lights came on.

I could feel the pyramid come alive. A low hum began to permeate the structure and the place seemed to warm a bit. Suddenly, I heard excited chatter coming from the pool of water I'd just left. I walked back to see what the racket was—a number of Dolla greeted me with their heads bobbing above the water. They began to speak.

"Father ... we ... like ... music."

I laughed. Music? What were they talking about? I bent down and stroked one on the snout. "Music? What music?" I asked.

"You ... play ... Dolla ... sing ... everywhere."

342

It dawned on me that they meant the pyramid—the humming. Possibly because it was underwater they could hear the vibration and considered it music.

"I'm glad you like it."

"Yes ... we ... rejoice ... all ... unison ... we ... come ... now ... join."

"That is good," I said, rising from the pool. "I'm glad you're enjoying the music, but I must return to my work."

I began to walk away, but something stopped me dead in my tracks. I had a curious thought. What did they mean, *unison, we come, now join*. I moved back to the water's edge and bent down close to the chattering faces that smiled back at me.

"Explain," I said. "What do you mean when you say we come now join?"

"Music ... good ... Dolla ... come ... to Father."

"You're telling me that more Dolla are coming?"

"Yes," they chattered happily. *"We ... come ... sing ... for ... Father."*

"From where? How far?"

"Everywhere," they responded.

The entire moon?"

"Yes ... we ... come ... sing ... for ... Father."

I could have danced a jig. The Gods had just handed me the answer I was looking for. I couldn't believe that it was going to be this easy. That the Dolla were the key—that through them I might be able to control the Aquella whether they liked it or not. I bounced back to the dais with a renewed zest and enthusiasm sweeping over me.

I immediately set to work reestablishing the controls on the pyramid. Barely anything worked; there wasn't even enough power to transport off Urlena. The system had to be reset and brought on line, a task I felt ill equipped for. It was only by trial and error that I managed to reestablish operations. I think the Visi had a hand in the process. It seemed that when I slept I was given insights into the pyramid's function and after two days of work I was able to get the holograph to appear. He was not very helpful at first, his abilities were limited, but slowly I was able to bring him up to full status. Things went smoothly after that, which was a good thing, as more and more Dolla were arriving every day. Already there were a million or more packed outside in the waters surrounding Aquilika. Their numbers had grown so vast that I could no longer swim outside and fresh food was becoming an issue.

Unknowingly, the holograph explained what the problem was.

"The core harmonics are out of alignment."

"The what?" I asked.

He shot me a look of disapproval. His programming was Aurian and it showed. He had an attitude.

"The core harmonics—the crystals embedded in the sea floor. They power everything. Can't you hear that humming?"

"Yes, but I thought that was normal."

"I would expect that from a Motula."

I ignored the remark.

"Can the harmonics be adjusted?" I asked.

"Yes, it can be done. I just need to find what is disrupting the energy flow. Once that has been confirmed I can realign the probes within the mantle, and harmonic balance should be reestablished, giving us full power to everything, including the transport."

A thought struck.

"Will the realignment alter the harmonic vibration we're hearing?"

"Of course," he snorted, "that's how I know they need to be adjusted."

"So, if the harmonic is changed, then the Dolla who swim these waters will no longer be affected by it. They won't be attracted to this place or under its control."

"No, I suppose not, but what does it matter? They can be controlled numerous ways—that's why we altered their genetics. It was our gift to the Aquella."

I wanted to strangle the holograph I was so angry. I felt as if I'd been slapped in the face with another example of how the Aurians had manipulated the moons for their own means—it was aggravating. Still, it didn't matter now, what was done was done. I just had to figure out where to go from here.

"What is the extent of control one can exercise over the Dolla? Can they be told to stay away from the Aquella—to disappear?"

"Yes, I suppose that could be done. But why would you want to do that? I see no meaningful purpose ..."

"Because they are my last hope for bringing the Aquella into the war against the Zecla."

I could see the holo was confused; his image actually wavered a bit. I decided it was time to fill him in.

"You have been off line for nearly two thousand years, Aurian—ever since the Aquella and your people destroyed the island of Aquilika and sank this edifice. Your race lost the war with the Zecla, as did all the moons. At the moment, the Zecla have regrouped. They have invaded Boutal and are only a short time away from the feeding. I am not Motula, but a soldier from another world sent here by the Visi to bring an end to the hostilities between the moons, but in order to do so I must stop the Zecla from taking over Boutal. Are you with me so far?"

The holo said nothing. I wasn't sure what he was doing, but I had the suspicion that he was trying to contact Aura. I waited. A moment later his attention focused back on me—I caught a glimpse of sadness in his eyes. I acknowledged his loss.

"I'm sorry. Much has changed since you were last aware."

He nodded. "I will try to help. What would you like to say to the Dolla?"

"For the time being I need the Dolla to avoid the Aquella at all costs. If you can tell them to dissipate—to hide—send them to the deepest parts of the ocean, or the poles, anywhere where they can run and escape the Aquella. It is the only leverage I have in forcing the Aquella to join in this cause."

"I will work on this immediately. I should have the command programming completed by the time I've realigned the pyramid's harmonics."

"Good. I have another question. What are your defensive capabilities?

The holo relayed to me the defensive weapons at his command. Essentially, he could prevent anyone from harming the inside workings of the pyramid short of outright killing them, which is all I needed. I explained why he might need such resources, along with the message I needed broadcast to the Anoni and Aquita.

☆ ☆ ☆

Two more days passed and I was ready for the next leg of my journey. I needed to reach the underwater transport on Boutal. With the Dolla gone, safely hidden in a region near the southern pole, it was time to prepare Boutal for the arrival of the Aquella. Adversely, this was perhaps, my most dangerous quest. The transfer point I was attempting to reach was called Arison, and it was located deep in the tumultuous waters of the horn of Myolic, an area I knew firsthand for its treachery. What made my attempt here so dangerous was that I had no definitive reason to believe that Arison was still a viable transfer point. It wasn't even a pyramid, but a small space station; an abandoned facility built by the Aurians for their initial reconnaissance of Boutal. The probe had been sent from their home world and sunk in the waters of the Myolic Sea, safe from prying eyes. From there, the hidden base was used for studying Boutal. Once the Aurians realized that the Motula were too primitive for their concern, they moved north to the ice fields where they studied the Solula. Afterwards, they chose a more hospitable location for a permanent transfer base—Luskia.

After Luskia was finished, Arison was deemed useless and they abandoned it. Since then it had lain dormant on the bottom of the ocean and I had no idea what condition the station was in. Was it solvent or had it been compromised by the sea?

Would I be trapped there? Even the holo was unsure. To prevent a total disaster I prepared a message for Oolat and gave it to the holo. If I was unable to confirm my safe arrival on Arison, the holo would forward my distress call to Luskia. I hoped that would not be necessary, but it was the best I could think of for the moment. In the meantime I assembled supplies, food, and water, in case I was stuck there for a while. Suddenly an alarm sounded.

"What is that?"

"A number of Aquella are approaching," the holo answered, while silencing the alarm.

"How many?"

"Six."

I suspected the worst.

"Water breathers?"

"It would appear so. I sense no artificial breathing apparatus."

I expected this—it's what I would do if faced with an ultimatum like the one I was giving the Aquella. Assassins were being sent to eliminate the threat. We had tried it with the Relcor and it had failed. I hoped for the same results here. I instructed the holo.

"You know what has to be done. Defend this facility at all costs. The Aquella must yield to my demands or face losing the Dolla forever. Five thousand Aquita are to be assembled and made ready for transfer. And make sure they understand that Salokka-ril from the Anoni must be brought to me unharmed and unmolested. Now open the transport and send me to Boutal."

I disappeared in a burst, reappearing instantaneously within the freezing depths of Arison. The ship was larger than I expected and totally different from any other Aurian facility I'd been inside. The ceiling was arched, and I felt trapped within a bubble of old, stale air. It was hard to breathe. I turned around, studying the ship. It was definitely spherical, smaller than the pyramids and very, very cold. I could only hope that everything still worked. My teeth chattered as I crossed to the main console. I pushed a seti stone into the panel and waited as the ship sputtered to life. The process was arduous—I'm not sure from where or how the ship drew its power, but it took forever. Finally, the lights flared, giving some warmth to the area, and the gem stones atop the console panel began to illuminate. A minute or two later a holo sprang to life. His form wavered and fluttered as his graphics solidified. He turned to face me. I was overjoyed with my success.

"How may I help you?" the holo asked, as his line of sight became fixed on me.

I was about to answer when suddenly he glared at me. He began yelling, pointing his finger and proclaiming, "You are Motula! What are you doing here? Intruder! Intruder!"

I knew immediately I was in trouble. The floor beneath me began to vibrate, the intensity increasing. The ship was drawing power and there were red lights on the console flashing. It didn't take a rocket scientist to understand that the holo was shifting to a defensive mode and I was the target. I spoke rapidly in Aurian, commanding him to disengage. I tripped over my words—I was still mastering their tongue, but it was enough. I felt the vibration in the floor dissipate and I continued explaining my presence.

"I am not a Motula," I told him. "I am Melelan, a visitor from another part of the universe. I am here on a mission for the Visi. I am here to prevent the Zecla from taking over Boutal."

The holo looked at me warily. "That is preposterous," he replied. "We've only just met the Zecla and they do not have transporter technology."

"Then contact Aura. They can corroborate my story."

The holo went blank—I waited. Soon he returned giving me his full attention.

"I still do not understand. My contact with Aura was unsatisfactory."

"I'm sure it was," I said. "And I beg you to contact Luskia and Aquilika for additional verification, but first let me explain things."

I then began to explain the history of things, bringing him up to date on all that had occurred since he'd been left dormant. The explanation seemed to quell his suspicions and he gave me access to Aquilika, where the holo there confirmed all that I said.

"So, am I to understand that my creators are gone?" he asked, in a somber tone.

"In their physical form," I answered, then adding. "But their essence lives on through the robots they have created on Aura. They are there now rebuilding. We're all trying to make things right again."

"What would you like me to do?"

"Can you bring in some fresh air? My lungs are aching. And warm this place up—it's freezing."

"Certainly," he answered.

I felt a surge of power again. It was followed shortly by a burst of chilly, cold air—at least it was fresh.

For the next hour I toured the ship with the holo. He took me through the various levels and I found that the ship held a resemblance to what I was used to. Its outer design was of course different, the spaceships of the Empire were not spherical, but it held familiar attributes inside. There was a galley, dining and sleeping quarters, and a helm from where the ship was piloted. There were also pressurized chambers located in the lower levels that allowed personnel and submersibles access to the sea outside. What I found most interesting was that the bottom half of the sphere was filled with water. The weight kept the ship locked in one place on the seabed—I found this to be ingenious.

The tour also revealed that the ship had been stripped of most everything. I surmised that since the Aurians had no plans for returning here, they took everything with them to Luskia. Fortunately, the one thing they left was a two man submersible. Luskia had no body of water nearby so it made no sense to take the sub. I looked the sea craft over, like the spaceship, it was old. The technology on-board was timeworn, perhaps three thousand years, and it had lain dormant for two thousand.

"Will it still operate?" I asked the holo.

"The seals are still waterproof, but I will need a power source in order to perform diagnostics."

"What type of source? Explain."

"This craft uses C-nine power cells, three of them, and they are missing. The data logs have a notation that they were taken to Luskia when Arison was abandoned."

"Great. And without them, analyzing this craft is impossible."

"That is correct."

"Are these power cells still in use? Perhaps at Luskia or Aquilika?"

"Unknown, but a possibility."

"What do they look like?"

The holo showed me a picture and a schematic of a power cell. I needed three of them to get this miniature sub back into operation—a feat I seriously needed to have happen. I set to work immediately, ordering the holo to send the schematics to Luskia. The holos there could search the pyramid's database to see if the cells even existed. There was always a distinct possibility that Aurian technology had changed over two thousand years and that these types of cells were antiquated. If I couldn't find them there, I would have to expand my search to Aura—if there was time. I was cutting it close. I'd been gone for days and I knew that the birthing of the Zecla would begin soon. I had to hurry if my plans were to work.

With the spaceship nearly ready, and the holo looking for new power cells, I was ready to return to Luskia. There were other urgent matters which required my attention, one of them being Casita. I left the Arison holo with orders to finish the re-powering of the ship—it had to be ready to accommodate the Aquella who would be transferring in. He assured me the work would be complete in a day or two and I could trust his programming to fulfill my request. The ship would be ready for the Aquella. Confident, I entered the dais and shot away in a burst of light, reappearing at Luskia where Oolat and the Aurian holo were awaiting me. It was good to be home, and I bolted from the dais, a flurry of questions exploding from my lips.

"Have the Zecla started to move? Holo, what is our present defense status? Oolat, what is the news regarding the battle between Phratis and Casita?"

The two of them both stood silent. Oolat gave me a quizzical look. "Are you all right?" he asked.

"Of course, I'm all right." I answered. "Now tell me, what is our present situation? Have the Zecla moved further north?"

"The Zecla have moved no further than they were four hours ago when you left," stated the holo.

"What? I've been gone for days!"

Oolat shot me a look of concern. He shook his head.

"You've only been gone four hours or so, my friend. The holo is telling you the truth. Nothing here has changed, except for the messages we have received from Aquilika and Arison."

I felt my body reel. I felt tired, but exhilarated, relieved and overwhelmed, but mostly very happy. I began to laugh, which must have made me look even crazier than I was.

"Yes, yes, YES! Thank you so much!"

I knew now what Leanna meant when I lay in her arms. I knew now what the Visi had done for me as their last gift. They had given me time. That's why the robots on Aura had moved so slowly. And why the Aquella submersible had moved so swiftly through the water. Time had somehow been suspended. They had given me the chance to set my plan in motion. I moved from the dais, a new series of commands crossing my lips.

"We have no time to waste."

I looked at the holo.

"How goes the search for the power cells?"

"We have nothing here that is a match. I have contacted Aura, as you requested, to see if they can help."

I looked to Oolat.

"My friend we have to journey to Casita again. It is time to put an end to their war."

An alarm began to sound. It blared through the pyramid, causing us to turn toward the dais. A bright light flashed and a robot appeared—it was Philip. He turned toward us.

"I found these in the archives," he announced.

In his hands were the power cells we needed. I stepped forward and took the cells, while introducing him to Oolat.

"Philip—this is Oolat, my warrior brother of Boutal. He is the leader of the Solula. Oolat this is my Melelan friend and Aurian benefactor, Philip Golan."

"I am looking forward to fighting by your side against the Zecla," said Philip, stepping from the dais.

He walked toward Oolat and held out his hand. The Solula warrior responded in kind and the two grasped each other by the hand and wrist. It was a most interesting meeting, seeing the two giants meet, and I was glad that both were on my side.

"I have three hundred robots ready to transfer, along with six hovercraft," noted Philip a minute later. "And I scrounged all of Aura for weapons. We have almost three thousand blasters, a thousand microwave rifles, and I managed to assemble two dozen vacuum bombs just in case, though launching them might be a problem. I hope it will be enough."

I nodded my head. "It will have to be."

For the next two days I worked with Philip, Oolat and the Luskia holographs, plotting our attack on the Zecla. Our biggest concern was avoiding the Brata that were migrating toward the Aritonian desert. From our reconnaissance we could see increasing numbers heading east—there were thousands, and this forced us to be very cautious. The Aurian robots were ideal for this purpose. They were invaluable in eluding the Brata, as they carried no scent and were masters of stealth and camouflage. We sent thirty of them south. Their purpose was to penetrate the areas held by the Zecla near the dome. There, they would set up a surveillance network using insect-sized spy drones. Another dozen robots were sent to the southern coast of Cassandra. Their task was to locate and select sites for the Aquella. These sites were to be placed at strategic intervals along the coastline, and furnished with supplies and weapons so the water breathers could rest, eat, and train as they made their way to the dome. The remaining bulk of the Aurians stayed at Luskia to aid with our defense, though I did send half a dozen to Casita. They were under orders to remain hidden outside the city until I arrived.

The next morning Philip, Oolat, and I rose early to begin our separate missions. The monsoons were upon us and it was raining heavily. Oolat headed north into the mountains where the majority of the Solula tribes were camped. He was to assemble them into an army and bring them back to Luskia where they would be armed for the trek south. Philip, in turn, was taking three quarters of the robots and heading for the Aritonian outposts. Our objective was to set up a small base there and establish contact with the other robots hidden near the dome. His team would also release insect spy drones, covering the desert to the west. We hoped to map out places in the terrain where our forces could hide unseen, and set traps for the Zecla. For myself, I was heading east to Casita. I had to stop the war between Casita and her sister cities and enlist their aid in the coming battle. If successful, I would then journey to Arison and bring the Aquella to Boutal.

I flew to Casita with a robot in the seat behind me. It was an uneventful flight and six hours later we reached Casita. Our arrival was well timed. The ships from Phratis and Coralis had just combined their forces upon the sea, and were now heading into the bay to assault Casita. I estimated there were at least forty ships, maybe more. It was a pity that many would be lost before the day was done. I remained high in the sky watching as the vessels moved into position. I then commanded the robots on the ground to make their way toward the city. They were under orders to harm no one. Their sole mission was to destroy the cannon towers that Casita had pointed toward the water. My job was to see that the ships upon the water caused no harm to Casita.

It was late afternoon by the time the battle began between the city states of Boutal and it lasted a half hour at best. As the robots entered the city and made their way toward the fortifications lining the shore, I flew in between the ships and vessels, blowing holes in their sides with the blasters we carried. The ships quickly succumbed to the damage and sank to the bottom of the bay, the men aboard swimming for their lives.

The people of Casita, Phratis, and Coralis were stunned by the turn of events that befell them. The robots entering their city were unlike anything they had ever seen and fear swept the population into a near frenzy. They had no idea what to think and they ran like children into hiding. Likewise, the sailors and soldiers aboard the ships were even more traumatized. As the ships sank beneath their feet, they were forced to abandon their vessels and swim for their lives. Most made it to the shore safely where they now faced the enemy they had hoped to conquer.

I took my flying craft in the direction of the castle and fired several shots at the cannons that were positioned along the fortress wall. They were either blasted into oblivion or rendered useless. I then set my ship down on the beach just out of reach of the arrows. Everything now came to a standstill. I climbed from my craft and stood on the beach, taking a few steps while strapping my sword to my hip. My robot companion followed behind. He took his place guarding my rear about ten feet back, his blaster ready. I yelled to the castle.

"I am here to speak with King Hazadek!" I yelled in Motula.

For a moment nothing happened, and then a voice called down.

"Who is requesting the presence of the King?"

"The warrior, Roolka," I hollered back. "I've come to demand his surrender."

If silence was a precursor to action, then this was it. I saw a lot of movement at that moment. Heads were bobbing, fingers were pointing, and voices were jumbled in chaotic tones and commands. The gates of the castle soon opened and I saw a number of armed men exiting. Hazadek was in the lead atop his polono.

I waited as the group marched out and when they were about fifty feet away, I yelled to them.

"That is far enough." I raised my blaster to show that I meant business—they stopped.

"What do you want?" Hazadek asked. He still did not recognize me.

"I am here to relieve you of your kingdom, oh great King." I replied. "You have inflicted enough damage on your people. It's time for them to be free."

I'm not sure what Hazadek made of the situation. He seemed a little bewildered by my boast. He looked at the men who stood on either side, trying to garner support. He laughed, then announced, so all could hear.

"You say you are Roolka. You lie. Roolka was black, like us—not a pale milk, like you. He drowned last year on a mission for me in the waters near the horn."

"I see your eyes are as weak as your heart," I stated.

Hazadek responded, sliding from the back of his polono. As his feet hit the ground he took a fighting stance, his right hand gripping the hilt of his sword.

I laughed, moving myself into position, my eyes locked on him.

"I did not die when I fell overboard, oh great King," I mocked. "I came back and took Leanna, your unwilling Queen, the woman you bedded against her will. She now sleeps in my bed. Her heart is mine. And now—now I come for your throne."

I caught the flash of hate in Hazadek's eyes; his blood was beginning to boil. I tossed my blaster into the sand while continuing to prod him.

"I see your knees are shaking, jackal. Is that your piss in the sand or your honor?"

My words hit home with that final insult. Hazadek bellowed like a bull. He pulled his sword and charged. I pulled mine and readied my stance.

He came at me on a dead run, his blade wavering high over his head, an obvious attempt to cleave my head in two. As he neared, he swung down hard. I sidestepped and countered his move, our swords smashing together in forceful anger. I whirled, ducking underneath his arms, my body twisting, my feet dancing away. The momentum gave me leverage and space to strike back. I whipped my blade toward his face; the tip of my sword nicking the end of his nose, slicing it—blood spurted from the cut.

Stung by the bite of my blade, Hazadek jumped back. He wiped away the blood dripping down his face. He was furious. Blinded by rage, he charged at me again. I met his advance with my hands clenched on my sword hilt, our blades locking together—our faces within an inch of one another. I taunted him.

"How does it feel to taste your own blood, jackal? Surrender now and I will spare your life."

Hazadek answered with an attempted knee to my groin. The move failed and I shoved him back. He stumbled in the sand, but quickly recovered. We closed in on one another, our blades hammering and clashing as we parried back and forth. Sweat rolled from our foreheads. For untold minutes we circled one another, with our faces taut, the fight intense. If the truth be known, I was relishing the moment, as were the men who were watching. The air was filled with a chorus of shouting and yelling. Some were lending their support to the King—others were on my side.

From the corner of my eye I took it all in. Everyone had a stake here, including my robotic companion. He was standing behind me, towering over everyone, watching and waiting. I knew intrinsically he had my back. I turned my attention to Hazadek and our fight ensued, the metal of our blades clanging in dissonant tones as we danced around one another. The fight was well fought and I was most appreciative that my blade was normal again. It had decimated the metallic robots on Aura as if they were butter, but this was not the case today. Today, my fight was true, a man to man battle, and I wanted this tyrant to lose without trickery.

Without warning, Hazadek charged at me blindly. He carried the angle of his blade toward my mid section. I turned and stepped quickly to one side allowing his momentum to carry him past me. As his blade flew harmlessly by, I struck out with my fist, catching him square on the jaw. The blow was solid and it felt good. I heard a sharp crack and watched as Hazadek crumbled onto the sand, where he lay panting. I walked toward him and placed the tip of my blade against the back of his neck.

"Yield now and I will grant you your life."

Amidst his labored breath, blood stained face, and the feel of cold hard steel pressing on his neck, Hazadek nodded in agreement.

"I yield!" he cried.

He released the grip on his sword and I kicked it away. The people watching us were silent. What was going to happen now? Even I wasn't sure.

I moved back, giving Hazadek room to rise. Some of his men moved toward him.

"Get back!" I ordered.

That brief distraction almost cost me. Hazadek used the diversion to charge at me, throwing a fistful of sand in my face. His shoulder slammed into my gut, knocking the wind out of me. I reeled back, my sword flying from my hand as I fell to the ground. He was on top of me in an instant, his fists flying. I struggled for my life, trying to fend him off, blind in one eye. Suddenly I saw him pull a knife, hidden from within his clothing. There was a flash of light, the shiny blade reflecting sunlight. He plunged it toward my chest. I knew I was dead and helpless to stop it, but the blow never came. Instead, Hazadek flew from atop me like a rag doll being jerked into the air. I watched in amazement as he dangled three feet off the ground, his knife hand caught within the grip of an Aurian robot.

Before I could utter a word, the robot took action. He squeezed Hazadek's hand like an egg, crushing it—blood and bones exploding between his metal fingers. The entire city of Casita heard the agonized scream of their King, his painful cry reverberating across the entire bay. The robot then dropped Hazadek onto the sand like a piece of trash. I watched as the King lay in a crumpled mass, sobbing in anguish as he cradled his useless hand. The robot approached me, and with the gentleness of a baby, helped me up.

"Thank you ..." I coughed out, "... for saving my life."

Though I expected to hear nothing in reply, I was surprised by the robot's response. "You are needed alive," he replied.

I looked over to where Hazadek lay whimpering like a baby—his hand a mass of twitching muscle and bone. He was in shock. I looked to his council.

"Get him to a doctor." I ordered.

Several of his men rushed to his side. They picked him up and began to haul him away. I turned to face the crowd who were bunched together witnessing the spectacle of their fallen King. Suddenly there was a commotion behind me. I whirled around to see Hazadek choking—he was spitting up blood. That's when I saw the arrow protruding from his chest. He'd been shot.

The men who carried Hazadek dropped him like a rock and ran for their lives. The crowd was becoming angry and unruly. I yelled at them.

"Stop! Everyone!"

For a second they held. I looked to see who might have shot the arrow, but there were too many people. There was no way to know. I couldn't even say if he had been killed out of mercy or for revenge—either way he was dead.

"Your King is dead!" I yelled aloud.

A murmur ran through the crowd. They looked at one another, confused. This was unexpected. What should they do? Some began to drop to one knee, lowering their eyes, as if to grant me Hazadek's throne. Some began yelling.

"Yield to our new King!"

I fired back loudly to the crowd.

"I am not here to take Casita's throne," I shouted. "The people of Casita must decide for themselves who will be their ruler."

"What would you have us do?" someone asked.

I motioned for the robot, which stood a few feet away, to come closer.

"Pick me up so I might address the crowd." I requested.

Without a word the robot hoisted me up and placed me atop his shoulder. I looked out over the crowd and motioned for them to come closer. As they drew near I clasped the seti stones I carried around my neck with my hand. I cleared my mind, hoping that with their Visi magic I might convey to these people the severity of the situation facing their moon. I began to speak, addressing the Motula of Boutal.

"People of Casita, Phratis and Coralis," I started, taking them all in.

"My name is not Roolka. And from my skin color you can easily see I am not a Motula. I am a stranger who has traveled from far away to bring you a warning. Boutal is being invaded by a race of insect warriors known as the Zecla. They have already landed and are setting up a fortress within the Aritonian desert from which they can attack. They are coming to take your homes, to destroy your way of life, to feast on your very existence. They are vicious creatures who have joined forces with the Brata and they intend to destroy all of Boutal. I am here with men and arms from the other moons of Tiiana to help you defeat this enemy. We have come to stop the Zecla, but our numbers are small. We need Motula, men who are proud warriors—men who know the sound of battle, men who are willing to lay down their lives for their lands, their women and their children. People of Boutal, the request is simple—join us. Save Boutal. Save your moon. Save your way of life."

A proud, boastful man would have relished the words I had just spoken. The truth was I knew it was the seti stones. Still, the results were as I hoped—thunderous. The men of Boutal were ready to defend their moon.

CHAPTER TWENTY ONE

Countdown

alokka-ril stood near the transfer dais, keeping his distance from me–he was nervous. Ever since his arrival on the Arison, his aloof actions had made me suspicious. He refused to take a seti necklace, preferring to speak to me through the Aurian holograph, complaining that the seti stone made his head hurt. I knew, instinctively, that this was a ploy. And though it made matters between us more difficult, it was not impossible to work around. I granted him his wish, and we spoke to one another through the holo.

In reality, I suspected that his motives were due to my recent actions–the kidnapping of the Dolla. My deed was bound to have repercussions both for him and his people, and it made me wonder if he was under duress. Perhaps he was being threatened by the Aquita or even his own tribe. That was a distinct possibility. Simple conjecture led me to believe that he'd been given orders to slay me, though he was remiss in following through. That would explain his worry over the mind link. It would confirm those orders and, in turn, I would have to kill him. It made for a sticky situation. I pondered my options; I needed to regain his confidence.

"I think I know what the problem is," I said, finally.

The holo translated for me and I saw Salokka-ril's face pale. "What do you mean?"

"You're not the first diplomat whose personal convictions are in conflict with those of his people. I just have to wonder how far you're willing to go when you know you are right."

"I'm not sure ..."

"Walk with me." I interrupted. "Let's analyze the situation together."

I took several steps, my movement followed by two robots that were standing nearby. Salokka-ril balked.

"Come," I motioned. "They won't harm you."

Reluctantly, the young Aquellian followed me, his robe dragging behind on the floor. The holo who floated nearby kept pace with us, translating as we moved. As we spoke, I kept my head turned so I could watch Salokka-ril from the corner of my eye, my hand resting on the hilt of my sword.

"My friend, I do understand your situation. I have been in the military far too long. I understand your duress. I know they told you that it's your duty to eliminate me—that it's your duty to protect your people."

The look on Salokka-ril's face confirmed everything. His eyes darted side to side—he wanted to run and hide in the worst way. I looked for a way to defuse the situation, to calm him.

"I find this ironic," I said, turning my back to him.

"Why?" he queried.

"You've been inside my head," I answered. "You know I mean no harm to the Aquella or Urlena. And you of all people know that I would never let anything happen to the Dolla—so don't you think that this game of intrigue is a bit misguided?"

Salokka-ril nodded his head. There was a look of relief in his eyes.

"How did you know?"

"The holo at Aquilika told me you carried a knife hidden in your robe. I can only assume that you carry it for a reason."

The young man nodded. "Yes," he answered, guiltily. "They asked me to slay you, but it's wrong. I just know it—and I have no stomach."

"I'm glad you feel that way. Now if you would, slowly lay the knife at your feet and join me."

"You're not going to kill me?"

I laughed. "My friend, that would accomplish nothing, and I need you very much alive."

Salokka-ril reached into his robe. I motioned to the robots to hold position while the Aquellian placed the knife on the floor.

"Come," I said, tossing him a seti stone. "We have much to discuss and we cannot solve our problems with closed minds."

Salokka-ril took the necklace and placed it over his head. Our link was established and we began to talk. I put the matter regarding the knife behind us. I needed to educate this man and bring him on board. I ordered the holo to bring forth a map of the moons. I then began to explain how things lay upon the moons of Tiiana.

My first point of education was to show Salokka-ril who and what the Zecla were. He had never seen anything like them before. I explained their biological processes and explained how this had led to the first moon war. With that, I brought him forward in time to show him Zin in its present state—nuked and rendered useless.

"These creatures are fighting for their very existence. They are wounded and have been backed into a corner. This makes them the most deadly of enemies. Right now there are eight to ten thousand Zecla on Boutal, but once the Queen hatches her eggs that number will climb into the hundreds of thousands almost overnight. And after they have devoured every piece of life on Boutal their numbers will exceed the millions. Where do you think they will go next to feed?"

"But our seas," he protested. "Won't they protect us?"

"The Zecla arrived on Boutal in rocket ships, and they will continue to build more. Their hunger will drive them to search for more food. They will search every moon seeking their next meal. How long will it take the Zecla until they locate the Dolla in your oceans? How long will it take to find the Aquella living underwater?"

Salokka-ril shrugged. He was becoming overwhelmed. I took a break from the holographs, and the two of us walked. I spoke to him as a father and mentor, perhaps overstepping my bounds.

"My young friend," I cajoled. "There are times in history when a man is asked to think outside the circle—to move beyond the confines of his home, to move past what is expected, and what is normal. This is one of those times. Your people are dying from Giragoc, a weapon created by the Zecla. Would you not like to rid your moon of that viral disease?"

"You could do that?" he asked.

"Not with absolute certainty. But if we can defeat the Zecla, we can access their knowledge. We can learn their science and find a way to turn Giragoc into a harmless gas. Your people could then rise from the sea and bask in the sunlight again. And you—you would be their hero, the one who led his people to freedom."

For a second the notion took hold. Salokka-ril nodded his head. It was a dream that any man would love to aspire to. Suddenly, his temper flared; he broke away from me. I sensed his anger at being played—toyed with by someone with more knowledge and more to gain. He wasn't stupid. He started to rip the seti stone off. I yelled at him.

"Go ahead! Rip it off. You're right. I can't promise you're going to be a hero. More than likely you'll be killed. We'll all be killed. Why? Because this is a war—a very dangerous war and it will take guts and determination to win. These creatures don't give a damn about your dreams or aspirations. All they want to do is eat—and they will move from moon to moon until everything is gone. And then, they will find a way to move beyond, to someplace where another helpless race lies unaware."

I stopped short.

"You know, Salokka-ril. The irony here is the fact that your people could help stop this. But then again I've seen what your people have become. I lived with your kind for better than two years, slaving in a Aquita mine, digging ore to pay tribute to a stupid cloud, while you–your people hide like infants under the water, too afraid to use their science to fight this thing. Go home, Salokka-ril. I will release the Dolla so you can pretend you have an existence. Go home. I will find another way to fight the Zecla without you."

"No!" he answered, shrilly. He moved close, shouting in my face. "No, I will not go home. My people are brave! We once had a civilization that rivaled the Aurians and the Visi! We built great cities once! And we will do it again."

"Then you will fight the Zecla?" I asked.

He nodded.

"Good," I replied, "then let's get to work. I still need to tell you of the Brata."

After educating Salokka-ril on the gargoyles we went to the lower levels where the sub lay in waiting. It had been re-energized with power cells and it was fully seaworthy. We took it out into the waters of Boutal and I showed him how it worked. Within a day he was piloting the craft as if he'd been doing it for years. I was impressed with his grasp of new technology.

For the next several days we made excursions to the coast of Myolic. He piloted the sub and I showed him where the drop points would be for food and water. These were places where the Aquita could come ashore to rest, eat, and drink. He noted their placement on the sub's computers.

"They must only come ashore at night." I instructed. "The Brata fly by day and if the Aquita are spotted, all might be lost."

Salokka-ril understood.

Upon our return to the Arison I knew it was time to take Salokka-ril to Luskia. There was nothing more that needed to be done here and we needed to bring everyone up to date in Luskia. Additionally, it was time for my Aquellian partner to meet the others involved in this quest.

When we appeared in Luskia it was early morning, and I was pleased to find that Oolat had returned from the north. With him was an army of six thousand Solula. They were camped throughout the mountains surrounding Luskia, and they were anxious to begin their trek—food was getting scarce. I introduced Salokka-ril to my warrior brother, Oolat. The Aquellian was stunned by Oolat's size and that of his brethren; they towered over him like giant, hairy trees. A short time later Philip arrived. He informed me that he and his robots had located the area we'd chosen to make our stance. It was approximately two hundred leagues south of the Aritonian outposts, next to a small range of mountains that overlooked the desert floor. The location was just out of visual sight of the Zecla's defense perimeter. It was here, utilizing the cover of darkness, that his robots had fortified the position, entrenching themselves in the sand. I was ecstatic. My strategy for three-pronged attack on the Zecla was coming together.

For the rest of the morning, Philip, Oolat, Salokka-ril and I discussed details for the coming engagement with the Zecla. I laid out our goals and field tactics—each group needed to be aware of their responsibility for meeting their deadlines and making their rendezvous points. Everyone needed to be on the same page if we were going to defeat the enemy. If we weren't coordinated many would die. My main concern was for the Motula. They were still assembling into a cohesive unit as they marched toward Luskia. Untrained and raw, they were the weakest link in our battle plan. We also lacked sufficient advanced weaponry. We were shorthanded, and we needed more if we were going to supply both the Aquella and Motula. I pressed Philip and the holos in the pyramid to locate more, but it seemed fruitless—none were available. That's when Salokka-ril spoke up.

Hesitant to add his young counsel to the three of us, he balked at first, but with some prodding, offered his insight.

"After you left Urlena," he began, "before you took the Dolla away—I was ripe with zeal in joining your quest to defeat the Zecla. I used my status with the Queen to enter the library where the old documents regarding our early history are kept. I was eager to learn more about what happened during the war."

"What did you learn?" I queried.

"There is an island, not far from Aquilika where the Aurians stored many items. I think it was a trade depot. The island lay at the center of several major trade routes."

"A trade depot?" interjected Philip. "I would think Giragoc would have plundered and destroyed such a place."

The young diplomat shrugged. "I cannot say. The island is small and the plans I saw indicate it was built deep within the ground, and Giragoc's abilities are limited. He cannot penetrate the soil by more than a few feet, whatever his whirlwind tentacles can stir up or lay bare. There is a chance that only the surface structures on the island were destroyed."

I looked to the holo who floated silently nearby.

"What do you know of this place?"

The holo fluttered and whirled in response to my question. "I will investigate."

His form dissolved; then reappeared several seconds later.

"The young Aquellian is quite right," he noted. "There was a depot located on Annullitope, it was abandoned during the war–the Zecla targeted it. I have no knowledge regarding its contents, though it was a rather large storage facility. Weapons could have been stored there, though I have my doubts that they would still function."

"If there are weapons they could be recharged here in Luskia," noted Philip.

I was thrown for a loop. It seemed there was an outside chance that a weapons cache might be available on Annullitope and we all knew that we needed more weapons. Eight thousand Zecla coupled with thirty thousand Brata was a formidable force, and we needed every advantage. I made a quick decision.

"I will journey to this island and investigate."

Without warning, Salokka-ril blurted out, "No!"

The three of us were taken aback.

"It is not your place," he continued, emphatically. "This is my home. These weapons, if they exist, are on my moon. And you will need Anoni subs to transport them to Aquilika. You cannot do this alone. My people must participate. You have the Aquita to swim the waters of Boutal and attack the Zecla, but my people need to make a stand as well. I insist that you allow me to return to my home and deliver the edict."

Philip, Oolat and I looked at the diplomat. I was pleased with his conviction, and he was right. Still, I cautioned him.

"You will still need support. If there are weapons buried underground you will need Aurian robots to dig them out. There can be no other way."

Salokka-ril acquiesced, and an hour later I joined the Aquella diplomat at the dais where we had a private conversation.

"When your people find out that you have failed in your attempt on my life they're going to be furious. This will be compounded further when they learn you have joined in the quest to fight the Zecla. I suspect there will be a price placed on your head."

"I have thought of this," responded Salokka-ril, "but I believe this quest is worth the risk."

"A piece of advice then. Trust no one—not even your best friend. A knife in the back has changed history many times."

"That is a chilling prospect. But how can I lead my people if I can't be free to move amongst them?"

I smiled and motioned to one of the Aurian robots who had entered the pyramid with me. The robot moved in our direction.

"This is Auraten. He's an Aurian elite, a guardian, and he's volunteered to be your personal keeper.

Salokka-ril eyes grew large. Even though Auraten was smaller than most of the other Aurian robots he still stood over Salokka-ril by a foot.

"Are you sure?"

I placed my arm around the young diplomat as we headed for the dais.

"This guardian is aware of everything the Aurians knew regarding Urlena. He is fluent in all the Aquella tongues, dialects, and your customs. He can listen and hear what you may not. Stay close to him, and listen to what he says. He will be your shadow guard. Do not allow yourself to become distracted or separated from him.

Salokka-ril nodded in understanding.

"Also, I want you to take this."

I handed him a sword. It was a small practice blade used by young fledgling Solula, but it fit Salokka-ril's size perfectly. He eyed the blade with wonder.

"I know you are inexperienced at sword fighting," I noted. "But it doesn't hurt to carry one at your side."

I caught Salokka-ril's sense of appreciation. He was pleased. We then watched as Auraten took his place on the dais. He disappeared seconds later, transferring to Aquilika to secure the pyramid for Salokka-ril's arrival. The young diplomat followed, taking his place on the dais. I gave him last minute instructions.

"When you arrive at Annullitope, allow Auraten to act as your intermediary. He can help coordinate the digging on the island and return the weapons to Luskia if they truly exist."

"It will be done," responded Salokka-ril.

"Good luck, my friend. I look forward to your safe return."

With those words the Aquellian disappeared from my view.

✵ ✵ ✵

With Salokka-ril gone and Philip coordinating the data on the Zecla, Oolat and I flew to the Cassandra Pass to check on the movement of the Motula. There were about six thousand men and women making their way through the pass. Their progress was slow and cumbersome, as they had a limited number of polono and they were dragging a multitude of wagons filled with supplies. I estimated at least another five days before they arrived in Luskia. The slowness of our preparations was weighing on me.

After meeting with the Motula leaders, Oolat and I flew back to the pyramid, reaching it by day's end. I was tired and my mind was a troubled knot. Seriously, it would have been a pleasure just to eat and get a good night's rest, but there were concerns plaguing me. Chiefly, I was troubled over my handling of the Aquella, and ruminations on my ability to lead. I think Oolat sensed my anxiety. He counseled me as we ate our evening meal, suggesting that we walk afterwards.

"I feel I have become like Hazadek," I confided to him as we walked from our camp and into the forest. "It seems I have conscripted the Aquella into this fight with the Zecla when they have no desire. Salokka-ril is the only one."

"You are trying to protect their moon," Oolat responded. "This is a great thing. They do not realize the danger they face."

"Does that justify my forcing them?"

Oolat stood silent for a minute, finally shrugging his shoulders. "Perhaps you should ask them," he answered.

I was enlightened. His response was simplistic, and yet, to the heart of the matter. I knew immediately he was right. After all, I had spoken to the Motula directly and they had accepted the challenge, as had the Aurians. Why wouldn't the Aquella, if they were given the same option? I knew now what had to be done.

"Thank you my friend. I will follow that piece of advice as soon as they arrive here on Boutal. Perhaps if they see a moon free of Giragoc they might think this battle worthwhile."

Oolat placed his hand on my shoulder. "And what other problems are weighing on your mind, Roolka?

"The Motula," I answered. "I'm afraid they have no idea what they're getting into."

Oolat laughed aloud. The roar of his voice echoed through the trees and bounced off the hills. It took several minutes for him to settle down—I was a little peeved.

"What's so funny?" I asked.

His eyes filled with tears, Oolat answered. "Hell, Roolka, none of us know what we're getting into. We'll be lucky if we can stop these creatures, much less survive."

His tone changed—he became serious. He looked me directly in the eye.

"My friend, I have seen the images of Zin that still lay fresh within your mind. I have seen a young warrior stung to death by these vile creatures and I have seen them in battle. I know in my heart they will strip this moon bare, as they have done everywhere else they have journeyed. Everything will be gone—that is why I am willing to die in this battle. I want to save Boutal. I want my children and my grandchildren to grow up free and unafraid in the mountains, breathing the clear night air. This is why I fight with you, my friend—and why every other race will fight with you, if you give them the opportunity."

I was moved, and yes, a little inspired. I knew now, without a doubt, that others felt that the moons of Tiiana were worth saving.

✧ ✧ ✧

It was late, sometime after three a.m. when I awoke. The fire next to me was but cool ash. My sleep had been troubled and restless—I was still bothered. There was a matter I had chosen not to discuss with Oolat, for it was a subject too serious for idle conversation. This was something I needed to solve by myself and I think the answer had come to me in my sleep. Peeling off the blankets and darta skins that covered me, I got up and got dressed. I made my way to the pyramid, pleased by the fact that no one had seen me enter or was privy to my conversation with the holos. The three ghost-like figures asked me if they could help and I instructed them of my needs.

"I must journey to Aura, but I want no one to know. Do I have your understanding and word that nothing will be said of this journey?"

"As you wish," the three answered.

I climbed onto the dais and disappeared, reappearing on Aura. The place was dark except for the overhead light that flashed with my appearance. I walked from the dais toward the control panel—I pressed a number of the gemstones, activating the room. Lights fluttered on.

"I need to speak with whoever is in charge," I said, aloud.

There was no answer. I spoke again—this time louder. "I said I need to speak to someone in charge. I know that there are Aurians here who are listening. Awake and face me—it is of dire need."

Several voices replied together. "What can we do for you, Captain?"

"I am here to talk about what is transpiring on Boutal. I am concerned that we are faced with the possibility of losing to the Zecla and Brata. We are unorganized and have a shortage of weapons—a mix that could lead to disaster. Of course, with your link to the holos and the one you hold with Philip, I'm sure you're already aware of this."

"Yes," they answered. "We are aware of the difficulties you are facing, but we have given you all that we can. We have no more robots to spare or advanced weaponry that might help you defeat the Zecla."

"You have one," I responded. "You could give me a nuclear weapon, like the ones Philip used on Zin. It would be used only as a last resort—to prevent the Zecla from taking over."

There was silence on the other end. I knew what I asked was dreadful; the very words rang hollow in my mouth. I hated asking, but if it meant saving Boutal ... it ... my thoughts were interrupted.

"We have no nuclear weapons," the Aurians announced.

"What? That's preposterous. How could you not have nuclear weapons? That doesn't make sense—what about Zin?"

"Those weapons came from you, Captain—your ship, the one that brought Philip here. Our moon lacks the essential elements from which to create fissionable material. The bombs used on Zin were created with material supplied by your world, with your technology—by Philip."

I was stunned, and yet, it made perfect sense. In our part of the universe, in our war with the Relcor; we used nuclear weapons as fodder. And if there was anyone who knew how to build them it was Philip. I felt foolish. I apologized.

"I am truly sorry," I said. "I have shown how weak my heart is."

"It is not weakness to care for a cause or a people–this we understand."

The room in which I stood was silent and I felt like a chastised school boy. There was nothing more for me to do except return to Boutal. I made my way to the dais. Suddenly the voices spoke again.

"Captain, if it's any consolation, you are not alone in your sentiments or your logic."

"What do you mean?"

I did not get an answer. Instead, I was informed that I needed to return to Boutal immediately; the Zecla were on the move. I bolted to the dais and disappeared in a flash, the parting words of the Aurians still playing on my mind.

I was not alone in my sentiment.

My arrival on Boutal completely threw my visit to Aura out of my head. There were alarms sounding and general confusion. The three holos whirled toward me as I leapt from the dais, all of them speaking at the same time.

"One at a time," I ordered. "What's going on?"

"Zecla," the Aurian holo answered. "We've just received a transmission from the field. A large body of Zecla are approaching the western outposts."

"How many?" I asked.

"Approximately a hundred ..." noted the Aquellian holo, "... they move with thirty Brata covering the sky."

I was alarmed. This was trouble, big trouble. What could they be looking for? Were they out scrounging for food or was this a probe—a military reconnaissance seeking the lay of the land, and possibly areas of resistance? Or were the vags readying for covert strike? Were they aware of Luskia? That seemed unlikely. We had been very careful with our movement, staying well hidden in the mountainous terrain. And the weather, it had been getting colder for weeks, and no Brata had been seen this far north in a month or more. My contemplation was inter-rupted by Philip and Oolat entering the pyramid on a dead run.

"What is happening?" they asked.

I filled them in.

"What are your orders?" asked Oolat.

"We should hit 'em hard," interjected Philip. "Wipe 'em out before they know what's hit'em. It'd be a hundred less for us to worry about."

"No," I answered. "The less they know about us the better." I turned to the Aurian holo. "Are they in communication with the dome?"

"I'll check." His form wavered for a moment as he checked his data. "Yes," he answered, returning to me.

I felt redeemed. If we attacked, a simple transmission would alert the dome that there was resistance. We didn't need that, not just yet.

"We'll hold our position and keep an eye on them," I ordered. "This will be our chance to see what their capabilities are ..."

"Ahem ..." The Visi holo interrupted me.

"Yes?" I asked.

"This may be just pure speculation, but if the Zecla con-tinue heading north at their present speed they will reach the Cassandra Pass in three days. That timing will put them on an intersect course with the Motula heading here."

"Shit!" was the only response I could think of.

The rest of the morning was a blur of makeshift plans and the rapid deployment of our forces. My first measure was to send several robots ahead in hovercraft to stop the Motula from advancing. I could ill afford a confrontation between the Motula and the Zecla at this moment. Our sec-ond effort was figuring out a way to jam the Zecla's commu-nications. Philip was most useful in this area. He explained that instead of trying to jam their communications from the pyramid, which might be detected, we should use the insect drones to incapacitate their hardware. I was perplexed as to how this might be done and he explained.

"When the Aurians saw that they were losing the war against the Zecla, they expanded their research and developed a rash of weapons, throwing everything they could at the Zecla. Small drones were just one part of the picture. While they used most of them for spying and reconnaissance, some of the insect drones were designed to inflict poisonous bites."

I think Philip read the look of confusion on my face.

"The poison is acidic," he interjected. "We can use it to disrupt the Zecla's electronic hardware by dissolving the circuits within their equipment."

I was pleasantly stunned. He went on. "If that doesn't work we also have a number of the insects with metallic frames, which can conduct electricity. Put enough of them together atop an electrical circuit and it'll short out."

"Incredible—how long will it take you to get them in operation?"

"A few hours at least. I just need to overwrite their programming. We can release them by air and they'll do the rest."

"Get started immediately. The sooner we have the Zecla blind and helpless the better off we'll be—and, Philip, thank you. I never would have thought of something quite so clever."

"I've had a little practice," he responded. He then turned and joined the Aurian holo at his console.

With Philip at work with the holographs monitoring the Zecla and initiating antithetic measures, Oolat and I were free to organize the logistics for our counterattack. We began by marshaling our forces outside. We assembled robots and Solula, handpicking two hundred to make the journey to the Cassandra Pass. Others were given orders for moving the microwave cannons and rifles. We pulled a number of the weapons from the cliffs and hilltops at Luskia, and placed them aboard our hovercraft. They were flown to the Cassandra Pass and placed in positions overlooking the valley. We had three days, and much needed to be made ready.

Unfortunately, we were hindered in our progress by the weather—another large storm was brewing. I'd been so caught up with the invasion of the Zecla, assembling an army and acquiring weapons, I was remiss in keeping track of the weather. It was already quite cold, with winter closing upon us fast. Perhaps this was why the Zecla were exploring the terrain. With the Queen set to give birth, they needed to find more food, and quickly; they weren't stupid creatures. They knew that Motula and Solula had to be around somewhere—surely; the Brata had given them that much information. For some reason, the idea that the Zecla were looking for food gave me comfort—that they weren't invincible. I just hoped that the coming storm wouldn't hinder our investigation.

Three days passed and we were as ready as we were ever going to be. Our troops were in position, camouflaged against the terrain. We had chosen a spot where the mountains created a bottleneck, separating the Cassandra Pass by only a couple leagues. It was here that we divided our strike force into two groups. One group, led by me, took one side of the valley, while Oolat took the other. We maintained communication through our headsets. To assist in our reconnaissance, Auranine flew high above us in one of the hovercraft.

From atop one of the highest hills I scanned the mountain pass below with my field glasses. I wasn't having much luck. The valley was wide and hilly; a rolling terrain covered by tall grass and brush. Complicating things was the fact that we didn't know when, where, or how the Zecla would appear. Auranine had already lost visual contact due to the storm building over us. He was lost in a flurry of thick, dark clouds with lightning rippling all around. The storm's discharge of ionic energy and static electricity was playing havoc with our equipment, making it difficult to get recon on the Zecla's movements. Even our verbal communications were getting spotty. Making matters worse, the wind was picking up and I felt sprinkles of rain and hail.

Suddenly, I caught sight of movement on the grassland. A small, dark mass was meandering its way across. I raised my binoculars. It was definitely the Zecla and Brata. They marched together like ants, huddled low to the ground, the guardian Brata floating a few feet overhead. I studied the formation, trying to see what armament they carried. That proved diffi- cult. The Zecla were heavily cloaked with outerwear, but the opposite was true of the gargoyles. They were struggling, lack- ing sufficient attire for this weather, and were being buffeted unmercifully by the wind and cold. It was no wonder they kept so low. I notified the others of the Zecla's approach.

"I've got 'em. They're making their way across about a half a league from our position. The Brata are with them, flying very low to the ground."

I heard Oolat's voice cut in. "No surprise. Too much cold and lightning."

I switched frequencies and contacted Auranine.

"Do you have a reading? They're right below you."

Auranine responded negatively. "There's too much inter- ference. I'll have to drop altitude for visual confirmation."

"No," I ordered. "Hold your position."

I didn't want him seen. I didn't want to risk any chance of him being spotted and that information being transmitted back to the dome—it was too risky. I peered back at the Zecla through my glasses; they had stopped moving. I watched as they coalesced into a circle. What were they doing?

I was frustrated. This was not what I expected. They were holding position in just the wrong place. I wanted to drop a vacuum bomb on their heads, annihilating all of them in one fell swoop, but the weather was impacting our ability to achieve a direct hit. If Auranine dropped too close to our position we'd be killed too. I sighed. It seemed I had little choice. We were going to have to attack the Zecla directly.

I issued the order. "Cannon leaders—sight your targets. The rest of you move into position."

I surveyed the battlefield as the robots and Solula in my command eased their way down the mountainside, keeping themselves to the trees and rocks. I waited. Once they reached the mountain's base I'd give the order to open fire. During the interim, Oolat advised me of his status.

"My tribesmen are moving toward you. As soon as we see your battle flares we'll attack from the other side.

I was counting down the seconds. My order to begin firing was but a breath away. Unexpectedly, there was a hoarse whisper in my ear. It was Philip. I whispered hastily back.

"Say again?"

"I think their communications are out. Nothing's been transmitted for over thirty minutes."

"Hold position!" I instructed everyone. I spoke again with Philip.

"What was their last transmission—what were they talking about?"

"Not sure. I think the weather is becoming a problem for them. It's too cold."

That observance brought a grin to my face. I raised my glasses and weighed the scene before me. The Zecla were still packed tightly together. Some of them seemed to be arguing with the Brata. The black gargoyles were flitting about in a chaotic fashion; a few had settled to the ground. I sensed that they were uncertain of what to do. Suddenly a sharp, cold gust of wind swept down across the valley. I shivered—it was freezing, and the temperature was plummeting. I pulled the hood of my jacket over my head, just as the drizzle overhead turned to slush. Damn. I slid over to a grouping of rocks for protection. It was getting really nasty. I peered through my glasses. The Zecla were still immobilized.

Oolat contacted me. "What is happening?"

"Nothing, they're just standing there. Wait a minute—I see movement. Holy frazza!"

"What?" he asked.

I yelled hoarsely into the headset. "The Brata are leaving. They just took off. They're leaving the Zecla behind. Hold all action! No one—I mean no one makes a move. Let's see what's going to happen."

The minutes ticked by like hours. The Zecla were alone now. The Brata could no longer take the weather and they had deserted the mission. I watched as the Zecla waited. What were they going to do? Suddenly it began to snow and the wind gained in intensity. The air around me became a curtain of white that was impossible to see through. I watched as the snow piled up around me, and I realized we were going to be stuck here for a while. Looking upward to the sky, I saw nothing, but dense white, and I wondered: Was this just nature taking its course? Or was this the work of the Visi? Though I knew they weren't Gods, they seemed to command a unique power. They were in tune with the natural order of things and they had said: *I would have time.* I think, perhaps, we'd just been given more time.

"Thank you ..." I whispered. "... to whomever I owe thanks— thank you."

☆　☆　☆

We were stuck in the snow overnight, and when the sun came up the next morning the ground was covered by a two foot thick, white blanket. At first light, I surveyed the valley with my field glasses, finding to my immense delight that the Zecla were gone. They had fled during the storm, retracing their steps back to the desert. We pulled from our positions and slowly made our way down the hillsides toward the pass. The day was beginning to warm, with Tiiana's red light peeking through the clouds. We converged at the bottom and quickly found that the Zecla were nowhere in sight. All that was left was their trail in the snow. I put Auranine into the air and told him to follow it. I needed to find out where they were. Thirty minutes later he radioed back and informed me that the Zecla had reached the desert lowlands. They were heading back toward the desert outposts.

I was pleased. We'd gotten very lucky. The first major storm of winter had proved too much for the Zecla; we'd been given a reprieve. I sent flyers east with new instructions for the Motula. I needed them to make haste and reach Luskia as soon as possible. It was time to marshal our forces and take the offensive. I then called to the pyramid and asked if anything had been heard from Salokka-ril. The answer was, no. This was discouraging. I still had no Aquella on Boutal, or weapons from Annullitope. It was almost to the point where we couldn't wait any longer. I ordered the Solula and robots back to Luskia. Unexpectedly, Oolat called me on the headset.

"I've found something I think you should see."

"Where are you?"

He gave me his location—a league to the west. I moved to intercept him and his brethren. When I arrived, I found them standing around something that lay half buried in the snow. Upon closer approach I saw it was a dead Zecla.

"What happened?" I asked.

Oolat shrugged. "I was headed in your direction when we came across this thing. It was lying here frozen in the snow. I cut its head off just to be sure."

I nodded; that was a wise precaution. I bent low and examined the creature. Under its covering were a number of wounds, mostly second and third degree burns. Some were partially healed, but some were still oozing pus and blood. The smell was awful. We rolled the creature over.

"Look at this," said Oolat, pointing to the creature's underside. It was a blaster, still harnessed its holster.

I was floored—the spider-wasp was armed. This defied logic. Why would the Zecla leave such an important weapon behind? I pulled the blaster from its holster and flipped on the power switch. To my surprise nothing happened. I immediately contacted Philip and relayed the story.

"Bring the Zecla and the weapon with you. And see if you can find anything else out there."

"Good idea," I responded.

I immediately saw the wisdom in Philip's suggestion. We put the dead spider-wasp on a hovercraft and had it flown back to the pyramid. I then had our troops spread out and search the trail left by the Zecla. Our search yielded several valuable finds, including a discarded communications device. Back at the pyramid, Philip and the holos went over everything we had found, and we garnered a great deal of information on our enemy. The autopsy told us that the Zecla had been exposed to one of the nuclear blasts on Zin.

"Radiation poisoning," Philip informed us. "He was close enough to the blast to receive a lethal dose, but far enough away for it to take its time in destroying his body."

"What of his weapon?" I asked. "Why won't it work?"

"The weapon's circuits were fried. I suspect from the nuke's electromagnetic pulse."

I nodded my head; that made sense. I then noticed a confused look on Oolat's face, and I quickly explained the science behind Philip's analysis. "E-M-P—it's a wave of energy, created by a nuclear explosion that can pass through walls, people, and buildings. It literally cooks electrical circuits like heat from a fire burns meat. That's why the blaster won't work."

Philip expounded further, pointing to the communications device we found in the snow.

"This is also why the Zecla were using this. It's a primitive two-way radio built with vacuum tubes and wires, and one of the few technologies able to survive an E-M-P without shielding."

I was overjoyed with the news I was hearing, but much more so, when Oolat surprised me with an intuitive observation of his own. "Perhaps this is what the Zecla you fought in the forest meant, Roolka. The mind-link you held with the creature spoke of their weapons and technology being destroyed. It would appear from this that much of their advanced weaponry was consumed in your attack on Zin."

I was breathless with optimism. Could Oolat's revelation about the Zecla's weapons be the answer I'd been praying for? Were they truly weaker than I thought? Was our battle now equal? I could only hope that that was the case.

CHAPTER TWENTY TWO

The Battle For Boutal

y elation over learning of the Zecla's technological weakness was short lived. The very next morning I was given the worst news possible. I received a transmission from Auraten informing me that Salokka-ril had been seriously wounded. I traveled to Aquilika immediately to see what had happened. My arrival there was the next test.

I found Auraten and three other robots awaiting me at the dais. As he had forewarned, Salokka-ril was hurt badly. He lay unconscious on the floor, his chest pierced by an arrow bolt, his body burned in several spots. There was an Aquellian woman tending him. I did not recognize her, but she seemed to know what she was doing and she was being guarded by the robots and the pyramid's holo. Auraten pulled me to one side and briefed me.

"We were ambushed by the Aquita and later Giragoc. I lost three of my men—the cloud ate them alive."

"I'm sorry," I said. I knew now for sure that the robots were not immune to the power of the viral cloud. "Who is she?"

"I think she is his lover. She joined us on our journey to Annullitope as did several other Anoni. The others were killed.

We were attacked shortly after reaching the island; the Aquita evidently followed us. We killed a number of them, but then Giragoc arrived and the battle went worse for all of us."

"I'm glad you escaped," I said.

"There is more," he continued. "We had several subs loaded with weapons, but they were taken by the Aquita. We lost all that we had gained, though we did manage to capture a number of Aquita when we escaped"

"How many—where are they?"

"Seventeen—they are secure in the room adjacent to us."

Auraten pointed to a doorway where a robot stood guard. Behind him I saw a number of bluish-green faces peering out at me—Aquellian Aquita.

I was vexed. All my plans for using the Aquella on Boutal with Salokka-ril helping me were falling apart. I now had a seriously wounded young soldier on my hands, possibly near death. What was I going to do now? The obvious answer was to get him to Luskia for immediate medical attention. We had supplies there and people who could help. I made my way to where he lay and knelt down across from the female who tended him. She looked at me fearfully, but stood her ground. I pulled a seti necklace from around my neck and handed it to her. Her hand trembled as she took the stone. Our connection was immediate.

"I mean you no harm," were the first words from my mouth. "My name is Rez Cantor. How is he?"

She nodded her head in understanding. "I am Luna-rilta. He is not well; the bolt is very close to his heart. He needs surgery, and will not survive without it. Can you help me get him back to Atorika?"

"I'm not sure that would survive in Atorika," I replied. "We do have a facility at Luskia though, complete with medicine and personnel who can care for him. I think both of you would be safer there."

She nodded her head again. "Your words are true. Are you sure you can help him?"

"We will do our best. Come."

I helped the young Anoni woman to her feet and I addressed one of the robots. "Please pick him up gently and bring him to the dais. We need to take him to Luskia."

The robot complied, picking up Salokka-ril slowly within his arms. The four of us headed toward the dais. I briefed Auraten as we prepared to leave.

"I will return shortly. Keep our prisoners safe, they will need to be interrogated."

With that, I left for Luskia with Luna-rilta, Salokka-ril, and the robot that carried his near lifeless body. We arrived in seconds and soon the young diplomat was receiving the best medical help we were capable of. It was fortunate that the Aquellian holo had a complete medical database to draw upon, and soon Salokka-ril was undergoing surgery to remove the bolt from his chest. Three hours later he laid resting, his wound stitched, his burns dressed, antibiotics and pain medication easing his discomfort. I was relieved with the success of the operation, as was Luna-rilta. Knowing now that her young Anoni lover would not succumb to death, she breathed easier and I took her on a tour of Luskia. We talked and filled each other in on all that had transpired.

"How did you come to join Salokka-ril?" I asked as we walked amongst the trees.

I felt her blush. "He and I have a long history. We hoped one day to marry, but my mother has reservations."

I smiled. "Yes, mothers can often complicate young lives. It happens even on other worlds. Who is your mother?"

"You've met her," she answered, matter-of-factly. "She is Iantikke, our Queen."

I could not hide my surprise. The young woman smiled.

"And you joined him in this venture?" I exclaimed in disbelief.

I felt the rise of her emotions. "He is most persuasive," she noted proudly. "He was willing to die for this cause. He believes that you can help us rid our moon of Giragoc—that our people can once again be given a chance to rebuild."

"Does your mother know?"

"I'm sure she does by now."

"She will be displeased?"

She laughed. "Furious, if I know her."

"Then what should we do? Would you like to return home?"

The young girl gave me a pensive look, then flatly stated. "I would like to take Salokka-ril's place."

I was again stunned. "Why?" I queried.

"He told me of your plan—how you needed him to lead the Aquita on Boutal. I could do the same."

I wasn't sure. She saw I was hesitant.

"I know how to operate the subs on Urlena—everyone of official rank has to learn. I'm sure I could master the one Salokka-ril told me about."

"I'm sure you could," I responded, "but that is not the problem. We have lost the weapons we were trying to acquire and I still have no army of Aquita. I need them if I am to take the dome holding the Zecla Queen. You see, that was where Salokka-ril was going to help. He was the bridge I needed to convince your people to help. It was never my desire to force anyone into this war. I had hoped that the Anoni and Aquita would see that it was for their mutual benefit."

"I understand ..." she said. "And you have many Anoni on your side, but you must explain your position to the Aquita—if you want their help."

"How?"

"Start with the men you hold at Aquilika. Most are reasonable beings—not all Aquita are mad with worship for the cloud God. Most just follow orders to survive."

I liked this girl. She had confidence and a mind of her own. I suspected it was inherited from her mother.

"You will help me to convince them?" I asked.

She nodded her head. And with that, the two of us left for Aquilika.

✻ ✻ ✻

The seventeen Aquita prisoners at Aquilika sat in a semicircle on the floor, their hands placed on each other's shoulders. It made the communications process easier and they were surprised by the fact that Iantikke's daughter was taking the time to communicate with them. That someone of her stature would speak to ordinary soldiers. Using the seti stone to augment her thoughts, she explained why she was there, and how she had come to believe that the time was right for the Aquellians to fight for Urlena and their future. It was time, she said, to end the conflict between the tribes. I followed her speech, showing the Aquita their history, Urlena's past and what the Zecla had done. I explained that the Zecla were coming and why they needed to be defeated. I offered them a chance to obtain freedom for themselves and their tribesmen. I even offered the waters of Boutal as a haven if my plan failed to rid their moon of Giragoc. They listened well.

Of all the seventeen, there was only one who was bitten by the religious fervor regarding Giragoc. He was a young officer and his mind seethed with fear and loathing. He could not accept the freedom I offered. Fortunately, his fear only bolstered our stance with the others. They saw how pathetic he was, how unreasonable his view—how his closed mind held them hostage. After conferring, we agreed that he should be held elsewhere until they could recruit others and regain our weapons. And with that, I sent him to Luskia where he was held prisoner. The other sixteen were then set free, giving me their promise to return with more men and weapons. With my trust in their word, I prayed for their success. In the meantime I took Luna-rilta to Arison where I showed her how to power the submersible.

Over the next few days I learned that more Aquita were joining our cause. They were arriving at Aquilika in small but steady numbers every few hours; I even garnered a number of military officers who were willing to lend their support. They became the new alliance leaders, and I met with them as my time would allow. It was refreshing to see so many joining of their own free will. Oolat was right. Most of the Aquita were tired of living in fear and constant war. They fled to our cause because it brought meaning to their lives. For others, it was the call of open and free water, a lure too powerful to resist.

By day four the initial sixteen Aquita we had captured at Annullitope had returned with the weapons taken from the trade depot. We now had an additional twelve hundred blasters and microwave rifles. They were loaded onto the dais and sent to Luskia where they were recharged. From there, Aurian robots flew them ahead to the drop points on Boutal. They would be waiting for the Aquita who were now arriving on Boutal. We were nearly ready.

During this time I was pleased to learn that Salokka-ril's health was improving. He was up and walking when I visited him and I brought him up to date on everything that was taking place. He was pleased with the news that the Aquita were joining the fight, but quite unhappy over Luna-rilta taking his place. I promised him that no harm would befall her. I would see to it that she remained far from the battle. He was still unhappy. The prospect of her taking his place was certainly not what he had planned, but there was little he could do. To placate his pride, I offered him a chance to help with coordinating the Aquita communications grid–his response was lukewarm. I left him to sulk. I had more important things to attend to.

At least one thing was in our favor. The timing for our taking on the Zecla was coming at just the right moment. The weather at Luskia, though harsh, had been a godsend. Boutal's monsoon rains and winter storms had kept our location safe and the Brata at bay. Ever since our near skirmish with the Zecla, arctic squalls had inundated Luskia and the Cassandra Pass with snow, including the hills and valleys to the south. The cold had given us time to organize and prepare, and now another major storm was headed our way. At the moment, six thousand Motula were knee deep in snow, encamped in the Cassandra Pass where they were being trained in the use of blasters and microwave rifles by the Solula. Still, things were coming down to the wire. Our spies in the desert to the south had alerted us that there was new movement taking place at the dome. It was time; we could wait no longer. I sent word to Wakula, the new leader of Casita and the Motula army–head immediately for the western outposts.

As the latest cold front moved over Luskia, we were del- uged with a new barrage of wind, ice, and snow. It was bitter cold and time to move out. I met with Oolat and Philip for the last time. We spoke only briefly before setting our battle plan into motion. The three of us knew there was no turning back. Philip and Oolat left, both taking command of their respective armies, heading for the Zecla dome from different directions. Oolat's forces took to the high terrain, cutting through the hills and forest while Philip's robots followed the Pass and lower plains, joining with the Motula who were approaching the western outposts. By morning's end only fourteen elite robots were left at Luskia with me, along with Salokka-ril, and the holographs. I was happy to see that Salokka-ril's attitude had improved, though he still wanted to join in the battle. It took all my skills and resources to convince him that I needed him here in Luskia. That I needed someone here who could relay infor- mation to Luna-rilta and the Aquita as our attack unfolded.

With Salokka-ril finally convinced, and Luskia empty, I moved into action. I flew with Auraten toward the ocean where I made contact with the Aquella. It was imperative that I be there to lend my support and leadership–they needed to be in place and ready. Unfortunately, I didn't garner the five thou- sand Aquella I originally wanted. Only two thousand Aquita came, but at least they were willing fighters ready to do battle to free their moon, and I was pleased to have them on my side. Every day they swam hard, making their way west against the currents, and I found their mood positive. They seemed to rel- ish the fact that they were free here. No one was ordering them to kill their own kind and they were free to leave the water with- out fear of Giragoc; a feeling none had ever experienced before.

At dusk when the light on Boutal began to fade, the Aquella climbed from the ocean waters and fed heartily on the food and drink we supplied. At these quiet moments I took the oppor- tunity to instruct them on how to fire the blasters and rifles. I even found my past prejudices weakening; these Aquella were soldiers, and an integral part of my plan. I was touched by their questions about the moons and stars overhead. Many wanted to know what had happened. How had their species fallen so low? I did my best to answer, though I knew my responses paled in comparison to the simple reality that they could sleep under the night skies as free men. I knew that that fact alone would make some of them want to stay forever. And who could blame them?

✳ ✳ ✳

A week passed and the storms covering our troop's trek south were fading like a desert mirage—it was time. The weather was getting warm and I knew from our reconnaissance and the spies we had in place that the Queen's eggs were near ready to hatch. I return to Luskia for a final briefing. It was then that I received horrifying news. The Brata had staged a massive attack—a daring raid along the coastal cities south of Casita. I learned that thirty thousand gargoyles had darkened the skies, sweeping down on unsuspecting towns and villages. Now I understood why so few Brata had been seen in our movement toward the dome. Aside from skirting the cold, the creatures were flying the southern, more populated routes, crossing terrain unimpeded by snow and ill weather.

I was sickened upon learning of the devastation caused by the gargoyles. Thousands of lives had been lost. Numerous coastal communities, farms, and ranches had been plundered and raped, as most were unable to give resistance to the Brata. Krata, polono, and crops, along with men, women, and children were taken as a food source for the Zecla, their Queen, and her unborn parasitic pups. I was disgusted by the thought of helpless children being fed to the Zecla and I knew the

Motula would be livid with rage when they learned what had happened.

Frustrated beyond means, I vowed that it was time for retribution. Reports were filtering in from the Aquella and Lunarilta that flocks of the gargoyles had been seen heading west back toward the dome. They were flying low, weighed down by their bounty. I knew this might be our only chance to exact revenge. The black-hearted gargoyles would be tired from their long, enduring flight, and the Zecla would be preoccupied with the birthing of their young. This was our moment to eradicate the scourge from Boutal forever.

I took command of the seven flyers we had in our air fleet, one piloted by myself and Auraten; the others by Aurian elite robots, including Auranine and Aurasix. We split the twenty vacuum bombs between us and took flight. We headed toward the desert hills where the Motula army waited. There, I met with Wakula and Philip. It was time to brief them on what had happened and finalize our battle plan.

The meeting was terse and heated. The men and women who were encamped amongst the small, scrappy pines and brush were furious upon learning that the Brata had laid waste to their homes and villages. The interchange was so ardent that it took all my vocal capabilities and the power of the seti stones to stop blind rage from creating a mob of six thousand. I spoke with heated passion, trying to convince these people that the outcome would have been no different had they been there. More lives would have been lost, and an uncoordinated attack right now would accomplish nothing. I implored them to follow our plan, that revenge would come, but right now we needed to keep our heads. To my good fortune, Wakula helped sway the other leaders. He agreed with my reasoning, and his voice fell to my side. He convinced his people that the plan to defeat the Brata and Zecla in the desert was of merit.

With tempers cooling, the army of the Motula took a final reprieve to prepare. The sun was setting and we still had another twenty leagues to cross. After a quick cold meal, the men and women of the Motula army gathered together their weapons and we began to move. Our march took us across the desert toward the dome. The journey itself wasn't difficult, though it was long and we were hampered by the lack of light, that, and the fact that we had to maintain total silence. Sound carried easily across the desert floor and we could ill afford to let the Zecla know we were coming. With the robots in front guiding our direction we made our position; a series of low rising of hills about four leagues back from the Zecla's defense perimeter. It was here that I ordered the Motula to spread out and make ready our cannon line. It was three a.m. and dawn was only a short time away.

As the bulk of the men and women spread out, I met with Philip one last time. Our discussion was short and to the point. He was leading an advance strike force of twenty-five robots and five hundred Motula forward another two leagues. They were going to position themselves on the doorstep of the Zecla's perimeter. Immediately after we dropped our bombs on the dome and compound, they were going to attack the forward towers. This attack was our ploy to draw the attention of the Zecla. We needed to draw them out into the desert where the rest of the Motula would be waiting.

As light dawned on the horizon, Auraten and I took to the air along with the other flyers. Bombs primed and ready, we took our position over the battlefield, hanging low against the gray clouds that covered the sky. As we waited for more light I glassed the area ahead with my field glasses. I could see the dome, though no movement from our enemy. In my final prep, I warned everyone below against making a move until after the vacuum bombs had been dropped. I didn't want to jeopardize our position, as surprise was our best offense. We had been graced so fortuitously on our entire approach I didn't need any setbacks now, though I must admit, I was chomping at the bit.

Eager to get things started, I cursed the cloud cover that was blocking out the sunlight. It hindered out sight. Perhaps it was nerves, but everything seemed to be moving in slow motion. I was unduly worried that the Brata would take flight at any second and we'd be spotted. In fact, I was surprised that they weren't already in the air circling the dome as they usually did. It was perplexing.

Concerned, I contacted Oolat through my headset.

"What is your position?" I asked.

"We're in position two leagues east."

"Any problems?"

"All dead," was his response.

"Any Brata?"

"No."

"Get ready then—we're about to move. And keep your heads down. You'll probably feel the repercussion from the blasts all the way back to where you are."

"May Ahska's spirit be with you," he said.

"And you, my friend," I countered.

I then contacted Luna-rilta. She informed me that the Aquita were ready, lying underwater a short league out from the shore.

"Remain underwater," I warned. "The water will protect you from the blasts."

"I will await your command to attack," she replied.

Knowing now that our southern and eastern flanks were ready, I pushed my ship slowly forward, with the others following. "We're going in," I announced.

In silent stealth, we cruised over the Zecla's defensive perimeter unobserved, Auraten briefing everyone on the logistics of our movement. Passing though the low clouds, I watched breathlessly as the dome grew in size, amazed that there was no resistance and so little movement to be seen. Why were there were no Brata in flight? I had my answer soon. With daylight peeking through the clouds, the terrain was suddenly illuminated, giving us an unimpeded view of what was transpiring below, and I was immediately struck with fear and revulsion. It was no wonder that there were no Brata in the air. They were on the ground feasting side by side with the Zecla, and the sands surrounding the dome were blood red with carnage. It was the most nauseating sight I'd ever seen—I was sickened. Thousands upon thousands of Brata and Zecla were packed together devouring the animals and people they had taken in their raid. The poor souls were cornered like livestock, being eaten alive, and I swear I could hear their screams even at this altitude. Worse yet, a hole had been ripped open in the top of the dome and there were streams of tiny Zecla pouring out like ants from a hill. They were racing into the melee joining in the feast of death. We had arrived too late.

Overcome with rage, I commanded the robots flying with me to ready their bombs.

"Spread out," I ordered. "Take formation—Auraten and I will take the dome. Six, take the towers on the west. Nine, take out the ones on the east. Everyone else drop on the compound. On my mark, strike hard and fast! Now!!!"

With those last words I slammed the controls of my ship into forward taking us down toward the dome at breakneck speed. I commanded Auraten. "Put one dead center into the hole atop the dome as I make our pass. I want everything inside that thing dead."

He said nothing. I knew he was busy configuring our speed and our descent ratio, everything needed for the drop. I flew steadfast. I wanted my pass to be direct and on the mark with a speed that would allow us to slip away before the bomb exploded. The other ships followed behind, spreading their formation to allow for maximum impact on the Zecla's compound.

As our ships screamed down from above I wondered if the Zecla or Brata knew we were coming. I hoped so. I wanted them to see and feel the horror of the death I was about to bring on their cannibalistic souls. My heart cried out for the Motula who would be caught in the firebrand. I wanted to save them, but it was too late for that. The best we could do was to keep them from experiencing the agonizing death of being eaten alive. Death by a vacuum bomb was much more humane.

At a speed of several hundred leagues per hour, Auraten and I dropped our payload with deadly accuracy. As we curved up into the thinning air of the stratosphere, I heard the explosions behind us, the detonations reverberating across the desert. Though not as powerful as a nuclear weapon, a vacuum bomb was the next best thing. The implosion sucked in everything, stealing even the air and cloud cover over the Zecla's compound. Turning my ship, I surveyed the carnage below. The dome was gone, as was everything inside and the other bombs had taken out much of the perimeter wall along with a number of defense towers. We flew in for a closer look. Thousands of Brata and Zecla lay dead, their bodies strewn everywhere, but there was still movement to be seen. I commanded a return pass. I wanted every bomb dropped. This time we met resistance.

Our return entry brought us fire from the Zecla's cannon, along with another surprise—missiles. On heading down we were met by a barrage of small rockets and I was surprised by the quickness of the Zecla's response. The volley was impressive and we were forced to take evasive measures. I felt the concussion from the warheads battering our ship as we flew down. It seemed the spider warriors had been quite busy since arriving on Boutal; they weren't as helpless as I'd thought. Three of our airships fell to the rocket fire, though we did manage to drop more vacuum bombs, inflicting further damage on the compound. It was the best we could do and we took to the air in retreat.

With no bombs left, I ordered the remaining flyers back to where the Motula army stood waiting. I then sent a command to Philip: Strike now. Almost immediately I saw rockets being launched from out in the desert. They exploded around the Zecla's defense towers lighting up the terrain. This was followed by microwave and blaster fire. With our ground attack initiated, I flew with Auraten high into the sky, so I could watch and coordinate the battle from overhead.

Below us, things were unfolding in the Zecla compound. Over ten thousand Brata were taking to the air, surging upward with spectacular speed. I watched as they came together, swirling in unison like an angry tornado, twisting and gyrating back and forth. At two hundred feet they broke apart, skirting the rockets and weapons blast that Philip and his men were firing toward them. Hot, with a furious anger they headed toward the desert, taking aim on the men who were attacking them. The Zecla were not far behind. From atop the defense towers I saw weapons fire, and on the ground, a flurry of movement. Hundreds of Zecla were pouring forth from underground bunkers and tunnels like a boiling cauldron of red ants. They quickly assembled into battle formation and took off after the Brata. I estimated a good five to six thousand were leaving the compound and I knew the real battle was about to begin.

"They're on the move!" I shouted into my communicator.

I turned my ship and watched as the Brata closed the gap between themselves and our first line of defense. In my headset I could hear the five hundred Motula warriors below shouting—the din becoming louder as they prepared to meet the Brata head on. Fire starters were running back and forth igniting more fireworks, filling the sky with thick, black smoke. The air popped with heat and sound, and I watched as the Brata became disoriented from breathing the sulfuric air. Taking the advantage, the Motula and robots blasted them out of the air with their blasters and rifles, but it wasn't enough. There were too many, and I ordered our first line into retreat.

The ploy worked. The Brata were confused and blinded by the smoke and sulfur, and shortsighted in their understanding of what was unfolding on the ground. All they saw were the Motula taking to the desert and running away. Eager to exact revenge, they pursued the Motula with a vengeance. This was exactly what I wanted. We needed to draw our enemy out into the desert and they were taking the bait. Instinctively I knew these creatures no longer feared the Motula. They had fought too many times, and the gargoyles were bolstered by the backing of the Zecla who were right behind. This brazened their impertinence.

Breaking through the smoke and sulfur the Brata flew with a violent fury down onto the men who were retreating. What they did not expect was Philip and his robots giving the men cover with their blasters, or the fact that an army of five thousand Motula and robots were rushing headlong to meet them.

In was in this new encounter that another thousand gargoyles fell to the blasts of Motula weaponry.

From overhead, I watched as the two forces met. They clashed together in a tight-fisted throng, fighting now with sword and dagger, the shine of their blades mirroring in the morning's light. The battle was violent and filled with hate on both sides; these beings despised one another. For minutes they pushed and fought, the battle seething back and forth, the Brata getting a real surprise. While they knew the Motula, they had never encountered Aurian robots before and they held no quarter against these metallic fighters. The robots cut them down with little effort, tearing their wings from their backs with their bare hands. Still, the Brata had the advantage. They kept coming, thousands and thousands of them, and through sheer force they drove the Motula and robots back. Things went even worse as the Zecla entered the fray.

The Zecla were probably the fiercest fighters I've ever seen. They were killers, honed over time to survive in a multitude of hostile environments, including bombardment by nukes and vacuum bombs. They poured over the robots and Motula like ants crawling on a dead carcass. They were vicious and savage, carrying out their ferocity with extreme prejudice. It quickly became evident that the Motula were no match for these depraved creatures. The men and women did the best they could, but they had no real chance. It was time to call for retreat.

To buy us time, I ordered our flyers into the fray. Taking my own ship low, Auraten and I blasted as many Zecla and Brata as we could from the air. Unfortunately, even this was not enough. There were too many; even the Aurian robots were overwhelmed. They were outnumbered fifty to one and the Zecla were dragging them down, pinning them in the dirt, and beating their metal bodies unmercifully. Some were even assassinated with their own blasters. I saw Philip fall and I prayed for his safety, but at this point I knew the battle was lost. All I could try to do was save the rest.

I began to yell into my communicator, "Retreat! Retreat!"

I hit the alarm on my flyer giving voice to a blaring air horn; the other ships did the same. Soon a crying wail could be heard over the pandemonium. The robots on the ground responded. They knew what needed to be done. Those that were still able made a renewed effort to cast off the Zecla that were holding them down. They banded together and raced in units punching holes in the Zecla's offense. I saw Philip in the lead, he was alive and giving his robots direction. They created a path, giving the Motula the space and time to flee. I raced overhead yelling at the men, spurring them on.

"Retreat! Run! Run! Get back to the cannon line!"

I turned my ship and fired my blaster, annihilating as many Zecla and Brata as I could, giving the men below a brief reprieve. Most needed no other invitation. They threw their weapons aside and bolted for their lives, yelling and screaming in terrorized panic. Many were trampled underfoot by the Zecla and Brata who flew after them, slicing and stabbing them with their swords. A number of the gargoyles even tried to take my ship. They encircled Auraten and I like an angry flock of birds trying to take us down. Their attack forced me to jam my ship's controls into forward. We shot high into the sky, shaking them off and escaping.

Free of the gargoyles, Auraten and I quickly returned to the fray taking our place alongside the other flyers. We fired salvo upon salvo down upon the aliens trying to give the Motula more time. The battle was a bloody disaster and our enemy was pressing forward with a renewed zeal—they smelled victory. I knew if I didn't act fast I would lose every one of them. I just needed to get them over the line.

Racing ahead, I took the lead in front of the men giving them direction. I waved my arms madly, pointing them to the cannon line we had established the night before.

"Run harder! Run faster! Come on!" I yelled.

I screamed until I was hoarse. We just needed a hundred yards more. The men shot beneath my ship, passing through the cannon line and out into the open desert. They ran as if Hell itself was on their heels, and I watched as the Zecla and

Brata blindly went in for the final kill, which is what I wanted. With the seconds ticking by, I watched as the men and women ran further into the desert, many stumbling and collapsing in the dirt from exhaustion. As the Brata and Zecla came down atop them there were cries for mercy and help; I then heard Auraten's voice in my ear.

"They're over."

With my emotions stretched to the breaking point, I raised our ship skyward and out of harm's way. I then yelled into my headset the order I was dying to give.

"Counterattack—NOW!!!"

The response to my order was instantaneous. And I watched as the desert floor beneath my ship began to shake and convulse as if it were alive. The quaking quickly erupted into an explosion of sand and rock hurling skyward, as a hundred and fifty Aurian robots rose from the ground like zombies escaping their graves. From behind the ranks of the Brata and Zecla, they moved immediately into formation, some kneeling, the other half standing—their weapons primed and ready. With light cannon and blasters armed and sighted they began to fire, volley after volley taking down the Brata and Zecla with extreme malice. It was an incredible sight witnessing the decimation of our enemy and seeing their shock and confusion. Chaos reigned as the Brata and Zecla realized they had been outflanked. At the same moment, from over the hills to the east, three thousand Solula crested the low peaks. They poured forth en masse, their voices giving off an eerie wail as they charged into the fray. I'm not sure what the Brata or Zecla felt or thought, nor did I care. It was just awe-inspiring watching the giants of Boutal overrun them. I watched with exultation as the Solula swept down upon the Brata and Zecla, their weapons thundering, their swords flashing in the light. With unbelievable speed they engaged our foe, cutting and slicing them unmercifully.

I was beside myself with pride. Today was the day that the Zecla met their match. As strong and aggressive as they were, they held no advantage over the Solula of Boutal. These natural born giants were bred for survival in the coldest and harshest of environments and they were the most muscular, powerful creatures living here today. They towered over the Zecla, out-weighing them four to one, and I watched with sheer delight as they cut the aliens down like a sickle cutting grain. The red-skinned Zecla fell back—they were being crushed—even the Motula were inspired. The men realized that the tide had been turned and they raced to rejoin the battle. It was awe inspir-ing to see the races of Tiiana combining into a single powerful force, driving the Zecla and Brata into a desperate retreat. It made me want to sing.

To the south, at the dome, the same thing was happen-ing. The other half of the Solula army, led by Oolat, was pour-ing over the hills attacking the dome and the Zecla who had remained behind. With the Solula drawing weapons fire from one side, the Aquella rose up and out of the sea from behind, blasting everything in sight. The Zecla were caught entirely off guard. They had moved all their weaponry toward the forward battle line, not expecting to be hit from the sea. I could only thank the Gods above that they were terrible tacticians and that the battle was going as I planned.

Now for perhaps the first time in their history the Zecla were forced to run—and run they did, for their very lives. We chased after them like the dogs they were and we slaughtered them as they had done to so many others in the previous moon war. I wanted them exterminated; there would be no quarter given. Even the Brata knew it was over. Those that could still fly were already fleeing. They took to the skies in small flocks abandoning the Zecla. They headed south, back in the direc-tion of their island continent. The Zecla were now alone. As we pushed the spider-wasps into the desert they tried to make a run back to their encampment, but they were cut off by Oolat and his troops as they moved toward us. We now had them sur-rounded on all sides.

There were less than a hundred Zecla now and they were falling one by one. We were inches away from total victory. Then suddenly, the most unexpected thing happened. The

Zecla stopped running; they collapsed and huddled together, binding themselves into a tight circle. Almost in unison they cast away their weapons and fell into submission prostrating their bodies on the ground. It was evident they were ready to die with no further fight–the move brought everything and everyone to an immediate halt. Bewildered, the Motula, Solula, and Aurian robots looked at one another–a number of them to me, awaiting my orders.

I lowered my ship to the desert floor, bringing it to a rest. I climbed out and moved to the front where I could observe the Zecla directly and decide what to do. This was completely unexpected–in my wildest expectations, I never thought they'd surrender. From the corner of my eye, I saw Oolat moving toward me. He pulled himself through the throng of fighters as they stepped aside.

"What is this?" he asked me, incredulously.

I wasn't sure how to answer. I was just as baffled as he. "I'm not sure," I answered finally. "I think they're trying to surrender."

"Is that possible after all they've done?"

My mind was reeling, my tongue tied. Of all the outcomes I had envisioned in this war with the Zecla, this was not one of them. As much as I wanted to destroy every last one of the filthy creatures, my ethics held me hostage. Never before in my life had I killed anyone or anything under a flag of truce, or an enemy in the act of surrender. And yet, how could we allow them to exist? They were far too dangerous.

Unexpectedly, I was given a reprieve. A loud noise suddenly assaulted our ears–a dull, grievous roar which grew louder with each passing second. It drew our attention and we were taken in disbelief as we stared in total shock at what we saw. It was a ship–a spaceship. The men surrounding me instinctively moved back in fear. The thing approaching us had the look of a blackened, misshapen eye, covered in an ugly green slime, water cascading over its sides. It did not look friendly and they had no idea what to expect. Was this a weapon of the Zecla?

"Hold!" I shouted to all of them. "There is nothing to fear. This is one of our ships—it is the Arison. I have brought it here. Now keep your eyes on our prisoners! Our business here is not finished!"

As brave as I hoped my words were, I was at a loss to explain or understand what I was seeing. How under the grace of Ahska had this come to be? It was beyond comprehension. What had inspired this ship into movement? Why was it here? And who was piloting it?

I looked to Oolat. I think he knew I was at a loss. He bent down and spoke to me in a low tone, so the others could not hear.

"What is going on? You brought this here?"

My smile was weak. "I wish I knew—old friend. I wish I knew."

Flabbergasted, the armies of Boutal watched as the giant ship slowly moved across the desert seeking a place where the sands were open. We watched as water gushed from the ballast tanks on its bottom, soaking the desert, rivulets of mud flowing in every direction. After several moments, with the sea water purged from its bowels, the ship came to rest. It groaned painfully as its weight pressed into the desert landscape. We then saw movement midway up the ship's frame. A door opened and a ramp extended downward to the ground and a lone figure appeared. Again, I was stunned; it was a female in a long, flowing dress. It was Leanna. A gasp rippled through the crowd. Some of them recognized their former Queen.

I heard one say: "It's the ghost of our Queen." While another asked. "What is she doing here?"

Suddenly, a large number began to fall to their knees. This was a miracle. They had thought their Queen to be long dead, but here she was alive and returning to them. Even I was befuddled. What did this all mean?

Leanna stood atop the ramp not moving. She seemed to be surveying the scene below in silent stature, too far away for me to read. Anxious to learn what was going on, I took a couple of steps toward the ship, but I quickly stopped. Too much attention was being paid to her and the ship and no one was paying close enough attention to our prisoners.

"Wake up," I yelled at the men. "Do you want these creatures to cut your throats while you pine over your Queen? Show her the respect she deserves. Do your duty, now!"

That command broke the spell and the men about me became refocused on their duty and the war we had just bravely fought. I saw their anger rising. Some wanted to finish the job and end this standoff immediately.

"Wait!" I commanded. "It will be up to the Queen. Let her give the command telling us what we should do."

I had no idea why I made that statement, except that it seemed to make sense. In the worse case, it bought me time, as I still had no idea what to do with the remaining Zecla.

Oolat prodded me. "Go," he said, "find out what's going on. I will stay here with our prisoners and make sure nothing happens."

I nodded my head, appreciative of his offer. I then gave a quick look to Wakula and Philip.

"You both better come with me. Let's see what this is all about."

The two leaders joined me and we walked toward the ship–Leanna still had not moved. I was vexed. This was not characteristic of the woman I knew so well. I was resigned now to the fact that she was gone forever. That realization hurt.

CHAPTER TWENTY THREE

Oratola

akula, Philip and I ascended the ramp and made our way toward Leanna. As we approached I saw her face lighten in recognition of us–she smiled.

"My Captain," she greeted, warmly. I am touched to see you well; especially after all you have endured. You are unhurt?"

I nodded my head. "I am unharmed and in good spirits. We managed to stop the Zecla and we hold the last of their kind as prisoners."

She smiled again and looked beyond me. "Wakula," she said, looking at the warrior. "You are here in the stead of Hazadek?"

The Motula warrior fell to bent knee. He lowered his head and answered. "Yes, my Queen. King Hazadek perished a number of months before our journey here and I have been granted leave by the people to speak for them. My heart is gladdened by your return–it is a great day. Our people will benefit greatly from your guidance and counsel."

Leanna reached down and touched Wakula on the shoulder.

"Please rise," she requested. "There is no need to bow before me."

Reluctantly, Wakula did as she asked. She looked him in the eye.

"Wakula, most honored warrior. I am venerated by the respect you show me, but I am no longer the Queen of the Motula. The course of my life has changed. My path now lies in a different direction. To a realm far removed from Boutal and the moons of Tiiana, and it is there that I must return."

"But, my Queen ..." Wakula stumbled, "... we need–"

"No," she interrupted, firmly. "The Motula need a leader with a true heart. One of their own kind. I cannot override that wish; you have been chosen to lead. Accept your destiny."

"Yes, my Queen. If that is your command."

"It is–however," she added. "I do have one small request."

"Yes, my Queen."

"How is my son?"

Wakula nodded in understanding. "He lives outside of Romanth, with the King's younger sister, Mezitra. He is in attendance in school there–with the monks. Do you wish to see him?"

I saw Leanna's face tighten a little–a touch of pensiveness.

"No," she responded. "It would do neither of us good. However, I do bequeath of you one request. See to it, Wakula that my son stays in good health and spirits. I ask you this from the bottom of my heart."

"Yes, my Queen. Ask no more. It shall be done—I promise."

Breaking away from the spell of her past, Leanna turned and faced Philip.

"And Philip of Aura. How are things with you?"

Philip said nothing, but I could see his blue eye pulsating back and forth as the two gazed at one another. I quickly surmised that they were communicating on another level, separate from words. It was disquieting though it only lasted a moment. She then gazed upon me again.

"My Captain, I sense the questions you have burning in your mind and I have come in answer to your plight. Shall we walk?"

She took a step forward and the four of us began to descend the ramp while she conversed with me.

"I understand your situation with the Zecla and the need for it to be resolved."

"Yes," I replied. "Their capture has presented a predicament. Their aggressiveness cannot be contained, and they cannot be released–to do so would only jeopardize the moons again in the future."

"Yes, that would seem to be the case. Unless–they were taken somewhere where conditions were different, someplace where the very factor of time and environment could alter their evolution."

"And where could such a thing occur?" I asked.

"On Vashia," she answered.

I was dumbstruck. "Vashia?" I exclaimed. "How would Vashia make a difference?"

Leanna smiled confidently at me. "Captain, you of all people should recognize that Vashia is not all she seems."

A visual whirlwind of my visits to the white moon swept over me–the breath of her words ringing true. Vashia *was* an enigma.

"What will happen if the Zecla go to Vashia?" I queried.

"They will evolve differently."

"But what about the transport on Vashia? What would prevent them from returning sometime in the future?"

"That will not be a problem. Philip has agreed to help us with that. Now come, I need to speak with the Zecla while time allows."

I shot a look at Philip. He said nothing as we continued down the ramp. I was most curious as to what Leanna meant. It seems I was facing another of the Visi's unspoken mysteries.

We reached the bottom of the ramp and walked the mud laden desert toward the Zecla. They were still bound together tightly, surrounded by a multitude of armed warriors. I was surprised that nothing had happened in our absence–that neither they, nor our men, had made a move on one another. It was odd, considering how heated the battle had been. I was eager to see how things played out, and I watched as the Zecla became more animated as we drew near. Did they sense something was about to happen? It seemed so.

Leanna stopped about ten feet away from the spider-wasps. She extended her hand to me. "Would you give me one of your seti stones?"

I complied, taking one of the necklaces I wore and handing it to her. She placed it around her neck, and then made another request. "And now, if you would, one for them." She gestured to the Zecla.

Hesitant to get within touching distance of the creatures, I took another necklace from my body and hung it on the end of my sword. I then extended my blade toward the creatures. For a moment nothing happened. I gestured to the necklace with my other hand and finally one of the creatures gingerly reached out and took it from my blade. I saw a sense of wonder cross their faces as the spider-wasps established communication with Leanna. I listened to the buzzes and growls of their speech as one amongst their kind spoke. For some odd reason, I understood nothing of what was being said. I was curious to why this was, as I still wore the other stones around my neck. But something was preventing me from listening in—I suspect Leanna was blocking the process.

I waited for Leanna to finish. Her conversation with the Zecla lasted only a few minutes and she returned her attention to the rest of us.

"They are willing," she informed me. "If you and your men will allow—they will board the Arison and return with me to Vashia."

Her words caught me by surprise. "You will return, won't you?" My heart felt heavy. I didn't want her to go.

Her answer gave me hope. "Yes, I will return," she stated softly, her hand touching my arm. "All is not finished here, my Captain. Much work lies ahead for Boutal and for Urlena. Things still need to be set right. Now, if you will, please introduce me to the leaders of the Aquella."

I led her to where Luna-rilta stood, along with the other leaders of the Aquita, and I introduced her to the Aquella who had helped me defeat the Zecla. This time I was privy to the conversation. Her speech was frank and to the point.

"I want to personally thank the Aquella for coming to the aid of Boutal. Your advent here was instrumental in turning the tide in this battle against the Zecla. You should be very proud—you have helped to set right the erroneous history that has crippled the natural evolution of all the moons. Thank you."

I sensed the Aquella's response. They were pleased to learn that their help was appreciated, but they were motivated by their own needs. They wanted to know about Giragoc. Leanna spoke again.

"Yes, Giragoc ... I wish I could tell you that the creature plaguing your moon would be banished on the morrow. That we held some secret weapon to eradicate him from Urlena, but that is not the case."

I sensed a feeling of betrayal, but that feeling was quickly quelled by Leanna.

"We will remove Giragoc," she stated firmly. "But to do this, all of your people must participate."

The Aquellians all looked at one another. "How?" they asked.

"For Giragoc to be removed, he must be starved. You cannot feed him any longer. The drive for his consumption must become so great that he will succumb to his own appetite."

"But he will tear our moon apart. He will ravage everything in his search for food," Luna-rilta interjected.

"So, he shall," answered Leanna. "But only through purging him will you be free."

"But if we die in the process, then what good—?"

"You will not die if you accept Boutal's hospitality. This moon can protect you while Giragoc is purged. He has no influence here." Some of the Aquellians seemed unsure—Leanna pressed her case. "Look around you. The waters here are clean, with an abundance of food, there is land and open shores. It is here that you will find harbor until Urlena is free."

I saw a consensus taking hold. The Aquellians were agreeable, but I had questions.

"What of the Dolla?"

"They may come as well," she answered.

"And what lands will be given to the Aquella for their residence?" I knew that the hearts and generosity of the people on Boutal would be pressed if they were again crowded by a new alien species.

"Bratola," she answered matter-of-factly.

"Bratola?" I was taken completely aback. "And what of the Brata?"

She looked me square in the eye. "They are to be sent back to Zin."

My head was spinning. We had just defeated the Zecla, and yes, the Brata were severely crippled by the war, but their islands were distant and numerous. And, there were still thousands of the gargoyles left. Attacking their homeland would not be easy. How could we remove them?

Leanna laughed like an impish child playing with my bewilderment.

"My Captain, you have accomplished so much. Why do you doubt your abilities now?"

I had no answer and it took Leanna's counsel to help me understand the direction she wanted us to head. The Zecla were placed on board the Arison and locked down in the empty ballast tanks where the water had been held. The quarters were cramped, but the creatures gave no resistance. To insure none escaped, I put guards around the entire ship. I was taking no chance that one or more of them would slip out—Leanna assured me that that would not happen. When I asked why, she informed me that the Zecla were being extremely judicious in their acceptance of leaving Boutal—their very survival depended on it.

She explained that unbeknownst to us, a young, immature female was on board the ship. She had been driven from hiding during our attack on the Zecla compound, and as the battle moved to our side she was forced out onto the desert floor with the remaining spiders. Upon her appearance, the Zecla came to realize that not only were they losing the battle for Boutal, but their entire species was at risk. That's why they bound themselves into a small knot and surrendered. It was self-preservation, their only hope for survival. Their progeny lay secretly hidden at the center of their enclave—without her survival, no Zecla would ever be born again.

I was quite surprised by this revelation and I wondered if this was why I was not privy to the communications Leanna had held earlier with the Zecla. At face value it seemed she didn't want anyone to know about the Zecla's inherent weakness until the creatures were safely secure. This was speculation on my part, so I bridled my irritation. It made no sense to get ruffled at being left out on the details of the Zecla leaving; it didn't matter. The black-hearted creatures were locked on board the Arison and soon would be off of Boutal for good. My sincere hope was that they would languish and wither on Vashia forever, and never be heard from again. I was tired of dealing with them. Unfortunately, at the time, I did not realize the cost of my wish, the price that would be paid for the Zecla's internment—if I had, I might have thought otherwise.

Still, with all that needed to be done, I had little time to reminisce or guess what the future held. There were too many issues that had to be addressed. In private, Leanna and I talked. She had me give instructions to Wakula and the leaders of Phratis and Coralis. They were to return to their cities, taking with them half the army. Once there they were instructed to rebuild their naval fleets. The rest of the army was to remain here with me, guarding the desert and the coastline should the Brata decide to return. Almost immediately, I had the men and women with me begin to build a township. We needed new quarters, wells dug, food gathered, crops planted, and a defense line put in place to protect ourselves. Additionally, we began to build our own fleet of ships. Aside from the sea being a vast food source, we were destined to join with the others when it came time to invade Bratola—our projected deadline was nine months.

The same day that Wakula and his army left for Casita, Leanna took off for Vashia with Philip. It was a bittersweet moment, a feeling becoming ever so common in our relationship. I missed her tremendously. I wanted to hold her in my arms again, but it seemed there was little I could do about it. The change given her by the Visi had sterilized her feelings. As for Philip, he seemed distant as well, not his usual pretentious self. I don't think he was entirely happy about leaving and I didn't know why. He did tell me that the robots would remain under my command for as long as I needed. I was pleased, as they would be instrumental in helping with the rebuilding process, especially in the refitting of our weapons–so many had been lost and destroyed in our battle with the Zecla. Philip also instructed Auraten on how to construct more vacuum bombs. He knew we were going to need them for the invasion of Bratola. He then took his leave, sailing into the sky with Leanna. It was the last time I saw him.

Over the course of the next nine months much changed on Boutal. Through dispatches from Luna-rilta and Salokka-ril I learned that the Arison had returned. The Aurian spaceship was resting once more on the sea floor, her transfer facilities reactivated, allowing Aquella and Dolla to come through. The purging of Giragoc was beginning. The compound built by the Zecla was fully gone, dismantled and replaced by our own military port and city. It was a bustling seaside village populated by Motula, Solula, and a fledgling race of Aquella. The city was given the name of Cantor in my honor, which put me at a loss for words, but not as much as my pining for Leanna. I missed her tremendously. She had said she would return, but I had not seen her since she'd left for Vashia and I was beginning to suspect that she wouldn't be back. I was ever so grateful for Oolat, my old friend and constant companion. He kept me focused on my duties and our forthcoming campaign against the Brata. He also buoyed my spirits when they sank too low.

Eight and a half months after leaving, Wakula returned to Cantor with a small fleet of eleven ships. Not long after, we were joined by flotillas from Phratis and Coralis. Combined with Cantor's contribution of seven vessels, our armada grew to a total of twenty-nine in number. It wasn't the largest fleet ever assembled on Boutal, but it was still an impressive sight, filling the waters surrounding Cantor. From overhead in my airship I admired the navy we'd built. The ships were smaller in size due to our time constraint, but they were nimble and deft upon the sea. Many of their improvements had come by Aquellian know-how. Salokka-ril and his people brought their sea knowledge from Urlena, along with historical drawings and renderings from their moon's seafaring past. I marveled at how the small adjustments made in our ship building and design had made our vessels more efficient. They cut the water faster and with more maneuverability than ever before. And I knew we would need every advantage maneuvering the volcanic coastline and islands of Bratola.

Two weeks after the fleet's arrival we were ready to sail for Bratola. We were fully loaded with armament, soldiers, and provisions. It was everyone's desire to bring the last leg of this journey to an end, and send the Brata home. Sailing out of Cantor I realized that this was the first time in their history that the Motula and Solula had ever sailed together. That was momentous. But even more consequential was the fact that this time the ships carried Aquella and Aurian robots as well. And, as historic our battle had been with the Zecla, this battle with the Brata would be one for the history books also.

In the skies above I flew with Auraten and the other robot pilots. We only had three airships left, but we carried enough vacuum bombs and microwave weaponry to convince the Brata it was time to leave. Even the ships below were armed to the teeth. No longer were we attacking the gargoyles with just cannons of powder and lead, but with blasters and microwave technology too. I was determined to see to it that this mission would not fail. I did not want a repeat of history where others had failed in their attempts to rid Boutal of the gargoyles. Still, as we flew south I had concerns; there were unanswered questions haunting me. Just how were we going to rid this moon of the Brata and get them back to Zin? Where was Leanna?

This was her idea. Was she going to reappear with the Arison and somehow whisk these creatures away? And would they go peacefully or was I going to have to exterminate the entire race?

As I pondered these questions I kept an eye on our fleet below. Our airships had a bird's eye view of the ocean, and we flew ahead scouting the islands that dotted the waters, our heading leading us to Bratola. I was surprised at how few Brata we came across. Their numbers were small and they were quite skittish. As our ships sailed toward each rocky atoll and island, the gargoyles took to the air in fearful flight. I played with the thought of zipping down and dropping them from the sky, but there were so few. They were meager targets at best, and they brooked no fight to instigate a response from us. Heady with my recent victory over the Zecla, I failed to realize just how adept they had become, how easily they escaped our notice. Even with our radar they deceived us, scattering like leaves to the wind, their swarthy bodies vanishing against the dark, swirling background of the sea.

Two days later I got the lesson of my life. We were still a hundred leagues out from Bratola and the ring of volcanic islands that protected her shores. It was dark, well before sunrise, and our ships were anchored with our sails down due to a strong head wind. Above in the air, our airships floated silently. I was sleeping while Auraten kept an eye on things.

I was awakened by his voice crackling through the headset. "I am seeing movement below."

I struggled to regain my senses. "What?" I responded.

"There is movement upon the sea—see for yourself."

I snapped to attention, glancing at my console. The sensors indicated that the wind was blowing at a good forty knots. The seas were choppy with large waves and swells, but there was something else. It looked like a large, dark cloud sweeping toward the armada. It took me a minute to recognize what it was and I was stabbed in the heart with panic; it was the Brata. They were riding the air currents en masse.

I began to yell into my communicator. "They're coming! They're coming!"

I didn't hear a response and I knew we were in trouble. I yelled to Auraten. "We need to get down there, NOW!"

I jammed our ship to full throttle and we raced down like a jet on a bombing run. We had to warn the ships that were languishing in the water. I pushed on my warning horn, sending out a blasting wail. The other airships followed my direction.

"Spread out," I commanded. "And contact the robots aboard the ships. They need to be awakened!"

As we plunged lower and hit the troposphere we encountered the wind, its force making our flight a struggle. Gale-like forces whipped around us and we bobbed and weaved on our approach to the ships, which I could barely see against the dark water. They were anchored with their sails down, braving the onslaught of harsh and howling wind, waiting for morning's light. Of course, this meant no one on deck. Everyone was below, secure in the safety of the bows or sleeping in the holds. These were wicked seas and no one was expecting an attack from the Brata at night or in this weather, including myself. In desperation, Auraten and I raced in between the ships with the other flyers, our warning horns blaring with little effect. They were a meager wail adding to the noise of the wind that was howling over the water—no one heard us.

Suddenly, the Brata struck. There were thousands of them racing in flight across the night sky and they were nearly impossible to see. With the wind at their backs, they dove down like small aircraft, ferrying with them a payload of destruction. Upon their bodies they carried slings laden with rocks and boulders; some the size of a man's head. In unison, and with amazing speed, they began to drop their stones like bombs, striking at the decks' of the ships. The attack was well coordinated and relentless; the impact devastating. Some of the rocks were still hot, with molten cores. As the lava rock smashed against the decks, it shattered and burst open, spewing sparks and embers everywhere. The hot cinders fell upon the rope, canvas, and wood, igniting into flame.

How the Brata had managed such a coup, I did not know, but we were now at their mercy as explosions of gunpowder ensued. The sound of the attack quickly brought the men on board the ships to life. Hundreds dashed out onto the decks only to be struck and killed by falling rock. It was only the robots that had a chance and they saved what they could of the fleet. Awakened from their stasis, they grabbed their weapons and began to retaliate against the Brata, blasting holes in their formation.

Auraten and I did our best to help. We used our blasters as well, striking down as many Brata as we could, but we were also vulnerable at this level. Rock and stone were falling all around us, many exploding as they hit the cold water. Additionally, we were surrounded by weapon's fire from aboard the ships. We needed to retreat. I called to the other airships, commanding them to pull back, whereupon we rocketed high, punching our way through the mass of gargoyles that flew over us. In the safety of the open sky I castigated myself. I'd been caught with my pants down and now lives were being lost. Unfortunately, there was little I could do. I didn't dare drop any vacuum bombs for fear of annihilating the fleet, and our microwave cannon were useless. The winds were too strong and there wasn't enough light to shoot them effectively. All I could hope for was that the Brata would finish and break off. If they took to open territory we might have a chance to retaliate. In the meantime, we were resigned to using our hand blasters, firing down upon them from overhead. Our counterattack held little sway, it seemed the gargoyles were everywhere and they were ferocious in their intent to destroy us completely.

To my further dismay, the onslaught did not end with the rock attack; it was just the first wave. Seeing that they had scored a tremendous blow, the Brata stormed the decks of our ships. There were thousands of them, and the battle soon became a bloodbath of hand to hand combat. The fighting was pitched, and it took everything we had to repel the gargoyles— it was only the morning's illumination that saved us. With the gathering of dawn's light, the robots and I were able to sight and fire our microwave weapons without fear of hitting our own people, and we were able to take out huge swaths of Brata, knocking them from the air. It was at this moment that the gargoyles began to bolt. With unbelievable precision and unity they leaped into the air, instantly dispersing, putting airspace between themselves and our ships. I couldn't believe how quickly they fled, now that their advantage was lost. It was an exodus equal to that of any military, precise and well executed, and one I had not expected in such primitive creatures. One minute they were there, the next, gone. They were now ghosts in the waning night, black shadows flying low against the sea, fleet and elusive to our aim. Though I wanted to follow and annihilate them, it was fruitless to try.

I moved toward the fleet. I needed to assess the damage, and I was crushed by what I saw. We'd been decimated. Nearly half our ships were incapacitated, a third sunk, some were still on fire and there were hundreds dead. I thanked God that there were Aquella on-board. Between them and the Dolla who were following our fleet, they were able to save many of the men who fell into the water—especially the Solula who could not swim the cold, blackish waters. We had been beaten soundly.

For the rest of the day I was occupied in the rescue and salvage of the fleet. My heart was laden heavy with regret. Aside from the devastation and loss of life, my old friend, Oolat, was missing. I feared he'd drowned during the battle. He was not on board any of the ships and his body had not been seen in the water. I was sick to my stomach—this war with the Brata had just become very personal and I was guilty of gross negligence. I had underestimated the enemy and I didn't know if I'd be able to forgive myself.

Later that morning, I held a meeting with Wakula and several other leaders who had survived. We were all acutely aware that our fleet had been decimated. Most of the ships were crippled, their sails torn and burnt, masts broken, and numerous weapons lost. Additionally, each ship was burdened with the weight of too many men. We'd lost our mobility, the very edge we needed to sustain an attack against the Brata. I was now faced with a difficult decision. It was obvious that we could no longer carry out our attack plans; survival was now our chief concern. My worst fear was that the Brata would return. We were sitting ducks out here on the water, ripe for another attack, and it wouldn't take much for them to finish us off. I knew something had to be done, our survival depended on it. I needed to find a way to prevent the Brata from attacking the fleet again.

In the interim, I gave orders for the armada to return to Cantor. We needed to put as much distance between ourselves and Bratola as possible. The further we got out to sea the harder it would be for the Brata to reach us. Though they could fly and use the wind, they still had their limits, especially if they were laden down with rocks. Unfortunately, the winds that had plagued us the night before were gone. We were having difficulty making distance, and I was worried.

With our anchors raised and the afternoon falling behind us, we limped toward open sea—our progress slow. To better help the ships, the robots and I used our flyers to pull the vessels through the water. Our attempts were meager. Our flyers were too light to have a major impact, but it did help, and we slowly gained access to deeper water.

As we sailed to safety, I seethed with anger boiling in my heart. This disaster was my fault and it didn't help knowing that the Brata could return anytime to finish the job. That thought caused me a measure of paranoia, and I spent a good deal of time flying high into the sky, taking a hard look to make sure we weren't being followed, especially with night falling again.

With my eyes glued to my console, I studied the data before me; nothing was registering except the wind. It was picking up again, a light breeze, but it seemed to be increasing and blowing toward us. I wondered if this was a nightly occurrence. It would certainly explain how the Brata were able to attack us with such ease. Using their knowledge of the wind patterns, they could easily slip across the ocean and strike at liberty. It was apparent they were not the stupid creatures I had originally thought. They were smarter than I imagined.

It was then that a realization struck. If the gargoyles needed the winds to reach us, then they were probably amassing right now. But in order to strike they would need to gather rock and fly a great distance. Presently the winds were light—too weak for hauling a heavy rock over a long distance. That meant that they'd have to gain in strength and intensity—perhaps in a few hours. Suddenly, an idea hit. If we flew quickly to Bratola we might be able to catch the gargoyles before they left. We might actually be able to knock them from the sky with our vacuum bombs before they could attack again.

I flew down to Wakula's ship and told him of my plan.

"Continue sailing home," I instructed. "I'm going to buy us as much time as I can."

He wished me luck, agreeing that my idea was worth a try. I then gave my command to the other airships.

"Move forward," I ordered. "We're heading for Bratola. Make ready your bombs."

With the cold air whipping my face and hair, our ships shot forward to maximum velocity, and we jetted across the night sky toward the continent of the gargoyles. Our journey was short. Within an hour we were cresting over the outer islands of Bratola where I studied the terrain through my instrument panel. The infrared was especially helpful; it allowed me to see where the Brata were amassing. There were tens of thousands of the creatures. They covered the islands like a living sand, mostly resting on the high cliffs where the hot volcanic air warmed their bodies. It was this proximity that drew my eye. I noted how the gargoyles were congregating around the lava flows and the boiling caldrons that covered the volcanic islands. They seemed to revel in the intense heat, which gave me an idea.

The islands below were a hot bed of activity, linked to one another through Boutal's tectonic plates. Just underneath the sea was a tremendous amount of pressure—pressure begging to be released. If things were timed just right, we could use that pressure to strike a devastating blow to the Brata—one that might eliminate them forever. I glanced in either direction noting the islands that were jutting up from the water. This was our chance. I informed the other airships.

"Break away; put a league of distance between each of us. Each of you, select an island from the chain below. On that island pick the largest active volcano you can find. Verify and send me your data."

As I waited, the other two airships took their position on either side of me. In turn, I set my ship over the behemoth that lay below me at several thousand feet. It was a volcanic monstrosity, a huge boiler-maker that churned in anger, shooting streams of molten rock and ash hundreds of feet into the air. Hidden in the night sky by the fog of rising smoke and steam, I waited as Auraten set the timing on our vacuum bombs. A few minutes later, we received the data from the others—it looked promising. Each ship was now resting over volcanoes that were extremely active and quite violent.

I put Auraten in charge, allowing him and the other robots to synchronize, for what was required was beyond my capabilities. To create maximum impact, our payload had to be dropped at precisely the right moment so the bombs would explode at the same time, deep within the volcanoes' fiery interiors. Eight seconds later we dropped the vacuum bombs, and I slammed the ship's controls forward, taking us into the night sky at full speed. As the volcanoes fell behind us, I prayed for our safety as we tried to get out of range. We needed as much distance as possible if we were going to escape the devastation that was about to encompass everything below. I was not disappointed.

The explosion that resounded below us was nothing less than the force of several atomic bombs detonating at once. The three volcanic islands blew up in every direction, with molten rock and lava raining down upon the sea and land in catastrophic proportions. At the edge of Boutal's stratosphere, where the air was thin and the sky still dark, I sat with Auraten and the two other ships. We watched in safety the fireworks below. The scene reminded me of Zin when Philip nuked the Zecla's moon—it wasn't pretty. I watched in slow motion as the volcanic explosions ripped a gaping hole in the sea, exposing a red hot scar of molten mantle. For a second it lay bare like a jagged wound before the sea returned, pouring cold water on a blazing furnace. There was another explosion, worse than the first, the moon itself seemed to shutter, and I was immediately concerned over what I had done. Had I just set in motion the destruction of Boutal? Was I destroying the moon I had come to love so well in order to rid her of the Brata? My heart was pained, and I prayed for Boutal to survive.

"What is the status of things below?" I asked of Auraten, my voice weak.

"Too soon to tell," he paused. "The Bratola continent is still intact. There are fires burning."

"What is happening to the east—in the sea?"

"Our sensors are having difficulty obtaining data. There seems to be a swell forming on the ocean floor, and air temperatures are rising; a mixture of volcanic ash and steam. It's hitting the cold air, and creating a powerful electrical storm. Winds are presently at sixty knots, but increasing. I project hurricane velocity within fifteen minutes."

"Will the fleet survive?"

"I cannot say. I estimate they are two hundred leagues out—the storm will definitely engulf them, but to what degree, I cannot say. My immediate concern is the tsunami that will sweep the Myolic coastline and Cantor.

"Tsunami!"

Auraten's words rang like an alarm in my ear, and I knew immediately that we had to get back and warn everyone. I'd seen the devastation created by tsunamis, and even though Cantor was a thousand leagues east, it was in serious peril. I pushed our ship forward and we plunged down toward the ocean, racing against time and the forces of nature. The other airships followed. Closer and closer our ship fell to the water. I could now hear the hurricane I'd unleashed, screaming as it crossed the ocean, gathering strength. It roared behind us in frightful anger, telling me that Boutal was going to pay for my misdeeds. My heart was filled with horror. Skimming over the top of the blackened clouds, we raced just ahead of the monster, lightning dancing at our rear, the crackle of her fiery energy chasing us. We were like board riders, cresting a wave with a furious beast looming behind. There was so little time.

I felt the ship beneath me straining to maintain speed as we cut through the crosswinds. I had to warn the fleet and Cantor. I knew that just underneath the water a wave was forming; a sea dragon swelling within the belly of the ocean, taking form with anger and purpose. It was rolling forward, gaining pressure and speed, and it would be unstoppable.

In the distance ahead, I caught sight of the fleet. The ships were bobbing chaotically atop the sea, battered by the wind and rough waters. I called to them with my communicator, hoping that I could get through, to make them aware of the coming hurricane.

"There's a storm coming!" I yelled. "Warning! Warning! Batten down and hold on for dear life!"

We flew past the ships. Rain was falling and the darkened skies were casting an ashen gloom over everything. I called out again, but got no response. I feared the worst. The men and women had taken refuge in the holds and bellies of their vessels. They were awaiting their death in floating tombs. They would die by my actions, in a storm I'd created. What had I done?

Auraten prodded me. "We need to gain altitude," he warned. "The storm is outpacing us."

I acknowledged his warning and took our ship higher. The other two followed. Behind, the storm overtook the fleet, swallowing it entirely. I could only imagine the hell the men and women aboard were experiencing. Their deaths would be unpleasant. Had it not been for Cantor and my need to warn the citizens there, I would have plunged a dagger in my own heart. A fitting end, marking my ignorant deed, but I could not do that—not when so many more needed to be saved. We raced on again, gaining altitude as the storm surged ahead. I called ahead to Cantor.

The message I sent was of immediate urgency. I told them to evacuate the city—there was no time to waste. I received no response.

"Am I getting through?" I asked Auraten.

"The signal is weak," he responded, "our power cells are down by half, still, they should be able to receive it—keep trying."

I followed his advice, my voice becoming hoarse as I tried to warn Cantor of the coming tsunami. We raced the storm through the night and coming dawn, the speed of our flyers slowing measurably as we used up power. We reached the coastline ahead of the wind and rain, but not the tsunami. I saw the water rise up—the sea dragon taking form. She was a giant of epic proportions, and we had to pull high into the sky to avoid being hit by the beast. She was nearly two hundred feet in height and her width took in the coastline for as far as I could see. I knew Cantor was doomed. There was no stopping it.

From our aerial vantage point Auraten and I watched as the wave crested over the city, crushing it. The swell of water and mud rolled onto the land for miles. As it pulled back, the undertow ripped the ground underneath, sucking everything into the water. The city was devoured completely. There was nothing left, except mud and remnants regurgitated by the ocean. It tore my heart to see the city go; its demise only deepened my despair. I had destroyed all I cared about.

With the sky blackened by clouds and rain falling in torrents, our visibility fell to almost zero. If there were any survivors from Cantor they would have to be found on foot. We landed our craft and commenced our search, but it was useless. The mud on the ground was thick, the winds almost hurricane in force, and the rain, icy in its bite and sting. Instead of being able to help look for survivors I was relegated to eking out shelter alongside our ships while Auraten and the other robots plodded through the quagmire, searching.

Shivering in my mud soaked clothes; I took stock of the situation. The land about me was dark and dismal, depressing my spirit. My best friend was probably dead thanks to my arrogant stupidity, our fleet was lost, and the city of Cantor destroyed. What would my Princess think of her Captain now?

I was sorely ashamed. How could I face her—or anyone? Awash in pity and self-loathing it came to me that I needed to leave.

At first light, as the winds and rain abated, I took leave of Auraten and the others. I instructed them to remain behind and look for survivors. There was still much of the coastline to be covered, and I knew they could do a better job without my human frailties hindering them.

"We will contact you if we find anything," said Auraten, in a soft, muted timbre—the tone in his voice making me feel even guiltier.

I wanted to respond, but I had nothing worthy to say. Instead, I watched in silence as he disappeared into the curtain of rain that consumed us. And I wondered—did he understand my shame or was his Aurian soul incapable? And did it matter?

Trudging through the mud, I took stock of our three airships. They lay near one another in a quagmire of mud and seaweed. All three were dirty, worn, and battle scarred with their power supplies dwindling. I chose the one with the largest reserve, threw my sword inside, and took to the air. I felt like a rat, deserting my post, leaving my companions with the dirty work, but I knew that others would come. Those in Luskia were already aware, and they would find a way to bring help. I just didn't have the stomach to face them.

The rain filled skies were dark and gloomy as I headed back out over the ocean, plotting a course back to Bratola. I wanted to find the fleet or what was left of it—perhaps there were survivors. Unfortunately, my goal was unobtainable. For the further south I flew, the more dreadful the weather became, and it was all I could do to keep my ship airborne. In every direction, there was nothing but black rain—a caustic mix of wet soot and ash that poured from the sky. It choked the air, a dank mass that made it nearly impossible to see, and I had too little power to rise above it. The black goo was sticky paste and it burned my flesh. It clung to everything, my face, my body, and the ship. I was forced to cover myself with a cloth and fly by instrument alone, and even that proved difficult.

Eventually, my power supply reached depletion and I was forced to land. Fortuitously, there was a rocky atoll protruding from the water about a league back. I had passed over it during my flight. Turning my ship, I made my way back, finding it just in time. It was a small island, barely twenty feet in length, just large enough for the ship. I set the flyer down and got out. Under the bombardment of rain I searched around for shelter, but there was nothing available except my flyer and bare rock. Desperate to escape the deluge, I pulled out the rock from underneath the ship, and made a shallow hole. I then crawled under the flyer. It was the best I could do for the time being, though the protection given me was meager at best. For the rest of the day and night I lay there praying for salvation. This was my penance—the restitution for my crimes. This catastrophe was a disaster of my making. In my zeal to kill the Brata, I responded with overkill. I hadn't fully considered the consequences, and I deserved punishment.

For twenty-four hours I lay under the ship, listening to the muddy rain as it slapped against the rocks and the water around me. I had no food and the water supply on the ship was nearly gone. I thought of entering the ocean and swimming, but there was nowhere to go. I became resigned to my fate, knowing that this was where I would meet my end. Somehow that thought brought me peace, so I lay back wallowing in the filth, drinking sips of water until it ran out. Two days later the clouds parted and Tiiana returned, her radiant form baking me. With no water I soon became weak and delirious—my mind began to play tricks on me. I huddled underneath the ship and awaited my death, fading in and out of consciousness. When lucid, I prayed for forgiveness, asking all that I had harmed to forgive me.

Unexpectedly, my prayers were answered. A soft, squeaky voice called out to me.

"Father ... sad ... come ... help."

In the depth of my soul, I recognized the voice, but in my mind I knew I'd gone over the edge. I yelled angrily, like a swaggering drunk. "Go a—way!"

From the lack of water, my speech was impeded, my tongue swollen, lips cracked and dry. I was thin, weak, and drunk with fever. Who would want to save me?

The voice answered.

"Father ... we ... save ... you ... as you ... save us."

"U no i-dea whaaat u-r talk-king bout," I answered, before passing out.

The next thing I remember through my delirium were hands touching me—water being pressed to my lips. Someone was caring for me—I had no idea who. When I finally regained consciousness I found myself still on the atoll, weak, but lying under the shade of an Aquellian membrane bag. There was food and water set near to me. Someone had brought them to me. It had to be an Aquellian. Who else could navigate these waters to bring food and drink? I fantasized on my benefactor. The water pouches looked like the ones used in the Aquellian slave mines. Perhaps my savior was Jazokee or Raktila, my former slave companions? That thought brought a sense of irony to me. It made me think again about the dark days I slaved in the mud tunnels of Urlena, how I yearned to escape and survive. It made me ask myself: Why was I giving up now? I felt a seed of hope growing within. There was a reason, a need, for me to survive even if I didn't understand why. I sipped from the water pouches and ate.

Over the course of the next several days I felt my strength returning, my head clearing. I never learned who my benefactor was, only that fresh fish and bota bags filled with water were brought and laid upon the rocky shores at night as I slept. Those rations, though raw and tasteless, were enough to get me going again. I was finally able to pick myself up and look over my airship. It was not in the best of condition. Like me, it was covered with dried mud, volcanic ash and black soot. I cleaned it as best I could, scraping out the muck that caked the insides with my bare hands. I then turned my attention to the power cells. They were drained of power. I washed off the ship's solar panels with sea water, hoping that the light from Tiiana and the sun would recharge the backup drive. Time would tell.

While the sun arced overhead, I bathed in the ocean, scrubbing the filth from my body. It wasn't the best bath, but it helped, though my skin was left tender and sore from the caustic mud. Afterwards, I returned to the ship, delighted to find that the power cells were charging. They were at ten percent, giving me enough power to run an internal systems check. I quickly checked the ship over, finding several functions beyond repair, one being communications. I could not send or receive any transmissions. Still, the ship internal drives were holding power. It appeared that the ship might fly, if it could build enough of a charge.

I waited another two days giving the solar panels more time to build, finally reaching fifty percent of their capacity. It was enough; I couldn't take another day on the atoll. I climbed into the ship and powered it up. Begrudgingly, the ship responded, rising slowly into the air. It held itself at roughly four feet, enough to keep me afloat over the water. I headed for Bratola. The flight to the continent took forever. I flew for hours seeing nothing but water and rocky islands. There were no signs of life, and no evidence that the Brata had survived or escaped the devastation of the volcanic eruptions or the tsunami. I flew on. Finally, I came within view of Bratola. The weather was calm, the seas tranquil, and I was pleasantly surprised to see greenery in the distance. As I got closer I noted that there were large sections of land still covered with vegetation. Trees, plants, and shrubs stood alongside dead zones, areas of land that had been completely wiped out. I was amazed to see how much had survived, and relieved that my actions hadn't destroyed everything. Turning my ship, I moved inland paralleling the shoreline, flying alongside the patchwork of greenery and dead zones that pockmarked the land. I was searching for signs of corporal life or habitation, but I saw nothing. I traveled for leagues, heading north toward the area of impact, where the robots and I had dropped our bombs. It was in this direction that I saw the most damage: storm ravaged beaches; areas buried under sheets of lava now hardened and caked to the land, charred trees and burnt grass. The devastation was incredible and ran for leagues back onto the continent.

Continuing on, I finally reached an area where the terrain became more mountainous. Here, the hills and valleys had protected land, and I soon found myself entering an expanse covered by a lush, tropical forest. I began to hear the echoing calls of wildlife. However, there were still no signs of intelligent life—no Brata, Motula, Solula or Aquellian people. I wondered: Was everyone dead? The answer came soon.

With the terrain dense with vegetation, and my ship unable to fly over it, I was forced to stay near the shoreline. It was here, flying over a thin strip of beach that I continued my journey, my heading taking me toward a peninsula about ten leagues ahead. Rounding its tip I encountered the surprise of my life. For there, looming in the distance some five leagues away was the Arison. She was resting upon the shore, her form obscured by a grouping of grassy sand dunes that lay in between. I couldn't believe my eyes. I pushed my ship forward, only to have sputter and cough. I was forced to land.

I set the flyer down on the beach and climbed out. It seemed the ship had reached its end. I checked the power cells, they were dead; the solar panels could do no more. I grabbed my sword and strapped it on. I then began to walk in the direction of the Arison. I couldn't believe she was here and I was anxious to see what was transpiring. With each step toward her I gave thought to Boutal and the other moons. Was Leanna with the ship? She had to be. Who else would be flying it? I then wondered how she was going to feel, seeing all the damage I had caused. The walk seemed to take forever, the white beach sand was thick and deep and difficult to navigate. I felt open and vulnerable. If the Brata were anywhere nearby they could attack me with impunity. I gripped my sword for reassurance.

An hour passed before I reached the dunes that were obscuring my view. I plodded upward; sweating with exertion— it was getting warm. Finally, atop the dunes, I gained a full view of the Arison even though she was still a league away. To my surprise I could see others on the beach. I could make out a small number of Brata, several Aurian robots, and of all things, a couple Zecla. I was floored by their sight. I thought they'd been quarantined on Vashia–what were they doing here?

Stunned, and yet ever so curious, I moved forward, closing the gap between myself and the ship. I even pulled out my sword, though none of the creatures seemed to take notice of me. They were too engrossed in some sort of parley, and I was sorely interested in what was going on. As I got closer I caught a glimpse of Leanna. She was standing near the rear of the group, protected on either side by two robots. I stopped dead in my tracks, uncertain what to do. Fortunately, she turned and looked in my direction. She waved; then left the group, making her way toward me. Hesitantly, I took a step forward.

The two of us met halfway on the beach. "My Captain," she said, warmly. "It is so good to see you."

I didn't know what to say. I must have looked like a dunce. She took me by the arm and walked me away from the Brata and Zecla. We headed toward the water's edge.

"This must seem a little confusing," she said, squeezing my arm. I nodded in agreement, but said nothing.

"Your attack on the Brata was most successful."

"I'm really sorry," I answered. "I had no idea that my plan would harm so many. Can you forgive me?"

"There is no need for forgiveness," she responded. "All that has happened was as it needed to be."

"I don't understand."

"No, you weren't meant to." She squeezed my arm again reassuringly. "You see, my Captain, for everything to happen here, it was necessary that the Brata sustain major losses. They are simple creatures who understand things on a primal level. For them to vacate Boutal willingly they had to be shown that they are not wanted here, that it is time for them to leave–that their survival depends on it. Your attack was the only way to bring an end to the cycle of violence between them and the citizens of Boutal. If thousands of Brata had survived, the conflict would go on forever. No one on Boutal would be able to build a meaningful culture, including the

Brata. They need to go home to their own moon. If they do, they will have a chance to evolve and take their place in the universe as a civilized culture."

"But what of Cantor and the fleet—all those people who met their death because of my actions?"

Leanna smiled. "They were evacuated a full day before the tsunami reached her shores. They are all safe, and many have already returned to rebuild."

"What of the fleet?"

"They were rescued as well. We took them aboard the Arison before the storm struck. They are safe here on Bratola, residing in a cove not more than fifty leagues up the coast. They await the final outcome of our talks with the Brata. Some have expressed a desire to remain here, to explore and build new homes—others are waiting to return to Casita, Phratis and Coralis."

I was hesitant to ask my next question—I think Leanna sensed it.

"Oolat is safe," she said. "The Dolla found him at sea and pushed him to safety. A flyer has been sent to his location. He is tired and hungry, but alive."

I was overjoyed at the news. A major weight had been taken from my heart. I looked toward the Zecla.

"Why are they here? I thought they'd been taken to Vashia."

"The two you see have agreed to act as ambassadors. The Brata know them, there is a measure of trust. It is through them that we hope to make the Brata see that their lives will be better served by returning to Zin."

"Can Zin accommodate them? The last time I looked, the moon's surface was still reeling from the devastation caused by Philip."

"It is repairing itself—and there is just enough room for the remaining Brata to make a fresh start. This is why your attack on them was so important. Their numbers had to be drastically reduced for our plan to succeed."

I was stunned by her words and the implication—*this had all been planned?* I felt used, like a pawn in a grand chess game. Leanna looked at me and I realized I was connected to her thoughts through the seti stones.

"Not a pawn, my Captain, but an integral part. And in the end I think you'll find that it was well worth it."

She suddenly turned and walked away, leaving me even more bewildered than before.

CHAPTER TWENTY FOUR

Home

tanding along the water's edge, I watched as Leanna
returned to the negotiations with the Zecla and Brata. I
wanted to follow her, but realized that was a bad idea. The
ongoing talks were probably tenuous at best, and if the Brata or
Zecla learned who I was, it could easily destroy everything the
Visi were working toward. We didn't need that, so I decided it
best to keep my distance. I headed back to the sand dunes I'd
crossed earlier. They were far enough away that I could watch
things without causing a stir.

It was there on the dunes that I sat, waiting for the negotiations to conclude. The process was slow and tedious and
I noted a lot of movement coming from the Brata. Without
knowing better, it seemed that they had some sort of relay or
courier system in place—it was confusing. I could see gargoyles
flying from the beach toward the forest, then back again. The
process was repeated endlessly and went on for more than two
hours. It was weary to watch, and though I had no real proof,
I was given to the notion that the gargoyles were reluctant to
accept the ultimatum being proposed by the Zecla. My suspicions were later confirmed when I spied an additional number

of robots approaching—they were armed and there was unusual movement taking place on board the Arison. Without warning, a number of portals popped open alongside the periphery of the ship, and through those openings, came a number of long cannons. They were pointed toward the forest where I assumed the stronghold of the Brata lay. I was surprised to see the ship so heavily armed and I wondered how I missed these weapons during my tour of the vessel. Suddenly several cannons blazed to life.

I was not surprised by what I was witnessing. It was evident that the Visi were tired of negotiating and they were taking the talks with the Brata to the next level. This new message came via a microwave cannon volley aimed at their stronghold. Deep within the terrain I heard loud thundering eruptions as the cannon blasts struck. The explosions were followed by a flurry of movement including terrorized screams and general panic. I saw Brata flying chaotically over the tree tops trying to get out of harm's way. On the beach there was also a reaction. The Zecla were animated in their movement, pointing angrily at the gargoyles, and then to the Arison.

Almost immediately two Brata left the Zecla. They bolted into the air and flew directly into the forest. They were only gone a minute or two when suddenly a mass of gargoyles flew out of the trees and onto the beach. They pooled themselves into a large group, appearing resigned and contrite. It appeared that the Visi had made their point and the Brata were willing to surrender unconditionally. I saw no further negotiation, and I watched as the gargoyles were led by the Zecla to the Arison, where they entered its interior. The process took only a short time and I was surprised at how few Brata I saw. There were perhaps only six to seven hundred who boarded. I wondered if that was all that was left of their entire species. If so, my genocide was unspeakable. I still had regrets over what I had done, even if Leanna said it was necessary.

After the Brata were finished boarding I saw the Zecla enter the ship. They in turn, were followed by the robots and Leanna. The outer door of the ship was then closed, sealing everyone inside. The beach was now entirely empty with the exception of one lone robot. He stood there like a statue, waiting as the Arison lifted from the ground. He then turned and walked toward me.

"I've been instructed to take you to the others," he stated flatly, as he climbed up the hill toward me.

"How are we to get there?" I asked. "Leanna said the fleet was fifty leagues from here. Are we going to walk?"

"I carry with me an additional power supply—cells that can be used to replace the ones in your flyer."

I was elated by his news. "My ship lies in this direction," I responded.

We began walking.

Later that evening I was reunited with the survivors of the fleet. For me, it was a personal revival. I was sorely pleased that so many had survived the tsunami and hurricane, and of course, everyone was relieved to hear that the Brata were gone. Their departure brought forth a bevy of moods, both somber and joyous. Too many years of fighting had passed with the Motula and Brata at each other's throat. And everyone had lost someone during their wars and skirmishes, but now it was over. The gargoyles had been banished. They would never attack again—for some, that reality was inconceivable.

A day later, my old friend and comrade, Oolat, arrived. He was thin and his fur unkempt, but he was alive. I was overjoyed that Leanna had found him, sending a flyer for his rescue. His large, hulking frame was a sight for sore eyes, and I was relieved that he'd made it back in one piece. I was even more surprised when I learned that I was not the only person eager to see him. It seemed that my old friend had been busy cultivating a new friendship during his journey across the ocean. His time had been spent with a young female, a graceful Solula woman with light brown fur and soft eyes. I could tell immediately that he was swept up with her and I was no longer the sole companion in his life. I was pleased—it was about time.

Between our joyous hugs and the dozens of questions we had, Oolat introduced me to Falia, the Solula daughter of

Tiera, a tribe from the Desert Mountains. She was the youngest daughter of the tribe's chieftain, and a head-strong woman who immediately took Oolat's care to heart. She broke us apart and brought him to her camp where she made him eat, drink and rest. I had to laugh. I had the feeling that Oolat was going to be the head of a large family sooner than he knew. And I was greatly pleased that he had found someone, as I knew my days on Boutal were numbered. Now when the time came for me to leave, I wouldn't be so concerned about my old friend. His life was going to be full and quite busy.

During the next few weeks a number of changes came to pass. I learned from Salokka-ril that the Arison had returned. The ship was once again submerged in the Myolic Sea, preparing for the transfer of the Aquita and Dolla. They were heading back to Urlena. Even now, most of the water breathers were leaving. They had a long swim ahead; the return to Urlena would not be easy. I also wondered how the Anoni were going to get back. We were leagues from any transfer point and we no longer had sea vessels to cross the water. I soon got my answer.

Early one morning an airship appeared over the waters of the cove where we resided. It was sleek and shiny and of a registry I knew well. Here was Philip's new design; the ship he'd constructed on Aura. I was overjoyed to see it finished. And for the first time in years, I gave real thought to the notion that I might return home. I raced toward the beach eager to greet my former nemesis, and see the ship that he'd built, but Philip wasn't there. Instead, I found Leanna and several robots piloting the vessel. I was quite disappointed and I inquired to where Philip was. Hesitantly Leanna explained that Philip was no longer with us.

"He's dead?" I responded. "But how, he was a robot. How could he be dead?"

"He gave his life so that a lasting peace could be brought to the moons of Tiiana," she answered.

"Could you be a little more specific?" I said, perturbed by her aloofness. "Why must all your answers be in riddles?"

"I'm sorry," she responded. "You deserve to know. My hesitancy comes not from my desire to avoid you, but out of respect to Philip. He was ashamed of his actions."

"Ashamed? Of what?"

"That his faith in you was misdirected–that you would fail in your efforts to stop the Zecla."

"I still do not understand."

"He built a bomb ..." she responded flatly. "... and hid it within his frame; a nuclear weapon ready to detonate at the given moment you failed in your quest."

I was stunned, this revelation, it ... my thoughts flashed back to Aura and the conversation I had with the Aurian leadership. I recanted their words: *You are not alone in your sentiments, or your logic.*

That's what they meant. Philip didn't think we could beat the Zecla, so he took it upon himself to create a contingency plan. I was distraught. If only he had known that I had asked for the same thing. Still, I didn't understand. How did this lead to his death? I queried Leanna.

"The bomb he carried was corrupt," she answered. "He was exposing everyone around him to an instant and horrible death. The bomb was degrading–he was losing control. Knowing that we could put his weapon to good use, we asked him to join with us and end the situation."

"What happened?"

"The bomb was detonated within the pyramid on Vashia, destroying everything. It was the only way to ensure that the Zecla would have no access to technology, to prevent them from rebuilding or escaping. They now have no ability to leave. Their condition now is one of survival. It will take everything they have just to weather their new environment and adapt. Conquering other moons is no longer an option."

I was amazed and at a loss for words. I couldn't believe what Philip had done. We had started out as enemies, and now I was left with nothing but good feelings for him. After all, he had given me the means to save Boutal and rescue Leanna, even though it felt like she was no longer mine.

"So, what is to happen now?" I asked.

"I would like your help in coordinating our efforts so we can get everyone home. Especially the Anoni, they need to be taken to Luskia so they can transfer back to Alanth."

"Will they be safe there? What of Giragoc? Is the pyramid in the dead city still viable?"

"Giragoc is alive though very weak. His condition should allow the Aquella to return with no harm befalling them. However, we do need to hurry. He must be removed as soon as possible."

Within a matter of days there were great changes taking place on Boutal. Wakula and the other leaders of Phratis and Coralis were returned to their cities along with all the other Motula who wanted to return home. It was the same for the Solula. Most had no desire for the warmer climate of Bratola, and they were eager to return to their homelands and tribes. They left with Leanna and returned to Luskia leaving the continent of Bratola nearly barren of inhabitants.

Surprisingly, not everyone wanted to leave, including my friend, Oolat. To my astonishment he had decided to stay in Bratola.

"Why?" I asked.

"When I was in the water, struggling for my life, the creatures you brought to our world carried me. They made sure that I did not sink and they pushed me onto a beach where I was able to survive. There came a day when I was foraging for food. I climbed a great hill and I saw what I never expected to see—great mountains far away, tall and covered with snow. They lie to the distant south, and I want to see them."

"You want to explore?"

"Yes," he answered. "Like you."

"And what of the young Solula woman who now tends your fire?"

He grinned. "She wants to explore as well—and there are others, perhaps thirty of us in all. I know there are darta and valleys filled with lush grass. There is much room here for building a village. It will be good."

I was incredibly pleased. "I am going to miss you, my friend. Without you, I never would have survived Boutal."

His embrace nearly broke my back. "And Boutal would not have survived without you," he responded. "Our village will honor your name and my first born male will be known as Roolka-ton, the warrior. I want him to be strong and of courage like you."

"I'm not sure if I will be lucky enough to have a son," I replied. "So, I am greatly honored by your pledge. I only wish I could return someday to see you with gray hair, a fat belly, and grandchildren tripping over your feet."

We said no more, but we shared the longest of hugs. He was one of my truest friends and I was going to miss him. The next morning he and the other Solula left, beginning their journey to the Southern mountains. I, in turn, remained on the beach alone, waiting for Leanna to return.

☆ ☆ ☆

Two days later Philip's ship arrived. It landed on the beach not far from our camp. I walked toward it, and took a ramp up to where I found Leanna waiting. She looked as beautiful as ever, though her response to me was unusually cool. I was taken aback. Following her into the ship, I pondered her aloofness. I was having trouble dealing with her mood swings. I didn't understand why they were happening or what triggered them. It just seemed that ever since her re-assimilation on Vashia, things had never been the same. It was disheartening to hear her say she loved me, and that she wanted to return home with me, and the next, be barely able to coax a smile from her lips. My only recourse was hoping that our return to Melela would change things. That once back on our home planet, amidst our own people, her sweet and cheerful nature would return for good. If only I could be sure.

It was then that I began to really think about Melela. What would we find there? Were we still at war with the Relcor? Had we been beaten thoroughly? Or had someone found a way to stop them? I glanced at Leanna with consternation in my heart. She was still the daughter of the Emperor and her safety was my responsibility. If we returned to Melela and found it torn asunder by religious fanatics, there would be a price on her head.

I followed Leanna through the spaceship, amazed at how much a blend of Melelan and Aurian technology was laid out before me. There was a lot I recognized, but much seemed different. The ship looked Spartan, its interior design austere. I had to remind myself that Philip was more robot than human when he designed and built the ship. On the other hand, Leanna seemed to have little problem adjusting. She took a seat in the ship's control center, looking entirely at home in the piloting chairs.

She turned and beckoned me. "Captain, if you would, please take a seat. It's time to go."

I nodded my head and joined her, sitting in the co-pilot's seat next to her. I felt my body sink into the padding, the chair molding itself to my frame. It was surprisingly comfortable. I then noticed instrument consoles rising up from the floor. There were two for each chair, one on either side; granting control and flight access to the ship. I watched as Leanna began working her two consoles. A series of lights came on, and with that, two arms rose up on either side of my chair. They encircled my body and tightened their grip, strapping me to the chair. I was now secure in my seat as was Leanna.

I continued to watch Leanna as she navigated the consoles, marveling at her ability to make it all work. There were so many instruments, lights and buttons—I felt a little inadequate understanding none of it. Suddenly there was movement in front of me, as three large panels opened up in the wall. They were view screens showing the forward and aft views of the ship. I then felt a vibration, the engines were coming online.

"It's time then," I commented, as we rose from the ground. "We're headed home?"

Leanna smiled. "Almost, my Captain, we have just one last task to complete. Giragoc's need must be fulfilled."

I was surprised by her answer, and even more perplexed as Leanna guided our vessel toward the Horn of Myolic. Arriving there, we hovered over the water, and I watched as the Arison rose from the depths of the ocean. It appeared that Leanna was controlling the ship through her console. We began to ascend skyward pulling the Arison behind us, fighting Boutal's gravity as we headed up. After several minutes of flight, the forward screen began to darken, with stars coming into view. We were entering space. I glanced at Leanna. She was totally engrossed in her piloting, and as much as I wanted to talk and compliment her handiwork, I was hesitant to distract her.

Thirty minutes later we were in orbit around Urlena.

"What happens now?" I asked, my voice echoing across the room.

"Giragoc requires nourishment," she answered, not missing a beat.

I was confused. "I thought the idea was to starve Giragoc?"

Leanna gave no reply, but instead, turned our ship's heading, keeping our trajectory constant near the upper edge of Urlena's atmosphere. I watched on the screens as the moon rotated below us—islands and water twirling slowly across its surface. Suddenly I spotted Giragoc. The viral cloud was sitting atop a small island. It looked nearly white, except for the pink tentacles that were stroking the land in search of food. The creature appeared very weak, perhaps even near death. Our ship began to descend, and I was perplexed by our sudden change in direction. We were now headed toward Giragoc with the Arison right behind. I then noticed our speed increasing. What in the name of the Gods was going on?

"What are you doing?" I queried Leanna, with my heart in my throat.

"Giragoc requires strength—we have a long journey ahead."

She said no more and I felt the ship bank sharply. We were shooting upwards again, heading back into the atmosphere. Behind us, the Arison followed like a ball on a chain—its form nearly colliding with the island, but instead passing directly through Giragoc. To my utter amazement, the viral cloud latched onto the ship like a magnet, and even with us accelerating it hung on. In seconds we were back in the thermosphere with the sky around us darkening, and still Giragoc hung on. He was eating, dissolving the metal from the Arison's outer hull. In total disbelief I watched as Giragoc absorbed the ship. With each morsel of metal devoured, the viral creature grew in size, its color deepening. Before my eyes it changed from white to pink, then to purple. It was amazing.

We entered deep space, and I was sure that I was going to see Giragoc begin to wither and die, but that wasn't the case. Surely, it couldn't survive here, could it? What happened to our plan? I turned and looked at Leanna.

"He'll die out here in deep space, won't he?" I queried.

"No," she stated, flatly, her eyes locked on the screen, and fingers flying across the instrument panel. "As long as Giragoc has metal to digest, the consumption will provide oxidation; he can live anywhere."

"What are we doing then?"

I never got an answer. Instead, an alarm began to wail. It was followed by a computerized voice and the announcement: "Warp engines online. Energy discharge in twenty seconds."

I looked at Leanna, and then the rearview screen. The Arison was nearly half gone, and Giragoc was already twice his size. If he kept growing at this rate he'd soon be on top of us. I looked back to Leanna only to see her face suddenly go pale, her eyes quivering as her pupils rolled up and back into her head. Suddenly, an odd voice began to issue through her lips.

"It is time for us to go," it said, as Leanna fell into unconsciousness.

Powerless to move, I strained against the chair arms that held me tight. I couldn't reach Leanna to help her.

"Leanna!" I yelled. "What's wrong? What's wrong?"

I tried to touch her arm, but we were too far apart. I then saw two small spheres of light extrude themselves from her body—one from her chest, the other from her head. The two glowing spheres paused for a second. They whirled about Leanna's face, caressing it—I recognized them. They were glowers, like the ones I'd encountered when I first arrived on Urlena. What were they doing here? The answer came quickly as the two spheres moved in my direction. Instinctively, I pulled back, though I was unable to escape their approach. They floated about my head, each one taking a position next to my temples. Immediately, a flurry of thoughts came rushing at me, assaulting my senses. I knew instantly it was Yllis and Ahska—they were sending a message.

"Your ship is about to enter warp."

"You have done well, Rez Cantor."

"Tiiana's moons will survive and grow well because of you."

"Now it is our turn."

"Philip's design lies at the heart of this ship—he will lead you home."

With that they were gone, winking out in the blink of an eye. I heard Leanna moan. I looked over to her beautiful face, but I was distracted. Giragoc was looming before me on the screen. His form was approaching rapidly, reaching for us, the metal in our ship calling to him. In utter fear, I watched as his finger-like appendages came closer, each whirling tunnel flashing with light and heat. He was ready to pounce.

I felt the ship lurch and I was certain that Giragoc had latched on. But, no—it was the warp drive. I could feel the warp engines surging and my head was knocked back against the seat. The pressure was extreme. I was having difficulty moving. I turned my eyes to Leanna—she too was pinned, helpless like me. Overhead, on the main screen, the universe turned into a blur as the space around us warped. We were leaving Giragoc behind and heading back home.

As I lay half unconscious in my chair I wondered how we would find Melela. They said Philip knew the way—but Philip was dead. How could he? Without warning, we fell from warp and entered normal space. I felt my body snap against the restraining arms—my body wanted to float, but they kept me back. I then heard a voice announce: "Course correction verified."

I then felt the warp drives kick in again and I was pushed back into my seat. I felt sick and a little stunned. I didn't remember this happening with previous warp jumps. Was something wrong? Was this ship functioning properly? And if it wasn't, what could I do about it?

The process of falling from warp to normal space happened three more times. And each time I heard the voice say: "Course correction verified."

I realized later that we were traveling an incredible distance and I recalled Philip's explanation: *The Relcor's nukes had ripped a hole in the fabric of space just as we were going to warp, the results sending us across the entire galaxy.* It was evident now that we couldn't return the same way, but how long was it going to take? A hundred and twenty light years was a long distance. How old would we be by the time we got home? We entered warp again and stayed there for quite a while—so long that I actually slept.

How long I was out I wasn't sure, but when I awoke it was to silence. The warp engines were idle, and we were traveling at sub-light and in normal space. I stared at the main screen trying to figure out where we were, but I saw nothing I recognized. Leanna was still unconscious and of little help. With little else to do, I relaxed, wistfully watching the stars pass by on the three view screens. It was at this point that I realized Giragoc was gone. We had evidently lost him during our warp transfers. I was relieved. There was great satisfaction in knowing that we ditched the entity somewhere in space—that its death would give everyone a reprieve.

Content that justice had been finally served, I started to shut my eyes and go back to sleep, when I noticed an unusual oddity on the main screen. There were two stars off to our right, both orbiting in close proximity to one another—a binary system. I took in their appearance. One was a dingy looking, brown dwarf, the other a yellow behemoth; a rather unusual pairing in my eyes. I searched my memory, hoping that these two stars would give me a point of reference to our where-abouts, but nothing came to mind. Oddly enough though, we seemed to be heading in their direction.

As we came closer to the binary system, analytical data began to appear on the lower portion of the main view screen. At first it was simple. A generalized listing of the two stars' composition, but that changed as we got closer and our view became focused on the brown dwarf. The dark, celestial body soon filled the screen and I saw it was a quirky dynamo, a solar enigma in its own right. Cool by normal star standards, it was rotating rapidly and giving off an inordinate amount of x-ray and infrared radiation. What surprised me more though, were the six planets in orbit around it—planets that we were seem-ingly being drawn to. This caused me concern as it made no sense.

With my curiosity piqued and my thoughts running ram-pant, I stared at the view screen reading every bit of informa-tion that crossed it. Most of it was simple data, as we were still millions of leagues out, but it told me that the geophysical makeup of the planets was relatively normal. The outer ones appeared to be comprised of either rock or ice, or held seas of cold, liquified gas. The third one out from the dwarf was differ-ent. It had a thin atmosphere comprised of nitrogen and oxy-gen mixed with trace amounts of methane and ammonia. That put it in the realm of being able to sustain life, and that possi-bility raised the hair on my neck. I began to wonder if our guid-ance system had failed, or if Philip had seriously miscalculated the journey back. Either way it made no sense that we were coming here. This whole area was too inhospitable for human life. I tried to wake Leanna again, but she was still out cold and of no help.

With little choice, I sat tight as we flew toward the plan-etary system. The first planet we reached was 1745 million leagues out from the dwarf. It was a barren, cold world of measurable size covered with thick ice and dark rock. We flew past it, rounding its exterior on a heading that was taking us deeper into the solar system. At that moment, I got the shock of my life. The view screen suddenly lit up with a new display of data—communications data. It appeared we were picking up some kind of transmission, though my first thought was that it was just electromagnetic radiation coming from the dwarf. That assumption faded quickly. The message kept repeating, broadcasting over and over with the same dashes and bleeps. Was it a welcoming beacon or a warning? Or perhaps a distress signal? I had no idea, but its sound didn't ease my tension, and my gut told me it was coming from the third planet.

The next planet in our flight vector was a gas sphere, a cool blue color, with ninety percent of its surface covered by frozen methane and ammonia. That in itself was no surprise, but what happened next was. As we cleared the planet's magnetic field, the transmission signal we'd been hearing got stronger. The bandwidth became wider and our sensors began registering an array of signals, including several vocal communiqués— faint voices murmuring against a background of x-ray static. I immediately began to get worried. Something wasn't right. I hollered over to Leanna, I needed her awake. It was imperative that we regain control of the ship. I heard her moan, and at that moment things took a turn for the worse. A small light on the bottom of the viewing screen began to flash. It looked to be a warning of some kind, but I wasn't sure. I then saw an artificial satellite appear on the forward screen. It was a large, metallic body, definitely man-made and moving in a defined orbit. I was uncertain whether it was for communications or defense, but one thing was for certain: We were definitely entering into someone's domain and I had no idea if they were going to welcome our intrusion.

Suddenly, there was a bright flash of light emanating from the ship—I blinked. What just happened? The view before the ship was now empty, the satellite gone, vaporized, leaving only debris. What the hell was going on? Suddenly the ship's engines kicked in and our speed began to increase. Something was afoot. I began to yell at Leanna in a panic.

"Leanna! LEANNA! LEANNA!!!"

I saw her stir and I yelled her name until her eyes finally opened. She looked at me.

"You need to wake up, NOW!" I shouted; my face red as a beet, my voice hoarse. "The ship—it's out of control. It's firing its weapons! You need to regain command."

Leanna looked bewildered beyond means. I saw her looking around, wide eyed, as if she were totally unaware of where she was. I knew then we were in trouble, realizing that she hadn't been the one guiding the ship, but Yllis and Ahska. Oh, we were in deep shit.

I glanced at the screen. Our speed had increased measurably and there were more satellites ahead. In fact, it looked like we were entering an area guarded by some kind of defensive barrier. There were hundreds of mines, stretching out in all directions, littering the space before us. Suddenly our ship began firing, striking satellite after satellite. One explosion seemed to trigger another, and soon the whole field was ablaze. We then banked and changed direction. We were now flying along the edge of the mine field, skirting its border. As we did, the ship fired repeatedly again, picking off hundreds more. It looked like Armageddon, and I got the distinct feeling we had just knocked on someone's door very hard.

A meek voice queried me. "Rez, what's happening?"

I looked over to Leanna. She was staring at the screen, watching the destruction.

"I don't know," I answered. "I just woke up and found us approaching this solar system. The ship's gone mad. It's firing at these satellites and I don't know why. Do you know how to regain control?"

Leanna shook her head. "I can't remember."

I sighed in resignation. Whatever was going on, it was completely out of our control. We were hostages in some maddening game, destined to watch as things unfolded. I looked back to the screen. We were now headed toward the fourth planet out; beyond it was the one with the atmosphere. I sensed, intrinsically, that that planet was our destination—if we didn't get blown up first. Suddenly, another mine field loomed before us, thicker than the one before. We penetrated it, blowing open a wide swath on either side of the ship as we made our way around the fourth planet.

Unexpectedly, a loud voice with a thick, Gatlic accent began bellowing at us through the console. *"Alien vessel— Identify yourself. You are in violation of Relcor space. You have five seconds—cease hostilities and respond, or you will be destroyed."*

A feather could have knocked me over. I was floored, totally floored—Relcor—this was Relcor? How? Good God. I struggled to find my tongue. But what could I say? I didn't even know what we were doing here. I glanced at Leanna, panic in my eyes. She too was wide-eyed and at a loss for words. Suddenly another voice shouted out across the chamber. It began speaking to the Relcor, demanding in turn, their surrender. It was ME?

"This is Rez Cantor of the planet, Melela," the voice said. "I am here to demand the unconditional surrender of Juc T'Krola and the Relcor Empire. YOU have ten seconds to surrender or face the full brunt of our invasion fleet. What say you, Relcor pricworm?"

I sat dumbfounded in my chair. How in the name of Ahska was this happening? How could I be speaking when I was locked up here, helpless in this chair? I realized then I had just threatened the Relcor's home planet with an attack fleet—we had no fleet. We were one puny ship with no real weapons. I never felt so stupid and helpless in my entire life. At that second, the Relcor planet flashed on the screen before us. It was a dirty, polluted world, clouded by ash and sulfur from volcanic activity. It looked like hell itself, but that was the least of my concerns. There was a bigger problem. Laid out before us was a sight beyond comprehension. Surrounding the planet was the entire Relcor fleet—battleships, starships, transports, carriers and personal flyers. The sight was overwhelming. There was so much armament it blotted out entire sections of the planet's surface. My guess was that there were a hundred thousand ships or more, most captured or taken from the Melelan Empire. I realized at that moment we were dead meat. Too many of those ships were igniting their engines.

A voice came across the console, thick and hot with anger. *"We will meet your fleet Melelan dog, and we will roast your soul, as we did your planet."*

My throat felt thick; I had trouble swallowing. It was obvious that we had set a fire under a hornet nest and we were about to experience the full wrath of our folly. I just wished I knew why. It was then that our speed and direction changed again. We were turning about and making a run for it.

I heard my voice speaking again—goading the Relcor on, calling them vampire sluts who feared facing a true battle. It was total madness. My alter voice was insuring our death. On the rear view screen I saw more and more ships moving into action. The chase was on and I swore under my breath.

"Go to warp. Go to warp, now." It was the only way we could escape.

As we flew back, retracing our flight path, the Relcor dogged us with taunts. *"Melelan pus worm! Fleeing is futile. You are surrounded. Surrender now or be destroyed!"*

Glancing at the rear screen I knew he was telling the truth. There were an untold number of ships gaining on us, a number already heading into warp. They were jumping ahead to cut us off. This was it. I looked over to Leanna.

"I love you," I said.

She nodded in return, her eyes wet with tears. She knew escape was impossible—we couldn't win. "I love you too, she replied softly. "I just wish we'd gotten the chance to start over."

If ever there were a moment in my life when I felt undeniable love it was then. I wanted to hold Leanna in the worst way, and tell her how much I cared, but I couldn't. Not because of the restraints, but because our ship was being pounded relentlessly by Relcor weaponry. How we had survived so far was a miracle. We were rolling, pitching, and bouncing through space, all at the same time—it was the end for us, or so I thought. In response to the attack, we increased our speed and I prayed. Finally we were going to warp. On the forward screen I saw more Relcor. They were waiting for us with a hundred ships or more just on either side of the fifth moon. I knew instantly from their strategic formation that we were effectively surrounded.

Readying myself for the end, I heard the voice of our ship speaking aloud: "Worm hole reconnect in four seconds."

True to the computer's words, I saw a worm hole take form ahead of us. It lay halfway between us and the fifth moon. I was surprised by its speed and size and at how quickly it was pulsating. For a second I thought we might have a chance, but it was too far away—and our speed was far too slow.

"We'll never make it." I muttered aloud.

Already the Relcor were on to us. They were moving in fast, trying to close the gap between us and the wormhole. They were not about to let us escape.

It was then that the voice of the computer broke in, issuing a new warning: "Evasive measures in three, two, one ..."

Evasive measures? What the hell? I was thoroughly confused, had been ever since arriving here. Suddenly, and without warning, I felt our ship bolt. It was an effect that I had never experienced with any starship before. We didn't exactly go to warp, and we didn't enter the wormhole either. We just slipped out of phase, pushing past the Relcor as if they were in some kind of frozen stasis. My only analogy was that we sort of puddle jumped across space itself. There were three quick bursts of energy and several sharp turns, but in the breath of an instant we were beyond the sixth planet and entirely free of the Relcor armada.

From our new vantage point, I watched to see if the Relcor were following us, but their position was stationary. They were still orbiting the fifth planet, wondering what happened, and where we disappeared too. But that was the least of their problems.

A grin the size of Tiiana overtook my face. I was witnessing a miracle, and I began to laugh and cry at the same time, all the while yelling at the top of my lungs.

"Yes! Yes! Yes! Get 'em. Suck the fuckin' pricworms dry!"

Thinking me mad, Leanna stared at me fearfully.

"Look at the rear screen," I yelled to her. "Look!"

She turned, and her jaw dropped. She saw what I saw—the beginning of the end for the Relcor. For in orbit, not far from the fifth moon, was the worm hole we'd opened. Only it wasn't a new wormhole, but the one we had used to get here. I couldn't explain it; the science was beyond my understanding. I only knew that the Visi, using Auraian's technology and Philip's genius, had somehow given the Melelan Empire the miracle it needed. Giragoc had arrived and he was famished. His purple-pink form literally exploded through the gaping wide wormhole, and he swept out over the Relcor's armada like a thick, dark cloud of corrosive goo. Explosions began to ensue as Giragoc fed, sucking the metal from each ship he encountered. I couldn't believe his rate of growth or tenacity, and I imagined the Relcor couldn't either. It was astounding.

With tears of joy flowing down my face, I cried. This was the most awesome sight I had ever witnessed. I couldn't begin to express my debt of gratitude to the Visi.

All I could say was, "Thank you! Thank you! Thank you!"

Theirs' was the most precious gift ever. Giragoc, the scourge of Urlena, had been hand delivered by us to the one place where he could do the most good. Defeating the force that had bonded its soul to hell itself—and I was ecstatic.

We watched for a minute or two as Giragoc fed and I marveled at what an incredible bio-weapon he was. The Zecla had done well creating it, and I was happy that we were far from its reach. From our distance I could see bolts of lightning and sparks shooting in every direction. The cloud was spawning space tornadoes; its fingers reaching out for more ships. And even in their retreat, the Relcor had no chance. They couldn't get away fast enough.

As we jumped into warp, I thought about everything that had happened. In a perverted sort of way I wished I could have stayed and witnessed, in its entirety, the hellish carnage that was taking place with the Relcor. Giragoc was undefeatable, his appetite so ravenous, that no matter what they threw at him, he would continue to grow and feed. I could just imagine his fiery tentacles reaching out, twisting and sucking the metal from each and every Relcor ship. Oh to see those pious bastards asphyxiating in the cold, dark vacuum of space, it delighted my imagination to no end. For me, it was a just reward for their betrayal of humanity.

I then thought about the Relcor's home world. It was surrounded by countless ships, satellites, and minefields. All that metal floating in space would lead Giragoc right to them. And once there, he would feed for centuries, perhaps a millennia or longer—who could say? The viral beast would feed upon them and their planet until nothing remained. It was indeed a prayer answered.

I saw Leanna smile at me. For the first time in a year or more, she looked happy, really happy, and her eyes they were bright and oh, so wondrous.

"Hi," she said, stretching her arms.

"Hello, my Princess."

"I've missed you," she said.

"And I you."

I wanted to kiss her in the worst way, but the two of us were still stuck in our seats, and I was unsure how we would get free. Unexpectedly we felt the ship drop from warp and we entered normal space. This time, however, we were far from Relcor. This time we appeared a quiet distance from a small, light green planet that floated gently in the dark waters of space. It was Melela and she looked like a beautiful green gemstone. I pondered for a moment why we had stopped so far away. The answer came quickly. I could see tiny fireflies of light flashing all about the planet—warp signatures from the Relcor's warships. They were being called home to help fight Giragoc. I looked at Leanna, gloating with glee as I spoke.

"It's a thing of beauty, isn't it? Witnessing the end of those bastards. Knowing that Giragoc will suck every last one of them dry. That the silver, pious pricworms are going to pay for everything they did to us.

Leanna nodded. "And now we can rebuild."

"Yes," I replied. "We can rebuild, together."

"Thank you my Captain, for saving Melela—and me."

I glanced at her, noting her admiration, and hoping I deserved it.

Unexpectedly, a recorded voice broke the air. It began to speak to us through the console. It was Ahska.

"Dear Roolka," she said. "It is with the full heart of the Visi that we thank you for all that you have done for the moons of Tiiana. You are a man of courage and fortitude and we hope that our final gift to you will save your planet and give you and your love a chance to rebuild. Like the moons of Tiiana, your corner of the galaxy deserves its chance to be free. It was the least we could do. For the moment, however, it will not be safe for you to land upon your home world. You must give Giragoc time to consume your enemy and your world needs time to heal; likewise it is time for you to rest."

Suddenly, I felt the room about us growing cold as mist began to seep in. I saw shadows moving in the background. Someone was here with us, but who? I wasn't sure if I'd ever know that answer, for sleep overcame Leanna and I. And there we lay in repose until it was safe to return home.

From the Author

To my readers,

I wrote *THE 5 MOONS OF TIIANA* in homage to one of my favorite science fiction writers, Edgar Rice Burroughs. Aside from his *Tarzan* series, many are unaware that E. R. Burroughs wrote an entire science fiction series featuring a dynamic hero known as *John Carter of Mars*. It was this series of novels that impassioned my boyhood years, taking me on numerous adventures to the red planet of Mars, while inspiring me with its courageous tales of *Captain John Carter*, and his quest for his beloved Princess, *Dejah Thoris*, the *Princess of Helium*. These were enthralling novels that gave great reprieve to the long, hot days of summer, and honed my love of science fiction. Little did I know at the time that the memories created by Burroughs' would bring me around to the day where I would write my own book about the moons of Tiiana and its hero, Rez Cantor. It is my sincere hope that I have been able to partially capture and impart the same excitement and adventure that so characterized *Edgar Rice Burroughs'* series while giving you, the reader an enjoyable experience of your own—to this I say, thank you.

Sincerely,
Paul T Harry

www.ingramcontent.com/pod-product-compliance
Lightning Source LLC
Chambersburg PA
CBHW051535250626
47157CB00001B/56